Back in Bliss

Other Books by Lexi Blake

ROMANTIC SUSPENSE

Masters and Mercenaries
The Dom Who Loved Me
The Men With The Golden Cuffs
A Dom is Forever
On Her Master's Secret Service
Sanctum: A Masters and Mercenaries Novella
Love and Let Die
Unconditional: A Masters and Mercenaries Novella
Dungeon Royale
Dungeon Games: A Masters and Mercenaries Novella
A View to a Thrill
Cherished: A Masters and Mercenaries Novella
You Only Love Twice
Luscious: Masters and Mercenaries~Topped
Adored: A Masters and Mercenaries Novella
Master No
Just One Taste: Masters and Mercenaries~Topped 2
From Sanctum with Love
Devoted: A Masters and Mercenaries Novella
Dominance Never Dies
Submission is Not Enough
Master Bits and Mercenary Bites~The Secret Recipes of Topped
Perfectly Paired: Masters and Mercenaries~Topped 3
For His Eyes Only
Arranged: A Masters and Mercenaries Novella
Love Another Day
At Your Service: Masters and Mercenaries~Topped 4
Master Bits and Mercenary Bites~Girls Night
Nobody Does It Better
Close Cover
Protected: A Masters and Mercenaries Novella
Enchanted: A Masters and Mercenaries Novella
Charmed: A Masters and Mercenaries Novella
Treasured: A Masters and Mercenaries Novella, Coming June 29, 2021

Masters and Mercenaries: The Forgotten
Lost Hearts (Memento Mori)
Lost and Found
Lost in You
Long Lost
No Love Lost

Masters and Mercenaries: Reloaded
Submission Impossible
The Dom Identity, Coming September 14, 2021

Butterfly Bayou
Butterfly Bayou
Bayou Baby
Bayou Dreaming
Bayou Beauty, Coming July 27, 2021

Lawless
Ruthless
Satisfaction
Revenge

Courting Justice
Order of Protection
Evidence of Desire

Masters Of Ménage (by Shayla Black and Lexi Blake)
Their Virgin Captive
Their Virgin's Secret
Their Virgin Concubine
Their Virgin Princess
Their Virgin Hostage
Their Virgin Secretary
Their Virgin Mistress

The Perfect Gentlemen (by Shayla Black and Lexi Blake)
Scandal Never Sleeps
Seduction in Session
Big Easy Temptation

Smoke and Sin
At the Pleasure of the President

URBAN FANTASY

Thieves
Steal the Light
Steal the Day
Steal the Moon
Steal the Sun
Steal the Night
Ripper
Addict
Sleeper
Outcast
Stealing Summer

LEXI BLAKE WRITING AS SOPHIE OAK

Texas Sirens
Small Town Siren
Siren in the City
Siren Enslaved
Siren Beloved
Siren in Waiting
Siren in Bloom
Siren Unleashed
Siren Reborn

Nights in Bliss, Colorado
Three to Ride
Two to Love
One to Keep
Lost in Bliss
Found in Bliss
Pure Bliss
Chasing Bliss
Once Upon a Time in Bliss
Back in Bliss
Sirens in Bliss
Happily Ever After in Bliss

Far From Bliss, Coming 2021

A Faery Story
Bound
Beast
Beauty

Standalone
Away From Me
Snowed In

Back in Bliss

Nights in Bliss, Colorado Book 9

Lexi Blake
writing as
Sophie Oak

Back in Bliss
Nights in Bliss, Colorado Book 9

Published by DLZ Entertainment LLC

Edited by Chloe Vale
ISBN: 978-1-942297-20-8

Sign up for Lexi Blake's newsletter
and be entered to win a $25 gift certificate
to the bookseller of your choice.

Join us for news, fun, and exclusive content
including free short stories.

There's a new contest every month!

Go to www.LexiBlake.net to subscribe.

Dedication

Logan's story is a long time in coming and I feel the need to say a few words about how he's changed and grown over the course of eight books and two different series. I didn't intend for him to be such a player. He was a throwaway character, meant only for comic relief. And the Russian mob came to town and he became so much more for me. Logan doesn't have a terrible background. There's no grand pain in his childhood. In fact, it was almost idyllic. I got to write a character from the moment he learned the world was broken to the moment of his realization that he has the power to heal. For me, Logan has gone from a silly boy to a man who can make the choice to survive and thrive—the same choice many of us make every single day. I thank you all for taking this journey with me and for becoming a part of my own personal heaven—Bliss, Colorado.

I hope we have many more adventures ahead of us.

Dedication 2019

It's funny how we move through time. I'm sitting here six years after the first time Back in Bliss came out. So much has happened. Great things. Bad things. Triumph. Unimaginable loss. I put Logan through the wringer all those years ago because I thought it would be interesting as a writer. I lied to myself. I put him through the wringer because not one of us gets where we're going without pain and loss and sacrifice. Because none of us gets there without finding people who stand up and give us strength we didn't know we had. Because even when we venture far from home, someone is waiting for us, has the light on, and prays for our return. There's still another book in this series—Sirens in Bliss—but in so many ways this was the last Bliss book I wrote during my years as Sophie Oak so I'm going to sum up a series.

Thank you to the town of South Fork, Colorado, for serving as ground zero for Bliss. You're weird and quirky and beautiful.

Thank you to Kim Guidroz for being there from the first word.

Thank you to the fans who loved this little town and its odd citizens.

Thank you to my mom and dad and my whole family.

Thank you to my daily support system—Liz Berry, Jillian Stein, Kris Cook, Kori Smith, Lila DuBois, and Mari Carr.

Thank you to Shayla Black who befriended a first-time author and lifted her up.

Thank you to my husband who only flinches a little when he finds stories about his childhood in these books—Maurice the Moose was real, except he was an elk and my husband would say way, way scarier.

Thank you so much to my sweet Bella who sat beside me faithfully as I wrote these books. Sometimes the love we need doesn't come from humans. Sometimes it comes from a gorgeous soul who happens to walk on four feet. I love you and miss you.

And finally thank you to Margarita Coale, champion of authors. Without you the roads to Bliss would have remained closed, a permanent detour going around my heart. Because of you we will have more adventures.

Here's to more stories, to always looking for Bliss.

Prologue

Bliss, Colorado
Fifteen years before

Seth

"Please don't tell his moms." Seth had to talk for Logan because his teeth hadn't stopped chattering yet. And his lips were the slightest bit blue.

Seth took a seat at the bar, the smells from the kitchen making his stomach growl. He always ate more here even though he lived on the Upper East Side of Manhattan. His mother liked to tell him that the world revolved around Manhattan, but he never got mac and cheese there. Ellen Glen-Bennett always made mac and cheese.

And chocolate chip cookies. Gosh, he liked cookies even though his parents thought carbs were the devil. He lived for the three months of the year he got to spend in Bliss.

Ellen frowned his way as she placed a steaming mug of hot chocolate in front of Logan. "I do not understand boys. I swear. What on earth got into your head, Logan? The river is still very cold even during the summer. Did you fall in? Were you boys horsing around?"

He and Logan looked at each other. No horsing around. Just

Truth or Dare. Jamie had bet Logan that he couldn't last two minutes in the cold waters of the Rio Grande, and Logan had decided to jump into the river rather than tell Jamie how often he masturbated.

Seth would have told him. He would have done a lot to avoid those chilly waters. He wouldn't have told the total truth, of course, but some approximation of it. But not Logan.

Ellen shook her head as though she knew she wouldn't get an answer out of them. "I'm going to get another blanket and throw his clothes in the dryer."

Ellen strode out of the kitchen toward the laundry room.

Logan trembled in the seat beside him, his head swinging toward Seth, teeth chattering as he spoke. "Don't tell Ellen about the dirt bike. We can fix it up."

It had been a summer of what his mother would likely call "very bad choices" and what Seth labeled as the best of his life. The week before, Jamie had taken their friend Max up on the bet that he couldn't drive his brand-new dirt bike up the mountain. He'd gotten it up, but he'd come back down really fucking fast. Like way faster than the bike. The bike had kind of smashed into Jamie's head.

It had been cool and funny, and Logan was right. Ellen would be pissed. She might not let them stay out at the man cave again. He loved the man cave. Sure, it smelled bad, but even that was kind of cool.

"How did you do it, man? That water was so cold." Logan had stood there and took it like a man while Jamie had counted down the seconds and Noah held a lasso ready to catch Logan in case the current swept him away.

Maybe they hadn't thought through that plan as thoroughly as they should have.

"The key is to survive ten seconds, man. You can survive anything for ten seconds. And then you go for another ten seconds and another and before you know it, you're done. I use it when my moms are lecturing me on getting my school work done, too." His voice was almost back to normal, but his hands were still shaking.

A heavenly aroma hit Seth's nose as Ellen returned with another blanket. She opened the oven and took out the cookies after tossing the blanket around Logan's shoulders. Noah and Jamie joined them, looking at their stepmom with worshipful eyes.

Ellen frowned as she opened a jug of milk and poured four glasses out. “So now that we know Logan is going to survive, would anyone like to explain why Jamie looks like he went through a meat grinder?”

She was so calm. If Seth had walked in like that, his mother would have had a conniption fit, not because she loved him and was worried about him, but because she would have been deeply concerned about what the neighbors would say.

Jamie shrugged. “I fell. It’s cool.”

He’d fallen down a mountain and they’d spent days trying to heal him.

Ellen sighed. “All right, but next time call me. I’ve got to start dinner.”

She turned away and disappeared into the pantry. The tension deflated and everything was normal again because everything was always normal in Bliss.

He felt normal in Bliss.

“Way to deflect the mom unit, man.” Noah held up his hand for a high-five.

Jamie slapped his palm against his brother’s. “That’s the way we do it, brother. I learned from our dads. That’s how you handle a mom. It’s how we’ll handle Callie one day.”

Noah’s eyes rolled. “We’re not marrying Callie. She’s like our sister.”

“She’s the most devious thing ever. We should totally marry her,” Jamie said.

Callie had been the one to come up with the plan to fix Jamie up. Sure, he was going to scar, but he was alive. Seth had to admit, Callie was pretty cute, but she had a thing for Max and Rye.

Noah gagged. “Not happening.”

Jamie sighed. “But I like Callie.”

Seth looked over at Logan. “Who are we going to marry?”

It was said with the trepidation of a boy who wasn’t sure of his place. He’d always been at the top of his class, but that wasn’t where he’d wanted to be. He wanted to be here. With his best friend and his family.

Logan shot him a grin even as he pulled the blankets tighter. "Do you really think we can find someone to marry us? I don't know. It's a tall order."

But it was everything he wanted. A family with his best friend. In his town.

"Damn, man. I think any woman would want to marry you after she finds out how long you can stand in the river," Jamie said with an admiring glance Logan's way. "We're going to call you River Man from now on."

"No, Captain Freeze because his balls didn't drop off," Noah offered and then frowned. "Tell me your balls didn't drop off, man."

And then they were all joking and laughing and downing chocolate chip cookies.

He only had twenty-two days until he had to go back to New York, and then a whole year would pass until he could come home again. He would count every single day off, marking it on a calendar. But one day…

"Yeah, we'll find someone." Seth was sure. It was his destiny. His and Logan's.

* * * *

Del Norte, CO
Two years before

Logan

"Sweetheart, you need to eat something."

Logan Green forced himself to look up at his mother. "I'm not hungry."

He didn't like to open his eyes. When he opened his eyes he was reminded that he was in a hospital. The world seemed too white and sanitary, a foreign place where he didn't belong.

Of course when he closed his eyes he was back on the desk.

His stomach turned and he wondered when the nurse would be back with his pain meds. He'd been lying in this hospital for two days and the only time he felt comfortable was the magical moment when the meds kicked in and he suddenly didn't care what had happened to him, could barely remember it.

The trouble was the meds always faded and then he would see that face looming over him. He would know that whatever came next would break him.

Had broken him.

God, he was so fucking broken.

"Logan, you have to eat." His mother looked older today. She always looked fragile, but that was a lie. Teeny Green was small in stature, but she had a mighty heart.

How ashamed would she be if she knew the truth about what had happened to him?

He forced himself to sit up, biting back a groan as pain washed over him. It didn't matter if he was still or in motion, the pain seemed to always be with him now. "I don't want to eat, Ma."

He saw her eyes flare with hurt but he couldn't find the will to apologize. He knew he should. This was his mother and she'd sacrificed for him. He could see it, see the love she had for him, but since that moment when he'd been tied down and shown the way of the world, there wasn't room for anything in his heart but anger.

His mother started to say something, but he was spared by a knock on the door. Caleb Burke strode in wearing the white coat he always had on when he was either in his clinic in Bliss or here in the hospital where he had admitting privileges. Caleb was a taciturn man, not at all known for his bedside manner, but he managed to smile at Teeny Green.

Because his mother was a light in the world. The only problem was Logan had so recently been introduced to the darkness.

"Good morning, Teeny. How are you this morning?" Caleb asked, clipboard in hand.

His mother turned to the doctor, a fine sheen of tears in her eyes. "He won't eat, Doc. How can he heal if he won't eat? He's always had such a good appetite but now he won't even try."

He didn't fucking want to try. He didn't care enough to try. He ached with every breath, and he wasn't sure that would go away no matter which parts of him healed.

Why hadn't he died on that desk? Why had Stef chosen that

moment to slip inside and save the day? If he'd been a few minutes later…

"Hey, he's fine, Teeny." Caleb's voice had gone about as soft as Logan had ever heard it go. "This is normal. His body has gone through a lot. There's a long road ahead, but he's stable. He's getting everything he needs through the IV for now. In a couple of days his appetite will be back."

"I thought he could come home later today." His mother looked at him and then back to the doctor. "Marie is making sure his room is ready right now."

God, he couldn't even think about going home. How could he ever walk back into his room and pretend like life was normal?

Caleb shook his head. "I'm sorry the nurses told you that. I need to keep him here for at least another two days. It's nothing serious, but I want to watch a couple of his incisions and since Bliss is so far from an actual hospital, it's best he recovers here."

"The doc's right. I'm not feeling up to moving right now." If he could put it off for a few days, he would do it. The idea of going back into his room, of seeing his house again, made panic well up inside him. He'd grown up in that little cabin. He'd lived there for as long as he could remember. That cabin was love and safety and comfort.

That cabin was a lie.

"You go and call Marie," Caleb urged. "Let her know you still have a couple of days. He'll be on his feet in no time at all, and you are the one who needs to eat. Stella tells me you won't leave this hospital. You need to rest. It's very important for you to take care of yourself, too."

"But he's my boy," his mother said.

"And he's going to be fine." Caleb gave her a nod and gestured toward the door. "Stella's outside. She wants to take you out to lunch. You need a break. He's fine here."

"I am." He loved his mother but she'd been hovering and it rankled. He wanted a few fucking minutes to himself. "I'm good, Ma. Like Doc says, I just need a couple more days."

She crossed the space between them and leaned over to kiss his head. "All right. I'll go and have lunch with Stella. But I'll be back."

He watched as she walked out of the room.

He didn't really want to talk to Caleb either, but the good news was the doctor was gruff and they could get through this conversation pretty damn quick. Then he could be alone for a while. Then he could wait for those meds.

"So I've got problems with my incisions? They feel pretty good, but I want to stay here until I'm totally healed." He wanted to stay where he didn't have to talk, didn't have to think about going back into a life he didn't trust anymore.

"No, you're healing perfectly but I know you're not ready to even consider going home." Caleb laid the clipboard down. "I know because I wasn't ready. Logan, I'm not going to tell you everything because I'll be honest, it's been years and I'm still not ready. I've been where you are. I was…let's just say I went through some bad shit and it lasted for months. I watched people die. I was pretty damn sure I would be next."

He could feel the bile at the back of his throat and forced himself to shake his head. "Nah, I knew someone would save me."

Caleb nodded as though he'd pretty much expected that would be his reply. "Well, I didn't. I was kept in a cage and I would be taken out and beaten and shoved back in the cage. I lived that way and I remember just wanting it to be over. I still felt that way even after I was rescued and I got home. Sometimes I feel that way today. You need some time and you need to give yourself permission to take it. I didn't want to be around my family afterward. But I came here and I'm finding some friends. All I'm saying is you should think about talking to someone, but probably not your mom."

"I don't need to talk about it."

"Logan, I know what really happened and I won't ever tell."

He sat up, his whole body going rigid. "You fucking better not, Caleb."

No one could know. He would go to his grave with that secret.

Caleb held up his hands, conceding. "I legally can't tell anyone, but Logan, there's nothing to be ashamed about. Nothing at all. You were attacked. That's the hardest thing about any of this. You want to blame someone and you end up blaming yourself. I know I do."

"I blame those fucking Russians." He was not doing this. "Where are my meds? The nurse is ten minutes late. How much pain am I supposed to deal with?"

Caleb sighed. "I'll call her in, but you should be starting to heal. Don't get hooked, Logan. It's the last thing you need."

It was the only thing he needed. "Don't become an addict. Got it."

Caleb picked up the clipboard. "Think about talking to someone. If I know anything about your moms, I think they'll try to pretend like everything will be fine the minute your skin heals. They'll try to make things normal for you, but nothing is normal. They'll tiptoe around you when they should poke and prod."

"I think I've been poked enough." He couldn't look the man in the face. "I'll be fine once I'm up and on my feet."

Caleb started for the door. "You won't and no one will know. All they'll see is that the scars on the outside will begin to fade. They don't understand how bad the ones on the inside are. Call a friend. Don't end up like me. I still…well, I can't have the things I want because I never figured out how to get out of that cage."

He slipped outside the door and it closed with a *whoosh.*

And he was alone again.

A vibrating sound caught his attention. His phone. His mother had made sure it was kept charged and by his bed in case he needed anything from her. Not that he would have to call her since she refused to go home.

God, he should be grateful but all he wanted was to wake up and realize this was a terrible dream.

He glanced down and Seth's name filled the screen.

He put the phone back on the table as he realized he hadn't told Seth. His best friend in the world was likely calling because he wanted to talk movies or he'd read a cool new book. He had no idea that Logan's whole world had changed, that Logan wasn't Logan anymore.

How the fuck did he ever face Seth again?

Or he could call him and they could figure out what to do. That's what they used to do. Things would go wrong and they would call each other and help find a way through the problem.

But this wasn't him dropping his ma's cell phone in the pond behind the Harper's place because he was skinny dipping with

Callie's cousin from LA. He didn't need Seth to tell him how to sneak into the cabin because his moms thought he was in bed when he'd really gone out drinking with Jamie and Noah.

How could Seth help him through this? Hell, he hadn't even seen Seth in person for years. Seth was a part of his childhood and it was past time to be a man.

He sat there as the phone vibrated and breathed a sigh of relief when it stopped.

* * * *

Willow Fork, TX
Eight months before

Georgia

Georgia took the mirror Kitten had brought her and looked at herself. Whoa. She totally looked like a chick who'd been kidnapped and shot and barely escaped.

"It's all right, Georgia." Kitten had shown up at her bedside this morning. "I brought your makeup kit. Well, part of it, but I'm sure I got the part that has your concealer. It's nothing more than a couple of bruises. You can swipe your magic wand and no one will see them."

"Or she can wear them like a badge of honor because she was a badass out there." Nat had come, too. "You should have seen her, Kitten. She mouthed off and Gretchen shot her and Georgia barely made a sound except to mouth off some more."

Mostly she'd been trying to breathe. She didn't like to think about how much it had hurt when the bullet had gone through her upper arm. She was lucky it had been the fleshy part and she'd barely required surgery.

Logan had acted like she was dying. He'd held her so tight and gotten her away. He'd ignored everything and everyone but her. He hadn't let her go until he'd put her on the gurney at the ambulance. Even then he'd insisted on riding with her. He'd held her hand and been irritable anytime one of the EMTs tried to get him to let go.

She hadn't ever wanted him to let go.

God, she was in love with Logan Green. He wasn't her type, but that might be a good thing since her type seemed to be asshole bad boys who didn't care enough about her to call. Logan was different.

She wasn't sure she'd actually known what she needed in a man until the day she'd met Logan Green. She wished she'd acted like an adult and not a ridiculous child.

"Are you really okay?" Kitten asked, setting the case on her bedside tray. "You haven't cried."

She didn't cry often, but this time she hadn't been holding it all in. She hadn't cried for a reason. "Deep down I knew my brothers would show up. I knew they wouldn't stop until they found us." She needed to be braver than this. "And I kind of thought Logan would be with them."

A brilliant smile lit up Nat's face. "I knew they would come for us, too. Logan came for you."

Kitten was grinning. "I realized Master Logan had a thing for Georgia very early on. She would annoy him but he couldn't take his eyes off her."

She hoped so. She could feel herself blush. "I don't know about that, but he was nice to me today. It felt like there was something between us."

She never talked like this. She never allowed herself to be vulnerable. Mean girls abounded in her world and she'd had to protect herself.

Nat and Kitten seemed different. They seemed like they actually cared about her. Nat was going to be her sister-in-law. She didn't want to have a cold relationship with her sister.

Nat's eyes were soft as she reached out and smoothed back Georgia's hair. "There is absolutely something between the two of you. Everyone can feel it. The chemistry between you is off the charts. But you have to move that chemistry to something more and that means no more tricks on the poor man."

She hadn't been exactly kind to the man when she'd met him. She'd taken one look at his gorgeous face and gone straight into her diva brat persona. It had been to protect herself from him because she'd known the minute she'd seen him that he could break her heart.

She would never know if she never tried. Wouldn't it be worth it if maybe, just maybe, Logan was the one man who could protect her heart, who could make her heart strong because of the love between them.

"No more tricks," she promised. "I'm going to try with him. I'm ready."

Somehow she'd found her calm when she'd gotten kidnapped. She and Nat had been taken by Nat's creepy stalker who'd threatened to sell off Georgia to the highest bidder. Held in a cage and then shot, she'd still managed to not break down.

She'd thought of Logan the whole time. He'd been her touchstone. When the panic would threaten, she would close her eyes and he would be there. In her mind, he would tell her to be brave, to survive, to wait for him.

He'd come for her.

She couldn't stop the smile on her face.

"I'm so happy for you." Kitten clapped her hands. "Master Logan needs some joy in his life."

Nat winked her way. "So does Georgia."

There was a knock on the door and then she wished she'd used the concealer because Logan walked in. He looked utterly delicious in jeans and a T-shirt that showed off his sculpted chest. The boy worked out. A lot. He was masculine and gorgeous, and she was super glad they'd disconnected her from the thing that beeped a lot because her heart rate had definitely gone up.

"Hi," she said and barely managed to not wince at the breathy sound of her voice.

Logan nodded her way, a grim expression on his face, but then he had that a lot. He didn't smile often. There was a darkness to him that she'd never understood. She knew something bad had happened to him on the job, but she wasn't sure of the details. He was a deputy so it could have been very bad. "Hi. Uhm, Nat, Kitten, can we get a moment alone? I need to talk to Georgia."

"Of course." Nat looked to Kitten. "How about we go see if there's anything decent to eat in this place."

"There is not," Kitten replied with her trademark grin. "But the coffee's all right. We'll be back in an hour or so, Georgia."

Logan watched as they walked out and the door closed quietly behind her friends. "You seem to be getting along with them."

They were part of his world. She was glad she could be friends with such wonderful women. "They're great. Obviously I'm thrilled Nat's going to be my sister-in-law and Kitten's wonderful."

"She's cool. Weird at first, but hey, we're all fucked up, right?"

She didn't like the way he wouldn't look her in the eyes. He paced at the end of her bed like he couldn't quite make himself stand still.

He'd kissed her. When they'd made it to safety, he'd knelt down and kissed her. She'd never been kissed like that before.

His mouth had dominated hers and she hadn't needed air to breathe. She'd only needed him.

"Did I say thank you for saving me?" And for holding her and kissing her and making her understand what she needed in a man.

He stopped and turned to face her. "It won't work, Georgia."

Her stomach twisted because she knew what that meant. Still, she couldn't come out and say it. Playing dumb worked sometimes. "It worked well. I'm not dead."

"You know I'm not talking about that. I'm talking about the two of us."

She was the one who couldn't look at him now. She stared at the chair beside her bed. Since she'd been brought to the hospital someone had always been in that chair, whether it was one of her brothers or Nat or Kitten. Someone had been there for her.

But it hadn't once been Logan. He'd stayed until her surgery was over and then he'd left. This was the first time he'd come back. It should have told her something, but she'd made up a million excuses for why he hadn't come to see her. It had only been a day and a half and he'd had a lot of things to do, including talking to the police. And he needed some sleep. And he was probably thinking about what to say after that incendiary kiss.

It had been the last one, but not in the way she'd hoped. He hadn't been trying to figure out how to ask her out. He'd been trying to find a way to tell her he'd made a mistake.

Now was when she would shrug and tell him to fuck off.

"Why?" The question came out before she could hold it back and the world suddenly seemed watery. "You kissed me."

His jaw firmed. "I shouldn't have. That was my fault. Georgia, it won't work. We're too different. We could fuck for a while, but I'm not ready for anything else and I don't want to hurt you. I'm not good for you."

But he was. He'd saved her and he'd made her want to be better. Of course that wasn't what he really meant. He really meant she wasn't good enough for him. She'd heard it a million times before.

She sniffled and turned away. "Like I would stay in this town long enough to fuck you." There was her brat-girl persona. She pulled it around her like it was a bulletproof vest. "You should go, Logan. Again, thanks for the save. You're right. It wouldn't work."

"I…well, take care of yourself."

She heard the door close again and knew he wouldn't be back.

What the man who'd kidnapped her hadn't been able to do with threats and bullets and fear, Logan had managed with a few words.

Georgia put her head in her hands and she cried.

Chapter One

Georgia Ophelia Dawson looked at her boss and gave him what she hoped was a brilliant smile. He was the best man she'd ever met, and he deserved this huge crowd that obviously idolized him. They admired him for his brilliant mind, but she was falling for the softer side of the man. "You know Seth Stark is a big deal."

Seth turned to her, the lights of the stage shadowing his face. He was so sweet, and she couldn't imagine how he was going to walk in there and talk to five thousand stockholders, but she'd made sure he looked damn good. His Armani suit fit him perfectly, and he'd been shined to a brilliant jewel. He was quite hot once she'd forced him to trade his glasses in for contacts and gotten him into the right clothes. And the man liked the gym. She hadn't had to fix his lean, six-foot-two-inch muscular body.

Seth's lips quirked up. "You make me feel that way."

She kind of sort of loved him. But she still couldn't get freaking Logan Green out of her head. Why was she stuck on a small-town deputy when she had a sweet-as-pie, brilliant billionaire in front of her?

Not that Seth was interested.

It was her damn brothers' fault. They'd recently gotten married. To the same woman. Natalie Buchanan-Dawson hadn't had to choose between super-brilliant Chase and sweet, stable Ben. She had the best of both worlds. Georgia was starting to think she wanted the same.

She winked at Seth as his name was announced on stage. The crowd went crazy, applauding and shouting. Seth had made everyone there a ton of money. He was smart and had a business head that blew her away, but still he needed her.

Yet even as he walked away, she remembered another type of power. It was the image she saw every night right before she went to sleep.

Logan Green looking down at her, his eyes smoldering with will.

You will never pull that shit again, Georgia. I'll put you over my knee. Do you have any idea what I'll do to your ass?

God, she could still hear his voice, see that handsome face staring down at her. She'd been working for Seth for eight months, living in absolutely no sin with him for seven, and she wondered if she could make it happen between the two of them.

She watched him as he started to talk about the new products they would be launching soon. He was confident and strong, like Logan. He'd built a whole company, a ridiculously successful business. Seth Stark was brilliant. He didn't truly need her. If she walked away, he could find another admin.

Had Logan found another sub?

"Hey, baby sister," a deep voice said.

Georgia gasped and turned, her whole heart coming to life. "Win!"

Winter Dawson stood in front of her, looking perfect in his ridiculously expensive suit. He was like all of her brothers—handsome and confident, completely alpha in every way. Win Dawson had never sat up at night wondering if there was a place for him in the world. He went out there and made one. "Hello, sweetheart. How are you doing?"

She winced inwardly. He was asking that because he knew she'd lost pretty much everything. Their distant and unloving father had finally decided to cut her off financially, and she'd been left with nothing. Her other siblings had trust funds from their mothers, but her mom had been a stripper the elder Dawson had hastily married and divorced, so there were no funds waiting for her.

She gave her oldest brother what she hoped was a winning smile. "I'm great. I love New York."

She loved parts of it. She loved the city and the rhythm she felt when she walked the streets of Manhattan. There was a pulse to the city that invigorated her. It started in her toes, and after a while, she was filled with an energy she'd never known in LA.

So why did she miss small-town Willow Fork? It was the ass end of the world, but while she'd been there she'd been necessary for more than filing paperwork and keeping an appointment book. She'd helped her brothers Ben and Chase track down a crazy, psychotic asshole who liked to sell women into slavery. Oh, sure it had been a terrifying experience, but she'd felt necessary for about two minutes.

"I'm glad to hear it," Win said, holding his arms open. She didn't hesitate. She walked into her oldest brother's arms and gave him a bear hug. "I missed you, brat."

She squeezed him tight. "You know, I know what you mean by that."

Her brother was a Dom. He was into all things BDSM, and he meant something different by the word "brat."

I will slap that ass silly, brat. Do you know what I want to do to you?

Logan Green had been a Dom, too. There was no way to mistake his domineering nature, the way he oozed authority. He'd been the one to pull her out of the fire, to hold her close when the going had gotten tough.

And he'd been the one to walk away.

"I assure you I didn't mean it in anything but a sibling way." Win frowned down at her. "Look, you need to tell me what Ben and Chase let you do because I didn't beat the shit out of either one of them in deference to the whole 'finding someone crazy enough to marry them both' thing. Don't get me wrong. I like Natalie a lot. She's a great girl, but I question the sanity of anyone who willingly marries Chase. Seriously, I sent in a shrink."

"Nat is perfectly sane." Nat was so awesome it hurt.

"That's what the shrink said, but I think Ben and Chase paid her." Win was six foot forever and towered over her. His normally hard expression softened as he stared down at her. "I'm worried about you, baby sister. Why don't you come back to LA with me? You can be my assistant."

And not be with Seth? The idea made her stomach turn. God, eventually Seth was going to get his head out of business and he would find a girlfriend, and Georgia would have to watch them. The girlfriend would almost certainly make her move out, and then she wouldn't be able to sit on the terrace with Seth and have her coffee in the mornings, and they wouldn't sit together at night and have a cocktail.

"Georgia? Are you all right?" Win stared down at her. "You went pale. Have you been eating properly? We can leave right now if you like. I can have you at my place in Malibu in a couple of hours. You don't have to work at all. You can go back to your acting classes. I'll take care of everything."

That was Win. He strode into any situation and took care of things. And the problem with Georgia Ophelia Dawson was that she'd been allowing it to happen all of her life. She'd always had someone to take care of her. It was nice to take care of someone else for a change. Yes, she lived in Seth's house and cashed his checks, but she had a job and responsibilities. It was a lovely thing. "I like it here."

"Then why did you go pale? Is it the Stark kid? Because I can handle him."

That was the last thing she needed. She wasn't about to send sweet Seth into a confrontation with her claws-and-fangs eldest brother. "Seth is great, and he's not a kid."

Cool gray eyes rolled. "He's twenty-six, Georgie. Trust me, he's a kid. I'm thirty-seven. Everyone looks like a kid to me."

She wasn't sure Win had ever been a kid. He'd been forced to watch out for them all at a very young age. Still, she felt the need to defend her boss. "Well, at twenty-six you weren't in charge of a multibillion-dollar business."

"No. It was sad. Mine was only multimillion," he replied with the patented Dawson sarcasm. "It took me another ten years to get to a billion."

Georgia shrugged. "Well, I guess Seth is smarter."

His face fell. "Shit. You like him."

"Of course I like him. He's my boss," she said as quickly as she could. She had to throw him off the scent right freaking now.

But Win was a wolf who rarely lost his prey. "No, sweetheart, this isn't about a boss. You think I don't hear that sigh in your voice? I've been your big brother for a very long time. That was the sigh you used when Brad Pitt came on screen or that idiot high school boyfriend picked you up. That sigh isn't about how much he pays you or how he treats you on Secretary's Day. How did he treat you on Secretary's Day?"

"God, Win. You're like back in the fifties, you know. I'm his assistant. It's Administrative Professional's Day, and he was very nice. He took me to lunch at Cipriani and then we saw a show." She didn't mention the pashmina he bought for her or the way he'd brought her breakfast in bed. It wasn't like he cooked it or anything, which was good because he couldn't cook to save his life, but he'd placed it all on a nice tray.

Those icy eyes of his grew grim. "So he wants you, too."

At least she could be totally honest, and it would save Seth so much trouble. "I like him a lot, but our relationship is not like that. I…god, this is stupid. I like him. He doesn't like me. I tried to kiss him one night and he said no." She'd had too much champagne at a gathering, and she'd kissed him in the back of the limo. He'd been a perfect gentleman, hugging her and saying all the right things, but she'd been in her own bed the next morning and they hadn't talked about it since.

He didn't want her. Seth would end up with someone sophisticated and smart and very, very beautiful.

And she would spend the rest of her life pining away over men she couldn't have. Maybe she should go back to California.

"Georgia!" Gus, Seth's driver, called out. He was standing backstage with the rest of Seth's staff. He always invited staff to these things since one of the ways he paid them was in stock. His staff members were also his shareholders, and they tended to love him for that. Gus's daughter was in college thanks to what Georgia had come to think of as the "Seth Stark college fund." "Come on. He's trying to get you onstage."

Seth's voice came over the loudspeaker. "Come on, Georgia. Don't leave me hanging out here. I swear, people. She really does exist. She's the best assistant in the world, and she's also gorgeous. I do not deserve her."

"Just boss and employee, huh?" Win said with a frown.

How did she make him understand? She probably couldn't. Win believed what he wanted to believe. "He's like this with all his employees. In some ways, we're his family. I have to go. Dinner tonight? You're paying or it's fast food, and even then, you're probably paying."

He ruffled her hair like he had when she'd been a kid and he'd been the only father figure she could count on. "Of course. But I should warn you, we're all in town."

She felt her eyes widen. "All? Like Ben and Chase and Mark and Dare?"

A ridiculously predatory smile lit her big brother's face. "All of us."

Shit. That didn't bode well for someone, and it was probably her. Her brothers only tended to get together when they were plotting. But hey, she would likely get some good meals out of it. And hopefully Nat was around and they could do some shopping with Ben's MasterCard. Yeah, she would take that. She could use some shoes. And clothes. And a new handbag. Visions of Chanel danced through her head.

Sometimes she missed being wealthy.

"Georgia? They are starting to believe you're a figment of my imagination. Stock is going down as we speak," Seth said over his mic.

"I have to go. See you later." She gave her brother what she hoped was a saucy smile, but all she could think was that once again her big brother thought she needed rescuing, and this time he'd brought in the big guns if he'd managed to get Mark and Dare and Ben and Chase all in the same room at the same time. She'd fucked up in their eyes, but then that seemed all she was capable of. She rushed to get to the corner of the stage. She couldn't leave Seth out there alone. He liked to call out his employees for recognition.

He was the best boss ever.

He was watching for her, his face frowning in consternation. He smiled as she came into view, his hand coming out to pull her onstage. She let him drag her forth and turned her head toward the bright lights. She'd been on stage enough to know how to handle them. She didn't blink, merely gave the unseen crowd a brilliant smile.

"See, I told you I have the most amazing assistant. Couldn't do it without her." He brought her hand to his lips, kissing it gallantly. She didn't take it personally. He was an affectionate man. She winked his way and waved to the crowd.

This, at least, she knew how to do. Smile and try to look pretty.

It was all she was good for.

* * * *

Seth Stark took a long breath before he pushed through the conference room door. Georgia was taken care of. She was off to Bergdorf Goodman and Tiffany with Nat Dawson, and then the two women would have an early dinner at Cipriani where the maître d' was waiting to treat them like queens. It would keep both women out of the way for hours. The men he was meeting had made sure of it. Of course, they had their reasons. None of the five Dawson brothers wanted their baby sister around for this takedown. Seth was sure they thought they didn't want her around because she would object to their interference in her life. Soon they would be happy they'd made arrangements for her to shop with her sister-in-law for different reasons—so baby sister didn't watch as they were all taken down a peg or two.

Seth Stark didn't play games and he didn't allow anyone to push him around, least of all the men who would one day be his brothers-in-law.

Begin as you mean to go. If he showed one ounce of softness, they would be all over him like a pack of wolves.

He was about to show them who the fucking alpha was.

They all turned in their chairs and he was faced with five Dawson wolves. Winter, the oldest, ran his own communications firm. DawComm had, at one time, belonged to Win's father. Win had won it over in a slick hostile takeover that had left his father blindsided and his business gutted.

To Win's left sat Ben and Chase Dawson. Trust fund private detectives, former SEALs. Ben was frowning, but Chase had an air of amused expectation about him as though he was looking forward to the upcoming drama. Across the table from the twins sat Mark and Dare. Mark was the older of the two but only by ten months. They were currently on a Delta Force team, and Seth had insider information that they were being recruited by the CIA. They were the easiest ones to take down, but in the end, he'd managed to find something that would force every one of them to back the fuck off.

Of course, he could be wrong and this could be a friendly "get to know you" meeting. He gave them his best "geeks are harmless" smile. He'd learned that being underestimated was sometimes his best maneuver. "Gentlemen. It's nice to meet you all."

Maybe they were here to check him out and they wouldn't give him hell. He would wait and see. He never played cards he didn't have to.

Win Dawson leaned forward, a menacing smile on his face as Seth sat down. "Thank you for agreeing to meet with us. Now, this is going to go one way and only one way. You are going to fire Georgia, and I'm taking her back to California with me."

Excellent. They were good cards. He really wanted to play them. He frowned, hoping he looked worried and a bit scared. "I don't want to fire Georgia. She's actually quite good as an assistant."

A low huff came from Win's chest. "I'm sure she's perfectly atrocious. Georgia doesn't take anything seriously. Look, I'm not stupid. None of us are."

"I don't know that I'd say that, Win," Ben Dawson said with a frown.

Ah, a crack in the brotherhood. Ben hadn't wanted to play it this way. He would have made a bet that Ben Dawson would be the softest of the five. It was good to know his instincts were perfect.

Win ignored his younger brother and plowed straight ahead with the surety of a man who always knew what he was doing and always got what he wanted. "Georgia has never been organized a day in her life. She rarely looks up from doing her nails long enough to do more than text her friends."

"You haven't been around her lately," Chase said with a shrug.

"Yeah, because Georgie got serious all of the sudden," Mark broke in. He was all shoulders and bulky arms. "I don't buy it. She goes from acting classes to being some tech guru's secretary? Not in this lifetime. She's fucking him. She's his mistress, and no man is going to fuck my sister over."

Ah, the military contingent. A sense of peace settled over Seth. A lot of men got a rush of adrenaline before they went into battle, but for Seth there was always a sweet contentment that came with knowing he was about to dismantle someone's life.

"Win is right. She needs to be home," Dare said. "She's not that smart when it comes to men."

"She's Georgie, Dare. She's not all that smart about anything," Mark said with a shake of his head.

And he was done playing around. Seth smacked a fist on the table and let go of his affable-geek persona because no one, not even her brothers, was going to insult his lady. "If I hear you insult Georgia's intelligence one more time, Mr. Dawson, we're going to fight, and you won't like how I fight."

Mark turned on him, canines bared. Yeah, he was going to be a peach of a brother-in-law. "Somehow I think we'll manage, Mr. Businessman."

"She's not dumb," Ben insisted.

"She's not." Win seemed determined to placate the most reasonable of his brothers. He sent Ben a long look, and Seth wondered how it would feel to be able to communicate with someone through a single look. Ben settled down. "She's not dumb, but she can be a bit naïve. She claims that she's not sleeping with him and there's nothing between them. Is that true, Mr. Stark?"

"I'm not sleeping with Georgia." He let a sigh of relief run through the crowd. He found it deeply interesting that Ben alone seemed upset by the news. And then Seth dropped his hammer. "I'm not sleeping with her yet. The time isn't right."

He stood because this wasn't as much fun as he'd thought it would be. He meant to marry Georgia Dawson, and now all he could think about was the fact that she seemed to love her brothers. He wasn't sure why, but she did, and she would be upset if she knew they were all fighting.

He didn't like it when Georgia was upset.

Seth made his way around the table, placing a file folder in front of each Dawson brother. "Gentlemen, if you would care to open the folders in front of you, we can begin."

Win pushed his away, a stubborn look on his face. "What the fuck is this, Stark? This isn't some business meeting. I'm not in negotiations with you. I've come to take my sister home, and there's not a damn thing you can do about it."

"What the fuck is this supposed to mean?" Dare held the contents of his folder up. He and his brother Mark were a very simple fix. His folder contained one phone number, a match to his brother's.

Seth settled back into his chair. It was time to get comfortable. "That's the phone number to the chairman of the Joint Chiefs of Staff of the United States. I recently did some programming work for the Pentagon. They were grateful. I have dinner with the old guy now and again. He's a nice man. Reminds me of my grandfather."

Mark rolled his eyes. "Awesome. You have a phone number. Good for you, buddy."

"This is stupid. I'm getting Georgia. I'll drag her home if I need to." Win started for the door.

"Brother, I would sit down if I were you. I think the little shit is serious." Chase frowned. "Is this what I think it is?" He held up a crystal-clear photograph of himself sitting at his computer desk, his back in full view.

"That was taken with a high-powered rifle from a building one block down from your office in Dallas. As you can see, there *is* a sniper position that works for your desk." He'd learned from Georgia that Chase was the smartest of all her brothers but had a paranoid streak that went a mile wide.

"Motherfucker. He's going to snipe me." Chase sat back, his hand slapping at the table. "I like him. You have my full support. Get at her, man."

Dare stared down at that number. "Are these ways you're planning to get rid of us? Is he serious?"

Seth shrugged casually. "Perhaps I'm not completely serious about taking out Chase. But I will spend an enormous amount of time and effort pointing out all the ways his security plans don't work.

He'll be like the little Dutch boy trying to plug all those leaks with too few thumbs."

"Dude, I told you I'm good. You're mean. We're going to get along nicely." Chase grinned, the only one in the room who seemed to be having a good time. "How are you going to kill Ben?"

Ben held up his note. It was blank. "I'm nothing to any of you."

"You're the reasonable one," Seth explained. Ben was deeply simple. If logic didn't work, he knew who to talk to. "And I do have a plan to deal with you. If you give me trouble, I'll talk to your wife."

Ben paled. "I'm with Chase. Go get Georgia. Don't look at me like that, Win. Nat can be brutal when she wants to be, and she won't like us pushing Georgia around. They've got that whole 'girl power' thing going."

"She's your sub. Tell her what to do," Win shot back. "Or have you two taken her collar? Do you understand the Master-sub relationship? Has Julian Lodge gone soft? What the fuck is he teaching you?"

"Yes, Julian is such a softie," Ben replied, rolling his eyes. "There's a reason you're not married, you freak. Keep it up, Win. I want to see how Seth handles you."

"I still don't know how this phone number is supposed to scare me." Mark seemed to struggle with the concept. Maybe they weren't as smart as he'd imagined.

"Dude, he's going to call the big brass and get you kicked off Delta Force." Chase shot his brother the finger, and for the first time in his life, Seth was genuinely happy he was an only child. The level of testosterone in the room was ridiculous, and the brothers looked like they were going to start throwing punches any minute.

"He can't get me kicked off." Dare stood up, leaning over the table. "Now he might have been able to get a sad little SEAL kicked out, but we all know you guys take it up the ass from anyone."

Ben got up, too, proving the reasonable guy could only be pushed so far. "I have something I'll shove up your ass, Dare."

"Shut up, all of you." Seth had been forced to shout down protesters before. He could handle this crew. He turned to the Delta contingent. "I assure you if I call and offer the United States military my expertise at no charge, with the only codicil being you and your brother's immediate forced retirement, you two will get kicked to the curb." He turned his gaze on the former SEALs. "Don't think I can't take care of you two. I can make Natalie think I am the greatest human being in the world. I recently set up a fund for victims of human trafficking. I endowed it with fifty million dollars and set her up as an advisor. I intend to let her know about the new charity this evening. Who is she going to think is best for Georgia?" And Win. Win was the hard case. Win was the one who wouldn't go down easy. "And you. Please read that file because I set that up so carefully. I want you to understand how far I'm willing to go."

Win's face was red, his whole body stiff and stubborn, but he sat back down and the rest of the pack seemed to take their cue from him. The whole group calmed, a détente obviously reached. Win opened his folder and began to read. His was the most convoluted, complex plan, but he would get the gist quickly.

Seth waited and wished Logan was here. Logan Green was his best friend despite the time and distance between them. They'd bonded at a young age. He'd been older than Logan, and it might have meant something if they'd met at Seth's school in New York. But in Bliss, those months didn't mean a thing. Bliss, Colorado, had been his sanctuary, the one place where he could be a kid, and Logan had been his brother in every way but blood. He'd spent each school year working hard so he would be allowed to spend the summer and Christmas break with his granddad in Colorado. If he'd earned even one *B*, his parents would have forced him to stay in New York and spend the summer with a tutor. Seth Stark had graduated with a perfect GPA. He'd been a National Merit Scholar and gained every academic award his private Manhattan high school had offered, and all because he wanted those months of freedom with his brother.

He was too close to having the family he wanted to screw it up now. He'd found the right woman thanks to someone named Kitten. He wasn't going to allow Georgia's brothers to fuck it up for him.

And he wasn't going to let Logan fuck it up either.

Win Dawson took a long breath and closed the file. "This is a long line of dominoes you've set up, Stark."

Seth had known Win wouldn't need a lengthy explanation. "Yes and they end in my hostile, but easy takeover of DawComm. I estimate it will take about ten months and a hundred and fifteen million or so, but I can have your company if I want it. I suppose you understand that I wouldn't keep you around."

He could see the minute Winter Dawson decided to take him seriously. "What do you want?"

That was the easiest question he'd had all day. "I want Georgia. I intend to marry your sister. I intend to make her my queen, and I won't allow you to come between us."

Win frowned. "Wait. You want to marry her? You're going to marry Georgia and take care of her for the rest of her life?"

"That's what marriage means." His parents' marriage had been a piece of shit, a cold contract between two wealthy people. Seth's marriage was going to be different. It was going to be about passion and love and friendship, and it was going to be the slightest bit illegal because he wanted a threesome and he intended to have it at any cost.

"Why the fuck didn't you say that?" Mark asked, rolling his eyes.

"If you're willing to marry her, we'll welcome you with open arms, man," Dare said.

"It's not as simple as that," Ben broke in.

"She's in love with Logan Green." Chase neatly summed up what should have been his problem.

"I'm counting on it." If she didn't love Logan, nothing would work.

Win groaned and let his head hit the desk. "God, I don't get the ménage thing."

Mark and Dare shared a high-five. "We do."

"Oh, because you're so fucking original," Chase said, shaking his head.

"We're the originals," Ben agreed.

He must be in love if he was willing to deal with these insane idiots, but they weren't exactly scaring him off. Family was important. He should know since he'd never truly had one. But a man couldn't pick his family. It tended to be thrust upon him, and the Dawson brothers were going to be his. Luckily, Logan seemed to have liked at least a couple of the Dawsons.

And if Logan hadn't wanted Georgia, he would sell his company stock for a penny.

Georgia was the most beautiful thing he'd ever seen. She was curvy and sexy and had a submissive streak that Logan would need. Seth required it, too, but not the way Logan did. Seth would be utterly content to quietly top her without ever acknowledging who was in charge. He would smile and tell the world that he was pussy whipped and happy to be so.

Win's eyes narrowed, and Seth realized this wasn't over. "How are you going to handle the whole acting thing?"

The rest of the room groaned.

"She's still auditioning occasionally. I've taken care of it. She was cast in an off-Broadway play, and I managed to get it shut down."

Ben frowned. "She got cast and you shut it down?"

"The director is known for fucking his actresses and tossing them aside. He cast her as Lady Macbeth. Do you honestly see her doing Shakespeare? And it was, shall we say, a nontraditional version with an enormous amount of nudity." That director had recently left New York when it had become apparent to him that he wouldn't be hired here again. Seth had made damn sure of it.

Ruining the lives of those who truly deserved it was his gift, and he genuinely enjoyed doing it.

All five brothers froze, predatory eyes zeroing in.

"Yes, I felt the same way," Seth explained. "He was using her because she's gorgeous and naïve, and so fuckable it hurts."

"Not to sound like my sister," Mark began, "but ewwww."

Seth shrugged. They should get used to it. "I think she's the most beautiful woman on the planet. I don't intend to allow others to use her. She's actually a quite horrible actress. She's brilliant at improv, but if you give her a few lines, she turns into a robot. I could get her parts on Broadway, but I haven't figured out how to bribe the entire world to say she's good. She would get her feelings hurt, and I won't allow it."

"You're a manipulative little shit," Win said with something akin to respect.

He wasn't that freaking little. He was six foot two, and he might not be the bulkiest guy, but he was strong. He worked out every day. He couldn't help it that the Dawson brothers were overgrown Neanderthals.

Logan was bigger than he was. Logan was more masculine. What if Georgia only wanted Logan? Sure there had been that one night when she'd tried to kiss him, but she'd had a bit too much to drink and he'd been playing a long game.

If he'd slept with her that night, she would have run the next morning, or she would have stayed but for the wrong reasons.

He stared at Win. Win was the hardass. The others would fall in line if Win gave the okay.

"I'm going to marry Georgia, and I'm going to share her with my best friend. I'll do it whether you like it or not. If you try to come between us, I'll bury you. I'll play it smart. She won't know what's happened, and she won't believe you when you try to tell her what I've done."

Win's eyes narrowed, and he saw the shark that lurked beneath Winter Dawson's three-piece suit. "If I want to, I'll make her believe."

"Do you want to start a war with me? Perhaps you could win, but your sister would lose a man who would die for her, a man who firmly intends to put her first, to take care of her. Make no mistake, I am in love with your sister."

Win studied him, the silence heavy in the room. After a long moment, he held out his hand. "Welcome to the family, Seth. Good luck with her. You're going to need it."

He was suddenly surrounded by Dawsons. They slapped him on the back and started telling all kinds of stories about Georgia's childhood and the trouble she'd been.

He listened, enjoying the feeling of being accepted, but it was hollow without his brother by his side.

Unfortunately, his "brother" was twelve kinds of fucked up. Logan was in a bad place, and it was up to Seth to bring him out of it because his long dark period was starting to look like a permanent state of mind. He couldn't lose Logan like this. And he wasn't about to lose Georgia.

Seth was going back to Bliss, and this time he would never leave.

And he damn straight wasn't going alone. The plan was already in motion. He was hours away from the call he'd been waiting for, and then he would take Georgia and start his real life.

Chapter Two

"Earth to Logan. Come in, Logan."

Logan Green opened his eyes and frowned up at Leo Meyer, who should know better than to interrupt a nice nap. He glanced over at the clock on the wall. It was barely three in the afternoon. He didn't have to be on the dungeon floor until nine. He had hours and hours to sleep. Though he probably shouldn't have tried to do it during a counseling session. "It's your fault, man. This couch is comfy."

Leo frowned. "Blame Shelley. She insisted on redoing my office. She said it wasn't patient-friendly enough."

Leo's office before had been a whole bunch of Asian stuff and weird rock garden tables. There was still a waterfall on the wall, but the rest of the room had been transformed into something infinitely comfortable and yet wholly masculine. Logan yawned. "I don't know that I need this anymore, Doc."

The talking thing didn't work for him. Talking about shit made him antsy. Now working the dungeon floor soothed him. Leo had been right about that. He'd managed to find a happy place where he could tie up a sub and spank her pretty ass and send her on her way and everyone was satisfied.

"I asked you a question. The customary reaction to having a question posed to you would be replying with an answer, not a snore.

Have you had your sinuses examined? I think there might be something wrong with you."

He'd always been a snorer. It didn't bug him at all since he didn't have to listen to himself. "I'll check into that, Doc. Are we done here?"

Leo frowned in a way that let him know he was rapidly losing patience. "I asked about the women you've been topping in the club. I was asking about any trouble you might have had."

Logan sat up. The one thing he took seriously these days was his job. "Did someone complain?"

His brain raced, trying to come up with a name. He hadn't had problems with anyone since he'd taken on the full-time Dom job after he'd left Kitten duty. He had several regulars, and he was starting to work with Wolf on training the new staff, both tops and bottoms. He'd never had a single complaint that he knew of.

"Yes, several of the women have been complaining," Leo explained.

He was a damn good Dom. He took care of his charges. He felt a fierce frown cross his face. "I haven't done anything bad. I've been careful."

"Yes, that's the problem. They've been complaining that you won't have sex with them." A smiled curved up Leo's lips now. "Not on the record, of course, but Shelley's been hearing it in the locker room. They're calling you the Priest. You'll hand out the discipline but you won't take any pleasure."

He couldn't. He couldn't get a fucking erection anymore if the woman wasn't a gorgeous brat with blue eyes and blonde hair and the sassiest mouth in the world. "I wasn't aware I should do that."

"I realize that you signed a contract that banned sexual relations with Kitten, but she was a special case. The women who come here have been fully screened both psychologically and physically. You can fuck any one of them who consents."

Logan groaned. "Do we really have to talk about this?"

"The women who come here tend to be looking for relaxation."

"Dude, you make me sound like a hooker."

"I believe the male equivalent is a gigolo, and now, obviously you aren't being paid to have sex and you don't have to have sex with someone to top them, but most men of your age would view The Club as a sexual free-for-all. I sure as fuck know I did." Leo leaned forward. "Now would be a good time to point out that patient confidentiality works both ways."

Logan nearly rolled his eyes. Leo didn't want his almost wife to hear about his former life at The Club. "I'm sure you were a legend."

"Maybe not a legend, but I did enjoy myself. After I got divorced, I cut quite a swath through the subs here. I didn't take sex seriously until I met my fiancée. I negotiated a lot of sex with submissives. You don't even talk about it with them. I have to admit, I was surprised. I expected you to become one of the dungeon studs. Is there something I don't know?"

"No." What the hell was he talking about? "Dude, I spent a summer fucking my way through half of Southern Colorado's female population with your brother. I get it. You had a ton of fun when you weren't like old and stuff."

Leo wasn't old. Leo was like thirty-five or something, but he also had his whole life together and was happily sharing an amazing woman with his brother and enjoying his dream job of fixing fucked-up people. Logan was one of those fucked-up dudes, so he felt the need to needle Leo about his age since it was all he had on the man.

"Nice, asshole. I'm not that old." Leo wasn't the most formal of shrinks. "And I've heard about your escapades with Wolf. That's why I'm surprised you haven't partaken of the pleasures offered here at The Club. I've heard Haven has been rather…persistent with you."

Haven Welch. Sweet girl. Pretty. Thin. Glossy black hair. Deeply submissive. "She's a nice girl. She's been complaining?"

Leo snorted. "Dude, she practically presents to you every time you walk in a room. It's disturbing. Seriously, you haven't picked up those signs, yet?"

"Uhm, I top her. That's the extent of the relationship. She filled out a form, and I do what I'm supposed to do." He hadn't thought to go any further. Had he fucked up? He was good at fucking up. He didn't think of Haven as anything but a client. She wasn't the woman who would spit bile at a man and pretend to toss his phone into a grove of fucking rosebushes. She wouldn't push his every boundary and make him fucking hard at the thought of getting her on her knees in front of him. Yeah. He would make her beg for his cock. She would fucking know who her Master was when he was done with her.

"Or maybe you really like her. Wow, that is a massive erection," Leo pointed out.

Fuck. Logan sat up, trying to shift so his cock wasn't poking out of his sweat pants. Damn her. "I wasn't thinking of Haven."

"Were you, perhaps, thinking of Georgia Dawson?" Leo asked the question in an innocent tone of voice.

He wanted to growl and punch something. That was what Georgia brought out in him. Georgia Ophelia Dawson. He could still hear her in that oh-so-proper voice introducing herself to him like he was the hired help. She'd turned that button-cute nose up at him and proceeded to talk on her phone, ignoring him until she wanted him to pick something up or help her out of the car. She'd been a snot-nosed, brat princess.

Who had nearly melted for him because it was all an act. He could still feel her arms around him, clinging to him as she cried and thanked him for pulling her out of that hellhole she and Nat had been thrown into.

I didn't think you would come for me. I wanted you, Logan. God, I prayed for you to come for me. Logan, Logan, I love you so much.

She'd sobbed into his shirt on their way to the hospital, and for a minute, he'd thought about keeping her at his side. He could have collared her in a heartbeat. She needed a Dom so badly, wanted a real lover who wouldn't let her get away with that bratty shit she pulled for attention. She was starved for affection, and he'd thought about marrying her in that moment and realized he couldn't. He couldn't take her home to his moms. He couldn't go home, and it wasn't because he was ashamed of her.

He was ashamed of himself.

He was a ball of hate, and he couldn't bring her into his world because any life here in Dallas was a half life.

Fuck it all. He wanted to go home, and he couldn't. He wanted Georgia more than his next breath, and he couldn't have her.

"That was a whole lot of emotion playing out over your face," Leo said with a self-satisfied smile. "Good. We're getting somewhere. So, this is about Georgia."

"There's nothing going on between me and Georgia." Because he wouldn't allow it to happen. He put his hand over his heart. The memento he'd had inked over his left pec had done exactly what he'd wanted it to do. It reminded him that letting her go had been the best thing for her. And him? All he truly deserved was that damn elaborate *G* he'd had tattooed on his body the day after she left. He'd been careful about the placement. It was hidden under the leather vest he wore, and he showered privately now. That *G* was his. No one else needed to know.

Leo sighed, a deeply patient sound. "We haven't talked about that day."

"Because there's nothing to talk about." Nothing he was willing to talk about. The minute he'd known she was in danger, his whole fucking world had stopped. He'd thought he'd been through some serious shit. He'd been brutalized, his whole being boiled down to pain and survival, but he realized he hadn't known real fear until Georgia had been put in the same position.

He'd been helpless, as helpless as he'd been when the fucking, goddamned, scum-sucking Russian mobster had tied him down and beaten him until he'd begged for death. Knowing that Georgia was in the same position had been worse. And he couldn't fucking talk about it.

"I've had sessions with Ben about that day," Leo offered.

Ben was a talky, touchy-feely kind of guy. Ben had never been tied to a fucking desk and shown the truth of the world. Ben had never prayed that the next second was the last, the end to his pain. "Good for Ben. I hope he feels better."

"I've had sessions with Chase."

Yeah, that news made him feel like the freak of all time. *Fuck.* Chase Dawson was one of the world's premier curmudgeons and he was talking about his feelings? Curmudgeon. He only knew the damn word because he'd had to help Seth with his SATs.

How long had it been since he'd talked to his best friend? How long was he going to duck Seth's calls because he didn't want Seth to know how low he'd sunk?

He'd told Seth everything. No moment of his life since he was seven years old had been real until he'd talked to Seth about it. But that day in the sheriff's office in Bliss, Colorado, had been hyperreal, and he couldn't discuss it with Seth.

He'd sent Georgia away because he didn't want her to know how fucked up he was. Was he going to drive Seth away, too? Would he end up with two tats on his body one day and absolutely no friends?

"Do you wonder where she is?" Leo asked.

Only every minute of every day and all night long, even when he managed to sleep. "She's got a job somewhere. Dude, it doesn't matter. She's a Dawson. She's rich and has a whole bunch of brothers and shit. She'll be fine."

"Really? What gave you that impression?"

A bite of uncertainty flashed through him. Georgia was fine. She had to be. "Uhm, she's a Dawson. They all have cash. She's back in LA becoming some sort of star."

She was beautiful enough to do it. One day he would be sitting in a movie theater and she would come on the screen, and he would tear up knowing that she'd been the one and he'd been too screwed up to take her, to hold her, to make her his. The truth of the matter was she deserved way better than him. He'd found out what a pathetic piece of shit he was that day he'd been tied down and tortured.

A sympathetic look crossed Leo's face. "I don't think you understand the Dawson clan. Georgia's father cut her off. She doesn't have a dime to her name. She left Dallas because she found a job in New York, but she wouldn't let Ben pay for her way. She went there on a bus. Ben and Chase didn't know about that at the time. To say they were upset would be an understatement. Do you know how expensive New York is?"

He couldn't quite catch his breath. Georgia was in New York, and she didn't have a metric shit ton of family money behind her? She was alone in a massive city? Where the fuck was she working? Panic threatened. He knew some people in New York. Seth was in New York. He could get Seth to find her.

"Where is she? Where is she working? I need her address."

How fast could he be in New York? There was usually a red-eye out of DFW. He could likely be there by morning. Two hours to get to whatever hellhole she was in and ten fucking seconds to pull her out of there. They could be back in Dallas by tomorrow night.

And then what?

Leo's eyes widened. "Do you understand how creepy stalkery you sound right this second?"

Probably really creepy because the way he felt about Georgia wasn't exactly normal. He didn't kind of worry about her and hope she was okay. She was a gnawing guilt in his gut. He tried to force himself to stay calm. He'd gotten good at hiding what he felt. He was pretty sure no one knew he was screaming on the inside most of the time. "She's the sister of my friends. It's not a big deal."

"Oh, I think it's a huge deal. She's the sister of your friends? Who do you think you're fooling? Look man, you can't consider yourself truly crazy about a woman until you've walked that slender line between 'checking in' and 'stalking.' Helpful tip—don't carry a camera with you when you're 'checking in.' It makes the cops crazy."

Logan stood, running his hands through his hair. Half the time he couldn't tell when Leo was joking and when he was serious. Leo was the most sarcastic bastard he'd ever met, and he'd met Zane Hollister. It was often best to ignore Leo's advice when it sounded like sitcom dialogue. "Dude, do you know if she's all right? Have Ben and Chase not been checking in on her?"

He would be shocked if they hadn't at least made sure she wasn't on the street.

"Chill out. She's fine. She landed a good job, and she's living with her boss, who also happens to be a billionaire."

He felt his face flush, his heart drop. She'd been gone for eight fucking months and she'd already found a billionaire and made her move? He could still see the tears in those crystal blue eyes as he'd pushed her away. Had they all been for show? And who moved in with their boss? A couple of nasty names flashed through his head, but he shoved them aside. She wasn't like that. Not deep down. She was bratty and used that rich-girl persona like a shield, but she'd been sweet and supportive with Nat and Kitten. He'd watched her when she thought he hadn't been looking.

Yeah, he'd done that a whole lot because the minute he'd gotten a look at that girl, he'd been hooked. It was a good thing he didn't own a camera because he really could have turned into creepy-stalker guy.

Who the hell was this billionaire motherfucker? He had to be using her. "Is she engaged to him?"

He might be able to handle it if the asshole was actually marrying her.

"Not as far as I know. According to Chase, she moved in with this guy about a month after taking the job. Maybe she's simply being a hands-on assistant. She might not be sleeping with him. It does seem farfetched, though. She's a lovely woman."

She was the sexiest woman on the fucking planet. It had been the hardest thing in the world to keep his hands off her, but he'd done it because he knew he couldn't give her what she needed. He'd done it because he cared about her. This rich bastard obviously had no such qualms. "And Chase let this happen?"

What the hell was wrong with him? Logan could see Ben screwing up like that. Ben would be all "she's an adult and needs to make her own decisions and we should support her." Chase was more reasonable. Chase should have put a hit out on the guy like any good brother would.

"I believe Ben and Chase are visiting her this weekend along with the rest of their brothers," Leo explained.

Thank god. He settled back into his chair. He'd only met Win Dawson once, and he'd never met Mark and Dare at all, but Win would haul her ass out of there and he wouldn't give a damn that it was the twenty-first century and women had rights. He would do what it took to protect his sister.

And who would save her the next time she got duped into a bad relationship? There it was. There was that nasty kernel of guilt. She needed a Dom. She needed a Master who would make sure she was all right. Her brothers couldn't do that for her forever. She needed a lover, a keeper, a friend.

It was the last part that he wasn't sure he could handle at this point. He could fuck her. God, he could very likely fuck her forever. He could top her in a heartbeat. He would love it.

But he wasn't anyone's friend now. It was precisely why he couldn't go home, why he might never go back to his job.

Because he still couldn't walk in that building without feeling the pain. He still couldn't hold a gun in his hand without visions of blowing Alexei Markov's head away.

"Good. I'm glad to hear Ben and Chase will take care of her." Now he could try to steer Leo away from the subject.

"Do you want to tell me why you shoved Georgia away when it's so obvious to everyone that you're in love with her?"

Or Leo could ignore him and push through. Logan snorted. "I'm not in love with her."

He wasn't actually capable of that now. He sure as fuck wasn't deserving. Something had gone wrong with him. Maybe it was his father's DNA. His dad had been a piece of shit coward who beat his mom and sent her on the run. Only Marie Warner had been able to save them. Marie. His other mom.

How ashamed would she be if she truly knew what had happened in that room?

"So Georgia doesn't have anything to do with why you haven't had sex in eight months?"

Leo's words forced him back to the shitastic here and now. "I don't know that my sex life is any of your business."

"It is. Everything about you is my business. I'm your therapist, but more than that, I'm your boss. You're in a position of power as a Master in The Club, and I have to understand the rationale behind any major changes in your behavior. Before you met Georgia Dawson, you enthusiastically fucked any woman who would let you have her."

It hadn't been that bad. He'd enjoyed himself. "You make me sound like a manwhore."

"If it fucks like a duck," Leo snarked, "it's usually a manwhore. Look, man, I told you I've talked to Wolf. I would have thought that maybe you preferred a ménage, but you had sex with plenty of women on your own here. So I have to wonder if you're in love with Georgia Dawson, and then I wonder why you pushed her away."

Because he'd never truly walked out of Nate's office. He was still tied down and dying, and he didn't know how to get off that fucking desk.

Leo leaned forward. "Logan, talk to me. We've been doing this for over a damn year, and we've never gotten to the heart of the problem."

"The heart of the problem is that some asshole beat the shit out of me, and I won't let it happen again." He still couldn't talk about it.

Leo shook his head slowly, leaning back. There was a calm about Leo that set him on edge. "No. That was the start. You've talked about everything that happened in clinical details, but you've never gotten down to the feelings behind it. And I'm pretty certain you've never once told me the whole story."

Feelings? Loneliness. Despair. Helplessness. Weakness. "I felt pissed that I was getting my ass kicked."

And no one needed to know the whole story. No one except Caleb. He hadn't been able to hide anything from the doctor who had put him back together, but Caleb had kept his mouth shut.

"See, your words betray you. What happened to you went beyond a Saturday night fight. You're still making light of it. Tell me why you don't read comic books anymore."

He rolled his eyes. "Because I'm not fucking twelve."

"You weren't twelve when you were reading comics. You read them up until that day and then you burned your whole collection. You can't tell me that wasn't a defining act."

"How the fuck did you know that?" He'd done it in his backyard a few weeks after he'd gotten out of the hospital. He'd doused three long boxes with lighter fluid and set his whole collection on fire. Twenty years of collecting up in smoke because every single one of those books had lied. There were no heroes. Or at least he'd figured out he wasn't one of them.

"I've had long conversations with all of your relatives and friends."

Betrayal bit into his gut. "What about that whole patient-client confidentiality you mentioned earlier?"

"That's only in play when it comes to me discussing my findings with them. They can talk about you all they like. I simply called and put a few questions to them, and then I listened. They were eager to talk about you because they love you. Well, most of them. That doctor hung up on me."

Leo listening was a powerful thing. "I want you to stay away from my friends."

"Are they your friends?" Leo asked. "You haven't talked to them in months. You've barely talked to your moms."

He was real damn good at one-word answers. Yes. No. Maybe. "They're okay."

"I don't think so. When I talked to them, they seemed a bit fractured."

His moms? No. His moms were solid. Always. There was one certainty in his life and that was that Teeny Green and Marie Warner loved each other. They were devoted. "What's happening?"

He hadn't called. He'd actually dodged their calls. And Seth's. And Nate's and Cam's and Callie's. And James's and Hope's. It was far easier to be here where almost no one had any expectations of him. Where no one knew who he'd been before he'd been shown who he really was.

"I can't talk about it. I can only say that your mothers miss you and want you to come home. You know it's their twenty-fifth anniversary."

He knew. "Yeah. I'll send them a card."

"You're not going to the party?"

Party? His momma hated parties. Marie thought they were a horrible waste of time. Of course, Teeny loved them and Marie loved Teeny so…maybe. "Are they having coffee at Stella's?"

"They're having a complete rededication ceremony. It's being paid for by the same man who paid for your…" Leo stopped, taking a long breath. "It's going to be a lovely ceremony, but it will likely be empty without you there."

A nasty suspicion played through his head. "Paid for my what?"

"I shouldn't have said anything, but you can't believe I'm doing this for free. Logan, you have people who love you."

That didn't answer the question. "I thought I was working off my debt."

It was why he worked five nights a week in the dungeon. Hell. That was kind of wrong. He loved working the dungeon. He would do it for free. Of course, now that he thought about it, the dungeon itself was membership-only. The other Doms either worked for Julian full time or they got reduced-rate memberships in exchange for their work.

And Leo's services weren't exactly cheap. *Fuck.*

"Who? Is it Stef?" The king of Bliss was a likely candidate. Stef

Talbot tried to take care of everyone, but the thought of charity rankled.

"No. It's not Stef."

Fuck all. His gut was in a knot again. "My moms can't afford this."

"I would never charge your mothers. Initially I was going to do everything pro bono, but you have a friend out there who didn't want you to be beholden. You have an actual lifetime membership to The Club in your name. And none of that matters. Logan, forget I said anything." Leo waved him off. "We have other things to talk about."

There was a loud knock on the door, but Logan ignored it as the truth swept over him. There was only one person who would swoop in and drop a wad of cash and never miss it and never mention it. "Seth."

It was Seth. Seth, who damn well knew how he felt about taking charity.

The door opened and Wolf strode in.

Leo's eyebrow climbed right up his forehead. "Hello, brother. Since when do you interrupt a session?"

Wolf stopped, rolling his eyes. "Dude. You're ten minutes over time. I've been waiting forever, and we have a lunch meeting with Shelley, if you care to remember."

Leo went a little white. "I remember. Jeez, don't tell her I forgot. We're supposed to be at Top in fifteen minutes." He stood up. "Logan, I'll see you on Thursday."

Thank god. He was done. He could stop fucking talking and hang out until he could get back to the dungeon. Except that now he knew he was here on Seth's fucking charity.

Wolf turned to him. "I don't know about that. Logan, I got off the phone with Jamie a couple of minutes ago."

Fuck. "What happened?"

"You know Cam and Laura and Rafe got married last weekend, right?"

He felt his jaw tighten. Yeah. He'd been invited. Cam had become one of his best friends, and he'd always had a thing for Laura, but they had gotten married in a ceremony that included Holly and Caleb and Alexei.

He couldn't watch Alexei find his joy. He fucking couldn't.

"Yeah, I know," Logan replied.

"Well, Cam and Rafe surprised Laura that day. They adopted a baby. Caleb and Stef made it possible."

Because they were billionaires and money greased a lot of wheels. But Laura had a baby. A knot formed in his chest that had nothing to do with hate and everything to do with that part of him that could still love. Laura would be a great mom. That kid was lucky. "Good for her."

"Nate's alone at the station right now. He forced Cam to take paternity leave, and there's no one else qualified. Rachel is pregnant again, and she's having a rough time. Rye won't leave her. Nate's been living at the station. I'm going to head back to Bliss. I have to help out."

Wolf was going to Bliss to do Logan's job? Nate had kept it open, but he'd known he wouldn't go back. Except that the thought of Wolf sitting at his desk kind of pissed him off.

Leo stood. "You can't leave. We have the engagement party in two weeks. Do you know how long Shelley has been planning this? She's going to be devastated."

Shelley. She'd been so sweet to him, inviting him to dinner, taking care of him. Was he going to let her engagement party get ruined because Wolf felt like he had to do his job? And then there was his moms' party. Twenty-five years of pure love and devotion should be acknowledged.

"I have to go. I owe these guys," Wolf argued.

Wolf didn't owe anyone, but Logan fucking did. Nate had helped him out when anyone else would have fired his ass and washed his hands of him. Cam had been a true friend. Hell, he owed James and Noah's wife, Hope, more than they could know. He owed Bliss.

"I'll go." The words dropped out of his mouth like a lodestone, dragging him down.

He owed his moms everything.

Wolf's whole demeanor changed, relaxing and showing some joy. "Are you serious? Because that would make my life so much easier. Shelley would be upset if I wasn't here for the party. Are you sure, man?"

He owed Wolf. It was time to man up and help out his people. He would survive it. He would go to his moms' party and help at the station, and when he left this time, his head would be held high.

And he could leave and not go back. And he damn straight would figure out how to deal with Seth.

"I'm sure."

Leo and Wolf looked at each other, having a silent conversation that only brothers understood. Jealously nearly split Logan in two because he knew what that felt like. He and Seth had that kind of communication once.

"If you're sure, then I'll have Kitten book the ticket out for you instead of me," Wolf said, but his tone had turned hesitant.

God, he hated that. He hated the whole sympathy-pity thing. And he was going to have to call Seth because he also didn't take fucking charity. "I'll be fine."

Because he was headed back to Bliss. Back home. God. He was going home.

He started out the door to go and pack. As he glanced behind him, he was almost sure he saw Leo and Wolf high-five each other.

Chapter Three

Logan turned the truck into town and drove right past the Trading Post. It was the store his moms ran and one of Bliss's great meeting spots. He'd grown up in that store, watched it go from a place where the people of the town could buy food and simple supplies to a one-stop shop for everything from eggs and milk on the first floor to clothes, camping gear, and sporting goods on the second. The Trading Post had grown as he had, his moms gaining more and more confidence in their business abilities every year.

He couldn't go there yet, hadn't even called to let them know he was coming. He'd had a single conversation with Nate where he'd arranged for his truck to be brought to the airport and then asked Nate to keep the whole thing on the down low. Only Nate and Zane knew he was coming back to town. They thought he was trying to surprise his moms, but the truth was he didn't want anyone to know until he'd figured out how it was going to work.

Cam had six weeks of paternity leave. He could survive six weeks. He had to.

And maybe he wouldn't even go back to Dallas. Maybe he would take off and find someplace where he didn't have to talk about shit and no one cared what had happened to him. He could start over since he'd fucked up this particular life.

Stella's was up ahead. He knew the roads like the back of his hand, but the sight of Stella's had him choking up. The sign was the same as it had been since he could remember seeing it. White letters on a red background. A little cup of coffee. *Stella's Diner. Bliss, CO since 1970.*

He remembered vividly the first time he'd eaten here without his moms at his side. He'd been with Seth. He'd been nine and Seth ten, and he could still recall how adult he'd felt sitting there and eating a turkey sandwich and fries with his best friend and paying for it himself. He'd been a real big man.

The sight of the sheriff's station up the street turned his stomach.

He hadn't been a big man then. No. He hadn't been much of a man at all.

"Holy fucking shit." A deep voice pulled him from those thoughts. "Am I seeing things?"

He glanced over and there was Jamie in the parking lot of Stella's. James Glen. He was standing with Noah, his brother. Hell, half his childhood had been spent knocking around the county with those two, and he'd skipped their wedding party, too.

It was right there—the urge to punch the gas and get out of town. He didn't have to deal with any of this. But then he caught the smile on Jamie's face dimming as though he realized what Logan was thinking. *Fuck.*

Logan pulled in and plastered a smile on his face as he shut off the truck. Before he got out, his hand went to his left pec, rubbing there. He did it almost unconsciously now, as though she was there in the lines and flowers of the *G*. Somehow, if she was with him, he could get through the bad parts.

He slid out of the driver's seat, and Jamie was on him in a heartbeat. "Logan! Oh, man, you have no idea how good it is to see you."

He let himself get pulled into a manly hug and managed to slap his old friend on the back. "Hey, Jamie. Noah."

Noah stood back as though unsure of his welcome. He'd only been home for a few months, but Logan hadn't seen him at all. God, Noah had come home and managed to get married and set up his veterinary practice, and Logan hadn't even called him.

He was a shit.

"Noah, my man." He pulled away from Jamie and held a hand out to Noah, but he couldn't help giving him hell. He'd heard some from Wolf about what had transpired, but giving his friend shit was something Logan lived for. "Heard NYC wasn't so great for you, buddy. So the whole 'marrying a complete ho-bag' didn't work out?"

Noah flashed Logan his happy middle finger and then shook his hand, pulling him in for a manly hug, the tension dissolving. "Yeah, well, I did better the second time around. What the fuck happened to you? When did you go all Incredible Hulk? You're huge."

A whole fuck-ton of weight training had transformed him from a lanky, six-foot-three, one-hundred-and-sixty-pound kid, into a man with two hundred and twenty-two pounds of pure muscle. He'd kept up the workouts in Dallas, never missing a day. *Fuck.* Where was he going to work out here? All of his equipment was back in his old room, and he couldn't stay there.

"Logan!"

A brunette ball of pure energy raced his way, and he braced for impact, a genuine smile hitting his face for the first time in forever. Hope. She threw her arms around him and expected him to catch her.

Which he would. Always. Because Hope had saved him that night.

"Hey, sweetheart." He hugged her close, deeply aware that he'd failed her, too. He should have been here, should have taken care of her. He owed her so fucking much. "I'm sorry I missed your wedding reception."

She squeezed him tight. "It's okay. I'm just glad you're back."

"Dude, if you don't let my wife go soon, I'm going to throw down with you," Noah said, his words hard.

Logan let go of Hope, allowing her feet to hit the gravel of the parking lot.

Hope turned back to her husband. "What is wrong with you?"

"It's cool." He understood the whole territorial-male thing. He wouldn't have BG. Before Georgia. God, he kind of measured his life in "befores" and "afters." There was all that time before The Incident. And there was a time Before Georgia and After Georgia. After Georgia, he totally understood Noah wouldn't want his wife held in the arms of another male, even if the other man thought of her as a sister.

Noah turned to his brother. "Dude, you got no problem with that? She wrapped her legs around his waist."

Jamie threw an arm over his wife's shoulder. "Naw. See, I know what Hope looks like when she's seriously wrapping herself around a man. I had an up close and personal experience with it about ten minutes back."

Hope flushed a furious shade of red. "James Glen. I can't believe you said that."

Noah huffed. "I knew you weren't going to wash your hands. You followed her into the bathroom for a quickie. Damn it. I wanted to do that but I was afraid Stella would come looking for us."

"You snooze, you lose, brother." Jamie had the smile of a perfectly satisfied man.

The Glen-Bennett family started arguing loudly amongst themselves over protocol when it came to bathroom quickies, but Logan got distracted. The door to the diner opened and he caught sight of honey-blonde hair and nice tits. Not as big as he remembered. She'd lost weight. *Damn it.* She was always trying to lose weight, and she didn't need to. She was perfect. He was going to make her march right back into that diner and he would pick out the biggest piece of chocolate pie he could and feed it to her by hand. She loved sweets. He hadn't missed the way she licked her lips when a fine piece of chocolate was put in front of her, but seventy-five percent of the time she pushed it away and claimed she was full when he knew damn well she wasn't. He would take her to the bathroom and spank her ass and then feed her that delicious chocolate pie. He would get it on his fingers and have her lick it off.

What the fuck was his Georgia doing with some scruffy asshole? The pretty blonde was joined by a guy in jeans and a T-shirt who immediately pulled her close. He was all over her. A wild, violent urge flared up.

"Dude, are you about to go all green and shit?" Noah asked. Hope and Jamie were still arguing over whether or not he should announce their forays into public sex, but Noah had moved closer, his voice going low. "That's Gemma. She's engaged to the man she's kissing. His name is Jesse. And there's Cade. They're new here but keeping up with our long tradition of sharing."

Not Georgia. God, he had it so fucking bad. As the pretty blonde turned her face up to the tall, dark-haired man, he could see plainly that she wasn't his Georgia. Not his. He had to fucking stop that.

He attempted to shrug it all off. The last thing he needed was to explain he was getting jealous over a woman he'd pushed out of his life. "Hey, nice to know the new kids are keeping up traditions."

Noah stared at him thoughtfully. "Is everything okay?"

"It's all good." He held his hand out and shook Noah's again. "I'll see you guys around. I'm going to go and talk to Stella real fast and then I have to check in with Nate. I'm taking over for Cam while he's on leave. Hope, will I see you tomorrow?"

Hope was the heart of the station house. She was the office manager. Knowing that he would get to hang with Hope had made the whole thing easier to take. Hope could keep him calm.

Hope's eyes widened. "No one told you? I quit. Gemma's the new office manager."

Excellent. The blonde with blue eyes who reminded him of Georgia was going to be around all the time. Awesome. Maybe she was mean. Yeah. That would be good. Except his *G* had been a little mean, too. *Fuck.*

Why was he here again?

To find a place to stay, and it wouldn't be the Circle G. The quicker he found a place to hang his hat, the better. The faster he could be alone for a while.

He waved good-bye and walked into the café only to be assaulted by the past. God, he'd loved this place. The smell of fries and baking pies lit up his system. This smelled like home. Tears pricked at his eyes, threatening to unman him, but he took a long breath and forced them back.

It was almost three in the afternoon. The lunch crowd was gone and the dinner crowd wouldn't be around for another couple of hours. Stella's was nice and quiet, just like he'd hoped.

Stella strode out of the kitchen, her boots ringing against the tile floor. She was dressed to kill in a red and white Western shirt, jeans, and boots that had been blinged out to an inch of their damn life.

Stella was a flamboyant woman with a helmet of teased blonde hair that he was pretty certain he could bounce a quarter off of. He felt another smile cross his face, warmth flooding his chest. Stella was one of the good ones.

Her eyes widened. "Logan?"

Was he coming back from the dead? People seemed to look at him like they'd seen a ghost. "Hey, Miss Stella."

She sighed and rushed to him, throwing her arms around his neck. "Thank god."

She held on to him, and he hugged her back.

"Do Teeny and Marie know you're home?" Stella asked, pulling him to a booth.

He shook his head. "No. I wanted to find a place to stay first. I know everyone thinks I should move home, but…"

She patted his hand. "You're a man now. You need your space. Of course. I can help you with that. Wow. What a coincidence. I got a call today from a broker looking for someone to watch over this cabin some rich guy built outside the valley. You know the land right next to Nell and Henry's place?"

He nodded. There was a big tract right next to the river. Prime property. He'd always wanted to buy that land for himself and build a cabin there. It had been his dream property. "Yeah. It sold?"

Not that he could have afforded it.

Stella nodded. "About four months ago. It seems like someone was slowly picking up all the land from Nell and Henry's almost into town. The whole town's been trying to figure out who it is. Everyone thinks it's some kind of movie star or something because that cabin went up fast, and it's a cabin in name only. That thing is ridiculous. I snuck inside and it's gorgeous. I swear, Stef is going crazy trying to figure out who it is. He's talking about redoing our whole house now. I think he's trying to keep up with that cabin. That boy likes being the richest man in town, I tell you. He likes it too much."

He held a hand up to stop her because Stella could gossip for hours, and he didn't have that kind of time. He had to be at work tomorrow and that meant finding a place to stay and getting some sleep. "I don't need some mansion. Can I take the apartment upstairs?"

Stella's had a small apartment over the diner that had been used by Stella for a while, and then several of the waitresses, and finally Hope. But Hope was at the *G* now. *G*. Georgia. His hand went right back to his pec like there was a magnet there. When was he going to forget her?

He would call Seth and lay into him and then ask him to find out what was happening with her. He couldn't truly rest until he knew she was safe.

"Hey. You're new." A dark-haired woman with outrageous curves stared down at him, a sparkle in her green eyes. "Aunt Stella, you didn't tell me about this one. Do you come with a hot friend? Because that happens a lot around here, I've been told."

"Down, Shannon." Stella sent the black-haired woman an affectionate stare. "Could you not jump on the man before you take his order?"

She unashamedly shrugged. "He's hot. I swear if you had told me about how hot the guys are out here, I would have come sooner."

She was gorgeous, but she wasn't Georgia, and he couldn't date anyone yet. *Fuck*. He might never be able to. He shook his head. "I'm not interested in food. I just came in to talk to Stella about the apartment upstairs."

Her eyes widened and a grin came over her face. "I've got room for you. I've been looking for a roomie, if you know what I mean."

"Go and refill the sugar shakers," Stella said in a firm voice.

Shannon frowned and winked as she walked off.

"So she's got the apartment." Logan groaned. He'd been counting on that tiny space. Now he might have to head out to the Movie Motel.

"Yeah. I had to bring Shannon in after that rat-fink bastard Nate stole my last waitress. I offered to trade Shannon for Gemma, but Nate said Shannon would just as likely flirt with his prisoners as keep them in jail. He's probably right. That girl is on the prowl. Her ex-husband was a low-life bastard who ran off with her best friend when she was…that's neither here nor there, but the long and short of it is the apartment isn't available, and before you think you can actually be Shannon's roommate, let me explain that she's all bark and no bite. She's a good girl under all that paint and pain."

"No. I'm not going to hit on her. I'm a reformed manwhore." He only wanted one woman, and he couldn't have her. "So what's up with this cabin thing?"

If he did go out to the Movie Motel, the first thing the owner would do was likely call his moms to make sure they were okay with him renting a room on his own. It wouldn't matter to Gene that he was an adult.

Then there was the fact that he'd almost died in the parking lot.

The fact that he had multiple places where he'd nearly died and been either beaten or shot was a good reason to not stay here for long.

"The broker says she wants someone to watch over the place, but that the owner could be there anytime, so you would have to be ready for that. You would have full use of the cabin and all the amenities. It's stocked with food and furniture and anything you could need. The broker goes out and makes sure it's always ready for the owner. That would be your job, but there's a household budget and everything."

"Why did she call you?" His mom had a real estate license. She usually handled all the deals in Bliss.

Stella waved it off. "She called Sebastian. He's got all the contacts in the world. He still couldn't get a name out of her. He wanted to see if that Michael fellow needed a new place. You know, the crazy guy who took up residence in that hunting cabin up on the mountain? I told Sebastian that I wasn't going to turn over that gorgeous place to a man who has been satisfied living with an outhouse for over a year. No way. He's crazy, and he's got way too many firearms."

God. Michael McMahon. Logan had been shot by his crazy-ass girlfriend, who'd then been killed by Holly, of all people. He was still hanging around? Did anyone ever leave Bliss?

He had a couple of options. Jamie would take him in, but watching all the happy threesomes out at the Georgia would make him crazy. And there was the fact that he'd called his friend's ranch the Georgia. Nope. He was passing. He could head home and get assaulted with everything he'd lost and have his moms all over him twenty-four seven. He loved them and he couldn't handle it. There was a reason kids moved away. Nell and Henry had a guest room, but that came with tofu and lectures on global warming and shit.

Damn.

"I'll take it."

Stella smiled. "Excellent. I'll get you the key. I'm happy you're back."

He nodded and hoped this wasn't the biggest mistake of his life. As Stella went to grab the paperwork, he pulled out his phone. He had to call his moms and let them know where he was.

And then he was going to call Seth and have this shit out. He was going to get a detailed accounting of exactly what he owed Seth.

And he was going to figure out who had their damn hooks in his Georgia and whether or not he needed to kill someone.

* * * *

The Bond Aeronautics jet came to a stop on the private airway Seth had commissioned when he'd bought his wretchedly large tract of land in Bliss. He'd had to wait, buying up piece after piece of land as it hit the market.

He'd bought his first few acres before his company had hit the big time. He'd had to scrimp and save, but it had all been worth it because now it was his.

Georgia came awake, her eyes opening, and she hid a yawn behind her hand. She smiled at him, her lips still a perfect red even after her nap. Fuck, but he wanted to see those lips wrapped around his cock. Eight months. Eight months with no sex because the minute he'd laid eyes on her he'd known he wouldn't let another woman touch him. Not for the rest of his life. If she died tomorrow, he would be celibate, a fucking monk worshiping her for the next eighty years or so until he could join her again.

"Hey, we're here." He bit back tears. *Damn it.* This place and this woman brought it out in him. He was a fucking emotional mess when it came to them.

She smiled, her eyes lighting up. "That was quick. You know I've been here once before, but I didn't see much. Who are we meeting?"

"We're going to a friend's anniversary party and meeting a business contact. And taking a couple of days off. I thought I'd do some fishing."

John Bishop wasn't technically a business contact. He was Nell's husband, although she didn't know his real name. Seth wasn't sure he knew the man's real name. The man he'd formerly known as John Bishop had been a CIA operative, and they knew how to bury an identity. So did Seth. When Bishop had fallen in love with Nell, Seth had buried him so far and so deep that no one should have been able to find him.

Except someone had. Someone had figured out that the man now known as Henry Flanders had once been John Bishop.

Henry was going to kick his ass.

Georgia's blue eyes flared and that bee-stung mouth of hers lifted into a smile that had his heart flipping. "It's going to be interesting to see how long you can fish before your cell phone goes off. I have to say, I'm not so interested in fishing, but you know I love a good party. What's the anniversary they're celebrating?"

"Twenty-five." Teeny and Marie were one of his inspirational couples. Never wavering. They had known they would be together when they'd met, and they'd stood the test of time.

"That's nice. I don't know anyone who's been together for that long." Georgia sighed and her chest came up as she stretched, her breasts moving. "I hope Nat and Chase and Ben stay together for that long."

He nearly reached up and ran his finger across that cheek of hers. When the time was right, he would reach out and haul her into his lap and kiss the hell out of her whenever he wanted to. "I'm sure they will."

She turned away, looking out the window. "Wow. It's dark here. And your phone is buzzing. Do you want me to listen in?"

He clicked the button on his phone and answered silently "no." Nope. Never. He shook his head as he clicked the voice mail button. "Naw. It's okay. I can take care of this."

Normally he wouldn't care if she listened to his messages, but not this time.

Georgia unbuckled her seat belt. The plane had seating for eight, but he'd sat right beside her, giving her no space at all. She brushed against him as she got up. Yep, that had his cock standing up straight as she shuffled past him and those hot breasts of hers brushed against his chest.

God, all he had to do was lean in a couple of inches to get them in his mouth. Sure there would be all that fabric between them, but he could make that disappear. He could bite down and have her nipples between his teeth.

They would be brown and pink, and her areola would be quarter sized or bigger. God, he fucking loved tits. He could spend an hour at those nipples, licking and sucking and tonguing and making them his. He wanted to rest his head on those breasts. Comfort and warmth were right there. He could rest his cheek against her soft skin and then he would rear up and ram his cock inside. Damn straight.

Comfort and hard fucking. That was what he wanted from Georgia. Everything. Yeah. Everything that could happen between a man and a woman and his best friend, who also loved the woman. That was it.

His phone. He needed to check his phone. It was still buzzing. He'd turned it off while they were in the air, but that beeping had started the minute they had touched down and he'd turned it back on. He quickly ran down the list as the hostess opened the door to the plane. He'd made sure there wasn't far to go from his private landing strip to the front door of his new, state-of-the-art house. It was fitting that he would see it for the first time with Georgia. He'd built it for her.

"Anyone special?" Georgia asked as the hostess passed her the Louis Vuitton roll-on he'd bought for her and convinced her he'd bought if from a "vendor" on Canal Street.

He smiled as he found a number he knew well on the screen. Logan. Damn straight. He loved it when a plan came together. "Naw. It's just some office stuff. I'll be with you in a second."

She gave him a smile and started off the plane, allowing him the privacy he needed. He pressed the button to start the first message and hoped all his pieces were in working order. It was a long row of dominoes he'd set in motion. There was always the chance that one had gone astray.

Stella's Western twang came across the line. "Hi, Miss Hill. I wanted to let you know that I found the perfect man to house-sit for your client. I've got the paperwork ready, but I went ahead and gave him the key. I know this kid. He's good people. Hope you don't mind. Call me."

He didn't mind. He'd totally planned it that way. He moved on and pressed the button that brought him to Logan's message. A deep voice came over the line, and Seth couldn't help but smile.

"Seth, you shitball. How dare you pull this crap with me. I'm paying you back. Every fucking cent. I know you're the one who paid Leo." He wasn't going to let that happen, but Logan's angry voice warmed him because it was the first time in two years he'd heard emotion in that laconic Western drawl. "You can't think I wouldn't fucking find out. I'm pissed as shit." There was a pause in the line. "We'll work something out, but I need a favor. Look, man, there's this chick I met out here in Dallas. She's in New York now, and I need you to look for her. She's a friend, but she's cool, you know? I like her. Not like like her, but like her. Like a friend. I want to make sure she's okay. So call me and we'll work out a payment plan and you can do me a solid. K?"

The message dropped and Seth sat back, a deep satisfaction running through his system.

No. Logan didn't like like her. God, were they back in junior high? Was Logan somewhere writing her name all over his notebooks? Yeah. Didn't like her. Not at all.

Seth got out of his seat as he dialed the number he didn't want to dial. There was more than one reason he was here. Oh, sure, he would have come no matter what, but he had an obligation.

"Hello." No matter how Seth sliced it, Henry Flanders sounded dark and dangerous.

Maybe if he didn't know what he knew, he would shrug and simply call that dark voice masculine, but the CIA operative Henry had been was still there, no matter how he tried to cover him up. Seth was one of three people in the whole world who knew that Henry Flanders, mild-mannered former professor, used to be John Bishop, CIA assassin.

"Henry, it's Seth."

A low chuckle came over the line, and Seth was struck by how far the man had come. He'd never laughed before he'd come to Bliss.

"Hey, man. How's it going? I read that *Time* article about you. The company is doing great things. I'm proud of you, Seth."

An odd feeling went through him, and he had to blink back stupid, dumbass tears. Over the years, Henry Flanders had been a source of strength. They'd talked often over the last six years. It had started out as Henry simply checking in to make sure his cover was solid, but at some point in time, they'd started talking about anything that came up. Henry had proven to be an excellent sounding board.

So he didn't prevaricate or drag out what he had to say. "Someone is looking for Henry Flanders."

Seth could practically hear the temperature drop. *Fuck.*

"Really? How deep does it go?" Henry's voice had gone silky and smooth, perfectly deadly.

And there was nothing he could offer but the truth. "I shut it down, but the search went deep. It's possible that you've been compromised. I'm looking into it. Whoever is trying to find you, they're serious. I've been running around like a dog chasing my tail trying to find this guy. He wants me to believe he's a twelve-year-old searching for his bio dad."

"Fuck."

Double fuck. "I'm going to take care of this."

A long pause. "Seth, this is my business. I'll take care of it."

As any halfway decent mentor would say. But Seth knew the value of a great father figure. He'd had a perfectly shitty one for most of his life, and then he'd had Henry. "I'm going to make sure this works out. I promise. I'm in town."

Henry's voice was back to normal. Henry and Nell were the only ones who knew he'd bought all that land. He'd even let Nell pick the builder so he could ensure that the place was as bio-friendly as possible and he could avoid any protests she might mount. "Well, hello, neighbor. The cabin is beautiful. I would love to see you. Tomorrow. Lunch at Stella's. Nell will be happy you're here, son."

The *son* comment hit him hard, and he promised himself that he wouldn't let Henry down. Nell had no idea what her husband used to do, and it should stay that way. After all, the dude hadn't eaten meat in like six years. If that wasn't love, then Seth didn't know what was. "I'll be there."

The line clicked off, and he took a long breath before pocketing his phone.

"You call that a cabin?" Georgia asked, poking her head back in the plane. "I was prepared for something small. What's the square footage on that gorgeous thing?"

Satisfaction coursed through his veins. She would like it even better when she walked through those doors. "Ten thousand. And I made sure your room is up to your standards. Tempur-Pedic bedding, thousand thread count sheets, and a walk-in closet to die for."

She smiled, but there was a shake of her head that let him know she thought he was a little out there. "I'm not sure I need a walk-in closet. And why am I coming on your vacation? Shouldn't you have, I don't know, invited a friend?"

"You're my friend." He took the stairs quickly, the chilly night air hitting his lungs. Yeah, he loved that. It was springtime, but the nights were still nice and cold.

"I'm your employee." Her mouth settled into a frown as she strode to keep up with him. She was wearing a hot-as-hell pair of Gucci boots with gold studs on the heel. She'd gotten them the day before with her brother's credit card. Ben had happily sent Seth the receipt with a note and a deeply sarcastic smiley face. It said that in the future, he'd be sending all of Georgia's receipts his way. He was sure Ben had laughed as he'd signed that note, but Seth had been more than happy to write that check. The fact that she was wearing clothes he'd purchased for her—from the St. John blouse to the killer Rag & Bone jeans, to those boots that would look good wrapped around his neck—did nothing but make him smile on the inside. And he'd paid for lunch, too, because he liked knowing that she wasn't hungry because he'd fed her.

He was sure there was a psychiatrist somewhere who would say his possessiveness bordered on the psychotic, but he didn't give a damn.

"Have you listened to a word I've said?" Georgia asked as the hostess carried out the rest of their luggage. Georgia didn't pack light, and he was going to have to haul everything up to the house because he hadn't brought along staff. He wanted to be alone with her.

"Sorry, my mind drifted." He was glad he worked out. He

stacked the two large rolling bags and lifted the third one. Damn. What had she packed? Her whole shoe collection? At least her brothers had done one thing right. She didn't protest that she should be carrying the luggage. She made a single attempt to get her own suitcases and backed off when he waved her away.

"I said maybe I should hop a plane to Malibu and visit my brother. I don't know these people. You should have brought a girlfriend."

Seth stopped because this wasn't going according to plans. *Fuck.* She was back to feeling bad about the kissing incident. He had to think and fast. "You know how work goes. I'm planning on relaxing, but something will inevitably come up. I need you here with me. It's only two weeks. If you still want to go out to Winter's place after that, then I'll give you some time off and let the jet take you out there."

She wasn't going to Win's place. At least not without him. He still didn't trust the bastard. For all he knew, Win might lock her away like a freaking princess in a castle.

In the low glow that came from the plane and the landing strip lights, he could see the indecision on her face as she kept pace with him. They walked toward the back porch of the cabin. The beautiful structure had three levels and some floor-to-ceiling windows that would offer a spectacular view of the river and the Sangre de Cristo Mountains. "I don't know."

The porch light wasn't on. Actually, no lights were on. Was Logan here? He couldn't see the front of the house so he wasn't sure there was a truck up ahead. If Logan was at Hell on Wheels, Seth was going to have to go drag his ass out. Damn it, he was supposed to be better. Seth hefted the suitcases onto the perfectly finished wraparound deck and prayed he'd remembered the key.

"It's going to be great." Where would the broker have hidden a key? He needed to get Georgia settled and then go after his crazy-ass best friend. He had to make sure Logan was sober and presentable enough for breakfast in the morning.

Georgia followed him up the steps. "It seems weird to go to someone's party. I don't know them. I'm your assistant, but sometimes you don't tell people that when you introduce me and they assume we have something personal going and I have to correct them.

I don't like it."

He set the bags down and realized that she needed him more than he needed to plot. He got in her space and was happy when she didn't back down.

"Can you have some faith in me?" he asked, staring at the face he was crazy about. God, she was so fucking pretty. "Can you believe that I want what is absolutely best for you, and I will do anything I need to do to make it happen?"

"I don't know why you would say that to me."

"Yes, you do." His lips hovered above hers. Maybe he shouldn't wait any longer. He was finally home. He wanted to commemorate the moment, and there was nothing better on the planet than kissing Georgia in the moonlight. He was jumping the gun, but god, she was so close and he didn't have the heart to shut her out again. He couldn't do it. She was his Kryptonite. Just one kiss. Then he would put her to bed and make sure she was safe and he would go after Logan's ass.

The sound of a gun being cocked wasn't completely foreign to Seth's ears. Nope. There was no way to mistake that fucking sound, and it made him stand still.

"Move an inch and I'll blow your head off," a familiar voice said.

Seth felt the press of metal against his head and realized that Robert Burns had been right. Sometimes the best laid schemes of mice and men came up against an idiot with tequila on his breath. Or something like that.

Chapter Four

Georgia held her breath. The cool of the night air suddenly felt thick along her skin, and she remembered how badly it hurt to get shot. She remembered the fire lashing along her flesh and the almost certainty that she was going to die, and it might be better for everyone that she did. That had been the worst part, the utter certainty that her life hadn't meant much. It hadn't been so terribly long ago. She still dreamed about it—dreamed about that stupid cage and how Nat should have let her go.

Now she understood Nat better because she couldn't imagine anything worse than Seth being in the same position.

She couldn't see their assailant. He was a looming shadow, but the metal of his pistol glinted off the moonlight.

Such a beautiful setting to die in.

"Please don't hurt him." Funny. She didn't think about it. She didn't think to plead for her own life or to use those feminine wiles she'd always fallen back on. They only worked part of the time anyway, and this was too important to play around. She couldn't stand here and watch someone shoot Seth. She couldn't. She wasn't even sure who she was asking. The assailant probably wouldn't care. Maybe she was simply pleading with the universe.

"He's not going to hurt me," Seth said in an altogether "too calm for the situation" voice. He dropped contact with her. Seth brought his hands up slowly as though he was showing their attacker that he wasn't armed with anything but that big brain of his. "He's going to put down the gun because he shouldn't be carrying while he's obviously toasted. Georgia, this is my friend. His name is Logan Green, and we're going to have a throw down the minute he gets rid of that gun. Or maybe he'll go ahead and shoot me since he knows damn well he's an instant billionaire if he does it. What's it going to be, buddy? Are we going to play out this IDTV special right here?"

Logan? No. No. No. It couldn't be Logan. Logan was in Texas. That massive shadow seemed to reform and now she could see those big, broad shoulders and muscled arms.

"G? Georgia?" His words seemed a bit slurred, but sure enough he tossed the gun aside and shoved Seth out of the way.

Logan. Oh, god, he was right in front of her. She could feel the heat coming off his body. He wasn't wearing anything but a pair of low-slung jeans and a white muscle shirt that clearly defined his too-die-for body. He was so big, so tall and strong. And he was going to be so pissed off. He would probably think she'd been looking for him.

"I didn't know you were here," she said quickly, forcing her hands to her sides.

He didn't seem to hear her. The smile that crept across his face was slightly loopy, like he wasn't altogether there, and yes, she could definitely smell the tequila on his breath. "I thought this was a shitty dream." He sighed as he moved in closer. "Thank god. It's a good dream. Seth, you can go away now. I'll deal with you when I'm awake."

He moved faster than a drunk should be able to and with far more grace and strength. One minute she was standing there waiting for him to get all mad Dom on her because she'd disobeyed his "never see me again" order, and the next her back was flat against the side of the cabin, her balance off, but he seemed to like it that way.

"Hello, Georgie. You miss me, girl?" He plastered his body to the front of hers, crushing her in between the cabin and his muscular form. His hips moved from side to side, rubbing himself against her like a horny cat.

And damn her, but she responded. Maybe he was right and this was a nice dream. She would wake up and the plane would be landing. It wasn't like she hadn't dreamed about him before.

He didn't wait for her to answer, simply put those ridiculously sculpted lips over hers and sucked her bottom lip straight into his mouth with a groan that had her insides lighting up.

No one had ever had this effect on her before. Logan Green was the match and her body was lighter fluid waiting to explode. He kissed her like she was made of sugar and he'd been on a low-carb diet for eight months. He licked and savored and drove his tongue deep, pressing it against hers and dancing all around. He practically inhaled her.

And she loved it. He'd only kissed her the once before, and it had been exactly like this. For a second she'd felt like a goddess, worshipped and beloved, like she was the only woman for him. The rest of the world seemed to drop away and she was surrounded by him.

He managed to circle his arms around her as he picked her up, leaving her no option except to wrap her body around his for support as he started to move toward the door.

"If you drop her, I will kill you, Logan."

Reality rushed back in. Seth. Oh, god. Seth was here and she'd nearly forgotten about him. What was wrong with her? And why the hell had her present and her past collided? How did Seth know Logan? Why had Logan been standing outside the cabin?

She pushed against Logan, but he wasn't letting her go. He cupped her ass and started moving into the cabin, his bare feet shifting along the wood. "Let me go, Logan."

"Already did that. Didn't work. You came back. Stop wiggling or I'll tie you down." The words came out as a silky, seductive threat.

Yeah, like she hadn't dreamed about that, too. If she thought for a moment that he honestly wanted her, she would have put her whole body into giving him exactly what he desired. She would have gotten on her knees and spread them, showing him the work she'd put in once she'd found out what he'd needed. Those days before he'd pushed her away had been spent with Nat learning how to submit to the man she wanted more than anything in the world.

But he hadn't wanted her then, and she wasn't sure he wanted her now.

Except his cock seemed ready to play.

"Logan." She had to find a way to get him to make a lick of sense.

A light came on overhead and his eyes fastened on her breasts. Her blouse had come unbuttoned and those big boobs of hers were trying to climb their way out of their punishing minimizer bra. She'd always hated those bras because it meant she couldn't wear most of the designers her so-called friends in LA wore. One of the casting directors in LA she'd seen had told her to try her hand in the Valley since her tits were made for porn, but only after she'd lost a few pounds.

His mouth was right back at hers, and she wondered how long he was going to be able to hold her. God, it felt good to be held, and he wasn't shaking at all. He was holding her like she didn't weigh a thing.

"I want you naked. We're going back to the bedroom and you're going to take off those clothes and spread your legs for me. Do you understand? You're going to get wet for me, and I'm going to give you everything I have. Fuck, baby, I'm going to fill you up."

Dirty words that should have her fighting to get away from him, but her whole body softened as he kissed her again, his tongue tangling with hers, strong and dominant. Always dominant.

"This fucking gun didn't have the safety on when you tossed it across the yard. It could have gone off." Seth's angry voice rang out as he walked back into the room and slammed the gun down. "And it's county issued. Did you get your badge back and immediately hit the liquor? What the fuck is wrong with you? I'm bringing in the luggage."

Seth. God, what must he think of her? And why hadn't he tried to take them apart?

"Asshole!" Logan yelled back. "Fucking messing up my one goddamn good dream."

She shook her head because he seemed to start coming out of it. "It's not a dream. Logan, you have to let me down. I need to help Seth with our luggage."

His hands tightened as if he wasn't willing to let go, but he blinked those green eyes once and then twice and slowly let her down. He scrubbed a hand across his slightly scruffy hair. It had grown out since she'd last seen him. And she could see the tendrils of a tattoo peeking from under the white of his shirt. The ink was new, too. But the cold look that hit his eyes was par for the course. "What are you doing here, Georgia? Aren't you supposed to be in New York?"

Well, that answered one question. She'd left without telling him where she was going, and it had always been in the back of her head that maybe he'd changed his mind and he would look for her. Oh, she'd known that all he had to do was ask her brothers, but she'd never been particularly rational when it came to him. She'd had the fantasy that he might hate not knowing where she was and come looking for her.

He'd known where she was and she'd not even gotten a call to make sure she was okay.

It was time to try to get back some dignity. She took a step away from him and let herself settle into her armor—a carefree smile and blank eyes. Just another rich bitch who knew how to put a man in his place. Thank god Ben had opened the checkbook yesterday or she would be in her Macy's bargain-basement clothes. Somehow having designer duds on felt like a shield. "I'm working. I do that, you know. Shouldn't you be back in Dallas banging whatever sub Julian Lodge tells you to?"

Damn, that seemed to be a direct hit. His eyes flared momentarily, and a low growl came from the back of his throat. "There's the bitch. Nice to see you again. Heard you had a cozy job boffing a billionaire. He seems to be keeping you right nice. Must be some kind of skills you have."

Well, that was the pot calling the kettle black. She happened to know for a fact that he actually did have sex on the job. She'd heard endless stories about how great a Dom he was from the women of The Club. "I'm his assistant."

Those gorgeous lips went faintly cruel as he looked her up and down. Before, she'd felt warmth from him, but now there was only cold assessment. "I bet you assist him a lot, baby. I bet you assist him with blow jobs and hand jobs, and just about any other job a woman of your type can handle."

A woman of her type? Bubbleheaded and dumb. He'd never had a whole lot of respect for her smarts. "Because I don't have a brain in my head. I must only be good for a cheap screw."

He chuckled, but there was no humor to the sound. "Hey, I never said you were cheap. I always expected you would be quite expensive."

Bitterness welled. This was the way it was between them. If he wasn't kissing her like there was no tomorrow and rushing in to save her life, they tore each other up. She'd gone along with it because it seemed to be the only way to get his attention, but she was tired of it. She was tired of hurting, tired of aching inside over what she couldn't have. She took a long breath and sank to the sofa. "Well, that shows what you know about economics, Logan. I'm sorry I said those things to you. I was caught off-balance. I didn't expect to see you here."

He strode across the room. She only knew he was in motion from the sound and, of course, he moved away from her. She heard the sound of glass hitting glass and a short swallow. "What are you doing here? I'm only going to ask once more. Why the hell are you in Bliss?"

No apology. No "let's meet in the middle and find common ground." "I told you."

"You're working for some asswipe billionaire." The reply came out draped in suspicion, and then he cursed under his breath. "Seth. Fuck me. You're working for Seth. God. What a clusterfuck."

"How do you know my boss?" She glanced around the cabin. Cabin? Hah. It was a mansion, a gorgeous monstrosity of wood and glass. That was Seth. He didn't do things by half.

Logan's red-rimmed eyes caught hers. "Boss? Seriously, Georgia. I know Seth. You're sleeping with him. Seth has never had a female assistant before. He's always hired dudes because he didn't want the distraction."

Logan fumbled, another sign that he'd had too much to drink.

"You should sit down." What the hell was she going to do now? She couldn't stay here with Logan. And was he right about the male assistants? At first she'd kind of assumed that Win had gotten her the job. She'd asked him if he wouldn't mind being a reference. Two days later, Stark Software had called and said they'd heard she needed a job.

She'd been surprised it was for the CEO, but Win had powerful connections. When she'd thanked him, he'd sworn he had nothing to do with it. She'd thought he was trying to make her feel better.

"I'm fine," he rumbled back at her, but he took the seat across from her anyway. "This makes my day complete, sweetheart. I get to come back to the scene of all my crimes. What fun. Where the fuck am I going to stay now?"

He could be a giant asshole. "Please stay here. I'll leave tomorrow."

"You're not going anywhere, Georgia," Seth said as he dragged in her suitcases and slammed the door behind him. "Except to bed. I apologize for the behavior of my friend. He's actually civilized when he's sober."

"Yeah, you don't know me that well anymore, man." Logan sat there, looking at her, his eyes blank like she wasn't really there.

All in all, it wasn't how she'd thought a reunion between them would go.

"I know him. We met in Dallas." Georgia stood up and wondered if she could find a hotel nearby. Did they have a cab that could pick her up? "We don't get along."

Seth set down the suitcases and met her halfway, a gentle smile on his face. He was Logan's opposite. He was all civilized good looks where Logan was a massive hunk of man meat. Seth was manly, but he was a metro tiger where Logan had never once left the wild. "You looked like you were getting along pretty well from where I was standing."

There wasn't a hint of jealousy in those words, and she sighed inwardly. Nope. Why would he be jealous when he didn't want her, either? "We have a bit of a history."

He reached out for her hand. He did that a lot. He was a touchy-feely guy. "I brought you here to meet him."

She frowned. "Why?"

"Because he's my best friend and you're…you're perfect." He kept his voice low as though he didn't want Logan to hear.

Emotions rolled through her, but mostly it was all confusion. "What is that supposed to mean?"

He pulled her close and, for the first time, wrapped his arms around her. "It means I think you can help."

She shook her head. "He doesn't want my help. Not now. Not ever."

And yet it was so obvious Logan needed someone's help. He sat there, his shoulders squared, but his eyes were old and tired. What the hell had happened to him? He was young. Younger than her, but there was a weariness to him that made her want to hold him, to lift him up.

"I came back to help him because I'm worried that if I don't break through his barriers, I'm going to lose my best friend," Seth whispered in her ear.

"Did you know I knew him?"

"How would I have known that?" Seth asked.

She'd never mentioned him. "You brought me here to set me up with Logan? Seth, I'm so sorry. He doesn't like me."

"But I like you." His eyes strayed back to where Logan sat.

Something fell into place. She'd talked endlessly about Chase and Nat and Ben. Once she'd realized Seth wouldn't judge her, she'd felt so free to talk about how much she admired what they had and the odd relationship of theirs. She'd been so sure he liked her. Like really liked her. She'd been so sure they were connected, but he'd put her off.

Her mind went back to that moment in the limo. She'd leaned over and tried to press her lips to his. All night long, he'd held her hand and showed her off like she was something other than his assistant. She'd felt like a princess that night, and he'd been the one making it happen. For the first time since she'd left Willow Fork, she'd forgotten she loved Logan and she'd known she had fallen for Seth.

And he'd turned her away, his lips finding her forehead instead of her mouth, and suddenly the words he'd said to her made a weird kind of sense.

It's not time yet, love.

"Seth?"

"I want to try," he said, pulling her close. "I grew up with him. This place was my heaven. Please. Give it a try for me. If it doesn't work out, we can go back to New York and I won't ever mention it again. Please. I just wanted the two of you to meet, to see if there was any attraction there, and you two were like a volcano. I had to walk away because I wanted to join in but I thought I would scare you."

She sagged against him. *Damn*. It was everything she could want and nothing she could have. She felt tears forming in her eyes and wished she'd taken Win up on his offer to leave New York, but no, she hadn't been able to leave Seth. Whom she loved. Seth, who needed a ménage with a man who couldn't stand her despite the fact that she couldn't get him out of her head.

"Give it a chance," Seth urged. "I'm sorry how it started. Do you know what happened to him? Do you know why he wouldn't come home?"

Walk away, Georgia. Walk away and save yourself. She had a deeply practical inner voice that she almost never listened to. Because it was boring. She was the dumbest girl ever. She was because she kept getting her heart broken and then begging for more. And she wanted to know Logan. God, he'd pushed her away and she still wanted to know him. "No."

Seth leaned down and brushed his nose against hers. "Give us a chance. I will make sure you're taken care of. Please trust me, baby. I'm not taking you back to New York as my assistant no matter what happens. I'm taking you back as mine. With him or without him. But I have to play this my way. I'm so sorry to bring you into a situation that makes you uncomfortable, but I still think it could work."

She shook her head, hating the tears that made her vision wobbly. "He doesn't want me."

"He fell in love with a woman in Texas. When I met you, I was sure you could make him forget her."

"I was in Texas. That was where we met, but he didn't love me." Except she'd thought he did. When he'd ridden in to her rescue, she'd been so sure he loved her. She would have bet her life on it.

"Are you sure? Or is he the kind of man who would push away the woman he loves because he thinks he didn't deserve her?"

"What are you two talking about?" Logan asked, turning his head their way. In the low light, she couldn't mistake the way his eyes narrowed. "If you're going to fuck, you should go to the bedroom."

God, why did she love him? She was a masochist. She obviously hated herself. She needed therapy.

"Stay," Seth said, his voice aching.

Go, that very practical side of her pleaded. *You don't need to know what happened to make Logan the walking human bomb he is. You can't save him. You can't save yourself and it would never work. You could never handle Logan, and Seth's world would eat you alive. You think LA casting directors are rough on a girl, try Upper East Siders.*

"Stay with me. Stay with us. We need you, baby." His lips brushed against her forehead.

"Okay. I'll stay."

She was the dumbest woman in the world.

* * * *

Logan watched as Seth returned to the great room after taking Georgia to wherever she would be spending the night. Seth strode down the gorgeous hall like he owned it.

Of course, there was a reason for that. He did. He owned every inch of this mansion. Hell, he was pretty sure Seth could buy the fucking world if he wanted to. Seth was smart. He'd always been so damn smart. Logan couldn't keep up with him. And now Seth had Georgia.

He hadn't missed the way that Seth held her, bringing his head to hers like they were nestled together. Like they belonged. And they did. Georgia was rich. Seth was rich. Logan had to take a job watching a house to have a place to live.

A house Seth had built and lived in, and for some reason brought him into because there was no way Seth hadn't had a hand in this shit. Because, like he knew—Seth was smart.

"So you're fucking her?" It sounded way harsher than he meant it to, but he'd had a shit ton of tequila. He hadn't meant to drink that either, but after an uncomfortable talk with Nate that included one of his twins spitting up on him while Nate replaced his badge and gun, he'd needed it. Oddly enough, his anxiety at that moment in time had nothing to do with the job or having to walk back into the station house. It had everything to do with the kicking kid that had been placed in his arms like he had a right to hold anything that precious. Nate had handed Zander over and gone about his business while Logan had been left looking into those completely innocent eyes and wondering if he'd ever get this—the sweet wife, the partner, the kids. Nate had a future right there in his hands. Two kids. Fuck. Nate had two kids and Logan hadn't met them. The closest he'd come before today was standing outside Nate's woefully small cabin and saying good-bye because he couldn't stand looking in on a future that wouldn't include him.

But the future he'd just seen had hurt so fucking much more.

Seth and Georgia. Damn, but they'd looked good together.

And he couldn't forget the way she felt pressed against him, her mouth open under his. She'd hesitated only the merest second and then she'd been all over him, her body softening like it should for her Dom. Damn. He was so drunk his cock shouldn't work, but the minute he'd seen her, it had come right to life.

"You're an ass," Seth said flatly.

He hadn't seen his best friend in forever, and yet the statement didn't shock him. It was the truth. "Tell me something I don't know."

Seth stalked toward him, a bottle in his hand. "Fine. I will. This fucking bottle cost twenty-five hundred dollars. Dos Lunas Grand Reserve. Did you like the tequila? It's a luxury liquor. You must really like luxury."

He couldn't help but laugh, but then he'd gone through a whole bottle of tequila. A wretchedly expensive bottle of tequila. "Tasted like tequila to me. Put it on my tab, asshole."

"And how about the gun?" Seth asked.

Logan groaned. Yeah, he was sorry about the gun. "There was some trouble earlier. Someone was walking around outside. I don't know. Maybe it was a deer or something, but they were making noise and I scared them or it or whatever off. I thought it had come back."

Seth stared down at him, looking way too much like a well-dressed father figure. Or any sort of dude who would totally disapprove of him. Which these days included pretty much any male who met him. "You were mean to my assistant."

What the fuck was this game? "Your assistant? If she's just your assistant, I'll shove that bottle up my ass."

Seth's mouth turned up, his lips curling in that son-of-a-bitch smile he'd used every time he'd come up with a brilliant plan when they were kids. "She has done nothing but help me with work."

"I'm not an idiot. She's…fuck. She's the one woman I've connected with and she suddenly turns up here in Bliss on the same day I have to come home, and she happens to be in the same house where I had to stay because it was the only place in town? Yeah. I see Seth Stark all over that shit."

Seth put the bottle down and crossed his arms over his chest. "She's the one."

Seth turned and walked back to the kitchen.

A growl started in the back of his throat. A vision of Seth fucking Georgia assaulted him. Seth could give Georgia all the shit she thought she needed. Fancy stuff. Designer stuff. All Logan had to offer her was dominance and hard, satisfying sex. God, he wanted to fuck her. The fact that she was in a bedroom in the same house that he was in had his cock straining. Eight months of nothing and he was in some serious pain. "You're a bastard. How did you find out about her? How many people do you have spying on me?"

He wouldn't put it past Seth to have hired some "friends" for him.

"We talking true now?" Seth asked, walking back into the great room. He'd found a bottle of his own. Naturally the cabin came with a bar that would put most Manhattan hot spots to shame. Nothing but the best for Seth Stark and his honey girl. Cîroc. It looked like it was fresh out of the freezer, the blue bottle covered in frost. Seth poured a couple of fingers into what was almost certainly Waterford Crystal and knocked it back.

True meant getting past all the bullshit. "Yeah, we're talking true."

"Will you remember this in the morning?" Seth sat back, one elegantly clad foot over his knee.

Logan rolled his eyes. "You think this is a bender? This is a fun Saturday night for me, man."

Seth's eyes narrowed down to slits of pure blue judgment. "I thought you stopped drinking."

"Drinking wasn't the problem." *Damn it.* Yeah, drinking was definitely the fucking problem now since he hadn't meant to say that, to ever admit that.

A long breath filled Seth's lungs, and he sat back. "How bad did it get?"

He didn't want to have this conversation. He never wanted to have this conversation. He'd been avoiding it with everyone. No one knew except the doc and Hope and Sawyer. God, he had to apologize to Sawyer.

"Logan?"

"I'm going to bed." But his feet didn't move. His arms stayed right where they were, clutching the chair like it was the only thing solid in the world.

"Are we done?" Seth didn't look at him. His face was turned down, staring into that glass.

"Tell me how you found out about Georgia." He couldn't walk until he knew.

"I got a call from someone. I thought it was you because it was your number, and for a minute, I got so excited because you don't call me anymore. But it wasn't you."

He sighed. "I'm never underestimating Kitten again. I knew I hadn't lost my phone."

"She explained the situation and said Georgia needed a safe place to go."

"So you took her in thinking you could use her to get me to come home." He could see exactly how that plan had gone through Seth's mind.

Seth was a manipulative, deeply possessive genius who hid a wealth of ruthless will behind that happy-go-lucky façade of his. Yeah, he'd known that even as a kid. Logan wasn't sure why, but Seth had clung to him and he'd…god, help him, but he'd craved it. He'd craved knowing he belonged with someone. He'd even liked how possessive Seth was of him. There had never been anything sexual between the two of them, but if Logan had been wired that way, Seth would have been the man for him.

"I fell in love with her the minute I saw her, Logan. She's perfect. I might have thought I was keeping her safe for you before I met her. Now I know I'm keeping her safe for us."

He still thought that would happen? He thought they could find the perfect woman and settle down? Seth had been banking on that shit for years, since they were kids. Logan wasn't a kid anymore. "Take her. I'm not interested."

He ached in a way no amount of high-end tequila was going to fix. His gut was an endless pool of self-loathing, and he was not bringing them into it. His hand went to his left pec. That was all he was going to get of Georgia.

"Bullshit. I saw what happened tonight," Seth argued. "And I saw how she reacted to you. I could have been dying on the floor and the two of you would still have gone at it."

Those few moments when she'd been in his arms had been the closest he'd been to content in years. He shook his head as he realized that was completely true, and his dissatisfaction hadn't come about after The Incident. He'd started pulling away when Seth stopped coming home, when he no longer got those summers with his best friend.

When he'd been left behind.

"She's a gorgeous girl, and I was noble the first time around because I got nothing to offer her." He wished he still had the tequila. Anything to numb him out. God, this was exactly how he'd screwed up. "Maybe I'll take her this time. Fuck her out of my system."

Seth shook his head as though he couldn't believe what he was hearing. "She's in love with you. Doesn't that count for something?"

"And you're in love with her." Now he forced himself to move, to make his body function, to get the hell out of here. "Good for the two of you. I'll send you a fucking toaster or something."

He walked past Seth. One foot in front of the other, placing distance between him and the long, shared history of their lives.

"Are you done with me?" Seth asked, his voice reminding Logan so much of that kid he'd been. Seth was still that kid who had gotten shipped to his granddad's place and had no idea how to fit in. He was still holding out his freaking hand and asking the boy next door to play with him.

He hated Seth in that moment. Hated him as much as he'd ever loved him. Seth got the money and the girl and the world where everything was perfect, where he never had to find out what a stupid, worthless bastard he was. "I'm not your boyfriend, Seth. I'm never going to be."

The glass Seth had been holding crashed to the floor, breaking through that horrible moment of silence that came after Logan's words.

This was another one. *Fuck*. This was one of those goddamn before and after moments, and he knew right then that he wasn't going to like the after that came with this one. He was going to hate it. Like a kid who had broken something precious, he scrambled to clean up the mess, praying that glue and tape could make the thing work again.

"I didn't mean it." He was righteously sober now. "Seth, I didn't mean that."

The minute he'd said the words, he'd known that he couldn't break the tie between them. He couldn't fucking lose Seth. He'd finally found that line he wouldn't cross. Now he knew no amount of tequila would be able to numb that loss.

"Yeah, you did." Seth stood up as they heard a door in the back open and feet scooting across the hallway floor.

"Seth, I didn't mean it." Maybe Seth wasn't the only ruthless bastard. Logan knew damn well Seth's dad called him all sorts of nasty names when he got snockered and one of them was "queer." Logan had gone straight for the weak point. The nasty bastard who'd taken up residence in his body had a laser focus when it came to dishing out the pain. "Please."

It was the first time he'd said that word and meant it in over a year.

"Seth? Are you all right?" Georgia rushed in. She was wearing a set of pajama pants and a tank top, her hair soft and skin scrubbed clean. Yes, she looked so beautiful and fresh, and he could see how quickly those crystal eyes summed up the situation and found the proper villain of the piece. "What did he do?"

He. Yeah, she meant Logan, and he knew it. And it would be easy to save face. He could shove his mask right back on and grab another bottle and walk away, and he couldn't do it. *God*. This was what he'd been dreading. The choice. This was why he'd avoided Seth. Because he would have to make the choice to break with his best friend or to try to actually get his head out of his ass.

"I said something horrible to him, and I did it because I'm an asshole, and I'll do anything to take it back." The words spilled out of his mouth, almost tumbling over each other, and he recognized his own damn voice for the first time in almost two years.

"It's cool." Seth had his patented smile on his face, the one he used for investors and his parents. Damn it. "Georgia, sweetheart, could you get me a dustpan? I need to clean this up, and I don't want you getting cut."

Georgia. She would get so cut up if she came into Logan's life. Like he'd cut up Seth.

Unless he stopped trying to throw himself off a fucking cliff.

"I'm sorry."

Seth's head nodded in a clipped fashion, with none of his natural grace. "I am, too. Go to bed, Logan. You have to work tomorrow."

"We'll talk then?" Now he sounded like the kid.

"Do we have anything to talk about?" Seth asked, his voice hollow.

"Do you want me to leave?" He was deeply aware that they sounded like a teenaged couple on the verge of a dramatic breakup, but for once he didn't give a shit. God. He'd finally found something to hang on to, and he was clinging. He wasn't sure he would leave even if Seth told him to.

Georgia banged around in the kitchen and a long moment stretched between them.

"No," Seth said finally.

Logan could breathe again. "Then we have something to talk about."

"All right, but go to bed now. I can't do this tonight." Seth put the bottle on the table as Georgia jogged back in, all fussy female energy and affection, though none of it was focused on him. It was all for Seth.

"Let me get that," Seth said.

Georgia shook her head. "It's fine. I want to help."

"There's glass everywhere." Seth put out a hand to try to stop her from coming too close.

"I'll be fine. I can see it," she insisted.

Seth was letting her roll right over him. Logan knew what to do. Before she could step too close to the shards of glass, he wrapped an arm around her waist and hauled her up against his body, her bare feet dangling off the floor.

"Let me down, you overgrown ape." She dropped the broom and dustpan.

He held her close. "When it's safe, I will."

She lit into him. When that girl wanted to go, she could spit some serious bile.

Seth set about cleaning up the mess, but when he looked up, he mouthed a "thank you."

Georgia went on and on about his parentage and the size of his penis—in her mind, extra small—but Logan felt something settle deep inside.

For the first time in forever, he felt necessary.

Chapter Five

Georgia came awake to the heavenly smell of breakfast cooking. She yawned, thanking god that it had all been a terrible dream and she was back in Manhattan. Yes, she could stumble out of her room and join Seth on the balcony for coffee. She hadn't made a complete idiot of herself. She would open her eyes and see her Upper East Side bedroom.

She opened her eyes and screamed because something horrible was staring in her window. It was big and brown and had monstrous nostrils that steamed up the glass.

The door opened in a flash, Logan slamming into the room, a gun in his hand. God, when had he gotten so familiar with firearms? He was wearing what he'd worn the night before, those low-slung jeans that looked about a size too small because they molded to his every muscle, and a ridiculously hot white muscle shirt that proved he was a meathead who worked out. Like a lot.

God, he was so hot.

"What is it?" He looked ready to kill anything that had invaded.

"Monster." She pointed to the window. Nature could be like that—filled with monsters. And there was lots of nature out here. She was more comfortable in the city.

Sure enough, the massive alien thing was pressed against her window, its enormous nostrils leaving gooey stuff all over the glass.

And Logan, rather than killing the thing like she kind of thought he should, laughed. A wide smile spread across his face and he looked young, so much younger than she could ever remember seeing him. He always looked like the weight of the world was on his shoulders, but in that moment, she could believe he really was twenty-five.

"Holy shit." He practically beamed at the thing that looked like it could eat her. "Seth! Seth, get in here!"

He went to the door and yelled for Seth again.

Seth ran in, his eyes wide and his body covered only in a towel. A little towel. A tiny white towel that contrasted with his tan skin and had been wrapped over ridiculously muscled hips. He had those notches, the ones she'd always been sure some artist Photoshopped onto male models because no one could be that perfect. His dark hair was wet, curling above his shoulders. Moisture clung to his every muscle and, holy hell, he had a lot of them. They hid underneath his perfectly tailored suits.

She forgot about the crazy-ass creature that had come straight out of some danger-in-the-wild documentary and watched the two gorgeous predators who had invaded her room.

She pulled the covers up to her neck, aware that she didn't look anything like they did.

"Maurice." Seth took a step forward. "Wow. How the hell long do moose live, man? It's totally Maurice. You can see where Hiram tried to take him down. There's a scar on his nose."

Logan moved in, too, and she could see the easy way the two men related. For a moment she saw the kids they had been, friends forever. God, she'd never had a friend like that.

Logan opened the window and she heard a loud chuffing noise. "He kicked Hiram in the groin. It was a damn lucky thing the man already had three kids because I heard nothing worked the same after. Hey, boy. You remember me?"

Another huff and she was about to believe the thing knew how to communicate.

Seth looked over at her, his eyes glinting. "We don't get a ton of moose around here. Maurice is a legend. The people of Bliss say that if he shows up at your place, you're blessed. Meant to be here. He's the welcoming committee."

Logan laughed. "What no one will tell you is he's a total snack whore. If you leave a Snickers bar on the porch, he will show up lickety-split. When Laura finally got comfy, I snuck some chocolate onto her porch so she would feel welcome."

"I'm glad she stayed. I heard she got married," Seth said.

Logan nodded. "Got a kid now. That's why I'm here. Her husbands need some paternity leave. I heard it's a girl."

Their shared history was right there, a palpable thing between them. It was almost as though she could reach out and touch it, feel the warmth of it. Logan and Seth felt like a family.

What was she doing here?

Once again, like most of her life, she was the outsider. Even among her brothers, she'd felt it. Chase and Ben had each other. Mark and Dare had been tight. And she and Win had been so far apart in age that they couldn't connect on a brother-sister level. She'd been alone. The only child whose mother wasn't up to snuff. The only one without money when the tide had turned.

Logan looked down at her, his eyes softening. "Georgia, I'm sorry about last night. I didn't mean a word of what I said. To either of you."

She nodded, feeling awkward. They were here in her bedroom. It was a bit surreal. She turned her attention back to the moose.

"So it's not something that's going to attack?" She kept the blanket around her neck. Yeah, that was another way she was different. She wasn't gorgeously perfect like them. She'd tried the whole diet thing, and she wasn't cut out for it.

"Maurice is a sweetie, but I won't lie. The first time I saw him, I peed my own damned pants and ran screaming for my mommas," Logan said on a laugh. He reached a hand out, pressing it against the screen, his eyes misting like he was reaching for his past. "He won't hurt you. He wants to say hello. And he probably smelled the bacon. Shit. My bacon."

Logan turned and took off at a dead run for the kitchen.

Seth touched the screen, too. "Hey, Maurice. Thanks for the welcome."

When he turned back to Georgia, he sported the sweetest smile.

He jumped onto her bed, not a hint of self-consciousness on his face as he settled in beside her. "How did you sleep? My bed's better, by the way. It's huge. Built for three."

"Good for you and whatever ménage you choose to invite. Could you go away so I can get dressed?" Last night seemed like a dream, and more than a little like a nightmare. God, what had she been thinking? Seth wanted her to tempt Logan into a ménage? He was insane. She was insane for not immediately walking out of the cabin and hoofing it to Malibu and the safety of Win's minicastle where she could make like Rapunzel. She would barricade herself in and then keep her hair cut because she was done with men.

He smiled, an intimate thing that threatened to curl her toes. "I thought we settled that last night."

She sighed and wished she was strong enough to not look at that towel, praying it would flop open and she would get a good view of what Seth had down under. Maybe it was small. Like tiny.

Did it matter? He was the sweetest man she'd ever met. He was kind and good. She wasn't about to reject him because he had a small penis. It wasn't like sex was all that awesome anyway.

Logan had a big penis. She'd felt it rubbing against her when he'd kissed her like there was no tomorrow. She thought about Logan's penis a lot. More than a lot.

Nope. She wasn't going to reject anyone based on penis size. She was going to reject them because she wasn't about to get her heart broken again.

"I don't think it's a good idea, Seth. It can't work."

He was lying right next to her, his head propped up on his hand, laid out like a centerfold, but he stared at her with his all-too-intelligent eyes. "It can work. You're scared and I understand that. But I meant what I said when I told you we're going to be together. I have no intention of taking you back to New York as my assistant."

She didn't exactly understand that either. "Am I supposed to go back as your girlfriend? I don't know how that would work. We would have to keep it quiet because my brothers would get upset if they decided I was some rich guy's mistress."

"I'll handle your brothers. And girlfriend is such a juvenile word." He scooted closer to her, his free hand reaching out over the blanket that covered her. "I'm crazy about you."

"You haven't been." Except she knew the minute she said the words that she'd been fooling herself.

"Really? You think I had my other assistants move in with me and have breakfast with me and dinner every night? You think I gave them gifts once a week and brought them their favorite latté every afternoon? I hired a barista to be on call for you."

Yeah. She'd been kind of dumb on that one. And the whole complete redo of her bedroom. He'd claimed it was in their contract. Which, of course, she hadn't read. She really could be a dumbass. Maybe her brothers had a point about her not thinking things through. "I thought you said you love coffee and needed your fix."

His hand moved up and he touched her cheek, his eyes roaming her face. "Hate it. I've never liked coffee. It seriously makes me want to vomit, but you love it so I made sure you could have it."

She felt her eyes narrow. She knew the answers to all of her questions but still felt compelled to ask them. Or maybe she simply wanted to stay close to him. Certain body parts definitely wanted to stay close. "And the clothing allowance? Did Bruce get a clothing allowance?"

Bruce had been the last assistant. And as far as she could tell, he'd quit because he couldn't handle working with Seth. Which hadn't made sense to her at the time because he was so sweet.

He shrugged as best he could. "Bruce bought his suits on sale and I didn't care. I don't know if you've noticed, but the software industry is kind of relaxed. My old version of dressing up was switching out my pajama pants for a pair of sweats. Do you honestly think I cared what he wore?"

Manipulative bastard. "You don't care how I do my job, do you?"

This job was all she had.

He moved fast, as though he'd anticipated her next course of action and sought to block her as quickly as possible. He rolled on top of her, trapping her under his body. It was pure proof that he was a great tactician because she'd intended to get out of bed, throw something at him, and stomp out. A great exit was totally necessary when she needed to keep her head held high.

He brought his face close to hers, their noses almost touching. "You are the best assistant I've ever had. You care about more than just keeping your job. You've taught me how to dress and you've charmed the world's nastiest geeks into submission with one smile. You light up my every fucking day, and I have zero intention of letting you go."

She was so confused. She'd settled into a future where she didn't get Seth. She'd let go of Logan a long while back, but apparently he was in the kitchen making breakfast. It seemed like a slope she shouldn't go down again, a long, slow trip to Wonderland where someone would inevitably lop off her head. Because she wasn't Alice. "It's not like you can hold me prisoner. It might be better for me to head to California. Win can find a job for me."

She wouldn't try the acting route again. It had been a huge bust.

"No." Seth breathed in, his eyes closing briefly as though he was categorizing the scent. "And I can keep you prisoner. This is my kingdom, Princess Georgia. Consider yourself a hostage."

His lips were curved up, his gorgeous eyes seemingly innocent. She rolled her own. "Yeah, I'm sure the moose is going to keep watch over me."

"Nope. He's completely useless as a watch moose, but I have other ways to keep you here. Let me kiss you. Do you have any idea how much I wanted to kiss you in the limo?"

But the time hadn't been right. She wasn't sure she liked being a chess piece in one of Seth Stark's games. "But the timing is right now?"

He was close, not respecting her space at all. His lips, those gloriously sculpted lips, were hanging right there over hers. She could smell the mint of his toothpaste, feel the heat of his body. "The timing is all screwed up. I meant to take a couple of days, to ease you into the situation, but Logan is a fucked-up asshole and he didn't follow the plan. Let me kiss you."

Logan, if he was anything like Georgia herself, had very likely had no idea there was a plan to begin with. Seth had been playing some deep games, maneuvering her into a position, and now cutting in for the kill with ruthless precision and stormy blue eyes. She'd been so stupid thinking he was perfectly nice and kind. He was a billionaire, and he hadn't inherited it. He'd been smart. There was a wolf under all that fluffy wool, and damn her, it made him that much more attractive. And it made her that much more sure that this couldn't work.

But her body didn't seem to be in line with her brain. Her body was turning all *bow chicka wow wow* and thinking, *hey, sex has sucked before, but this could totally be different. Let's give this penis a try!* Her vagina was in full-on cheerleader mode, and her nipples had totally joined the party. Her girl parts were overly optimistic in the worst of times, plain dumb in times like this. She had to shut that shit down before the girls took over and slipped a nipple in his mouth and she was down for the count.

"What did Logan say to you last night?"

Seth rolled off her, and she could have sworn her nipples deflated, their protest obvious. "Nothing. It was nothing."

Well, at least she could breathe now. He walked back to the window and, for a moment, she wished she'd listened to the girls.

Excellent. Ditch your clothes and throw yourself at him. Call out and ask Logan if he wants to join in. None of your friends has ever had a hot ménage with a moose witness.

Her nipples had perked right back up at the first sign of weakness. She decided to silence her inner idiot. "It wasn't nothing. You broke a hundred dollars' worth of Waterford over what he said."

She could still remember rushing in and feeling the tension between Logan and Seth. The idea that they were fighting because of her had made her stomach churn. She'd quickly figured out that it was nothing more than Logan being his jerkfaced, never-give-a-girl-a-reason-to-love-him normal self. She'd been ready to lay into him when she'd seen the shocked look on his face. She knew that look. She'd had it on her own face from time to time when she said something she didn't mean to save her pride. It was longing. He'd desperately wanted to take back what he'd said and Seth had been all kinds of cold, and she'd done the only thing she could think of to fix the situation.

It was something she'd done from childhood when her brothers would fight. She hated it, needed calm and peace among the people she loved. When they started fighting, she would do something dumb, and then they would all turn on her and unite to save their idiot sister.

She'd attempted to walk straight into the glass like she didn't have a brain in her head, and Logan had responded accordingly. She'd known damn well that Seth would try to reason with her and that big gorgeous Neanderthal would do something brutish. Neither one of them would let her walk anywhere near that glass.

It had worked beautifully. She'd seen the moment Seth had thanked Logan, a bit of their peace restored.

"I don't want to talk about it." He was staring out the window as the moose slowly lumbered away.

It was time to lay a few ground rules herself. She wasn't going to do whatever he wanted. She couldn't. Well, she was almost certain that she couldn't. She would eventually hike out of this town and make for civilization, but just in case she made the horrible decision to stay, she needed to make sure there was a real place for her. She couldn't be Seth Stark's china doll, another piece of his collection who didn't truly mean anything. She was damn tired of keeping her mouth shut and trying to look pretty.

Not his china doll. His fuck doll. They actually make them in Japan, but he seems to want a warm one. And he apparently wants to share you with Logan. Yeah, you could be their sex toy.

She needed a serious therapist. "If you didn't want me to ask questions, then you shouldn't have taken a way-too-curious captive. Look, you pulled the rug out from under me, Seth. You say you want me? Well, you can't keep me around only for the good stuff."

She'd had enough boyfriends who wanted to have sex and go to sleep and not have a lick of intimacy between them. That was what she'd loved about being close to Seth. She'd felt like she was a part of his world.

He was silent for a moment, staring out the window with nothing but the sound of the river rushing by. "He told me he wasn't ever going to be my boyfriend and I should stop hoping."

That was what it felt like to get the breath knocked out of her. Wow. She could hear Logan saying it, his lips faintly cruel. She should have taken that fucking broom to his head. What an ass. And yet… "Do you want Logan?"

A low huff came out of Seth's chest.

She scrambled and found quickly that she couldn't stay away from him. She wrapped her arms around his lean waist, and that move had nothing to do with the girls and everything to do with that other stupid part of her. Her heart was every bit as dumb as her girl parts. And her brain was working about a million miles a minute. What if Seth really only loved Logan and he thought that bringing a woman into the mix would get him his guy? She hated the idea, but then realized that she didn't care. She still loved this man. "I didn't mean it in a bad way. I wouldn't think less of you if you did. Sweetie, we need to talk because I don't think he's gay. I think that's a heartache waiting to happen."

She knew all about heartache when it came to Logan Green. She let her hand rub up Seth's chest. God, he was lovely. It felt right to be near him, but she was worried that her near lover was about to become her gay bestie, and damn it if her heart wasn't breaking all over again. This might be the last time she got to hold him like this. The first and last.

His hand came up and covered hers, holding it to his heart. "Logan's not gay. I can't tell you how many women we managed to run through after he decided his sex drive was worth risking his moms' wrath. Sometimes two and three at a time." She started to pull away, but he tightened his hand. "Don't. You want me to start being honest with you? You're going to have to handle the damage. I didn't share those women with him because I was secretly hoping he'd do me instead. Not even close."

He didn't sound like a man who was lying. He pulled at her other arm, gently forcing her to wrap him up. A low growl came out of his mouth. Nope. He didn't sound like a man who wasn't interested in women.

"But you do care about Logan?" She was trying not to think about how good this felt. And she was definitely not thinking about what it would be like if Logan walked into the room and took up position behind her. Nope. That was not a vision running through her head at all.

"I love him, Georgia," Seth replied, his words a confession. His hand rubbed against hers in long strokes. "If I was wired that way sexually, I would have been all over him, but it's not like that.

Sometimes I think it would have been easier that way. Did you ever have that one friend who being around them was like the most peaceful thing in the world? A friend where you didn't have to be anyone except the person you are deep down? I've tried to come up with a hundred different words for it. I've called him my brother, my best friend, but it's not exactly right. He's my soul mate and I'll never kiss him. I don't want to. But I want to share a life with him, and that makes me wrong for a lot of people."

She blinked back tears. Damn. What he hadn't managed with his seduction play, a few aching words had done in a heartbeat. Because she'd never had a friend like that. She'd grown up surrounded by prep school girls who wouldn't let her forget her mother had stripped for a living and she was a piece of trash. She loved her sister-in-law, but she still held back, a piece of her worried that she could wreck something special for her brothers.

You wrecked everything, her mother had said. They'd been the last words she'd said to Georgia. She'd only been five, but she could remember them. She'd wrecked everything by being born because her mother hadn't wanted to be a wife. She'd wanted to be a lover. Carrying Georgia had ruined her body, and she couldn't stand to look at her own daughter.

But with Seth, she'd felt like she could help. Seth was the first person she'd felt at peace with, and she suddenly knew that she couldn't give him up no matter how smart it would be to do so.

"Do you want me? Do you think you could care about me?"

He turned, flipping around and hauling her close like a shark who had finally scented sweet blood in the water. Ruthless bastard. It was deeply sexy, and she needed to call that therapist because her body was already singing again. "I am crazy about you, Georgia. I've been crazy since the moment I saw you and that's true. I want you so bad it hurts, and I want to give you everything you need."

But she couldn't *be* everything he needed. "And if Logan can't be brought around?"

"Then I'll be satisfied we tried." He hugged her close, his forehead rubbing against hers. "I'm going to be so good for you, baby. I'll take care of you. I won't let you down."

She sighed, all of her girl parts singing a happy chorus in her body.

If we're going to do this, you guys are going to have to get with the diet and exercise program.

And she had to stop mentally talking to her various body parts.

He was about to brush his lips against hers when she heard the door open and the sound of a smoke detector start to go off.

Logan stood in the doorway, a steaming, smoking pan in his hands. Her nose was assaulted with the scent of ruined bacon. "I think I killed the kitchen."

He paled as he noticed how close they were standing. She started to pull away, but Seth dragged her close again, not putting an inch of distance between them. "I'll come in and start opening the windows."

Logan turned back around and groaned. "Dude, put that shit away. What's wrong with you? You're a billionaire and you can't buy towels that cover your junk? You know they make them extra big now, but no. You like slapped a washcloth over it so the girl couldn't miss it. Do you think I don't know that play? Fuck, man, I invented that play."

She'd been totally wrong. Wow. Seth's rather intensely large and totally erect male member was poking out of his towel.

Told you.

She watched as Seth and Logan started back down the hallway, pushing and bumping each other like toddlers at play.

Yeah. This was going to be a ton of fun.

Chapter Six

Logan looked up at the building that housed the sheriff's department like it was a damn mountain he was about to climb.

He was dressed in his khakis and boots, a Stetson planted on his head and his stomach somewhere around his knees. He didn't want to walk into that building. Not today. Not tomorrow. Not ever.

What the fuck did he think he was doing? He wasn't this guy anymore. He'd never truly been. He'd been a dumbass kid playing at being a hero, and he'd figured out real damn fast that heroes didn't exist. He'd found out how flawed he was. He'd learned how easy it had been to break Logan Green.

"It's scary, isn't it? I've heard it's haunted by like a ton of ghosts and shit."

He turned, and there was the woman he'd first mistaken as Georgia. Blonde hair, blue eyes, but definitely more slender and willowy now that he was really looking at her. She had a big black bag at her elbow, one of those quilted things Georgia used to carry, but there was a more worldly look to this woman. Georgia, when she thought no one was watching, always looked so fucking innocent.

The way she had this morning when she'd looked up at Seth like he was Superman and he'd rescued her from certain death.

What the fuck game was Seth playing? He should have walked

out the night before, but Seth knew how to work him. He was staying until he heard the plan. He was staying because he couldn't do anything else.

"Not a big talker, then? We're going to get along so well."

So this blonde could be as annoying as Georgia. "You must be the new receptionist."

She groaned. "Yuck. He shoots, he fails. Office manager. I'm the office manager and all-around, one-stop lawyer shop. I find it's the best way to meet new clients. I can help process them in, and by the time they actually make it to the cell, I usually have them on retainer."

Logan stared down at her. Had Nate lost his damn mind? "Nate hired a lawyer? I thought we had an injunction or something."

"Oh, I learn fast, buddy. And I had Nell to coach me on how to get through a town hall meeting. The key is once you have the microphone, to filibuster the shit out of Hiram. After an hour or so, he wants a nap, and he'll give in to anything. So now I can practice law right here in Bliss. Not that it's impressive. It usually involves me talking Nate out of doing stupid shit. He's unusually cranky even for a law enforcement officer."

Well, it was good to know marriage and a couple of kids hadn't slowed down Nate's crabbiness.

"Are we just going to stand out here?" Gemma asked. Jamie had called her Gemma.

"You can do whatever you like. You can walk in at any time." She was starting to annoy him. "I need a minute."

"Seems to me like you've had more than a minute. More like a year or something. You think another minute is going to make a difference? I don't think this is about a minute so much as making up your mind. You're either in or you're out, and another minute won't change it."

"Are you this obnoxious when Nate's around?"

A brilliant smile curved her lips up. "I am the best office manager Nate Wright's ever had, and he won't tell you any different. Now, I've been forced to keep that desk of yours just like you left it since Nate and Cam seem to think it's some sort of shrine. I was actually surprised to find out you weren't dead, merely on some form of extended vacation."

"I was in therapy." Why was he answering her?

She shrugged. "Oh, my bad. I thought people in therapy were encouraged to like call and shit. You know, to update the people who love them on how they're doing. They don't usually leave them hanging unless they're real assholes."

"You got a problem with me?" It was a dumb question. She obviously had a problem with him.

She was perfectly calm as she started up the steps. "Look, man, I'm fairly new here, but I've grown to love this town, and I definitely love Nate and Cam. Consider me a protective and territorial female. You've hurt them. Everyone else might want to treat you with kid gloves, but I don't do the glove thing. I'll tell it like it is, and I've had to watch them stare at that desk every day I've been here. It's like you're a ghost that hangs over this place, and no one will let me call an exorcist."

And she didn't even know the right terminology. "An exorcist is for demons. You need a medium for ghosts."

She snorted. "Wow, they told me you were a total geek. I thought they were joking when you showed up all big and brawny, but there's still a dweeb in there somewhere. Maybe there's hope for you, Green. You like coffee?"

He loved it. Couldn't make it to save his life. He'd gone from his mom's coffee to Shelley's, to this morning when he'd looked at the machine and tried to figure out where the cup things went. Seth hadn't been any help at all. The big tech guru who'd bought the thing stared at it like it was a monster about to attack. Logan had killed the kitchen and he hadn't had an ounce of caffeine, and he couldn't get the sight of Georgia wrapped up in Seth's arms out of his head. Or the fact that all he'd wanted to do was walk up and cuddle behind her and slowly maneuver her back to the bed so they could start the morning right. Maybe if he'd eaten some of Georgia's pussy, he wouldn't need breakfast.

"It's a simple question, man."

But for now he had another obnoxious blonde to deal with, and this one seemed to hate him as much as the first. "Yeah, I would love some coffee."

"Good. Nate's waiting for you in his office. He has a meeting with some law enforcement from local cities in an hour or so and he wants to talk to you about it. How do you take your coffee?"

Sweet. Like he thought Georgia's pussy would be. "Cream and lots of sugar."

Gemma opened the first of two doors that led into the station house. Logan felt stupid standing there, so he followed her. "I can do that. Nate likes his coffee with a little motor oil. I swear that man has an iron gut. I've been making him double espressos, and he claims they're not strong enough. The things I put up with."

"Uh, the coffeemaker here kinda always makes coffee like that." It was why he'd consistently made sure he had a thermos of his mom's coffee before he went to work. And there had always been coffee around The Club. He was kind of spoiled.

Georgia liked coffee. No one had made coffee for her this morning. Or breakfast. Julian Lodge had done his job well. The Dom in Logan was feeling shitty right now because it was his job to make sure his sub was taken care of.

Georgia wasn't his sub. She obviously was going to belong to Seth. Seth. What the hell was he up to now? Seth had to have a plan. Seth always had a plan.

"Oh, I assure you, we've got a new coffeemaker. I threw the old one out." Gemma pushed through the doors and a laugh filled the room. "Thank god. It's been a week since he arrested anyone. I thought Nate was going soft."

Two familiar faces looked out from the twin jail cells. There were only two cells, and most of the time they were completely empty. Not today.

"Logan, dude. Damn, no one told me you were coming home." Max Harper thrust a hand through his cell bars. He wasn't in his usual jeans and Western shirt and cowboy boots. He was wearing a blue gown. A hospital-type gown. "Damn, when did you get all extra extra large? It's hard to believe you came out of Teeny. She's like three feet tall and weighs ten pounds."

"I would explain to you how babies get made, you dickwad, but I'd rather put my fist through your face again." Caleb Burke was in the other cell. He was perfectly dressed, but there was a fine spray of blood across his scrubs and his nose looked like it had taken a beating.

"I know how babies get made, Doc," Max shot back. "I just don't want to make one with you."

The doc growled. "It's called an exam, asshole. And next time I will let you get testicular cancer. See if I give a shit if your balls drop off."

"You can't grab a guy's balls, Doc. Not unless you expect to get clocked." Max turned to the doctor and Logan was the one who was groaning because those stupid exam gowns didn't cover enough.

"Max, you're flapping in the wind, buddy. Cover that shit up." At least at The Club he hadn't routinely caught sight of male parts dangling or dude butts outside of the dungeon floor. It was kind of a way of life in Bliss.

Max turned quickly, his hand reaching for the back of his exam gown, his normally taciturn expression going positively prudish. "I can't help it. Doc makes everyone wear one." He leaned toward Logan. "Are we sure he's not a pervert?"

Caleb slapped the bars of his cell. "God, you're an idiot. I swear there is brain damage. Hell, I don't have any actual evidence that you have a brain. You can find another fucking doctor."

Max clutched his gown, trying to hide his naked backside. "Come on, Doc. That can't be the first time someone's punched you in the face because you treated their balls like the handle on a slot machine."

Caleb glared back at him. "I was gentle, asswipe."

Max shook his head. "We have two different versions of gentle."

Gemma held a hand up, looking deeply amused. "Hey, hold up, you two. So, I get why hot buns is in here. By the way, don't you hide those on my account. Just spices up my morning."

"Thanks," Max said with a wide smile. "I really do work on my glutes."

"Max has a 'frequently jailed' card laminated in his back pocket, but what's your story, Doc?" Gemma asked.

Logan could take a wild guess on that one. Some things never changed. "Max punched him, and Doc ran for his tranq gun."

Caleb grunted. It was his version of agreement. He'd learned Caleb mostly communicated through a series of grunts and rude hand gestures. He was the perfect doc for Bliss. "I didn't have to run. I keep it in my exam room ever since my blood pressure monitor sent Mel into an alien abduction flashback. That old man is strong, let me tell you."

"Yeah, well, I'm fast," Max explained. "The minute Doc went for the gun, I hightailed it right out of there and started back up the mountain. Unfortunately, Doc holds a mean grudge and he followed me, and apparently we scared the shit out of some tourists. But only some of them. The rest were busy taking pictures. I think there might be a video on *YouTube*. Do you think I can use that to sue Doc here, Gemma? I can give you a retainer when I get my pants back."

There was another grunt out of Caleb, but Logan thought this one was Doc's "fuck you" grunt. "You are never getting those pants back. I told Naomi to toss them in with the medical waste."

Max's eyes went wide. "Damn, man. Those are my favorite Levi's. They don't make them anymore."

Caleb shot him the bird.

Gemma shook her head. "I think I'm going to pass on suing Caleb. He's the only doc around here, and one day I'm going to want to have babies. Besides, Jesse told me he was very gentle when it came to his balls."

"See, I'm damn good with balls," Caleb shouted. "And I'm gentle with the rectal exam, too. I'm a motherfucking artist."

Max turned to Logan. "Doc wants to play with my rectum. Can you get me moved to solitary?"

"We don't have a solitary. You're going to have to stay to one side." Yep. Now he was remembering the job. He spent half his workday simply containing the chaos. "I'll call Rachel and Holly."

"Don't! Call Rye. Please call Rye," Max pleaded.

"Naomi's already on her way. Holly and Alexei are in class." Caleb sighed and lay down on the cot like this was merely another part of his day.

Alexei. *Fuck*. He hadn't heard the name in a long time and that was a good thing. He'd avoided saying it, tried not to think it, but he could hardly expect to not hear about the motherfucker here. And apparently he'd gone to college. Logan had wanted to go to college. He'd had the applications in his desk drawer the same day Alexei had sentenced him to hell.

"Logan, good to have you back." Nathan Wright stood in the doorway to his office, his even voice pulling Logan back to the here and now. "Max, Caleb, we'll get you processed out real soon. Naomi's five minutes away. And Rachel is right here."

"Max Harper, this is the last straw!" A five-foot-four-inch ball of pure fury blew through the double doors, her strawberry blonde hair flying behind her.

"Logan, come on into my office. This is going to get ugly." Nate gestured him back. "Gemma, I need a triple, please, and could you get the paperwork done to process them out?"

Gemma gave the boss a jaunty salute. "Will do."

"I ask you to do one thing!" Rachel was yelling. "One damn thing. Get a physical so we can get life insurance so we can protect our babies. Babies. We have another baby on the way, and you want that baby to be left with nothing if you die."

Max's blue eyes went wide. "No, baby, no. I just want to protect our child from unneeded rectal exams."

Rachel's eyes narrowed. "Are you kidding me? We're here because you're afraid of having a single finger shoved up your ass so we can make sure you don't have cancer?"

"Baby, it's unnatural."

"Max Harper, you are never getting anal sex again. Not for the rest of your life. And the vaginal sex is in question, too."

Max got to his knees, his hands on the bars. "Baby, no. I can't live on oral alone."

Rachel turned. "Leave him in there. I've got pregnancy hormones to deal with. I can't deal with him, too."

"Rachel, baby, I love you!"

Rachel stopped briefly to look up at Logan. "Logan, welcome home. It's good to know you got your head out of your ass long enough to come back to where you belong. Your mommas have been very lonely. I expect to see you out at the house for dinner on Sunday."

"I'll have to check my schedule," he replied because he wasn't sure they would be back to normal by Sunday and if Rachel was annoyed with Max, dinner would be uncomfortable.

Rachel's eyes narrowed. "Really?"

He knew damn well why she was surprised. He would never have thought to reply to her with anything but a solid "yes" before because Rachel was a ballbuster. She could freeze a man at fifty paces, but he wasn't the same kid who'd left. "Really. I have a lot of obligations while I'm here. If I can, I would love to come out to the house, but I have to check with my roommates."

God only knew what Seth had planned for them. If he really had balls, he wouldn't care. But the thought that he would get thrown into something with Georgia…damn, he couldn't pass that up. He knew it was wrong. He knew it made him a fucking masochist, but he couldn't help himself. He'd tried to stay away from her, knew he couldn't be with her long term, but he wanted to worship her from up close while he could, and he wasn't going to let Rachel Harper's iron willpower get in his way.

Rachel smiled and gave him a wink. "Good for you. I'll give you a call. What's your friend's name? Seth, I think? He's welcome, too, and the pretty blonde. Nothing gets past Callie, hon."

"Rach?" Max sounded so sad.

Rachel growled. "I'll be at Stella's. I need some pancakes."

As Rachel walked out, a gorgeous, curvy woman with coffee-colored skin and a deep frown on her face walked in.

"I don't know why I work for you."

Caleb smiled. "Hey, Na. You rock. Ten percent pay increase."

A brilliant smile crossed her face. "Yes, there it is. Where's Gemma? I have to get you out of here. You have a ten o'clock sonogram with Jennifer Talbot."

"She's in the back," Nate said, pointing toward the break room. "Logan? Park your stuff at the desk and get in here." He turned away, disappearing into his office. "We have weird shit going on in the county. Well, weirder shit than normal."

Max and Caleb started yelling at each other again. The woman who seemed to be named Naomi walked back to find Gemma, and Logan was left in the one place he'd been pretty certain he wouldn't visit again.

He drifted over to the desks. There were three. The big one in the middle of the room had always been used by Nate's assistant. He glanced down and could tell that Gemma was different. Hope had kept her desk pin neat, with no personal touches at all, but Gemma had a bunch of pictures of people all over her desk in pretty frames. He recognized the men she'd been with outside of Stella's, her arms around them. There was a picture of her with Hope and a pretty, really pregnant woman he thought might be James's partner's wife.

He moved past her desk and was caught by the big framed picture on Cam's desk. In the center of the frame was a tiny baby with a tuft of black hair. That baby was in Laura's arms, and she was shining in the picture, her blonde hair a virtual halo around her head. Rafe and Cam were beaming down at the woman and child. Hell. Cam had a baby. Cam had been his friend, and he didn't know what the baby's name was.

"She's pretty, huh?" Gemma was behind him, a mug in her hand. "Sierra Rose. Cam brought her up here yesterday to show her off and he left that picture here. He was so happy. I'll admit, it makes me think even I might be able to have scary pooping rug rats. Here's some coffee. I've got to go and deal with a shit ton of paperwork. I hope Max never gets sex again."

He took the mug, and the amazing smell hit him. Damn, that wasn't Hope's coffee. This was brown gold. He took a long draw as he sat down at his old desk. Gemma had been right on two fronts. One—her coffee was worth more than money. It was beautiful and might actually change his life. Two—his desk was exactly how he'd left it, right down to the pencils he'd left by his phone.

Damn. It was like he'd never left. It was like he'd never done all the shit he'd done. Never walked into Hell on Wheels and…fuck. He didn't want to think about that. He set his coffee down and opened the right drawer. It was where he kept his notebooks, but that wasn't what he saw when he opened it.

Comic books. A big stack of comic books lay at the bottom of the drawer. Superman and X-Men and Fables and Spider-Man. He'd missed these when he'd burned the rest of his collection. They'd been buried in his desk. He stared at them for a moment.

He'd loved those books. He'd spent hours reading them.

He'd been an idiot then. His childhood flashed before him. He'd spent all his time dreaming about being some freaking superhero, and all he'd gotten out of it was the final realization that he was nothing.

He slammed the drawer shut.

Maybe certain things hadn't changed around Bliss, but other things had. He had. He'd changed irrevocably and there was not a damn thing anyone could do about it.

He turned away and started toward the room he'd lost his innocence in. Nate's office. His personal version of hell.

Fuck, he hated everything.

* * * *

Seth loved everything about Bliss. This was paradise, his true home.

Manhattan might have been good to him, but Bliss was paradise. Of course, even paradise had its issues.

"Seth." Henry Flanders held out his hand and Seth shook it, holding it probably two seconds longer than necessary because he'd missed Henry.

"Henry." Seth forced himself to let go. He'd only been back in Bliss once since the time he'd met John Bishop, aka Henry Flanders, but they had kept in touch. It had been awkward at first, but then they'd settled into talking once a month, their long conversations filling something deep inside him. Henry was always the one who called, and Seth often wondered if Henry had put that call on a schedule.

"What's wrong with you, son? Get up here and give me a hug." Henry held his arms open.

Seth practically jumped up and hugged the man he considered a father figure. "It's good to see you."

"It's been a long time. I was starting to think you wouldn't come home again."

He stepped back, sliding into the booth as Henry took the place across from him. Henry's hair was longer than it had been six years before. When he'd first met Henry, he'd had a short, neat cut, and his clothes had been straight out of Professor Retail. He'd been uptight, but the man who sat in front of him now was relaxed, his brown hair brushing his earlobes. His clothes were fairly loose and laid back. He would bet they were all organic cotton.

A waitress stepped up, winking Seth's way. She took their orders and walked back toward the kitchen.

"Still eating vegan, huh?" Seth asked.

"Always. Good for the body. Good for the soul." Henry leaned forward, his easy smile disappearing. "How bad is it?"

Seth frowned. This was the shitty part of his visit. "I think I stopped it, but I can't shut down everything. If I do, it could actually make things worse."

"I understand. Should I expect a visitor?"

Seth shook his head. "I don't think so. According to all the records, Henry Flanders lives in Seattle. I keep a place out on Bainbridge Island in your name."

Henry smiled again. "You're such a devious thing. We should all be damn happy you're not a criminal."

"Hey, some people would disagree. Have you read the *Times* lately?" The *Times* seemed to have it out for him, claiming that his current domination of the software market was bad for businesses and consumers everywhere. They likened him to the old railroad tycoons who had a stranglehold on transportation in their time.

"It's always hard to be on top. So any ideas on who's looking for me?"

"I traced some of the inquiries back to DC." In his mind, it was the absolute worst-case scenario.

Henry took a long breath. "Langley. The Agency."

"Yeah. I don't know how or why they would start looking, and I damn straight have no idea why they would be looking for Henry Flanders. There weren't any loose ends that I can think of."

"Oh, I can think of one." Henry sat back. "I shipped out of Colombia on Henry Flanders's passport. At the time it seemed like I was starting a new life, but now I can see where I was lazy. When I left Bliss, I switched to another passport so Henry Flanders left Colombia, but he never entered the country according to airport records. I could fake the stamp on my passport, but I couldn't fake the airport records. The authorities don't like messy passports. And sometimes they like to run checks. It's entirely possible that the passport got flagged."

"After all these years?"

He shrugged slightly. "Identity is a funny thing. And so is intelligence. Things can be very fluid in that world. The way things were set up, I was killed by a cartel and they took my body. If the next operative got in good with the cartel, he might have investigated. The Delta agent who set up my exit could have had a change of heart, though I would be surprised at that. He seemed solid. I suspect they found something, some thread I left behind, and now they're seeing how far it will unravel. Don't worry about it. They're fishing. They don't have anything or they would be on my doorstep and not on the Internet."

How was Henry not losing his shit? Seth was almost always calm, but the idea of someone looking for Henry had his stomach in knots. He'd worked so hard to keep this all under wraps. Nell didn't even know that her husband had a past life as a CIA operative who went by the name John Bishop. "I'll keep an eye on the situation. And I have someone watching the Bainbridge house to see if anyone's casing it."

"You know the Agency would have loved to have you. You're a genius when it comes to laying out a plan. So Nell and I own property on Bainbridge Island, huh?"

Seth chuckled. "Don't try taking her out there, man. I bought the place off a junk bonds king. The housekeeper says he was a true believer in gold fixtures and mounted animal heads. She hasn't gotten around to earth friendlying the sucker up."

The very flirtatious waitress set a pot of tea in front of Henry and a water for Seth before winking at him as she left.

It made him uncomfortable. He was already taken. He just wasn't wearing a ring yet.

Henry poured the tea with a practiced hand. "You haven't even seen the place?"

He shook his head. "Nah. I didn't buy it for a vacation."

"No, it was part of your plot. So tell me, that monstrosity of a house next to mine…what plot is that a part of?"

Seth sat back, a little startled. "It's not a plot. You know I've always meant to come home."

"You haven't been back in almost six years."

"I was working. I finished school and I started Stark Software. It was intense. The programming was only the beginning. And then contracts started rolling in. I've barely looked up from my computer for the last six years." It had been a whole lot of hard work, but everything was in place now. He could breathe again.

"It was funny. I rather think we all believed you would move out here after college, or at the very least spend some time with Logan. That first summer you didn't show up was a surprise."

Whoa. He'd always thought of Henry as the father he wanted, but now he was sounding way dad-like with the guilt tripping. "Granddad died. My dad sold the place right out from under me. I think granddad thought that my father would do the right thing and keep it in the family, give me a chance to make some money and buy it, but Dad sold the cabin two days after we buried him. I've been working my ass off so I could come home in style."

"I don't think anyone was worried about style," Henry murmured. "We wanted you home. I think Logan's felt like you abandoned him."

"You wouldn't know it. It's not like I didn't call. I called at least once a week, and then two years ago he stopped talking to me. Oh, he would answer the phone, but I got nothing out of him. The only way I knew he'd been in the hospital was Momma Marie called me."

"But you didn't come to visit." Everything Henry said was with an even, calm tone.

"He told me not to."

"And you listened to him?"

"He promised me he would come to New York and then he went to Dallas instead. God, Henry, I didn't know how bad it was. When Marie talked to me about it, she said he'd been in a work-related incident."

Henry's eyes went slightly cold, and Seth could see that John Bishop was still in there, buried deep. "Marie has a habit of understating things. He was brutalized. He was tortured for hours by a member of the Russian mob, and I think it broke him in ways not even he understands. I was happy to hear he's been working with a therapist. That's why he went to Dallas."

He'd known it was bad. He'd suspected Marie was understating it. Why hadn't he come home? "I know. Jamie called me when some guy named Wolf wanted to set up a deal with the counselor. Logan was supposed to go there on some sort of payment plan, but I didn't want him to have to worry about money. I paid for his membership at some club that the therapist insisted on. A BDSM club. Apparently the therapist uses BDSM to help control impulse issues. I've been studying up on it, actually. I've been to a Manhattan club."

Henry watched him for a moment. "I wouldn't pick you for a lifestyler."

"I probably wouldn't be but Logan needs it, and I think the woman I love needs it, too."

Henry pointed at him triumphantly. "Ah, there's your plan. I knew it would be in there somewhere."

Damn it. Why did that make it sound cheap? "It's not a plan. I'm trying to bring us together."

"Let me see if I can guess what's going on here. You've found a woman you like."

"I've found a woman I love," Seth corrected.

"Fine. You've found a woman you love and you're ready to move on, but you want the ménage you've always dreamed of and Logan's not where he needs to be. So lucky you. You manage to find a naturally submissive woman. Logan is a trained Dominant male. You intend to ask him to teach you how to top your girlfriend. Are you going to give him rights to her body?"

Guilt was gnawing at him. It sounded dirty when Henry put it like that. But it was going to work. It had to work. "Yes. It won't work if he doesn't have sex with Georgia."

"Sex could bind them together. For the female, it will be difficult for her not to fall for him."

He was sick of feeling like the bad guy. It brought out the beast in him. "Oh, Henry, you see this is where you've underestimated me. You want to make me the villain? You haven't gone far enough. Georgia knows Logan. She spent time with him eight months ago, and I believe they fell for each other then, but his mental state kept them apart. Well, that and her deep stubborn streak. I was lucky enough to find her. I intended to simply hire her and keep her safe for Logan, but I took one look at that blonde with her bratty mouth and her soft heart and I knew I would keep her for myself if I had to. Eight months. I've kept my hands off her for eight months until the time became right for me to bring us all here and under one roof. I will maneuver them both into a situation where they are living together, sleeping together, playing together, and I will get what I want in the end."

A slow smile crossed Henry's face. "There's the Seth I expected. It's an interesting play. Where do you fit? If Logan is the Dom and this Georgia is the sub, what's your role? How do you know that once you manage to get them together, they won't need you anymore? Ah, there's the rub."

Henry had gotten obnoxious since he hit forty. John Bishop hadn't talked this much. Of course, John Bishop had also tried to kill him once, but Seth had been cock blocking the man, so he understood.

"It won't happen."

"It could happen. You could end up feeling like the second dick or worse, the guy they keep around because they feel guilty."

This hadn't gone down the way he'd hoped. He utterly lost his appetite. He felt his body flush, and he took a deep breath to banish the unwanted emotions that threatened to take over. "Well, I can see what you think of me. Uhm, I'm going to get back home. Give Nell my love."

Henry's hand shot out, grabbing his wrist before Seth could stand. "Don't. I know you thought you could walk back in here and everything would be roses and moonlight, but if you want to live here, if you want to be a part of this family, you're going to have to change your expectations. I know you think of me as a father figure."

This was the part of the day where he would normally tell whoever was making him feel like crap to fuck off and walk away. If it had been his biological father, he certainly would have done that. "If you don't want me to bother you anymore, Henry, I won't."

"See, this is what I'm talking about. The minute you come against something you can't barrel your way through, you drop it like a hot potato. Stop. Take your little boy hat off and listen to me. You think of me as a father figure and I love you like a son. That means I'm going to poke at you and try to make you the best you can possibly be. It's what parents do. I'm worried about this. I'm not worried that you won't have a place in this relationship you want. I'm worried that you won't see it. You get so damn caught up in a problem that you don't see the emotional ramifications of what will happen when you get what you want. You're obsessive and you tend to let the rest of the world fall away when you're focused. I think this relationship could be very good for you. I think you and Logan have always balanced each other, and you two got into serious trouble when you no longer had the other to count on. You drifted into your work and he could not cope with having his innocence stripped away. You two need each other. Don't look at this like one of your plots, Seth. It's too important."

"It's everything," Seth concurred, relief flooding his system. He hadn't realized how much he'd come to depend on Henry being there. "I understand what you're saying and I appreciate it. I'll consider everything you've said, but I think we all need this."

"All right." Henry sat back. "Looks like breakfast is here. Scrambled tofu and veggies. Damn. Nothing gets a morning started like that."

The waitress put a plate in front of Seth, but he had to force himself to eat. As Henry started talking about everything that was going on around the county, all Seth could see was Logan, battered and bruised. What if he was wrong? What if he didn't understand what the problem truly was? What if love couldn't cure Logan?

Chapter Seven

Georgia stuck her head out of the door and wasn't immediately assaulted by a giant raging beast.

It was the first thing that had gone right all day long.

She stepped out on to the deck that faced the river. She wasn't all nature girl, but there was no way to not find that view spectacular. The river was wide and the sound of it rushing by soothed her. It was the sound that had put her to sleep the night before.

It wasn't like she'd never camped in her life. Her brothers had loved camping, and despite the fact that she'd been so young and had gotten into trouble a lot, Win always made sure she came along. At first she'd thought he felt guilty about everyone else getting to go because her brothers all went together, but later she learned that he'd left her behind once and when he'd gotten back her nanny was in bed with their father and she hadn't been fed in two days. He'd never allowed her to be alone again.

She felt alone now. Was she always going to be that kid other people had to look out for? A burden. An afterthought.

Seth and Logan had practically run out the door this morning as though they couldn't stand being there with all the tension between them.

Jerks. If they'd stayed, they would have gotten her world-class frittatas. She'd offered to make breakfast, but they had both turned a little green and went running out the door. Seth had a housekeeper in New York and when she'd known Logan, they'd been at a resort. Neither man knew she could cook, and it looked like it might stay that way. She'd cooked her own breakfast, read the manual for the single-cup coffeemaker, had some awesome coffee, cleaned up, and then decided to bake some cookies because she was bored out of her mind. She had a horrible sweet tooth and baking soothed both her need for sweets and her nerves. She liked the kitchen. It was big and had every type of tool she could possibly want. Whoever Seth had hired to fill the place had known what she was doing.

After clearing up all of Seth's e-mail and requesting some changes to the quarterly reports, she'd stuck her head in the fridge, found a whole chicken, dressed it with garlic and basil and stuffed it in a Crock-Pot for dinner. It was an old trick she'd learned in college. If she could get a chicken in early enough, it would be tender and perfect by the time dinner came around. There were potatoes in the pantry, and at three o'clock she'd peeled them and cut them and put them in the pot. She'd found fresh asparagus and steamed it with some garlic and citrus and made homemade biscuits, cut with a juice glass because the only thing she couldn't find was a biscuit cutter. She'd grown up in LA, but their longtime cook had been born in New Orleans. Georgia had spent long hours of her life with Rene in the kitchens learning how to make roux and properly shuck oysters.

She'd spent the day wandering around because no one had come home and no one had called her to ask her to meet them. It was like they'd forgotten she existed. At least in New York she had a job to do. She had a purpose. Here all she had was her e-reader. She'd restarted J.R. Ward's books, organized her makeup, hung up her clothes, and wondered what the hell she was doing here.

She wondered if they would even try her meal. Logan probably wouldn't. He'd made it plain that she wasn't good for much, and she'd probably reinforced the idea because she could be nasty when she felt threatened.

She'd gotten dressed in her nicest jeans—the ones with the most bling on the butt—her Elie Tahari blouse and new Gucci boots, and placed her brown sugar blondie cookies in a basket and headed out to meet the neighbors.

She stopped, staring at the cabin next door. She didn't have long before dinner would be done, but she didn't know when Seth and Logan would be back. She didn't even know if they would be back at all. Maybe they would have dinner somewhere else and she would be alone tonight.

What was she doing? She didn't live here. Seth lived here apparently. Logan definitely lived here. She was only passing through. So why did she have the most insane urge to make a good impression?

Because these people mattered to Seth and Logan. Because even if they didn't care about her, she cared about them.

She looked back at the door. She should go inside and hide. She didn't belong here.

What was that? A footprint?

It was there on the side of the deck, a thick muddy print. She moved across the deck and stared down at it. It wasn't Seth's. He'd been wearing size thirteen Louis Vuitton loafers. These were much smaller. Maybe a men's nine. Logan was a ridiculously overgrown fifteen. No way it had been his foot that made it. The print was round and curved in the middle before coming back out and rounding at the back. Sneaker. There was a second print, but it was only of the toe and pointed right under the big window that graced the living area. Someone had gone up on their toes, right foot dangling off the deck, as they tried to look into the cabin.

Maybe it was a worker. Seth had mentioned that the place had recently been finished.

Yeah, that had to be it.

Except it felt wrong. She shouldn't follow her instincts. Did she even have instincts? Usually her instincts were about men and sex, and they were almost always wrong. But it wouldn't hurt anything to look around. The tracks came from the yard, and apparently the ground was soft enough that the imprint was still there. Had it rained in the last couple of days?

The tracks led off to the west. It couldn't hurt to follow them. They likely led to the driveway. Except they didn't. She could see clearly where the tracks led back to the river. Someone had walked up to the cabin from the river.

"Hey, baby." Seth walked around the house. She hadn't heard the car pull up.

This morning she'd discovered that he'd had an Escalade purchased and waiting for him in the drive. The keys had been on the bar. She'd walked him out to the car because she'd kind of been hoping he'd take her with him, but all that had happened was he'd found a nasty note about the vehicle's fuel efficiency taped to the windshield. She'd been offended, but he'd smiled and folded the note up and shoved it in his pocket like it had been a love letter.

Logan's truck was parked in the garage. He'd gotten a ride in from Seth. Apparently he would be coming home in a county vehicle.

"Hi." She felt so damn awkward. What the hell did a girl say to a man who was her boss and had also made some sort of plans for them to become boyfriend and girlfriend in the future? She kind of wished he'd given her an exact date when that would happen. She nodded toward the comfy-looking cottage next door. "I'm going over to say hi to the neighbors. I baked some cookies for them. I'll be back in a bit."

He practically leapt onto the deck. "No. Oh, Georgia, honey, that's not a good idea." He tugged the basket out of her hands. "That's Nell and Henry's place. They are total vegans. They don't eat cookies. I'll set these aside for me and Logan. Now, how about you get ready and we'll head into town and have dinner and drinks."

"I made dinner."

She flushed with embarrassment as he obviously tried to figure out how to get out of eating at home. She could see the way his brain was trying to find any possible out.

"You did? Well, that's great. Uhm. I thought we would go into town."

She heard the crunch of gravel this time and didn't wait around to hear all the reasons Seth didn't even want to try her food.

Logan parked his massive SUV. It was another Escalade, but it had county colors on it and was emblazoned with the words *Bliss County Sheriff's Department* and had a set of lights on the top. "Dude, is this your doing? Because this ride is so fucking boss."

Seth walked out behind her. He'd stashed her cookies somewhere because his hands were empty. "I thought the county could use an upgrade. I bought four and donated them to Nate. He was pretty happy with me. I might be able to avoid a ticket for a week or two. I've heard the dude is crabby."

The two met in the middle and slapped hands and then did that guy thing where they halfway hugged and then proceeded to beat the hell out of each other's backs. She stood in the background, completely ignored.

They started talking about everything that had happened during the day as they walked back toward the house. The tension from the night before seemed to have passed, and it was easy to see that they had been friends for a long time. Seth reached out for her hand, but he let her go without a protest when she stepped back.

They walked into the cabin, neither of them bothered by the muddy footprints on the deck. She probably shouldn't be either. She frowned when she saw that Seth had set her basket behind the woodpile like he was trying to hide it. She picked it up and followed them inside.

Logan's hat was on the bar, and Seth had set his keys down. Seth had the refrigerator open and passed Logan a beer.

"So I thought we could talk tonight. Maybe head into town. You said there was a new tavern, right?" Seth asked.

"Trio," Logan replied. "It's Callie's place."

Seth smiled. "We grew up with Callie. She's a complete sweetheart, Georgia. You're going to love her."

She bet she would. She bet that if Callie had cooked dinner for them, they wouldn't be planning how to get out of eating it. She sat down at the bar. They didn't seem to need her input.

"What exactly is it you want to talk about?" Logan asked, his voice tightening.

Seth set his beer down and took a long breath. "I want to talk about D/s."

She heard him vaguely, but her mind was wandering. Guys changed when they got around other guys. Seth had been so sweet when they'd been in New York. She'd felt like the center of the world. She didn't need to be the center of everything, but she hated this feeling, like she wasn't in on the joke. Or worse, like she was the butt of the joke. She got that a lot. Guys could be great when a girl was alone with them, but sometimes when a guy got with his friends, he changed. Seth seemed to be changing.

"Georgia?" Logan was staring at her, a serious look in his eyes.

"What?"

"Are you sure you want to go along with this?" Logan asked. "What he's asking for is some serious shit. It would be very serious for me."

Serious? What had she missed? Did she want to admit she'd drifted off? Wouldn't that make her look that much dumber? *Stall them, Georgia.* Maybe she could figure it out. "Sure. Uhm, why don't you go over it again while I get the plates out for dinner?"

Logan grimaced. "I thought we were going to Trio."

"We don't have to go out. I cooked."

Seth reached out to touch her hand. "Sweetie, it's our first night here. Let's go out. We can have your dinner tomorrow night. Or we could save whatever you cooked for lunches and leftovers."

"You have to eat a thing to have leftovers." That answered one question. They didn't want to take her seriously at all and they weren't willing to be polite to save her feelings. "Why am I here?"

Logan sighed. "I told you she wasn't listening."

Fine. She was dumb as dirt. Her stomach was getting tight, and anger was starting to boil. "No, I wasn't. I was thinking about something else. So tell me why I'm here. Because I wasn't brought here to work, and Seth left me alone all day, so I wasn't brought here to meet your friends. Why am I here?"

Seth's whole face softened. He was like a gorgeous puppy with perfect abs when he got that look on his face. It had worked on her before, every single time. "Baby, I can't wait for you to meet my friends. It's not the time yet. I thought I would give you a couple of days to get settled in."

"I unpacked. I think I'm settled in." She was on the fence. He could be very thoughtful. Maybe he was honestly trying to give her time.

Seth patted her hand. "Uhm, maybe you need a little time to kind of figure out the social situations around here. Tomorrow we'll talk about small-town life. This isn't New York. You have to act a bit differently around here if you want to fit in."

"What he's trying to say is that your big-city princess act won't fly around these parts," Logan clarified. He was watching her with hooded eyes as he tipped back his beer.

She got the subtext. Seth didn't want her to embarrass him. He'd never minded in New York, but it suddenly struck her that he didn't have anyone in New York that he actually cared about. She'd never seen him hug a friend in New York or smile the way he did here. He'd shown her off in New York because it didn't matter. Now that they were someplace that it did matter, she wasn't good enough, and he thought he could change her.

She'd thought he was the guy for her. Logan was a pipe dream. She wasn't even sure what she'd felt for Logan had been love. It had been a crazy hot attraction. It was still there. Every time she looked at him, she felt like that dumb moth who kept circling the flame, getting closer and closer with every pass. He'd saved her once. He'd kissed her silly and made her feel more than she'd ever imagined, but he'd made it plain that she was way too much trouble.

Seth had been reality. She'd fit into his world, kind of, sort of. She'd thought he liked her the way she was, but that had been another lie. He liked the way she looked. Some guys went for the blonde bombshell thing because they thought the way she looked meant she was good at sex. Seth had a curvy-girl fetish.

But it was obvious he didn't truly like her or he wouldn't be hiding her away.

"That isn't what I'm saying at all," Seth said quickly. "I'm saying Bliss can be a bit of culture shock."

Logan shrugged. "If she can't be who she is, there's no damn reason for her to be here."

She rather agreed, but the way he said it stung. Tears threatened, but she wasn't going to cry. Dawsons didn't cry. They were tough. She'd watched her brothers. They were her only role models. Oh, she'd had a parade of stepmothers, but they were cold for the most part, and she'd seen that crying didn't work with men. Anger worked. And she was definitely angry. Rage clouded her judgment. Win had been right. She should never have come out here. Now she was alone.

"Try the food." She didn't make it a polite request. She wasn't feeling polite. She stared at Seth because Logan was a lost cause.

Seth stopped and studied her for a moment. She could see that big brain of his working, trying to figure out exactly how to handle her. After a long moment, he nodded. "All right. I would love to try it."

He was a good liar. He'd even managed to say the words with a smile and an emphasis on the word "love." She walked over to the Crock-Pot and picked the best parts of the chicken, ladling on some of the rich gravy that had formed. She scooped up some choice potatoes. The plate was pretty. Probably not what he was expecting, but then she was about to show him she didn't always do what he expected her to do.

"Dude, she's about to pull some shit." Logan's eyes had narrowed. He didn't move from his seat, but he was watching her like she was a dog growling his way.

She set the plate in front of Seth. Logan didn't matter. "Eat it."

Seth's shoulders squared, his face tightening, and for a second she caught a glimpse of the real man behind the sweet façade. He was ruthless, and he didn't like being ordered around.

Logan never took his eyes off her. "I'm telling you, man. Shut this shit down now or I'll have to do it. You want me to teach you how to top her? It's not going to be easy."

Top her? Seth wanted to top her? Well, if he'd wanted to easily do that then he should have stayed her boss. She'd done everything he asked of her then. "I'm not a sub."

She wasn't going to admit any of her fantasies at this point. She wouldn't admit that Nat had talked to her about the possibility that she would be happier in a D/s relationship. She definitely wasn't going to mention that before she'd left Dallas, Julian Lodge had offered to find a Dom for her.

She'd thought about it. And then left because she'd only wanted one Dom.

"Oh, you're a sub." Logan said it with an arrogant smile that made her stupid heart pound faster. "That's what we've been negotiating. Seth wants me to train the two of you so you can have a D/s relationship. You're just fighting it. You're a little sub who likes to rage against the machine because you haven't found a Dom yet who has the patience to handle you."

"Well, we both know that's not going to be you." He'd made himself plain enough.

The smile vanished. "I might have made a mistake back in Texas, Georgia. Seth wants to explore the lifestyle. I want you. This plan of his gives us all what we want."

Damn, she should have paid attention. He wanted her? He wanted to be her Dom? God, she'd fantasized about it because Logan was right. After a lot of talks with Natalie and Kitten, she was pretty sure that she was probably more submissive than she wanted to admit. She just hadn't found anyone she could trust. Was she misreading the situation? She took a deep breath and forced herself to take the leap. "Do you really want me?"

Logan shrugged, his eyes sliding away. "Sure. You're sexy as hell. But you should understand that it's a training relationship. There's no 'happily ever after' here, so don't get that look in your eyes. Seth is generously allowing me access to you while you're in training."

"Do you have to make it sound so nasty? I think it's something the three of us can enjoy." Seth had the fork in hand, but he hadn't taken a bite. "I think it's a good way to explore a relationship. We don't have to place arbitrary boundaries on it."

Well, it certainly seemed to work for the boys. There was only one problem. She wanted them to love her, and they'd proven that they couldn't. Did they expect to keep her here like some dirty secret? What would happen when they went back to New York? He'd said he wouldn't take her back as his assistant. Was she supposed to go back as his submissive? Would he keep her in the apartment for sex and then go about his job and his life like she didn't exist? Was this his perverse way of firing her?

She wanted to cry. God, she wanted to wail, but it wouldn't fix anything and it would only make her look weak. Her father had hated it when she'd cried, told her how pathetic it made her. She couldn't cry, so she leaned on the one thing she could always fall back on. Anger.

"Eat it, Seth." She was determined that he would take one fucking bite and then she would leave. They could take their plan and go to hell. She would have to suck it up and admit to Win that she'd gotten played. Again.

"I'm telling you, man. This is about to go south," Logan said. "That's the voice she uses right before she starts throwing shit."

Because he knew her so well.

Seth looked between the two of them like he couldn't quite decide which one to obey. He finally sighed and took a bite of chicken and potatoes. He stopped, chewing thoughtfully, and finally a smile crossed his face. "Georgia, this is excellent. Seriously, Logan, you should try that. It's really good. Sweetheart, you never told me you could cook." He used his fork to pull off another piece of the chicken. "This is falling apart it's so tender."

Well, she was glad he liked it. And that was all his ass was getting. She pulled the plate out from under him, marched to the trash can, and dumped the whole thing in. He could afford new plates. He was Seth Stark. If he saw something he wanted, he bought it and used it and discarded it.

"Hey, I said it was good." He was staring at her like she'd grown another head.

He'd never once seen her mad. It was a damn good thing she was leaving because after this, he would likely throw her out. Now that she knew what he was after—a pretty, trouble-free sex toy—she knew she didn't fit the bill. She'd been careful around Seth, desperate for him to like her, but all that good behavior had been for nothing. He didn't want her around his real friends even when she was playing nice. Well, except for Logan, but she was some sort of sexual sacrifice to him.

Stay. Maybe it could work out. And if it doesn't, at least you'll know if the sex would be good.

Those voices were back again, but she wasn't listening. She grabbed the Crock-Pot and chucked that, too.

"Georgia!" Seth had his hands on his muscular hips looking every inch the disapproving male. "Stop it right now. I get it. I was being an ass. Now sit down and we'll talk about it."

"She's not going to talk. No way, no how. You're lucky she didn't dump the contents of that Crock-Pot on your head," Logan pointed out.

Okay. That would have been a better idea, but she was kind of done with all of it now. Logan looked amused by the situation. She was so glad she could entertain him. Tears kind of blurred her vision as she looked at them.

"Georgia?" Logan asked, frowning and putting his beer down. He sighed. "Come on. Do what Seth says. Let's sit down and talk this out like adults."

Because she certainly wasn't one of those. She was a toy to be kicked around and used up and tossed out when she was no longer pretty or useful. She'd seen it a hundred times before. Her dad had been crazy about her mom until he wasn't and he'd kicked her out. He'd done it with four different wives and countless girlfriends, and finally he'd been done with each of his kids.

There was only one man she could count on. Win. Ben and Chase didn't need their obnoxious sister hanging around with their new wife. Mark and Dare were god only knew where. She had one place to go.

She turned on her heels and started for the door.

"Georgia!" Seth yelled.

She grabbed her bag. Maybe he would be nice and send her things to her in Malibu, but he was just as likely to throw them away.

It didn't matter. All that mattered was getting the hell out and never seeing either of them again. She had to hope she could find her way into town. But there was no way she was staying a second longer.

* * * *

Logan put down his beer and hopped off the barstool. Seth was staring at the place where Georgia had been standing before making one of her trademarked exits.

Except she hadn't yelled at them or thrown crap at their heads like she usually did when she was throwing a hissy fit, brat attack. She'd stared for a minute like she'd lost something and then she'd turned and quietly walked away. She hadn't even slammed the door. He didn't like how quiet she'd been.

"Are you going to go after her?" Logan asked, praying the answer was yes because he was pretty sure if Seth said no, he would still be walking out that door. And the minute he laid hands on her this time, he wasn't sure he would be able to stop until he'd stripped her down and spread her wide.

Damn. The minute that evil glint had hit her eyes, his cock had gone to full fucking mast. His whole body had been ready for a fight, ready to take her down, but the quiet exit had him near to reeling. That wasn't his Georgia. His Georgia would have tossed something at his head as she spat bile his way.

She'd looked hurt. He'd handled her like crap. Again.

"What the hell was that?" Seth asked. "She's never once behaved like that."

He frowned at his friend. "You don't know her, do you? She's a brat. She hides a whole lot of hurt under that mouth. Tell me something. Was the food actually good?"

"It was great." Seth started moving toward the door.

"How have you lived with her and you didn't even know she could cook?"

"I have staff. She doesn't have to cook."

"Well, you don't have staff here. And you left her alone all day?" He wasn't in a huge hurry. She hadn't grabbed the keys to either of their cars and she wouldn't get too far in those heels she was wearing. God, the woman was wearing four-inch heeled, fuck-me boots out in the middle of the wilderness. She'd gotten all dressed up and she'd cooked dinner and made cookies. And they'd kind of been assholes. Total assholes. *Fuck.* Seth needed some goddamn training, too.

"I had stuff to do. I couldn't take her with me." Seth's face became a grim mask as he opened the door.

"And you wanted to figure out how to handle her before you shoved her out into Bliss," he surmised.

"She's lived in a big city her whole life and it shows," Seth said quietly as he walked out onto the deck.

He knew it. Damn Seth. "She'll be fine. She can talk shoes with Laura and art with Stef and Jen. Tell me something, were you going to let her talk at Trio? Or were you going to pick the booth in the back and hide her away?"

The idea pissed him off. If Georgia was his, he would show that fine woman off everywhere. He would even sic her on some of the other women when they got too aggressive. Rachel and Laura could flay a man alive at times, and he wouldn't even go into what his mommas could do. If Georgia was his, he would hide behind her designer skirts at every given opportunity. Conversely, he would beat the holy living shit out of any man who treated her poorly.

Like he and Seth just had.

Seth's brows came together in a frustrated *V*. "I thought I would give her some time to adjust. I wasn't ashamed of her, damn it. I have to go get her. Where the hell does she think she's going? And I told her the food was good."

Logan followed Seth across the back deck and caught sight of her stomping across the yard. She was actually making excellent time in those boots of hers. And she was going the wrong way. She was about to pass Nell and Henry's and make her way up to Hell on Wheels. He would die before he let her walk into that bar. But he had a couple of minutes to tell Seth a thing or two before they went after her.

"I want you to think about it for two seconds, Seth. God. This is how you work, you know. You make a person feel like they're the most important thing in the world and then something else comes up and you expect us to be sitting around waiting for you to come home. She's not a puppy. You can't lock her up for the day and expect her to wag her tail and be happy to see you. You have always fucking done this. She got prettied up. She cooked dinner. She made dessert. And we both treated her like it didn't mean shit. We both thought there was no way she could cook, and then we told her what she was good for."

Seth went pale. "Sex. Shit. We told her she was good for sex."

"Yeah. And you're surprised she's walking out."

Seth turned. "I have to stop her. I have to make her understand."

"Let me get her. If this thing has half a chance of working out, we need to set ground rules now." Seth had no idea what he was in for. Georgia wasn't going to listen to sweet reason. They'd blown past that point. Now that he was looking back on the last ten minutes, he could see how patient she'd actually been. They'd had a couple of chances to avoid Hurricane Georgia. Now they had to deal with the winds.

"No. I have to apologize." Seth took off after her.

Logan groaned. An apology wouldn't work at this point. Seth

should be ready for a full-on brat attack, with flying nails and screams. It was how Georgia dealt with this level of hurt. It actually didn't bug him all that much. He kind of understood it. Georgia had never had real boundaries. She'd had land mines, but no firm and loving boundaries. She'd had men she worshipped like her brothers, and every other damn man in the world had been a douchebag asshole who let her down, including her father, according to Ben. Georgia was a textbook case of needing a firm but loving hand. He was sure Seth could give her loving, but he wasn't so sure about the firm part.

He stopped at the edge of the deck, his boots hitting some encrusted dirt. Someone had been all over the deck the night before. Had he made that mess?

"Go to hell!" Georgia's voice carried over the sound of the river.

Logan looked out as Georgia rounded on Seth, taking him down with one swing of her ridiculously oversized handbag. What the fuck did she carry in that thing? She said something he couldn't hear but he would bet she was probably questioning Seth's parentage, and then turned right back around and started across Henry and Nell's yard.

Seth sat on his butt for a minute before getting up, obviously willing to give it another go. "Georgia, baby! Come on."

Oh, he was asking for trouble. When Georgia got wound up like that, she was begging for some boundaries. She was desperate for someone to stand in front of her and say "no." She wouldn't feel safe with some weak apology. He would bet she'd heard a million of those lame-ass, "I won't do it again, baby" apologies. What she hadn't heard was her Dom telling her to stand down and act like the intelligent woman she was.

Unfortunately, he wasn't her Dom. Seth was her Dom-in-training. *Damn it.*

He should let this play out. Georgia would likely leave, and then all of his problems would be gone. Well, all the ones he had tattooed on his chest.

Georgia turned, a look of unholy rage on that gorgeous face. Seth nearly tripped on his own feet.

Fuck. They needed him. Seth was being an idiot, and Georgia was too stubborn to let go of her anger. If he didn't get involved, she would walk away and Seth would lie around like a mopey-ass billionaire.

And he would never know what it felt like to sink into Georgia Dawson's body and lose himself there. He would never know what it felt like to share a woman who mattered with his best friend in the world. Seth was opening a door. He was letting Logan in without a real commitment beyond the training. The training could last as long as Logan said it did. And they would always need follow-up sessions. And play sessions. He could be fucking Georgia on a regular basis for the foreseeable future. They were young. Even if Seth married her, they probably wouldn't have kids for a while. As long as there weren't kids, he could come to their bed.

He would go back to Dallas because he wasn't good for anyone, but he wouldn't have to worry about Georgia. Seth could take care of her. At least financially. He'd done a shitastic job on the emotional stuff today.

"Georgia! You stop this right fucking now!" Seth shouted as she swung her purse around again. But he did a sissy thing where he ducked and tried not to let her hit him.

Logan growled. Yeah, he couldn't watch another minute of this. Georgia was hurting, and she would lash out at anyone she could because she didn't know how to handle it.

He was going to show her.

"You're trying to make me into a prostitute!" Georgia screamed.

Nice. She was going there. It was a good play. Especially since Logan realized they had an audience.

Henry and Nell were sitting in lawn chairs. Each had a glass of what Logan suspected was organic wine in their hands, and they were watching the action. Nell sat forward the minute she heard the word *prostitute*.

"I'm not going to pay you." Seth's voice held the kind of horror Logan had heard before in victims of terrible crimes. "God. What do you think of me? I mean, I'll pay your living expenses and you'll have a credit card you can always use and you won't have to work, but you're not a prostitute."

Yeah, that had been the right thing to say. God, Seth had gone to all the best schools, but they hadn't taught him a damn thing about not pissing off a chick.

Georgia sort of primal screamed and started swinging her bag in a hard arc.

Logan took two steps and managed to do what Seth hadn't. He caught the bag and pulled it away in one neat twist, leaving her without a weapon to beat them with. He tossed it away before she could protest. "Stand down, Georgia."

"You asshole. That's a Prada bag." She was in full-on crazy mode. "You want to make me a prostitute, too."

"Logan." Nell was standing up now, her mouth turned down. "Are you trying to turn this young woman into a prostitute? Because while I uphold a woman's right to do what she wants with her body, I have to protest it when a young woman is forced into human trafficking. Not just young women. Any women. And men. And animals, too. Don't think it doesn't happen. I've seen it on the Internet."

God, if he didn't get this under control, they would all get a lecture on the evils of human trafficking. Still. He couldn't resist. He'd grown so bitter and sarcastic in his old age. "I'm not planning on sending her around the world, Nell. And I'm not going to make her a prostitute. I'm going to teach her how to be my sub so she won't smack me upside the head with purses anymore."

"It's a handbag, asshole." Georgia turned to Nell, obviously sensing that Nell was the weak link. "He is totally trying to turn me into a prostitute. He wants to share me with his friend."

Nell smiled as though deeply relieved. "Oh, thank god. I was worried for a minute. Welcome to Bliss."

There were some advantages to living in America's freakiest town.

"You should put a collar on that one, Logan. She looks like the type to run away." Luckily Nell already had a Dom. Henry didn't move from his chair. "Although she wasn't going to get far in those heels. Still, you should get her a collar and a leash."

Fuck. He'd just realized that. Henry fucking Flanders was a goddamn Dom. Now that he'd been properly trained, he recognized all the subtle signs. Henry was a quiet top, but Logan would bet he was nasty in the bedroom.

Nell sent Henry a look that could freeze the balls off a gorilla on testosterone. "You can't put a woman on a leash. You would never do that to me."

Henry simply sat back, a smile curling up his lips. "Oh, you have your leash, my love. Why do you think I buy you new Birkenstocks every couple of years? No one can run in Birkenstocks. They keep you tethered to me."

"You're a son of a bitch!" Georgia didn't seem to care about the secondary conversation. She was going straight for the throat. "Did you think I would spread my legs? Did you think you could treat me like crap and I would still fuck you?"

She had a point there. He'd treated her like she didn't exist because it hurt to look at her when he couldn't touch her.

But he'd made a deal with Seth, and he could touch her now. She was in so much trouble. They all were. And honesty was the best policy.

"You're right. I was an asshole and I'm sorry. I would go home and have the very lovely dinner you cooked if you hadn't already tossed the whole damn thing in the trash. Now turn that sweet ass around and get back to the cabin so we can sit down and have an adult conversation about this because it's serious. It's not something we should be talking about on Nell and Henry's front yard."

Henry smiled. "Don't mind us. We don't have cable. This is the best entertainment I've had in a while."

Nell frowned his way. "Henry!"

Henry shrugged. "Tell me you're not taking notes, baby."

Logan tried to ignore them. "Come with me and we can do all this privately."

"Fuck you." She said all the right words, but she didn't move. In fact, she leaned toward him, every action her body made calling to his senses.

His blood was pumping, thrumming pleasantly through his veins. This was where he wanted to be. And she was damn straight the woman he wanted to be here with. He had to give her every option. He couldn't sit down and negotiate with her. Not yet. Not until Hurricane Georgia had passed. "I am giving you the rules right here and right now. You can walk back to our cabin and stand near my SUV and I'll take you into town and find you a way out of here."

"No," Seth practically yelled. "No. She's not leaving."

Seth could be so dramatic. Of course she wasn't leaving. She wasn't going anywhere because she *wanted* this fight. She wanted to be taken down. She was practically begging for it. If she gave him one single tell that she didn't want this, he would back off. All she had to do was say no, move away, turn her back, walk over to his SUV. But there was a glint in her eyes and worse, her nipples were rigid against that thin shirt she wore.

She didn't take a step back. Her lower lip came out, and she moved even closer to him. She utterly ignored Seth's outburst. "Fuck you, Logan. You can shove that SUV up your ass."

Heat sizzled through his system. Why did this one woman make him crazy? Why couldn't he find a nice, easy submissive and settle into a relationship where no one screamed at him or fought him like a scalded cat? He'd watched his moms and they never had moments like this. Their relationship was a placid lake of calm and a source of deep strength for both of them. What he and Georgia had was a flash fire that threatened to burn them both. He couldn't see it lasting forever. He couldn't live like that, but he also couldn't let her go.

And if he couldn't walk away, then it was time to take control. For all three of them.

"Georgia, are you sure?" He felt a certain peace come over him. Oh, his cock was hard as a rock, but he could see everything playing out now that he'd made the decision to take charge.

"I'm sure you've got a tiny dick hiding away in those khakis." Georgia wasn't calm. Georgia was completely out of control. That much was clear.

He gave her a slow smile, loving the way that gorgeous face kind of screwed up because she couldn't seem to figure out why he was smiling. He had her confused, and it was about to get worse. "Your way, baby. Not mine. I was going to do this easy, but I think you like it rough."

She opened her mouth, but before she could spit more bile at him, he lunged forward, sank his left shoulder right across her belly, folding her neatly in two for easy transportation.

"What the hell are you doing?" She screamed, and he felt her fists on his back. Maybe not so easy transportation, but it was quicker than dragging her caveman style. Though she'd be real cute that way. Especially if she was naked first. Yeah, they would have to try that later.

His cock approved of the image. Hell, his cock didn't even mind that his back was being forced to take one for the team. He kept her off kilter, holding her thighs tight to his chest. Damn, but he could actually smell her arousal. She was as turned on as he was. Why the hell had he waited? She wasn't some virginal priss who didn't know the score. He and Georgia could have some nasty, filthy, gorgeous sex and then he would turn her over to Seth, who could handle loving her. "Nell, Henry, I hope you have a pleasant evening. You'll excuse me, but I have a sub to discipline."

"If you lay one hand on me, you fucking meathead, I will call the cops on you," Georgia vowed.

"I am the cops, darlin'." He smacked her ass hard with his free hand.

She gasped, a breathy, sexy sound. And then she seemed to remember that she was the victim here and screamed. "You pathetic, craphole, idiotic fuckmeister!"

Logan smiled at Seth, who was staring at her with wide eyes. Yeah, he hadn't met Hurricane Georgia until now. "She has a way with words when she gets like this." He smacked her ass again, this time harder. "But she's going to learn to keep it sweet, aren't you, baby? You wanted the bull? You gotta take the horns, too. You are going to get a whole lot of horn tonight."

Logan winked at Henry and Nell as he walked off. The day had been a shitstorm of crap, but the evening was looking up.

Chapter Eight

Seth stared at Georgia, her blonde hair flying around as she yelled and tried to beat the shit out of his best friend's backside. He felt like he'd been through a fight. She was so sweet, and she'd always been kind to everyone around her. His staff adored her. Never once had she thrown stuff around or tried to take his head off with a handbag.

Death via Prada. It was almost how he'd gone down.

Logan was walking away with her. Logan hadn't been surprised at all. Logan had strode right in and tossed her over his shoulder and taken charge. Seth had stared down crabby investors and lawyers and bankers. He'd ruthlessly handled the sharks of Wall Street, and he'd been utterly at a loss with what to do with one blonde in high heels.

"Is that your girl?" Henry had moved up behind him, settling a hand on his shoulder.

Seth kept staring as his best friend and the love of his life moved away from him. "She's never acted like that before."

"What was she upset about? The idea of being shared?"

Seth shook his head. "No. I ignored her all day and then I hit her with the D/s stuff. I think I scared her. I was so sure she would be interested. Her brothers are all lifestylers."

"I don't think she's afraid. Logan gave her every out he could, and she waited until he scooped her up." Henry smiled as Georgia's curse-laced screams carried across the yard. "I think that's just the way those two are going to play. Did you see how relaxed Logan got? I've never seen that kid so confident and happy as he was when he tossed her over his shoulder. They have a connection."

"A connection?" Seth was worried Henry had gone soft in the head.

"Yeah. She'll come around. She wants this. She wants Logan to take charge. If he's half the Dom I think he might be, he'll have her purring by morning." Henry turned to him. "You should think about this. You seem disturbed. Perhaps this isn't the lifestyle for you. D/s can seem cruel to some people."

He wasn't exactly a tourist. "I've played before. I've done pretty much every sexually deviant thing a man can do."

Henry winced. "I don't know that I needed to hear that."

"I love her." He just wasn't sure he knew every side of her. There hadn't been anything deliberately cruel about Georgia's rant. Well, the needle-dick charges leveled against Logan had been uncalled for and untrue. "It caught me off guard."

Henry slapped his back in a gesture of manly affection. "All I'm saying is you should think about it because she obviously needs this. I don't know that Logan is ready for anything on a full-time basis. That girl needs a Dom. She needs one so badly that I wouldn't hesitate to find her one."

An unholy rage filled Seth, churning his gut and making him stand taller. "She doesn't need a goddamn thing. I swear we're going to have trouble if you try to match her up with someone you know. I will make sure he's not fucking breathing by the end of the night. Do you understand? She's fucking mine. Head case or not. She belongs to me."

His heart was pounding, blood beating through his system. The very thought of someone coming between him and Georgia made him goddamn insane. So, no, her hissy fit hadn't thrown him off her. He'd been a bit surprised, yes. Her anger had shocked him, but it wasn't truly anger, was it? It had been passion. Georgia was passionate. She gave a shit. Of course, she'd freaked out. He'd ignored her, and what woman worth her weight wouldn't get pissed? His mother would have rolled her eyes and moved on to the next lover, but his Georgia had let her position be known, and Logan was handling that shit. It was completely unrealistic to think a relationship wouldn't require work. A woman like Georgia deserved to have her man work for her.

Henry was smiling at him despite the fact that he was pretty sure he'd bared his teeth at his mentor like a damn mountain lion looking for a meal. "Excellent. You sound like a caveman. Go get your girl. Don't let Logan have all that sugar. Come by for dinner sometime this week and bring your Georgia. I'm sure Nell wants to talk to her about those boots."

He looked ahead. Logan was trying to open the door to the cabin, but Georgia was wiggling, her legs kicking and her hands reaching for…damn, it looked like she was trying to get at Logan's dick with those gorgeous claws, and not in a hot, sensual way, more like a rip-it-off way. He felt his palm twitch. She was asking for the flat of his hand on her ass.

Fuck all. He might actually be a Dom. It had always been play before, but with Georgia, all those instincts were coming out.

"You thinking about spanking her?" Henry asked with a grin. "Because she's begging for it."

He felt his lip curl up, his shoulders straightening. He'd played in clubs, but this was the first time he'd felt a righteous indignation with a sub. She wanted to question him? Oh, he had some answers for her. She wanted to shock the fuck out of him with a side of her nature she hadn't allowed him to see? Maybe it was time he showed her his inner shark. "Yeah, she is. We'll come over for dinner sometime this week. I can't promise you that Georgia will be able to sit down, though."

Seth stalked the distance between them, his anger growing with every step. He'd done nothing but treat her like a precious angel up until this afternoon. Yes, he'd been an asshole, but his prior good behavior should have bought him something more than a Prada bag to the head.

He jogged the distance between Nell and Henry's place and his own. Not just his. Theirs. His and Georgia's and Logan's, whether Logan wanted to admit it or not. His heart was pounding, adrenaline pumping as he walked through the door.

It was perfectly silent, and for a moment, he wondered if one of them was dead.

Georgia stood in the middle of the great room, with its magnificent floor-to-ceiling windows and views of both the river and the mountains. He didn't give a shit about any of it. All he could see was her, her blonde hair wild around her face as she stared at Logan. Logan was sitting on the couch, his body relaxed as though he hadn't carried a woman away.

Maybe he could still save this. They weren't screaming at each other. He could mediate. The Dom in him snarled at the thought, but he couldn't start yelling when she was looking so fragile. "Georgia, would you like to explain to me what all of that was about?"

"Seth, would you like to go fuck yourself?"

Logan laughed. "You're making it worse."

She tossed him a quick middle finger and then turned away from them both.

His inner Dom was howling to get out. She thought she could pull the rug out from under him? Yeah, he'd invented that play. And he was finally comfortable with the fact that Logan and Henry were right. She was in a corner and she didn't know how to get out. Oh, there was a wide hole she could go through, but it took her away from them. She wanted this, but she couldn't ask for it. "Every time you curse or make a rude gesture when we're trying to behave like adults, you'll take another ten."

It was time to get the rules out in the open.

She turned on him. Her face was red and tears pooled in her eyes, but she wasn't crying. "Do you know what my brother will do if you lay a hand on me?"

He practically growled. It occurred to him how happy he was that this was coming out. If she'd been hiding her psycho side, he'd been covering up his ruthless-bastard side. It was time to show her there was a little Hyde in his Jekyll. He moved into her space, daring her to back up. "Are you talking about Win, baby?"

She refused to move, but he could see the way her eyes widened. "Yes. He'll take you apart."

Logan snorted. "I'd like to see him try."

"He already did," Seth said with a deep sense of satisfaction.

Her eyes widened. "What do you mean?"

He loved how breathy that question sounded. "You didn't think they came to New York for a visit, did you? Oh, no. They came to bring you home. Win wanted to save you from the big bad wolf."

She shook her head. "Did he threaten you?"

"Fuck, man. How bad off is he now? What did you do?" Logan asked, proving how well he knew Seth.

Georgia looked over at Logan. "Don't joke. You don't know Win. He can be brutal."

"And you don't know Seth, honey," Logan shot back. "I've never met a man who could be more nasty and manipulative than my best friend."

"No, Seth is sweet. Win could hurt him," she insisted.

Sweet. He fucking hated that word. "Your brother backed off, Georgia."

Her mouth dropped open. "Win never backs off."

Seth stared down at her, not ever losing contact with those wide blue eyes. "He backed off damn fast when I explained, in neat and very clear details, how I intended to take over his company and leave him with nothing if he ever tried to come between me and you again. I explained to all your brothers how I would take each of them down individually. They know I will ruin their lives and raze everything they care about if they attempt to take you away from me."

"Ah, there's Seth." Logan had the faintest smile on his face. "I thought you had gone all soft on me, buddy. Georgia, he's always been this way, ever since he was a kid. Seth always had a plan, and he always got what he wanted."

She closed her eyes, taking a long breath. "You threatened my brother."

Fuck. "Yeah."

"You told him you would take DawComm away from him?" Every word that came out of her mouth was precise, as though she was trying to grasp the idea.

Damn it. He was in for a penny though. "Yes. I planned out a way that would cost me over a hundred million dollars, but I could do it. I also threatened to get Mark and Dare tossed off Delta Force, and I might have inferred that I would have Chase sniped."

Logan's laughter split the room. "You did your research, man."

"A hundred million dollars?" Georgia's eyes opened. Wary,

questioning. "You would spend a hundred million dollars to make sure I didn't go back to Malibu with my brother? You would threaten them and go to war with them? Over me?"

There was only one answer to the question. If she was offended, well, then he'd overplayed his hand. "Yeah. I would."

"That is the sexiest thing I ever heard." She went on her toes, and before he knew what was happening, she brushed her lips against his, a shy kiss. "I can't be your mistress. No matter how nice I think it is that you would fight for me, I can't be someone you sleep with and hide whenever anyone who matters comes around."

His whole soul softened. He caught her in his arms, dragging her to his body. Those heels of hers brought her to exactly the right height. "I am sorry you felt that way today. I'll take you out tomorrow and you can meet anyone you like. I'm proud of you. I'm also slightly scared of you now, but that's a good thing. I think we're finally being honest with each other."

She bit into that incredibly sexy bottom lip. "You don't only want me for sex?"

Time for flat-out honesty. It was the only thing that would work here and now. "I knew I would marry you about five minutes after you walked in my door. And how can you say I don't want to show you off to anyone who matters? Besides you, no one matters to me more than Logan. I don't have any family I care about. My granddad died and my mom and dad don't care about me. I have Logan and I have this town."

"I can't not matter," she said, but her head found his shoulder.

"You matter, baby." God, she'd come to mean everything to him.

"Okay. I'm sorry about the stomping out thing." She gave him the sweetest smile, and he felt his inner Dom start to fade.

"It's okay." He let his hands run down her torso to her hips, his cock hardening at the thought that he could have her. Soon. Very fucking soon. Like minutes from now.

"Are you serious?" Logan stood up and his hands were on his hips, a sure sign he was irritated. "She gets away with that? Man, if that's the relationship you want, then I should pack up and head out to the Movie Motel because I can't do it. You set a rule and you hold that line. Just because she turns those gorgeous eyes up and bats those lashes at you doesn't mean a thing."

She turned, glancing back at Logan, and there was no way to mistake the heat in her eyes as she stared at him. "What are you saying?"

"I'm saying, pull down those pants and get over my lap and take your punishment and then we'll talk about sex. Then we'll talk about setting you on the bar and forcing you to make up for the fact that you threw out our dinner. We'll have to eat your pussy until we're full."

Her whole face flushed, her skin turning pink and her breath hitching. "You want to spank me."

It wasn't a question. He had a hunch that Logan had probably mentioned the whole spanking thing before. It seemed to be a theme with him.

The thought of Georgia willingly pulling down her pants and placing that round, sweet ass over his best friend's lap to take some discipline made him worry that his cock was about to go off. "Yeah, he wants to spank your ass, baby. And he's not the only one who missed dinner. I want to eat your pussy, too. I want to make you scream and forget that we were jerks tonight. Tomorrow we can start all over again. And in a few days, we'll go to Logan's moms' anniversary party and you'll be on my arm and there won't be any question that you're my girl."

Georgia took a long breath. "But I have to let Logan spank me."

"No." He wasn't going to blackmail her. "If you're not interested in this lifestyle, then we can go straight to bed and I'll treat you like a lady. I want you any way I can have you."

"I'm crazy about you, Georgia, but I can't promise you what Seth can," Logan said, his voice firm. "I can promise that as long as you and Seth want me in your bed, I'll be there, but I can't play it vanilla. The funny thing is, if it was anyone but you, I probably could. I'm going to be here in Bliss for a couple of weeks before I head back to Dallas. I want to spend that time with you. It's selfish as shit. I was right when I let you go, but I can't do it again, and that fucker you're standing with knew it."

Georgia shook her head. "He didn't know we were connected."

"Of course he did. Like I said before, Seth always has a plan. He wants you and he wants to share you with me. He wants the family he never had." Logan stood there, a completely immovable object.

Seth felt broken. He almost didn't recognize his friend. Henry's words came back to him. He'd left Logan alone. He'd gotten lost in his own plans and empire building, and Logan had suffered without him. He'd been so busy thinking of the future that he'd ignored the present when he should have been helping his friend.

So he couldn't leave him hanging out there. "I knew. Kitten told me. I was going to take care of you because I knew how he felt about you, and then I met you and I knew you were the one. Yes, I plotted. Yes, I threatened the fuck out of your brothers. Yes, I brought you here because I think you still want him. And yes, I want you to pull those pants down and lay across Logan's lap."

He had to hope that getting close to Georgia would change Logan's mind.

She stood there for a moment, her whole body tense, and he was almost certain he'd lost her. Then her hands went to the fastener of her jeans. The fly was a big rhinestone to match all the bling she had on her ass.

She stopped and Seth's heart almost did, too. He waited for the words that would kill his plans, but she merely frowned and knelt down and unzipped her boots. She set them aside and stood back up, her hands trembling as she undid the button of her jeans.

Logan sat back down, and Seth felt his heart in his throat.

His life, the one he'd waited for all these years, was finally beginning.

* * * *

She was taking off her pants. She was taking off her pants so Logan could spank her butt.

If her friends could see her now.

Except she didn't have friends. She had actresses in LA she'd competed with and mean girls she'd tried to fit in with. Natalie and Kitten were the first friends she'd made since tenth grade when Lisa Jacobs had moved away because her dad got a job in Florida.

What was she doing? God, she wanted to get naked and lie down over Logan's lap and find out why her sister-in-law smiled so much.

And she was terrified to do it. She had totally lost her cool and freaked Seth out and then found out he was kind of a supervillain and that was so hot, but neither one of them had seen her naked. She wasn't wearing pretty lacy panties. She was wearing heavy spandex to make her look thinner than she was because she couldn't seem to lose that extra twenty pounds everyone seemed to think she needed to. Her undergarments claimed to take ten pounds off, so once she'd put on three sets just to see if the effect was cumulative, but that experiment had ended with her passing out at an audition and Win thinking she had an eating disorder.

And she hadn't looked that much thinner.

Could he spank her in Spanx? He probably couldn't do the pussy eating thing while she was in Spanx. Although it did have a convenient hole in the crotch. Maybe he could put his tongue through there and then he wouldn't have to see her belly.

"Georgia?" Logan had moved in front of her, those green eyes staring down. Without her shoes, she barely made it to the middle of his chest. He was so big and broad, and Seth was standing beside him. She felt safe with Seth. Even the fact that he was a manipulative freak made her feel safe. All five of her brothers hadn't managed to convince him to leave her. That meant something.

But what if they took one look at her body and ran? Or worse, continued on because they were being polite.

She couldn't do it. If they didn't like her, she wouldn't be able to live with it. It was better to maybe find a way to be friends with them. Sex wasn't worth it. She buttoned her pants back up before they saw the tan panel the spandex formed. Yeah, that was sexy. "I think I'll, uhm, go and see about cooking something else. Seth has plenty of food. I can come up with something. I'm actually a good cook."

Before she could move, Logan had caught her, his right hand cupping her chin and forcing her to look up. "What are you afraid of? Is it me?"

He terrified her, but not because of the spanking thing. She shook her head. "I don't think the sex would be worth our friendship."

The sexiest smile ticked his lips up. "We aren't friends. We never have been. We've fought and kissed and you've made me utterly insane, but I can't be your friend."

That thought made her heart ache. "And you don't want to be my boyfriend."

A cloud passed over those green eyes. "That's Seth's job. I want to be your Dom. I don't want to cause you heartache, girl. I don't, but I'm also starting to think I don't want to go through the rest of my life without knowing what it feels like to be inside you. I don't think we would work long term. I think we're too different, but this heat between us is like nothing I've felt before. I want you."

She felt the heat, too. She'd felt it the minute she'd laid eyes on him. But he was a Greek god and she was just a woman.

"You might not want me if you saw me, really saw me. I wear a lot of makeup and I spend a lot of time on my hair, and I dress so I look way thinner than I am. My breasts are in a minimizer bra. Do you know what that means? It means they're bigger than they look and they sag already." She sniffled, her usual brat-girl persona failing her for once. "And I'm not good at sex. I know I look like some fifties pinup girl when I'm made up, but trust me, I'm not the sexy siren type. I can't even get masturbation right, so I think I should spare us all the disappointment."

"Show me." Seth's jaw was set, his eyes slightly narrowed. "Take off your shirt and that bra and show us your breasts. Be brave, Georgia. You want this. You don't want some stinking half life where we're 'friends.' Whoever told you you weren't sexy was wrong."

"Show us." Logan's eyes dropped to the place where her neckline touched skin, his fingers drifting from her chin to her neck. "He's right. Be brave. If you get rejected, then at least you tried."

But she'd learned not to try so long ago. Taking that first step seemed like willfully dropping over a cliff, and yet what were her other choices? Did she think she could be "friends" with Seth? Logan would be gone, back in Dallas and nothing but a memory, but was she willing to leave Seth and go live like some nun at Win's mansion? Her brother would take care of her, but she would be a burden to him. Or she could stay here and fight and try to make a place for herself.

She slowly pulled at the bottom of her blouse, wincing all the way. The tight spandex she wore beneath her clothes covered her stomach all the way up to under her breasts.

"That's good, Georgia." Logan stared down at her. He reached out and touched the fabric that still covered her torso. "You don't need this."

At least he didn't look horrified. "It smooths me out."

Seth was suddenly behind her, his fingers at the back of her bra. "You don't need to be smooth, baby. Come on, let's get this off and give the Dom his due so we can get to the good part."

The back of her bra came apart with a twist of Seth's hand, and she had to catch the front before it slid off. "I think y'all should know that I've never gotten to the good part before. I might not be able to, but I want to try."

"What are you saying?" Seth's hands were sliding around her torso, slipping up toward her breasts. She could feel the heat of his breath on her neck, making her shiver.

"She's saying she's never come before. You're not a virgin, are you?" Logan asked, his fingers smoothing her hair back.

God, they were surrounding her, and she was finding it hard to get a full breath. Her girl parts were starting to sing. Every inch of skin they were touching felt like it lit up, and she was getting an achy, restless feeling between her legs. "No. I've slept with men before."

"Not if you haven't come, you haven't. You've slept with selfish boys," Seth said against her ear. His fingertips eased under the wire of her bra and her nipples perked right up.

"Seth is right." Logan forced her to look him in the eyes. "I won't stop until you're screaming. Do you understand? Half of my pleasure will come from feeling that pussy clench down and damn near strangle my dick because the orgasm I give you is going to make your toes curl. And then Seth is a competitive son of a bitch and he'll try to best me."

"I'll do it, too," Seth vowed.

"He'll need to make sure you come, too," Logan continued. "No matter how long it takes, you're going to come for us, and we're going to teach you to never settle for less than being worshipped by men who care about you."

Every word he said was like a drug invading her system and softening her up. Maybe this time it would work. Maybe this time she would feel like a woman and not a used-up thing at the end of the night. She let go of the bra and it fell to the floor. She heard Seth's sigh of pure pleasure as his hands cupped her breasts.

"That's better." Logan stepped back, his eyes taking her in. His khakis had been a perfect fit before, but now they looked way too small. His cock pressed at the front of his pants, tenting them and making her feel bad for her previous, totally uncalled-for comments.

"I'm sorry for calling your penis small. It's obviously not small. It seems to be pretty big." Maybe penis size would make the difference. The men she'd been with before were way smaller than the monster that seemed to have taken up residence in Logan's pants. God, even that stupid polyester uniform looked hot on him. She had a sudden vision of him doing a deep-cavity search on her.

Logan sat back, and the grin on his face made him look so young and alive. He always seemed closed off, older than his years, but that grin was pure joy, and for a second, she got a glimpse of the boy he'd been. She'd put that smile on his face. "Georgia, do you know what I thought about when you insulted my poor dick?"

Seth was making it hard for her to think at all. His hands were rubbing over the mounds of her breasts, his thumbs flicking at her nipples. "I suspect that was when you thought about spanking me."

"Oh, no, baby. I thought about spanking you about two seconds after I met you, and I haven't stopped thinking about it since. Every time you open that bratty mouth of yours, I think about the flat of my palm against your ass. I think about spanking you until you cry real pretty and beg me to take you. No, when you insulted my poor aching cock, all I could think about was how you would feel when that mouth was filled with my pencil dick and I forced you to take it to the back of your throat before I came right down it."

Her pussy pulsed at the thought. Wow. Where had that come from? Seth rubbed his cock on her backside, and she was reminded that he didn't resemble any slender writing implements, either. "I'm not so great with that. Blow jobs and stuff."

"I'll teach you," Seth whispered. "I'll explain, in wretched detail, how to suck my cock, and I'll learn how to please you. Sex isn't something that just happens. We need to learn each other. Like now, I know you like to have your sweet nipples pulled on. I know because I can smell how hot you're getting. God, Georgia, I can smell you through all those clothes."

"Seth, show me those breasts. Now this is how it's going to work. I'm the top. I'm the Dom. Seth tops you," Logan said, his voice deep and husky.

"I don't get to top anyone, do I?" She was pretty sure that was his plan. But she was also pretty sure she didn't care because what Seth was doing felt incredible. Sex had always been fast and messy, and now she had to wonder if she'd done it for all the wrong reasons. She'd slept with the first guy shortly after she'd graduated from high school because she was so crazy about him and she wanted him to love her back. She'd sacrificed her virginity to gain his love and caring.

But this felt like love and caring, and it sure as hell didn't feel like sacrifice.

"No. You are not a top," Logan said. "Seth, move your hands. Let me see her nipples." She felt Seth's hands move down, and he cupped her breasts as though offering them up to his friend. Logan was staring at her breasts and he wasn't running the other way. He shifted as though he had to move to get comfortable again. "Yeah, that's what I want. Fuck, you're beautiful, G. Goddamn gorgeous. And that thing around your body offends me. Take it off of her."

He looked like a king sitting on his throne, waiting for his chosen lover to be perfectly presented to him. It totally turned her on. Seth's hands moved down her body. She felt him kiss her hair and the nape of her neck as he began to drag the spandex off her. His thumbs hooked on her jeans and he pulled them down as well, inch by careful inch, as though she was a present and he was afraid to damage any piece of her. All the while Logan watched. He was perfectly still, except for his cock. It twitched slightly in his pants as it lengthened and stretched.

Seth took his time, lowering her pants down with the same patience he used when working on a line of code. Precise and patient, and so, so perfect. Sex before had been harried and quick, but this aching slowness was opening up something deep inside her, a wanting she'd never felt before. Something was building inside her, a heat she couldn't deny. It was a dangerous slope she was heading down, but she couldn't pull back. She had to see where it went.

"Stop right there. That's perfect." Logan stopped Seth when he'd gotten her remaining clothes around the middle of her thighs.

The jeans were tight, but the spandex was tighter, holding her thighs together. "I can't move."

Seth's hands ran over the flesh of her ass. Oh, god, she hated her butt. He didn't seem to have the same issues with it. His palms cupped her and smoothed over her skin. She felt him get to his knees, his lips brushing the small of her back. She'd never been kissed there. It wasn't a sexy part of her body so previous boyfriends had ignored it the way they'd ignored the back of her neck and her shoulders. It had been all boobs and vajayjay and the occasional sloppy French kiss. She'd had one lover awkwardly kiss her pussy, but he'd seemed so uncomfortable that she'd told him she didn't like it.

She was beginning to get the impression that Logan and Seth weren't going to be awkward about anything.

"Oh," Logan began with a leering sympathy. "Is my poor girl trapped? Can you not fight me anymore? I might have to take back what I said about that thing you're wearing. It might qualify as fet wear since it's binding you as tightly as any rope I could put you in. I will be tying you up later, Georgia. I'll wrap my rope around your body like a dress that puts all the best parts on display. Those luscious tits. That pussy. I can see it gleaming from here. How is her ass, Seth? It looked incredible in a pair of jeans, but now I find out she's been hiding it, trying to bind it down. It's better than I thought, isn't it?"

"Damn straight." Seth's lips moved across her cheeks, his hands holding her still.

She was caught. She couldn't run or kick. She had to take what Logan gave her. She was naked in front of him. So vulnerable, and yet she stood there waiting for him.

"Bring her to me."

Seth got to his feet and hauled her into his arms before she could take another breath. He hooked his arm under her knees and picked her up like she weighed next to nothing. She let her arms float up around his neck.

Seth's handsome face was flushed, his voice soft as he spoke to her. "It's going to be okay."

For the first time, she almost, sort of, kind of believed him.

"Pick a safe word." Logan moved forward, making a place for

her on his lap.

"A safe word is…" Seth began.

She didn't need an explanation. She'd picked out a safe word when she'd started dreaming about Logan Green. "Rosebush."

She'd pretended to throw Logan's phone in a rosebush all those months ago. She hadn't really done it. She'd pocketed the phone and that prank had saved her life because Chase had been able to find them thanks to Logan's mom tracking his phone.

"I never spanked you for that." But he was smiling again.

"Rosebush?" Seth asked as he set her on her feet in front of Logan.

"It's an inside joke. I'll tell you the whole story later, but for now, I need to get her punishment out of the way. Just a spanking tonight, but I'll want a contract between the three of us."

That sounded so formal, and she was about to argue with him when she saw him start to shut down, like he knew what was going to happen. He needed the contract. He needed her to sign something to believe she would take it seriously. "All right, Logan."

"Sir." He relaxed again. "When we're playing you call me Sir. What you call Seth is up to him, but at the end of our training period, he should have the right for you to call him Master."

But Logan would never be her Master. Not in life. Not in play. He was letting her know that their connection would only go so far. But she couldn't go back. She would regret Logan Green one day, but maybe that was better than never having had him. She wanted to see if this lifestyle was for her, and she couldn't imagine going on that journey without Logan. And if she wanted to be with him, even for a little while, she had to think beyond her needs. If Logan needed a contract, she could sign a contract. If he needed to be called "Sir," she could do that, too.

"All right, Sir." She turned her eyes to meet Seth's and was shocked at how vulnerable he looked. Like he was afraid of getting pushed to the side. She couldn't walk to him because she was trapped in her pants, but she could reach out to him. Somehow it was easier to let go of her anger when she'd realized they wanted to be here. They wanted her. "What do I call you, boss?"

He shook his head. "Don't call me boss. Not ever again."

He was not thinking long term. "So we can't play out my 'billionaire throws down with his secretary' fantasies? Because I thought it would be fun if you could chase me around my desk on occasion."

There was his sexy smile. "Okay, you can call me boss then, but I'd like to hear my name now. So settle yourself across Sir's lap or he's going to get mad, and I want to get to the part where I put my tongue on your pussy."

She wanted to get there, too. And so did all her pink parts. They were cheering deep inside as she started to awkwardly move to Logan's lap. Seth was right there, helping her down.

Oh, god, she was on Logan's lap. She could feel his cock against her side, the hard lines of his thighs against her belly. She wiggled, felt how helpless she was, but it was all right because she trusted them. She was safe with Logan. He might rip her heart out in the end, but she trusted him with her body. She could still feel his arms around her as he carried her away from that dingy club where she'd nearly died.

"Are you thinking about it?" Logan asked, his voice deep and soothing. He hadn't smacked her yet, merely allowed his hands to explore her skin. His fingers traced the line of her spine.

"Yeah." Honesty. Nat had explained that honesty was everything in this type of relationship, and that was way scarier than any spanking.

"Are you scared?" Seth asked.

Seth knew what had happened that day when she and Nat had been taken and she'd been shot. The funny thing was, she rarely thought about the fear she'd felt. Somehow she'd known she would live. What she thought about constantly was how it had felt to have Logan rush in and scoop her up and, for a moment, she'd felt loved and protected and precious.

"No. I'm thinking that he promised me a spanking that day, and he never gave it to me."

A sharp flare of pain flashed across her skin, making her scream and forget to breathe. The sound came after, a loud crack that split the room. Her head reeled as she tried to process the sensation. That sound was Logan's hand hitting her naked ass.

"Do you have any idea how scared I was that day?" Logan's voice had lost its smoothness.

Tears burned her eyes as he slapped her butt again, three times without a break.

"You almost died. You got fucking shot. That motherfucker shot you."

Another couple of smacks jarred her. She wasn't sure how many. Pain made her grab Logan's ankles, squeezing tight. Holy fuck that hurt. And he kept it up, like it had been building in his system from that day, waiting to boil over. Tears dripped from her eyes, and she realized she hadn't cried. Not once that day. She'd held it in and sucked it down and she'd been so afraid. So damn afraid.

She'd been lying to herself.

"And all because you had to prove you were smarter than me." *Smack. Smack. Smack.*

"I wasn't trying to prove I was smarter." The words were said on a desperate huff. She could barely breathe through the tears. Somehow she couldn't hide the truth from him, couldn't lie when she was so exposed, when the tears were finally flowing. "I was trying to get you to pay attention to me."

He smacked her again. "You have my attention, Georgia. You've had my damn attention from the beginning. How do you like my attention?"

Another volley of smacks and she thought about screaming out that safe word because she couldn't handle another minute of it.

"Logan, stop. She can't take this." Seth's sharp command broke through the pain.

"Back off." She was damn surprised those words hadn't come out of Logan's mouth but hers. She stretched to look up at Seth. "You wanted me to work things out with him. This is it. Back off. You don't get it both ways. If he's in our bed, I have a relationship with him. It won't last forever, but while he's here, he's mine and I won't let you come between us any more than I would let him dictate my time with you."

Holy shit. She'd sounded halfway adult, competent. And all because no one was going to tell her what she could or couldn't take. If she let Seth, he would run her life as surely as any of her brothers would. He would be worse than Win ever thought about being because he could sweet-talk her and get her in bed, and before she knew it, she would be a trophy for his wall and she couldn't be that. Never. Her mother had been that, and she was never going to follow in those footsteps.

Smack. Smack. Smack.

"I want a promise out of you." Logan growled as his hand covered her aching ass. So much heat and yet now she had an oddly comfortable floating feeling. Like she'd survived something, come out the other side and was better for it.

"What?"

"You don't ever pull that shit again."

She sagged against him. "It turned out for the best."

"It did not turn out for the best. You nearly died or you would have been sold and then you would have died because you are so obnoxious that your new owner would have killed you straightaway."

"What?" Seth nearly yelled the question. "Kitten told me she got involved in Natalie's kidnapping but she was fine. The shooting was an accident."

"Oh, it was no accident," Logan replied. "Georgia ran her mouth. And she was only there because she distracted me so I couldn't protect her."

"I think I should get to spank her, too," Seth said.

She had to laugh. Her blood thrummed through her system, adrenaline giving her a high. Logan's hands moving all across her tender flesh were making her soft and submissive. Yeah, she definitely felt submissive. And honest. "If I hadn't distracted him, he would be dead and so would Kitten."

"I'm damn hard to kill," Logan shot back. "And I don't think further spanking is going to help. She's already a nice deep pink. She'll have trouble sitting tomorrow. Now, let's see if the spanking had the intended effect."

If he meant would she ever throw his phone again, well, no. She would probably avoid it in the future.

She felt someone, likely Seth, pull at her pants and suddenly her legs were free and she could feel cool air all over her body. She was naked. Naked and pinned to Logan's lap. One hand held her there while the other delved between her legs.

She wiggled as his fingers split her labia and started searching deep. She moved, trying to adjust to the feeling.

Those fingers came out almost immediately and another *smack* cracked through the air. The pain flared, so horrible and then so hot it made her moan. Somehow the pain morphed into arousal and a sensual high.

"Don't move. This is my time. You're over my lap, accepting my discipline, and you will be still." Logan's voice washed over her like warm water. His hands moved back to her pussy, fingers playing along her sensitive flesh.

She wanted those fingers. More. They were too small. She needed something more than those fingers. For the first time in her life, she was starting to understand what it meant to ache for something, and not in an emotional fashion. She totally understood that, but this physical ache was different. The physical ache made her feel alive, different than she'd been before.

She forced herself to be still as Logan's fingers started to penetrate her.

"She's wet." She could hear the wealth of satisfaction in Logan's voice. "So fucking wet. That's what I wanted."

She'd never been so wet. Logan's fingers slipped easily around her pussy, but he had to push to get inside.

"How tight is she?" Seth asked.

She felt herself flush and wanted to say something about embarrassment, but she suddenly realized there wasn't a place for that here. They had agreed to this. She'd agreed, not merely to the sex, but to the play, and that was something these men took seriously. They weren't going to laugh at her or treat her like a disposable toy to be used and thrown away.

They could call it play, but this was serious.

"She's so tight. I can barely get a finger in there." Logan pushed against her, his finger finally sliding deep. It took everything she had not to move against it. She could feel a delicious pressure building.

"I think she's been a good girl, Logan. Can we put her out of her misery now?" Seth asked, his voice tight.

Logan's finger fucked in and out of her in a slow motion. "Don't you mean you want me to put you out of yours?" He laughed at something she couldn't see. She would have bet a lot that Seth had given Logan his happy middle finger. "All right. She took it far better than I could have dreamed. Get the bar ready."

"Not the bar. Follow me and bring her with you. I think you'll like this."

She found herself being turned, her sore backside hitting Logan's legs. She winced as she was moved into his arms and he stood, not a single sign of strain on his face. No. That gorgeous face of his smiled down at her. "You'll wince like that for days, and every time you do, my cock will jump and I'll have the satisfaction of knowing you took that burn for me."

She cuddled against his chest, knowing there was no way he would drop her. She'd never been carried around in her whole life, and now she'd had it twice in one day. It was well worth the sore bottom. "Did you really want me back in Dallas?"

He started to move toward Seth's section of the house. She'd been in another wing the night before and Logan had stayed in the guest bedroom. "Yes. Why do you think your snitty attitude just about killed me? Why did you act that way? You don't act that way around Seth. He wouldn't be crazy about you if you were always on the phone or doing your nails or looking down that little nose of yours at him."

How to explain? "I wasn't looking for something with Seth. Not at first. I was still thinking about you. And I guess I wanted you to think I was a big deal or something. I pretended to talk to my agent about all the parts I was up for. Logan, I don't have an agent. She dropped me because I couldn't lose weight. She said I wasn't fat enough for the fat roles and that I was way too fat for the real roles."

His face hardened. "I'd like to meet that agent of yours."

She couldn't blame her. Her agent had been right. She was twenty pounds too big for any leading role, and she wasn't that great an actress anyway. She'd hated the business world with a passion despite the fact that she'd gotten through college with a high GPA. She'd only done it to please her father. Who had cut her off anyway. "Besides I needed the job with Seth. I found out how much I liked him later on. Do you think he thinks I'm a crazy freak now since he's seen me in meltdown?"

She'd kind of hoped Seth never had to see her that way, but now she could see how careful they'd been around each other. It was the opposite of the way she and Logan had been. There had to be some sweet medium.

Logan walked through the French doors and nodded Seth's way. "I don't think you put him off, baby. Unless you're talking about his clothes. You definitely put him off his clothes."

Seth was naked. Gorgeously, stunningly naked. And she'd been right. His penis looked more like a club than a pencil. A big, long, thick club that was supposed to go into her apparently tight vagina.

"What do you think?" Seth put his palm on the marble half wall that separated the sitting area from what looked like the biggest bed ever. It wasn't any kind of a standard size. It had to have been custom made. Seth was always an optimist.

"Did you actually measure?" Logan had a grin on his face as he moved toward that wide, smooth wall.

"Damn straight. Though you've got two inches on me so you might have to lean over. But I promise it's going to be perfect for me. Up you go, baby."

Logan placed her right on the smooth marbled top. She squealed at the cold, but then it settled against her flesh and took away the sting of the spanking. It was as wide as a bench, and she felt like she was suspended in midair.

"Spread your legs. Put your heels right at the edge and bring your pussy toward me," Seth commanded.

Logan had moved to the side of the wall that now seemed more like a sex apparatus than an architectural piece. And she could see plainly what they were talking about when they discussed the proper height. She was in exactly the right place for Seth's mouth.

"Damn. Do you know how long I've waited to get my hands on these?" Logan's breath huffed as he palmed her breasts. Even as high up as she was, he loomed over her, her larger-than-life, Western lawman.

"And I've been dying for a taste of you, Georgia. I need you to know I haven't touched another woman since the day I met you. I had a date that night, and I canceled and told her I couldn't see her again, and I've been a very good boy since then. I want you to know that even though I've kept my hands off you, I've been yours since that moment." Seth's hands pulled at her ankles. "And god, baby, it was worth it. You're so fucking beautiful."

He was staring at her pussy, but she wasn't thinking about anything but the words he'd said. No one. She even remembered the day she'd met him. He'd taken her out to dinner, saying they needed to talk more so she could have a handle on the job he wanted her to do. Just before, he'd stepped away and made a phone call. He'd broken it off with his date to be with her, and he hadn't had a woman since.

"I haven't slept with anyone either." He should know that. Of course, at the time, she couldn't because her mind had been playing the Logan channel twenty-four seven, but after a few weeks, the only one who could compete was Seth.

A fierce look came over his face. It was the look she associated with him making a very shrewd business deal. "Of course, you didn't. I made sure of it. I deflected the men who were interested in you and the one who wouldn't go away, I fired."

"Seth Stark!" She opened her mouth to start a tirade against his now seemingly constant manipulation, but he leaned over and swiped his tongue against her pussy and she lost all coherent thought.

Pure pleasure licked along her flesh.

"Thank god. I've been wondering how to shut that mouth of hers forever. Now I know. When I want to shut you up, I'm going to shove my tongue up your pussy and take your breath away. But since Seth is already taking care of that job, I'll have to improvise." Logan leaned over and sucked her nipple into his mouth.

Heat sparked through her. Heat and pure sensual ecstasy. Between Seth's tongue sliding through her and the sultry suction of Logan's mouth, she couldn't think past the next feeling, the next sensation.

Seth speared her, his tongue foraging high inside while his fingers started to move, parting the folds of her labia and finding the nub of her clit. His thumb ran over it, and a spark flared through her.

"Oh my god." It felt so good. Past fantastic. Past real. Her whole body was a live wire, threatening to spark in the most remarkable way. Any minute. Any second. One more touch. One more lick. One more suck.

She was on the edge, caught in the most amazing place she'd ever been. She was completely alive. She was in the moment. This was all that mattered. This moment and these men. The past didn't matter. She couldn't think about the future. There was only a glorious present where she didn't have to worry about anything but giving them what they demanded from her.

"Come, Georgia. Let go. This is what sex is about, baby." Logan groaned against her skin. "Sex is about your men making sure you scream for them because they can't think of anything better in life. Give it to us."

Seth sent his tongue high into her while his thumb pressed down on her clit, and she dropped right over the edge.

Electricity seemed to flow through her body, flaring and sparking, making her cry out and press her pussy against Seth's mouth. It was deeply unladylike, and she didn't give a shit. She was flying. She was free in that moment. Her body was light and floating and her blood thrummed happily through her system.

Seth's head came up, his tongue running along his lips. "God, you taste good. You're so sweet, Georgia. I could eat you every day."

She let her head fall back, her body lush and satisfied.

This was why Nat smiled every morning. This was why women giggled and joked about sex. Because sex was a drug and now she was addicted.

"Don't you go to sleep." Seth kissed her pussy one last time. "You have men to please."

She felt herself being picked up again. Such a good life. She didn't even have to walk.

She cuddled against Logan's chest and got ready to please her men.

Chapter Nine

Logan couldn't believe she was in his arms. How fucking long had he waited for her? How many times had he woken up, his cock in hand, because he'd been dreaming about Georgia Dawson? All he'd had for the last eight months were cold showers and his goddamn fist, and now she was here, warm and sexy and so damn fuckable.

And she was more than he'd thought. When she'd told Seth not to come between them, he'd realized for the first time that she could handle this relationship.

He was the one who couldn't. And he couldn't walk away either.

He laid her down on the god-awful, amazing fucking bed Seth had obviously ordered to custom specifications. Logan had always slept with his damn feet hanging off the bed, but this monstrosity had been built for three and long enough to handle him. *Bastard.* Seth was baiting a trap guaranteed to lure Logan in, but he couldn't stay caught. He had a life in Dallas.

Didn't he? His head was reeling, but he didn't even want to think about those kinds of decisions right now.

He had Georgia and, for the moment, he could keep her. He had weeks with her. Weeks to lose himself in her.

He settled her against the fluffy comforter, her curvy body calling to him. She looked sweet and soft and cuddly. He couldn't tell her how much he loved the whole of her, the crazy-ass bitch who yelled at him, the trickster who tossed his phone, the woman who'd been friends with an easily misunderstood Kitten, the badass who told Seth to stay out of her relationship with him. She was such a mystery to him, a complete puzzle that he could spend the rest of his life working out.

But he wasn't going to spend his life working out all the layers and plumbing the depths of Georgia Dawson. He was going to go back to The Club where he would eventually get to the point where he could fuck the subs he trained, and it wouldn't mean a damn thing.

Great freaking life.

"Logan?" She stared up at him, her crystal blue eyes narrow with worry. She started to reach for the covers, to hide all that beauty from him.

"Don't you dare cover up. I can't spank you again tonight, but I can tie you up and make you feel the burn. I can keep you on the edge all night." He turned back to Seth. "Are you ready?"

Seth stood back. Strange how he was actually comfortable with Seth being all skin out, but then he'd had his first sex with Seth on the other side of the woman they'd chosen. He and Seth had torn through Creede and Del Norte that one summer they'd had before Seth had decided to take over the Western world and had forgotten to come home.

God, he had to get over that. He wasn't twelve and waiting on his best friend, counting down the days until summer.

"Take her." Seth tossed his body down on the bed and rolled close to Georgia. "You want him, right?"

What? Logan went on full alert. No. He couldn't take her first. He wouldn't stay with her. Seth was going to stay with her.

Fucking take her. She's yours. She was always yours.

He shook his head. "No. She's your girlfriend."

"I want to watch you with her. You've known her longer. You've wanted her forever. Do you know the heat the two of you put off?" Seth wasn't ignoring Georgia. The whole time he was talking, his hands were on her body. He leaned over and kissed her, his mouth coupling with hers. Logan couldn't help the way his cock twitched at the site of their tongues tangling. Seth was sharing the taste of that pussy with her. After a long kiss, Seth rolled away, lying on his side and looking up at Logan. "Go on."

He wasn't stupid. He knew damn well what Seth was doing. He was offering Georgia up like a gorgeous sacrifice. And she was. He thought she was hot in a pair of jeans and a tight shirt. Holy hell. Naked, she was his every wet dream. Big, soft breasts, hips that curved for days, a plump, wet pussy, and all that honey-blonde hair.

She reached up, a siren calling to him. "Logan, please."

Fuck Seth. Fuck everything. He couldn't leave her like that. It was wrong, but he couldn't let her think for a second that he didn't want her with every cell of his being. She'd been rejected before. That was why she had all that armor around her. He wasn't going to be one more idiot man who couldn't appreciate all that she had to offer. If Seth hadn't been there, he might have had the strength to walk away. But Seth had always been smarter. He would stay and take care of Georgia. He would have a lifetime with her.

Logan only had the now. He'd learned that two years ago on Nate's desk when he'd discovered his true self.

He shoved the memories aside with a vicious will. Georgia was all that mattered in this moment. Getting inside her, feeling her all around him. Seth wanted to give up being the first? Who the hell was he to turn that down?

He nearly tore his shirt trying to get it off. Thank god he had a tank under it or she would have seen the tat and he would have some explaining to do. He didn't bother with his slacks. He simply undid his belt and shoved them down. "Where are the condoms? You have to have condoms."

If Seth didn't have condoms, Logan's heart might explode. He didn't wait for a response, simply pulled at her ankles, dragging her down the bed. Seth had gotten a taste of that pussy. He wanted one, too. He'd been craving her for months. Her pussy was gorgeous. Perfectly shaved and groomed like the rest of Georgia, but now it was sopping wet from her orgasm. Her first real orgasm.

He touched those plump folds, petting them. "You poor girl. No one's taken real care of you, have they? I will."

"Are you talking to me or my girl parts?" Georgia was staring down her body, watching him.

He intended to give her a show. "I'm having a conversation with your pussy, baby. I think I'll just talk to it from now on. It doesn't spit bile at me." He drew his tongue from the entrance to her pussy to right below her clit. "Seth was right. You taste so good."

His cock was dying, but he needed to memorize that pussy. He had weeks with her, but he was desperate to know her now, to commit her smell and taste and feel to heart so he could pull the memories out in later years and remember what it felt like to be truly passionate about a woman.

He licked and sucked, drawing both sides of her labia into his mouth, giving them equal attention and affection. The flesh was perfectly pink and softer than any silk. And she was so hot and sweet under his tongue. She wriggled, but he allowed it. Later, he would tie her down so she couldn't move an inch, so she was forced to take what he gave her for however long he wanted it to go on. It would be all his way in those moments. She would be his submissive, her goal to obey him so he could give her pleasure like she'd never known.

He sank his tongue deep as his mind was swamped with images of Georgia. In bondage, her nipples in clamps he'd placed there, his collar around her neck. He could dominate her in play, but she needed a top in other parts of her life, too. She needed confidence, and a good top could give that to her. A Dom could teach her to value herself.

Seth. Seth would have to do all those things because Logan wasn't that kind of Dom. He was the kind of Dom who fucked a sub and sent her on her way. He couldn't help anyone with their problems when he was such a fucking mess himself. He was good for a lay, but nothing more. Not for anyone. But he could try with Georgia.

"You taste better than anything, baby." He fucked his tongue straight up inside her, softening the way for his dick. He was so hard, and her little pussy was tight as a damn drum. He took his mouth off her but allowed his thumb to make long, slow circles around her clit, not enough to send her over the edge again, but the perfect pressure to keep her there. "How long, Georgia?"

Her lips were trembling as she looked down at him. Her blonde hair was tousled around her shoulders, the tendrils touching her nipples and making her look so sexy he had to take a breath. "So long."

That wasn't an answer. He used his thumb and forefinger to flick at her clit. His cock jumped at the desperate whine that came out of her. "Try again. Be specific."

Her breath hitched again. "At least a year, year and a half. I kind of gave up on trying. And I didn't get asked out all that much. Not by nice guys. And then apparently Seth has been scaring the nice guys off since I got to New York."

"Damn straight I did." Seth hopped back on the bed after tossing a string of condoms Logan's way. His hands were on her breasts in an instant, his mouth lowering down to her nipple. "You don't need a nice guy, baby. You need a me. And a him."

God knew he needed her. And eighteen months was way too long for that body to go without being loved and worshipped and adored. He got to his knees, kicking off his pants and ripping open a condom wrapper.

He didn't want anything between them. He'd never had sex without a condom, but it played through his head that if he took her, she wouldn't fight him. She was too far gone. She wasn't thinking about anything but the next orgasm, the next sweet high he could give her. She would accept him into her body, and if nature took its course, then that was the way it went and he wouldn't be able to leave her. He wouldn't have to be noble. She would be stuck with him.

And so would that kid, and that was why he rolled the condom over his cock. If he wasn't good for Georgia, he couldn't possibly be good for a kid. Knowing what he knew about himself, he couldn't be someone's dad. How could he explain to a kid what kind of man his dad was? No. That was for Seth. Seth would be the dad. Seth would be the one to marry her.

But Logan could have her now. He could try to make sure that he held some tiny place in her heart, even if he was nothing more than a fond memory of pleasure she'd had.

"Are you sure?" He had his cock in his hand, stroking himself as he asked the question.

"Please, Sir."

He couldn't resist the "Sir," but then he would never have been able to resist her. This had been inevitable from the moment he'd stumbled on her last night, maybe from the moment he'd met her.

Georgia Dawson was it for him.

He moved between her legs, settling himself in, lining his cock up. Later, he wanted to feel her mouth on him, try all sorts of nasty positions, but tonight all that mattered was being inside her.

"Take off your shirt." Georgia reached for his tank.

This was one of those times when it was good to be the Dom. "I'm in charge. And there's no time."

He pushed in and her eyes widened as she clutched at his biceps. She wasn't thinking about what was under his shirt anymore.

Seth moved in behind her, her back to his front. It brought her closer, nestling their chests together, and Logan realized he wanted to be skin to skin with her, but he wasn't ready for her to see the tat. He settled for kissing her.

Her lips were soft, like spun sugar, fluffy and sweet on his mouth. She melted underneath him, opening for him and inviting him in. He slid his tongue inside even as he started to ease his cock deeper.

Heat and a thrilling tightness squeezed his dick. He had to take her inch by inch, gently working his way in. Gain an inch, ease back out. Thrust a little harder. All the while, he had to take charge of his brain because he wanted to mindlessly fuck her, to thrust in and not stop until she was coated in him, completely branded as his.

But he had to make this good for her. He had to be slow and steady.

"I feel so full." Her head rolled against Seth's chest, but her ankles hooked around Logan's waist. "More. I want more."

She surprised him at every turn. "You want more? I got more for you."

He took another inch with a quick thrust. And then Georgia's hips shifted and drew him in further, finally taking him to the root. He was surrounded by her heat, his skin flashing with fire. She felt so good, so fucking right. He twisted his pelvis against her clit in a long, slow grind. Her chest hitched, her eyes dilating with pleasure. Her nails bit into his flesh, but he liked that bite of pain. He liked the fact that she was leaving a mark on him. He would feel it all day tomorrow and remember how she tightened up when she came all over his cock.

He forced his dick up, trying to find her sweet spot. Over and over, he thrust in and pulled out and ground down. Georgia's hips moved with his, her body finding a rhythm. He'd expected that sex with her would be a fight, that he would have to force pleasure on her, but again, she threw him for a loop. She worked with him, his name on those luscious lips, her eyes watching him. There was no fight in those baby blues. There was affection and a sweetness that pierced through him. She was his because she gave herself to him, not because he could take her. What she offered him wasn't something that could be forced or stolen. It was a gift.

"Oh, baby. I…I'll take care of you." While he was with her, he would make sure she wanted for nothing. And when he was gone, he would watch over her from afar.

"I'll take care of you, too." She wrapped her arms around him but moved her face up to look at Seth. "And you, Seth. I can take care of you."

Seth pressed his lips to hers. "You take such good care of me. Now take care of our girl, Logan."

In other words, move it along, man. He wanted his turn. He couldn't help but smile because it would be dirty anywhere but here. Sharing a woman with his friend like she was a toy was nasty, except when they cared so damn much for her that they were willing to work for her pleasure, her happiness. He could be a part of that for now.

She was ready. Her pussy was still tight but welcoming now. He had to fight his way in, and he groaned at the way she tried to keep him, but she wasn't feeling any pain. It was evident in the way she shoved her hips up and rolled them, keeping in time to his slow grind.

Over and over he fucked up inside, pressing down and pulling out and making them both insane. He loved how hard she clenched around him, her pussy, her legs, her nails. He forced his dick up, fucking as high as he could into that hot, amazing pussy. His spine was tingling, orgasm on the edge of his consciousness, and then her pussy clamped down, nearly strangling his dick. Her pussy muscles milked him. She screamed out his name as she went over the edge, dragging him off that cliff with her.

His body stiffened, his balls drawing up, and he looked down at her, his eyes helplessly watching her as he came. Her face was so soft, so happy. He'd given her that peace, that joy, and it informed his own. He spurted his semen into the condom, but his brain was envisioning something different. He was pouring all that life into her, his hopes and their future spilling into her womb.

He let his body go, falling across hers, her breasts a perfect pillow. Her arms wrapped around him, no hesitation there. She wrapped herself around him and pressed her lips to his cheek. So sweet. So goddamn innocent. He'd just had her, and all he could think about was how innocent she was. How she needed a man to protect her, even from herself. His every dominant instinct was engaged with this one woman. She made him want to be a better man, to be more than he was without her.

Logan laid his head on her breast, reveling in the way she smoothed back his hair and held him close.

"That was beautiful." Seth kissed her temple. "How do you feel, baby?"

"Utterly content." She had one hand on Logan and one on Seth.

Just for a minute, Logan let go of everything and let himself be in the moment. He settled down on Georgia's breast and rested, peace flowing over him.

Everything was perfect. If only he could stay here, in this one moment, his world would be perfect, too.

* * * *

Seth rolled over and ran a hand over Georgia's waist, hauling her back against him. Early morning light streamed in through the roman shades he'd had installed in this room. It was enough to illuminate how freaking gorgeous his woman was.

And to remind him that they were alone in the huge bed he'd had built for three.

She stirred beside him, her backside coming into hard contact with his cock. Damn. How many times would he have to take her before he could be calm when she was naked and cuddled against him? The night before had been perfection. Even watching Logan take Georgia had stirred something deep inside him, and it had nothing to do with jealousy. He'd loved watching them together. He'd practically come just watching how deeply connected they were. He wanted that. He wanted to be the third piece to that trio, and it was all in his reach. All he had to do was take care of his Georgia and convince Logan that he wasn't as fucked up as he obviously was. He could do it. He could be very persuasive.

Georgia yawned and her backside wiggled against his cock. *Fuck.* His dick twitched and grew to obnoxious lengths. Even after taking her last night, he needed her. After Logan had pulled his vanishing act—the motherfucking coward—Seth had made love to her, wiping away her tears and making her forget that his best friend was an idiot.

"Good morning." He kissed her cheek, running his hand down her arm and threading their fingers together.

She rubbed back against him. "Good morning."

His cock jumped at the husky sound of her voice. He pulled her close, bringing his cheek up to meet hers. "How are you feeling this morning, gorgeous girl?"

He was feeling spectacular. He'd gotten inside his Georgia last night. He'd fallen asleep with her all happy and satisfied, with her head on his chest.

"I'm good."

Yeah. He didn't believe that. There was a hitch to her voice that made him hesitate. "Georgia?"

"Do you think Logan's okay?"

There it was. Fuck Logan. How could he have made love to her the way he had and still walked out on them? He'd watched Seth make love to her and then awkwardly said good night, explaining that before they did anything else, he would need a contract. A fucking contract. Like they were a business deal.

Seth took business seriously, but this was so much more. This was their life, the one they could share if Logan would let them. If Logan would let them in. "He's fine, baby. He's taking that Dom thing very seriously. He wanted us to have some alone time."

Logan had gotten up after the initial sex and made sandwiches. They had needed their strength. Seth had followed and tried to ask him about the new scars on his arms. There were white scars on his wrists and forearms that had obviously been there long enough for

Georgia to have seen them before. She hadn't reacted at all, not to the scars on his wrists or the nasty circles on his biceps. Cigarette burns. He recognized them. His mother used to put out her cigarettes on the furniture when she got drunk enough. But she'd never treated Seth like her ashtray, and someone obviously had with Logan. He'd tried to ask about the scars, but Logan had completely shut down. He'd brushed off the questions and walked back into the bedroom, leaving Seth to finish the sandwiches. When he'd walked back in, Logan had been all over Georgia, fucking her like a man on a singular mission.

What was he thinking? Georgia had to be sore as hell. If Seth knew one thing, it was that Georgia needed someone to take care of her. He kissed her cheek. "I'm going to go start the shower for you. Nice and hot and then I'll see if I can figure out the coffeemaker. Do you want to go into town for breakfast?"

"Sure." She smiled up at him, but there was a hint of sadness in her expression.

And all he could do about it was coddle and love her because he couldn't promise that Logan would come around. He had to admit that Logan might not be easy to win over. Seth kissed her again and rolled out of bed, making his way to the bathroom.

The bathroom was a marble monstrosity. The builders had done an amazing job. Why had he allowed this whole place to be built without ever coming down here and checking it out himself? Why had he let Henry make all the connections? Until he'd come here with Georgia, he'd only seen the place in pictures and the artist's rendition. He'd stayed away because he'd wanted to come back to town as the conquering hero, but Logan had needed him.

How the hell did he figure this out? This wasn't something he could write a check for. Logan's problems wouldn't go away because he'd bought a bed that would fit him or because he'd built a house for them. He wasn't even sure Georgia could solve Logan's problems. He only had a few weeks before Logan would have to decide whether to go back to Dallas or stay in Bliss, and suddenly Seth wasn't sure at all that a couple of weeks would convince him.

Years. He'd let years go by with only phone calls and e-mails, and online game play. And he'd only done that when he could be convinced to stop writing his code. After the code had been complete, he'd set about building his company and he'd spent even less time with Logan.

"Is the water warm yet?" She'd slipped into one of his T-shirts. She stood there in the doorway looking slightly wary, as though morning had taken the sexy, confident woman and turned her back into a vulnerable girl.

He hadn't bothered with clothes. It felt right to be naked with her. He gave her a tired smile and cupped her cheeks, lowering his head to hers and kissing her softly. "Yeah, baby. It's a steam shower built for an army. It warms up fast. And the towel racks are heated."

"It wasn't built for an army. It was built for you and me and Logan, wasn't it?"

He nodded. "I'm sorry he's not here with us. Maybe when he gets his contract, he'll feel more comfortable."

She bit into her bottom lip, those blue eyes looking up at him. "I want to try with Logan."

"I know." And he wanted her to have what she wanted. What the hell was he going to do if Logan walked out? He didn't want to let Georgia down. It was no way to start a life together.

"But, Seth, if he doesn't want me in the end, do you think you would try to find another woman? Would you try to find someone he could want long term?"

"Georgia." He breathed her name as he gathered her close. He wrapped his arms around her. "Georgia, you're it. Do you understand me? You're the be-all, end-all of my existence. I'm never letting you go, and I don't mean that in a creepy-stalker way, though you should know I could turn into a creepy stalker if you dumped me."

He felt her smile against his skin. "You would be the creepiest, stalkeriest ex-boyfriend ever. I want to try with Logan, but Seth, if he doesn't want me, I don't want this to go away. I need you. I need this relationship. I was willing to give up the sex part to stay your friend because I need you in my life."

And he needed her, too. More than anything. "I'm not going away. And you were only willing to give up the sex because you didn't know how good it could be."

"You're so arrogant." She slapped against his chest, but there was laughter in her eyes as she looked up at him. "I guess my only question is why me? I don't want to sound like a whiny girl, but I have to wonder. I don't know if you noticed, but I can be a handful."

"And you can be amazing. The fit yesterday kind of threw me off, and it also did something for me. You're not some cardboard cutout who I'll always know how to handle. You'll challenge me and keep me on my toes. Life is exciting with you. You make me laugh, and there is such grace in you. You could be anything you wanted to, you know. You just have to figure out what that is. When you know what your passion is, when you find that one thing you want to leave to the world, damn, baby, I want to be there. I want to be beside you. I want to be the man who helps make those dreams come true. You always give me that pep speech before I have to go into a big meeting. What do you say to me?"

Her eyes rolled. "Seth Stark is a big deal."

She'd started it one week after he'd hired her. She'd retied his silk tie and made sure his new Armani suit was smooth, and she'd given him a smile before he'd faced a reporter. He was the billionaire and she'd been the one to lift him up.

"Georgia Dawson is a big fucking deal. She's the biggest deal in the world to me. I love Logan. I want Logan with us. But if he doesn't stay with us, I'll feel bad for him because we can have a great life."

She nodded and took a deep breath then stepped toward the shower, her hand pulling the T-shirt off and letting it fall to the floor. She opened the shower door and turned her head toward him. "Are you coming?"

His dick was right back up, but the situation hadn't changed. "Baby, you have to be sore."

"Oh, I am so sore. I think we should wait a little while before Mr. Happy plays with my girl again. But maybe I could help you get cleaned up." She winked as she disappeared.

Fuck. There was no way he would refuse that invitation. Even if all that happened was she ran her hands all over him and got him so hot he couldn't stand it, it would be worth it because this was intimacy. Waking up next to her, spending the day with her, showering with her. This was what he wanted. This was what had been missing from his life.

He got in the state-of-the-art shower with its nine showerheads.

He pressed a button and released the citrus steam.

"I love that smell. It makes me think of mornings." She reached out for him, her hands covering his chest, slowly moving across his muscles. She hadn't been allowed to explore the night before. He and Logan had taken charge. They had pleasured her, but there was something about the curious way she ran her hands over his pecs and down to his abs that made him think they had missed something. The water beat against his back, heat stinging against his skin, loosening him up. "I want you to teach me. You know, what you promised to teach me last night."

His eyes nearly crossed at the thought. "I promised to teach you how to suck my cock last night."

She flushed, pink creeping across her face. Her blonde hair darkened as it got wet, and it reached almost down to her waist. "Yeah. That."

Inner Dom was flaring back to life. He wanted more from her than that. He wasn't teaching her how to suck any cock. He was teaching her to suck his, and that was different. If he had his way, she would be sucking his cock for the rest of their lives. "Ask me."

"What?"

"Unless you're not interested in the lifestyle. I rather thought you were from your reading material. If you're interested in submission, then we should start now. This is sex, and I'm in charge of sex when Logan isn't around. I top you and I want you to ask me for permission to suck my cock."

Her lips turned down. "You didn't ask for permission to…do all that stuff to me."

"No. I didn't ask for permission to eat your pussy because your pussy belongs to me and I'm in charge of this part of our lives. I want you to think about the last six months. Who was in charge of where we ate lunch and what the chef made for dinner? Who was in charge of my calendar and forced me to take weekends off and then basically planned out those weekends for me?"

A mischievous light came into her eyes. "All right. I can play by those rules. Seth, would you please teach me how to suck your cock?"

Pure pleasure flooded his system, hotter than the water. "Yes, I will do that, baby. On your knees."

He held her hand, helping her down.

She looked right at his cock. She stared for a while and then her eyes came up. "Is it weird if I say I think you're beautiful?"

He put a hand on her head. He loved her like this, when everything was stripped away. When all the makeup was gone and she couldn't hide behind those clothes she wore, that was when she was at her most beautiful. "I'm deeply grateful, baby. And I think you're the most gorgeous woman I've ever laid eyes on. Kiss me."

She didn't pretend to misunderstand. She simply leaned forward and pressed her lips against his aching cock. Sweet brushes of her mouth that covered his flesh. She kissed the head of his cock and moved along his stalk all the way to the base.

"Kiss my balls, too." He tried to keep his voice at that deep command Logan seemed to find during sex. It must have been part of his training because Seth was worried he sounded like a kid whose voice was changing.

She did as he asked, dropping lower to kiss his balls. They tightened at the touch of her lips.

"Lick them." He'd never done this with a lover, never truly taken charge because he hadn't necessarily cared before. He'd pleasured lovers, asking them what they needed and taking his cues from their bodies, but this was different. He was training Georgia on how to please him. Because she was his. She wouldn't move on to the next lover.

All fucking his.

He put a hand on her wet hair. "Come on, baby. I want you to suck me. Suck the head of my cock, and then I'm going to work my way into your mouth. You can take me. We'll work at it, but you'll be able to suck every inch down."

She sucked his cockhead inside, her tongue whirling around it, tracing the ridges and lines and smoothing over the *V* on the underside of his cock. He felt a pulse of arousal leak from his cockhead, and she sucked that up, too. She pulled back slightly, lapping at his slit as though trying to draw out another bead of salty liquid.

"Fuck, Georgia. How can you say you're not good at this?"

"Because I never tried before. I want to be good now. I want to be the best you've ever had. I can be a good student. I just have to care about the subject. I care about Cock Sucking 101." She wrapped her palm around his cock. "Well, I guess I really care about pleasing my instructor, but it's all the same. I want to ace this particular exam."

Oh, she was going to be so damn much fun to play with. Boss and secretary. Teacher and student. If Logan would play along, they could get a damn fine game of dominant cops and cute robber going. "I think you're going to be fine. Keep doing what you're doing. Suck me. Hard. I want to fuck your mouth."

She leaned forward and started to eat up his cock. He couldn't help but stare down, watching as his dick disappeared behind those sultry lips. Something eased inside him, and he realized that he'd been worried she wouldn't want him the way she did Logan. The sparks flew off those two, but he had a different relationship with her. Not lesser, merely different, but still important. Logan had claimed that he couldn't be friends with Georgia, but Seth was. He'd laid all that groundwork, found a happy companionship with her. The fact that she sucked his cock like no one had before was a plus, but not the center of their relationship. He wanted to hold her hand and see the world with her. He wanted to have children with her one day—way in the future. Because he wanted this time with her.

He gripped her hair, pulling her forward. She could handle this. He'd been afraid she would only respond to Logan, but she wanted him, too. She needed him, and he wasn't going to hold back. He fucked into her mouth in short strokes, her tongue moving along his flesh, getting him harder and harder, pushing him closer to the edge. She fought him, sucking to keep him inside when he would pull out.

He kept control, wanting the moment to last.

But she had something to say about that. She sucked hard, her hands moving to cup the cheeks of his ass. She used the leverage to force him deeper.

He felt the back of her throat, loved the growl reverberating around his dick, and then she swallowed and he was lost. His balls drew up and shot off, pouring from him into her. She drank him down, swallowing everything he gave her. He came for long, delicious moments and sighed when he finally popped out of her mouth.

Her confidence was back. That was clear in the sexy, satisfied smile on her face. Damn, he might have made a monster.

He reached for her, pulling her up to him, rubbing his chest against hers and kissing her long and slow, tasting himself on those lips.

"Come here and let me take care of you now." He picked up the shampoo. It was the type she preferred. He'd made sure the agent who stocked the house had bought all of her favorite brands.

Georgia leaned back, allowing him to wash her, to clean her hair, to be with her.

Everything he wanted was right in his grasp.

Almost. All he needed was his brother.

Chapter Ten

Logan walked back out of the bedroom with a knot in the pit of his stomach. Seth was in the shower with Georgia, and they weren't just getting clean. They were getting dirty.

He'd stood there with the mug in his hand. It wasn't like he'd managed to get the coffee thing going. He'd given up and walked across the yard to knock on Nell and Henry's door and beg them for coffee. He needed to bring something to Georgia, and he'd proven yesterday that he couldn't handle himself in the kitchen.

He'd walked back in hoping to wake her up with the smell of organic French roast, but he'd heard her laugh and then he'd heard Seth groaning.

They were together without him and that was good. That was how it should be because he was their trainer. He wasn't a permanent member of the family. He was going to teach Seth how to top Georgia, and then he would likely be invited to their private collaring ceremony or their wedding.

One minute the mug was fulfilling its purpose and the next Logan was covered in coffee and there were ceramic pieces everywhere. *Motherfucker*.

He had a bone to pick with Nell. That coffee wasn't cruelty-free. It was hot as hell.

He jogged into the kitchen and wiped down his forearms. *Damn it to hell.* He'd wrecked his shirt. He had to change. He was going to be late.

Seth was fucking Georgia, and he couldn't walk in there and take what he wanted because he was the trainer. He hadn't slept next to her because he wasn't the boyfriend. He was the fucking trainer.

And he'd dreamed about it again. He'd woken up in a cold sweat, his heart slamming in his chest and a strangled scream in his throat. He'd taught himself to not scream, to stay quiet. To keep his fucking mouth shut. Even when the asshole had taken to burning him over and over again. Sometimes he could still feel those burns biting into his flesh. The pain would flare at first and then it would almost go away, but that was merely his nerves overloading. They would come back online and he would feel a circle of pain. And he wouldn't scream.

He still woke up every night, no matter how much he talked about it with Leo or how much time he spent working out to completely exhaust himself.

Leo couldn't do his job properly because you never told him what really got to you. You never told him who the real villain of the piece was.

He ripped open his shirt and was so happy to see the stain was on his tank as well. When he fucked up, it went straight to the bone. He reluctantly tugged it off, too, eager to get the soaked fabric off his skin.

He needed to get that damn mug off the floor and then he needed to hightail it out of here. He couldn't sit with them and watch Georgia and Seth hold hands and glow at each other.

The doorbell rang. *Fuck a duck.* They could wait. Hell, whoever it was could go away. He didn't need company.

"Son? Logan? Are you in there?"

He seriously considered running, but his momma was too fast. And apparently Seth had given her a key. Momma Marie strode in. She never simply walked. She swaggered like she was the lead in an old-school Western, and there was some truth to that since she was usually packing a handgun somewhere on her body.

"Hey, Momma. How is everything going?" God, he loved that woman, and she still scared the holy pee out of him at times. When she walked in the room, he was twelve years old again and praying his momma didn't find out all the dumb crap he did.

She could never, never know what he'd been willing to do.

"Is he in there?" A softer voice followed. Mom. Teeny Green stepped in the room carrying a big basket. She'd aged. Somehow in his head she was always the same vibrant woman she'd been when he was a kid, but there was no way to miss the lines around her eyes or the steel in her hair. She was a slight woman, her bones tiny, but he knew how strong she was. She was a woman who wouldn't break. Not ever.

Yeah, she couldn't know either.

"Logan." Pure pleasure tinted his mother's voice. She set the basket down and walked right up to him, throwing her arms around his chest.

"Ma, I'm covered in coffee."

"I don't care. It's so good to see you. I can't believe you're here." His mom squeezed him tight.

"I can't believe he's been here for two days and he didn't think to come by the house to say hello." Momma Marie always got straight to the point.

Guilt bit at him. He'd started to drive home, but he'd found himself pointing the truck here because he couldn't step back into the house he'd grown up in, couldn't be surrounded by the evidence of his childhood. That dumbass Logan who had read comic books and played online games and pretended to be a hero had died on Nate's desk, and the Logan who had been left behind couldn't stand to be reminded of what he'd lost.

"I'm sorry. I got in late, and Nate needed me at the station house. I tried calling the house, but no one answered. I was going to come over after my shift this afternoon. I promise."

Momma Marie's eyes narrowed as though she could see right through him. "And you're here in this monstrosity of a house why? Your momma cleaned up your room and got everything real nice for you when she found out you were coming home."

He couldn't back down from that particular fight. "I'm an adult. I can't live at home. I need my space."

"It also looks like you need laser tattoo removal, son." Momma Marie was shaking her head like she was ready to go and grab a laser herself.

"The tat stays, Ma." He heard the growl in his voice. He was never getting rid of that ink.

"Fine, it's a generational thing," Momma Marie said. "But you don't need to stay here. You're going to come home where we can take care of you."

"I'm taking care of him."

Logan winced at the sound of that soft voice. Georgia. She was standing in the hallway dressed in a tank top and stretchy pants that molded to her every curve. Her hair was still wet, and she wasn't wearing an ounce of makeup. She looked younger and more vulnerable than he could remember her being. She was a brat of the first order, but she would wilt under Momma Marie's gruffness. There was no contest.

"You're after my boy?"

Georgia's brows drew together. "Marie? Are you the one I talked to on the phone that day? You called the Willow Fork police and helped save me?"

His mother lit up. "Marie, do you know this girl? Oh, my heavens. Are you that sweet girl who got caught in the slavery ring?"

Georgia shook her head. "I didn't because Ms. Marie called in the cops." She smiled and the whole fucking room lit up. She walked right up to the scariest woman in Bliss County and wrapped her arms around her. "Thank you so much, Ms. Marie. You saved me."

To his eternal surprise, his gruffest momma hugged Georgia back. "No need to thank me. I got the cookie bouquet. It was real nice, darlin'. Now tell me what you're doing here. I thought you took some big job in New York City."

"She's with me, Momma Marie. And what happened in the hallway? Did a mug spontaneously explode?" Seth had put on a pair of jeans, but he'd managed to place them somewhere around his hips so all the douchebag parts were exposed like he was some sort of male model.

"I had an accident," Logan replied with a long sigh. "I was trying to clean up when the world decided to join us for breakfast."

A shit-eating grin hit Seth's face. "I'll take care of it. Nice tat, brother. I think I should get one, too."

Georgia turned, her eyes going straight to his left pec.

"It stands for Green." He was reaching. "I did it in honor of my mother. I'm going to get a *W* on the other side."

His mom shook her head. "I never much liked the last name Green. I kept it because it connected me to you, but I have to say, it's not the best last name."

"Yeah, it stands for Green." Seth shook his head, his eyes rolling slightly.

"Hello to the house," a familiar voice called out. Henry. Awesome. He would be bringing Nell with him. Yeah, the house was filling up.

"Teeny, Marie," Nell said as she walked in. "It's so nice to see you."

Nate walked behind Nell, his uniform in perfect condition. "Morning, y'all. I was talking to Henry and Nell about their upcoming protest schedule and it seemed like a nice time to come see this new property."

In other words, Nate was curious.

Georgia went straight to that obnoxious coffeemaker. "Can I get anyone coffee? I'll start breakfast if anyone's hungry."

Mom shook her head. "I brought some muffins. Enough for everyone. Seth, hon, I made your favorite. Chocolate chip."

"Sweet." Seth sat down at the bar like the whole damn world wasn't going out of control. "Sheriff Wright, I'm Seth Stark."

Nate got the widest grin. "Hey! Thanks for the rides, man. Four Escalades. We love them. The Broncos kept breaking down, and I couldn't get the mayor to open the purse strings to buy us new vehicles."

"No problem, man. I was happy to do it." Seth hopped on to his barstool, his eyes straying to Georgia.

"Stef was so pissed when he figured out someone else had bought the department new vehicles." Nate grabbed a muffin. He was never one to turn down food. "He immediately wrote the department a check so I have the sweetest new chair. It's like a recliner masquerading as an office chair. I can actually sleep in it. It's perfect. And the first person who has sex in my chair is going to jail. I'm putting it on the damn books. It's a law. No screwing in the sheriff's chair."

"I don't know if I think that's right, Nathan." Nell was shaking her head. "Your chair is truly county property. I think the taxpayers have a certain right to have access to that chair."

"No, they damn straight don't, Nell. That chair is now sacred to me. I have the right to sit in a chair that wasn't a place of conception."

Nell and Nate were arguing whether taxpayer money gave the citizens of Bliss the right to use Nate's new chair as a cheap motel. Henry started talking to Seth, and both of his mommas began a long, slow circle around Georgia, who was powering up the coffeemaker and sliding in a cup. She smiled up at his ma like she didn't know what was about to happen.

Momma Marie leaned in for the kill. "Tell me, Georgia, are you sleeping with my boy?"

"Momma!" He didn't have to take this. He was an adult. *Damn it.*

"I have the right to know," Momma Marie insisted.

"No, I am not sleeping with him." Georgia looked up to his mother, her blue eyes wide. "He made love to me and then refused to sleep in the same bed. I have to admit it did make me wonder if maybe I wasn't skilled enough. I haven't been with many men, Ms. Marie. Do you think he would have slept with me if I was better in bed?"

Seth choked on his muffin. "Holy hell."

Momma Marie's eyes, which only a moment ago had been narrowed in suspicion toward the woman she'd discovered in his place, now turned to Logan's with a cold disapproval. "I raised you better than that, son. How can you take this sweet young thing and use her like that?"

"I slept with her." Seth put his hand up like they were fucking five and he had the right answer to the teacher's question. "I cuddled her all night long."

Georgia didn't even blush. She simply gave Seth the sweetest smile. Logan hoped her backside hurt. She was going to get another spanking. Little brat. Damn, why did he go so fucking crazy for her every time she trumped him? She was a righteous bitch, and everything that was male inside of him responded to her. It was right there, the deep desire to walk up to her and put his stamp on her in front of his mommas. But he couldn't.

"Ma, it's not some great romance. It's a training relationship. I told you what I was doing in Dallas. I'm doing it here now." He said it with as little emotion as he could. The last thing he needed was a fight with his mommas.

"Training?" his ma started.

Teeny put a hand on Momma Marie's arm. "Let it be for now, Marie. He's home. He's safe here with Seth."

His ma backed down, but those eyes narrowed again. "All right, but I don't like the idea of him training young ladies, and Seth doesn't look like he needs any training at all. What is wrong with those jeans, Seth? You're about to fall out of them. Can't you afford jeans that properly fit?"

Thank god. She was off and complaining about Seth's jeans and the fact that he looked like a douchebag male model.

Georgia passed him a mug of coffee. "Well played. Do you have another uniform or should I see if I can get the stain out of this one?"

It was too sweet, too domestic, the idea of her washing his clothes after she'd made him coffee. He took the mug because he couldn't turn her down again. Not after yesterday, but he wasn't about to let her think she had to take care of him. "No. I've got five sets. I'll wash this one later. Thanks."

He practically ran down the hall to the room he'd been bunking in. He shut the door behind him and thought seriously about getting in his truck and heading out. Maybe if he went somewhere no one knew him, had no expectations of him, maybe he could find some peace. Maybe he could forget.

But his feet moved to the closet, and before he knew it, he was dressed again and ready to start a rousing day of dealing with tourists, talking down the crazies, and keeping threesomes off of Nate's new chair.

He picked up his hat and looked into the mirror. Sometimes he didn't recognize the face that looked back at him. He was older and harder.

His mother had looked so frail. He'd been her boy for so many years, her only child, and he'd walked away and barely said a word to her for a year. How much of the new gray in her hair was his fault? How many of the lines around her mouth were from frowning over his fate?

How much more would he disappoint her?

He couldn't walk back into that cabin he'd lived in all his life. That cabin had been full of love. Even when they'd struggled, he always knew his parents loved each other. They'd stood by each other, hands entwined. They'd tried to raise him so right.

What was so flawed in him that he'd failed that day?

"I like the blonde. She's got spirit." Momma Marie stood in the doorway looking in, her stern face frowning. He didn't take that to heart. She always frowned, even when she was happy.

"I think Seth is going to be real happy with her."

She shook her head. "Don't try to fool me, son. And don't even try to pass that tattoo off as a tribute to your last name. You know damn well the only reason I didn't adopt you was for fear of your biological father's parents possibly using the fact that your momma was with me to take you away."

He shrugged. "Maybe I'm more like him than you guys ever thought."

He said it like it didn't matter, like it was a throwaway line to annoy his mother, but it was his secret fear. From all accounts, his father had been a brutal man. He'd taken out his anger on the sweetest woman to walk the earth, and it had only been Marie Warner's stalwart love that had saved Logan from being raised by a killer.

Momma Marie was suddenly in his space. Though she was four inches shorter than he was, she got right up on him, her hands on his shoulders, forcing him to look at her. "Don't you ever say that. What the hell is wrong with you? Your father was a cold, calculating man. He couldn't even love your mother. If you can't love that woman, you can't love anything in the world. I need you to start talking, son, because I get the feeling that if you don't, I'm going to lose you."

"I'm not going anywhere." He'd thought about it. He'd thought about it a whole lot that night at Hell on Wheels.

"But you're not here, either." Marie took a long breath and

looked closer to crying than he'd ever seen her. "Logan, I don't talk about myself much. I don't see the point in it. But I need to talk to you about this now because I have to know that you're going to be okay."

He stopped breathing for a moment. His momma never talked like this. Never. "What's happened?"

"I had some tests run. Damn Doc insisted on it and Teeny finally made me go in. I haven't told her this because I don't want to worry her. My heart is failing. Doc says if I don't change my ways, I'll have a heart attack in a year or two. If you weren't in trouble, I wouldn't mention it, but I need to know you'll be here for Teeny when I go."

Momma Marie? No. She was stronger than anything. She couldn't have a weak heart. She couldn't. It was always so strong, so damn steady. Panic threatened to set in. He couldn't imagine a world where Marie Warner didn't stand tall and proud. It shook the very foundation he depended on. "You need to do what Doc tells you. What did he say? Did he give you guidelines? You have to tell Ma."

If she needed to change her diet, then that was what would happen. She did tend to treat a pound of bacon like an appetizer.

Her chin firmed stubbornly. "I am not telling your ma. And yes, Doc gave me all kinds of things I can't do anymore. If I follow his advice, I'll end up eating Nell's cooking from now on. I don't think this old dog can learn any new tricks."

She wasn't taking this seriously at all. "You damn well can and Ma will help you. We all need to sit down with Doc and talk about this. You have to change. We need you."

She shrugged. "Well, we need you, too, but you don't seem ready to try to change."

Oh, he was surrounded by devious women. "Momma, you can't put that on me. And I am changing. I have a steady job and I haven't beaten the shit out of anyone in months. I'm trying."

"No, you're not. You're biding your time. I might have a weak heart, but my eyes work fine. You're in love with that young woman and you're going to let Seth walk off with her. Do you think I don't know that you and Seth always planned to find a girl and settle down? You've practically got her name tattooed over your heart. But you say you're just 'training' her? The way I figure it, it's all the same. It's hard to do the work it takes to fix what's gone wrong. You're so young and strong. I'm not. If you can't do it, there's no damn hope for someone like me. That's how I see it."

His stomach flipped over. She was putting him in a horrible position. She was shoving him in a corner, but he wasn't going to be the only one hurt if he didn't come out of it. "You can't do this. This is blackmail. You can't put your whole damn life on the line."

"For my son? Oh, for my son I can do anything. You don't have a drop of my blood in you, Logan. But I put my soul in you. You think I won't fight? I'll fight and I'll die if I have to, but I won't leave you to this. I won't. I don't show it the way Teeny does, but I love you. You're the best thing I ever did, and I'll bet everything on you." She patted his arm and took a step back. "I'm going to get to know your girl. I think we'll have a lot in common. Both of us are waiting for you to wake up and realize that this life means more than what happened to you. What we gave you, the life we made for you…it means more, Logan. I have to believe that a lifetime of love means more than three hours of pain. I have to." His momma took a step back, her face set in stubborn lines. "I think you need to stay here in Bliss. You've done all the work you can there. I think you need to find a way to forgive Alexei Markov. You can't move on until you do."

He felt his jaw tighten, his hands becoming fists at the mere mention of the man's name. "I can say the words all day if you want me to."

"The words don't mean anything if you can't let go of that hate that's in your heart." She was almost to the door. He was almost home free. And she turned. "I want you to ask yourself some hard questions. If you love that girl in there and she was in danger, would you put Seth in the same position if it was the only way to save her? You don't have to answer me now. Just think on it."

"We're going to have to talk about your health, Momma. You can't keep this from Ma." She couldn't walk away from this.

"Well, I guess if you want to tell your ma about this, you're going to have to come out to the house and have a long talk. I think we have a lot to discuss."

She turned and walked out, and he could hear the laughter

coming from the kitchen. Seth said something and he could hear Georgia and his ma break into peals of laughter. The smell of coffee wafted through the house. Muffins and coffee and his family. They were all within reach. All he had to do was walk out and they would welcome him and try to make him comfortable.

But they couldn't because his momma was right. He couldn't feel at home here. He'd chosen to sleep alone in this room where his damn feet hung off the bed. Not that he'd slept much. When he wasn't dreaming about what had happened, he'd been sitting up wondering what the hell he was going to do.

He moved away from the door and turned to his window. It was typical of the whole house with its spectacular view of the river. He stared out. This was exactly the place he and Seth had talked about building when they were teens. He remembered it like it was yesterday. They'd sat by the river and talked about finding a wife and how they would build a life here in Bliss after they both got out of college. Seth was going to move down here after graduation, but that hadn't happened. After Seth had gotten perfect scores on his SATs, MIT had come calling and then he'd built his business and Logan had refused to let Seth pay for his college.

And somewhere along the way they'd drifted apart, except Seth didn't seem to notice that they were on two different planes of existence. Seth seemed to think that all he had to do was waltz into town, build a dream home, offer Georgia up on a platinum platter, and Logan would fall in line.

Logan set his forehead against the windowpane. It was smooth and cool. He was stuck, and he was rapidly discovering that he had a choice to make. His momma couldn't be serious. She couldn't. Except Momma Marie never lied. She couldn't be bothered.

If she was sick, he would have to stay, and if he stayed, he wasn't sure he could watch Seth and Georgia get married and settle down.

He had to figure a way out of this corner.

He caught a glimmer off the river, a glint that told him someone was watching. He brought his head up, his eyes focusing on a spot across the river. It was nothing but forest past the water. National forest land with deeply restricted hiking and camping protocols. Logan expected bears and moose and elk to walk out from there, but not humans with cameras—or scoped rifles.

Nothing else would make that glint. Nothing natural.

Someone was watching the house. Someone was taking pictures or taking aim. One of the two.

He damn well intended to find out.

Chapter Eleven

"Are you sure I should be here?" Georgia walked into the back room at the Trading Post, following after Momma Marie. The older woman had insisted that she call her Momma Marie and she was going along with it, but not for the reasons Seth thought. Seth had held her hands and promised that Marie Warner wouldn't actually kill her. He'd acted like he was sending her off to some sort of battle he wasn't sure she would return from.

Seth was scared of the gruff woman and Logan had gone a little green when she'd turned on him, but Georgia didn't see what the big deal was. Marie was rough on the outside, but there wasn't anything scary about her, not really. She sort of reminded her of Win. Oh, Marie had claws and fangs, but she wouldn't use them except to protect.

"You're practically a member of this club, honey. You didn't shoot a son of a bitch, but you did get shot by one."

Georgia couldn't help but laugh. She was pretty sure she should be all PTSD'd out, but the thought that there was a club for women who had gone through hell, and it had lemon crème cake, was actually kind of cool. "It was quite painful."

"But the way I heard it, you made it through real good. Even after you were shot, you had to make your way out of that hellhole."

She'd had Nat. Nat had given her the strength to get up that damn ladder even though her arm hadn't worked at the time. And she'd wanted to see Logan. Even after she'd been shot, all she had been able to see was his face. When she'd been struggling up that damn ladder, all she'd been able to hear was Logan's voice telling her to get the hell on that ladder and get herself to him. She'd done it. She'd made her way up that ladder, and she'd promised herself that no matter what happened, she'd find a way to live through it. "But it was my brother who shot the guy who shot me. And it was Logan who came in and saved me."

Marie shook her head. "Just staying alive in the face of adversity is impressive, girl. And if you're going to be with Seth and my Logan, you should start getting to know the women of Bliss. We stick together here. We have to protect this town. Oh, the men think they protect the town, but we know the truth." Marie stepped through the doors into a big room that had been decorated in lace and antique furniture in one section. The rest was a bunch of organized boxes and looked like the back of a retail store, but there seemed to be a small salon in there as well. A group of women were already sitting around, coffee mugs in hand, talking amongst themselves. "You see the men like to think they're in charge."

Oh, she knew all about that. "Absolutely. It's best they don't know they're being manipulated, but I thought all the law enforcement around here were men?"

Marie winked her way. "Not a one of those women in there would put on polyester to save her life, but you don't have to wear a badge to shoot a son of a bitch. You see the woman with strawberry blonde hair? That's Rachel Harper. Two husbands and she still had to take her son of a bitch down. All she had was a gun and her dog and cold steel in her veins. Callie there, that's the sheriff's wife, and her other husband is a big mean-looking son of a bitch. Who had to save them when the chips were down?"

"The woman with the baby shot someone?" She didn't look like she would hurt a fly.

"She took down a DEA agent." Marie nodded. "There's Holly right there. She had to kill a US Marshal gone bad, but only after my boy had taken down a paid assassin. Yeah, that was a rough day. Hope and Lucy there didn't actually shoot anyone. They took down their son of a bitch with a paring knife and a chair. They tag-teamed the nasty bastard. Real proud of those girls."

Georgia gulped. That was a whole lot of body count. "What did their bad guy do?"

"He was a horrible human being," a familiar voice said from behind. Nell Flanders practically floated into the room. She was ethereal with brown hair and wide eyes that reminded Georgia of the fairies in some of the games Seth played online. Oh, he tried to shut them down when she walked in a room, but she'd seen them. Dweeb. Hot dweeb. Stinking hot, make-her-crazy dweeb. God, she loved geeks. Why had she spent all her time on douche-nozzle jocks?

She forced her attention back to Nell, who was talking. "He pretended to be an environmentalist to bilk people out of money."

"He ran a cult," Marie said flatly.

"Not all environmentalists are in cults, Marie."

"You say potato," Marie shot back. She slid Georgia a look. "And Nell is an ancillary member. She never shot a son of a bitch."

"No. I'm completely nonviolent, but I do support the right of all creatures to survive. Therefore, I support this group. And I have been shot at by a…person of ill repute."

"He was a son of a bitch," Marie corrected.

Nell shrugged. "What she said. I'm not so much into cursing either. Do you think those shoes are good for the environment?"

Georgia heard a gasp coming from the salon. "Those are so pretty. I love the color."

It had come from the woman with the strawberry blonde hair. She was lovely, but there was a red rim to her eyes that told Georgia she'd been crying. Not recently, but she'd cried hard enough that her face was still slightly puffy. Damn. A woman only cried that much over a man or a broken heel.

"Thanks. I got them at Nordstrom. They're Puccis." She loved the five-and-a-half-inch platforms. Seth had seemed to like them, too. He'd stared at them for a while after she'd gotten dressed and muttered something about how they would look around his neck. They were gorgeous and hot pink, with silver buckles and perfect leather soles.

"I have no idea how you walk in those, but they're pretty," Callie said with a smile. She patted her baby on the back. There was another identical baby asleep in a car seat at her feet.

"Do not let Laura see those," the redhead named Holly said. "She likes to have the best shoes in town. You're about to be the foot queen of Bliss."

Actually, that sounded kind of nice. All the women were looking at her with smiles, and they seemed awfully welcoming.

Of course, sometimes people could smile and then turn around and stab a girl in the back, but suddenly it seemed like her heart was as optimistic as her pussy had been. Her pussy had known deep down that all she needed to do was keep trying until she found the right penis. What if it was the same with friends? What if all it took was to survive getting beaten down until she found a place where she belonged? She'd always thought it would be a big city, but she'd woken up this morning with arms wrapped around her and hope in her heart, and she'd known the mountains and river were the setting for her rebirth, not the city. Seth loved it here. Logan had been raised here. Clearly there was something beautiful about this place. "Thanks. I brought a bunch of my shoes. You should see the Pradas my sister-in-law gave me this year. They're white Italian leather mules with pretty gold studs."

"I have no idea how you walk in them, either," Nell said with a sad frown and a shake of her head.

The room groaned collectively.

Georgia waved her off. Oh, she knew where Nell was going. Nell was wearing Birkenstocks and a cotton skirt that obviously needed an iron. Yep, she was a very polite granola, and there was only one way to handle a granola. Never engage. Smile. Talk a little dumb. Never give a granola a target they could fixate on. The good news was, granolas were almost never cruel. They were kind and sweet, and they would take her Emilio Pucci heels from her cold dead hands.

"It's totally easy. These have a two-inch platform, so it's really like I'm walking in three-inch heels. Easy, breezy." She gave the Rachel girl a smile. "Do you want to try them?"

Georgia was a sucker for a teary girl. She'd been the girl who cried in the bathroom way too many times.

Rachel shook her head. "Oh, no. I couldn't. I haven't worn shoes like that in years. I'm pregnant. I can't walk in heels."

But she had worn them once. There was a look of longing on her face. Georgia would bet that she'd been quite the fashionable girl once. She pulled the shoe off. "I'm an eight."

Rachel's eyes got a little sparkle. "Me, too."

The granola wasn't done. Nell got in between them. "Do you like those shoes more than the earth?"

A totally easy question to answer. She made sure she looked deeply unthreatening as she responded. "Oh, absolutely." She passed the shoes to Rachel. "The shoes are gorgeous and never tried to kill me. The earth is actually quite violent. Earthquakes. Volcanoes. Poison ivy. The poison ivy was the worst. I got it up my hoo-ha. Seriously horrible. None of my shoes have ever made me want to scratch my own vagina off. My brothers used to take me camping. They didn't always remember toilet paper." She turned back to the strawberry blonde. "Those look awesome. Look how tall you are."

Rachel was smiling, her eyes lit with happiness. "They do feel nice. Wow. Laura would be so jealous." She looked down, admiring the heels. "I bet I'm as tall as Max and Rye now."

Sexy heels could give a woman so much confidence. "They look great on you."

"I think we should talk about how those shoes are made. And the sole is obviously leather." Nell had a look of deep consternation on her face.

Never engage the granola. Georgia gave Nell a big hug. "I'm so glad you noticed. You're so nice, Nell."

Nell sputtered, but her arms wrapped around her as though she couldn't possibly resist a human hug no matter whether said human was mad about leather or not. "Thanks."

"I'm so glad we're neighbors." She pulled back and winked. "We can be such good friends."

Nell nodded and found a seat in the salon.

Marie was suddenly next to her. "I think I might love you, Georgia. You might be the daughter I never had."

Rachel was shaking her head. "I've never seen anyone who was able to shut down Nell. I'm in shock. You kept right on talking. I never thought to do that. I always try to argue."

And that was where Rachel went wrong. "Oh, no, you can never win an argument with a granola, but that's okay. They're nice and stuff, so you have to hug it out. If you hug them enough, they totally lose their powers." Georgia turned a smile up to Marie. "Thank you for bringing me here, Momma Marie. I feel so at home."

Marie stopped, her face flushing, and then she nodded stiffly. "Well, you're a sweet girl, Georgia Dawson. A damn fine girl."

She turned and walked away.

"Holy shit. I think I saw a tear in those eyes. I didn't think Marie had working tear ducts." Rachel's mouth was hanging open as she watched Marie start toward the podium. "You are a miracle worker. And you're Logan's girl?"

She'd been feeling so happy before. She'd seemed to actually fit in with these women. But she didn't because she could never truly live here when it was Logan's hometown. Someday he would come back here and he'd bring his pretty subs with him or worse, he would get married and bring home his wife and she would look nothing like Georgia, be nothing like her. She would be classically lovely, and she would likely never scream at him and beat on his back as he had to carry her away. "No. I'm sort of dating Seth Stark, I think. But I might still be his admin. He hasn't actually gotten around to firing me. When I think about it, he shouldn't fire me. I should be allowed to quit gracefully after what I did to him in the shower this morning."

A wistful smile slid across Rachel's face. "I remember times like that. Once you get started in with having babies, those times are few and far between."

"Is this your first?" Georgia was far from having babies. No. Maybe when she hit her late thirties. Maybe. Babies were cute and sweet, but she was still a baby.

Rachel smoothed a hand over her barely there bump. "My second. Paige is with her daddy, well, one of them." She started to explain.

Georgia waved a hand. "Oh, I totally get it. Two husbands. Twice the sex. Twice the laundry. Twice the putting up with their shit. That's what my sister-in-law says. Of course, she also says twice the love. She's happy with my brothers. They're twins."

"So are Max and Rye. Max is giving me hell, actually." She sniffled. "I don't see why he can't take anything seriously. Yesterday he was supposed to get a medical exam so we could get life insurance, but instead he punched Doc in the face and got himself arrested."

"Oh, he sounds like he's acting out. I used to do that all the time to get attention from my brothers. They would get so involved in their lives, and my dad was never around, so I would pull some stupid crap at school to get Win to come home for a while. It wasn't fair. I should apologize to him for that." It hadn't been fair, but at the time, she hadn't known what else to do. She'd been selfish. The night before seemed to have changed something in her. She'd gotten a lecture from Logan about halfway through the night. He'd been buried deep inside her, his hips rolling in a lazy, deeply sensual rhythm. He'd talked about communicating. He'd told her she had to talk to him or it wouldn't work. "Maybe your husband is trying to get your attention."

Like she'd been trying to get Logan and Seth's yesterday. She'd tried to please them by dressing up and cooking dinner and making things nice, and when that hadn't worked, she'd thrown a fit.

Maybe next time, she'd just get naked. They seemed to like her naked.

Rachel's eyes widened. "Do you think so? I have to be honest. I've been worried that maybe he was bored with the whole family thing, and this was his way of having fun. I can treat him like a kid half the time. I don't mean to. I get in mom mode and I start in on them both. Rye will turn me over his knee and show me who's boss when I start in on him, but Max seems to pull away. I don't know why. He would put anyone else on their ass."

She could guess. "Because he loves you. I don't think men are always as rational as women are. He could feel as lonely as you are. I've heard having kids can be hard on a marriage. My dad tended to get divorced every time he had a kid."

Rachel's hands came up, her eyes flaring in obvious revelation. "So he's doing what he knows to do. Oh god. He's acting out because he's trying to get my attention. When we first started dating, we had this deal, Max and me. When he acted like an idiot, he owed me sexual servitude."

She wondered if she could get Logan and Seth to agree to that arrangement. Sexual servitude sounded nice. "If I had to guess, that's what he's doing. Trying to get your attention."

Rachel smiled and gave her the biggest hug. "Oh, I'm so relieved. You're a lifesaver. Why don't you come out for dinner sometime next week? Bring Seth and Logan. We would love to see them." She turned. "Marie, I need to go find Max and lay down the law. Can you handle this without me?"

"Sure thing." Marie stepped up to the small podium and everyone seemed ready to start this meeting thing.

"Oh, I almost forgot." Rachel started to take off the shoes.

But Georgia was enjoying playing fairy godmother. She shook her head. "No. He'll think the shoes are hot. You can borrow them for a while. I'll use yours."

They weren't what she was used to, but they looked comfy. And they fit, and it was worth it to know she'd made someone happy.

"Thank you." Rachel gave her another hug and ran out the door as fast as the heels would allow her.

Nell was standing next to her. "I do not approve of your footwear, but that was a nice thing to do."

"Thanks." She looked Nell up and down. "I love making people over. It's so much fun."

"Well, you obviously dress well. I prefer cruelty-free clothes, though." She ran her hands along her too-long-for-her skirt and shuffled those totally cruel-on-the-eyes shoes she was wearing.

Oh, someone else needed a fairy godmother. "I think I can help you there. I just need my credit card and a computer. This is going to be so, so much fun. I love a good makeover!"

Holly's head turned. "Did someone say makeover?"

Lucy and Hope turned as well.

"That sounds like fun. I've never done makeovers before," the one named Lucy said. "We should have a party."

Georgia could totally do a party. She did kind of have the biggest cabin in the town, after all. And if Logan and Seth didn't like their hideaway being invaded by makeup-loving women, then they shouldn't have chosen her as their girl.

Marie was standing at the podium. "I think that would be fun for y'all. Now it's time to get started. Miss Naomi has graciously agreed to teach us all about first aid today."

A beautiful curvy woman with rich, dark skin and the loveliest hair stepped up. She had a secretive grin on her face, like she was in on a joke no one else knew. "Just in case the son of a bitch you shoot next turns out to be your neighbor. Because that can happen, ladies. Now I've brought some supplies and I have a slide show. Let's get started."

Georgia took a seat next to Nell and tried to look like she was listening. But her mind was whirling with menu possibilities and how she would set up her party.

Friends. She was making friends, people who thought she was nice, who thought she was worthy.

Nell leaned over. "Do you really think I could find pretty shoes that don't harm the environment?"

Georgia was a little surprised when Nell actually reached out and grabbed her hand. Tears threatened. She'd been in damn LA so long, she'd forgotten how nice it was to hug and hold hands with friends and know that she would be accepted. "I promise, I will find them. I recently heard about a company that makes shoes out of recycled water bottles. We'll see if they're cute."

Naomi started to talk about exit wounds and CPR, but Georgia was making lists of appetizers and wines she needed to buy for her party.

Being with friends, helping them and becoming meaningful—that was everything she could hope for.

And if she couldn't find pretty shoes for Nell, she would make them herself. She was a Dawson, after all. And Dawsons persevered.

* * * *

Seth slapped a branch back and wished he'd switched into boots for this particular outing. "Are you sure you're not being paranoid?"

Logan followed the man in front of him, never looking back. "I know what I saw."

"Well, it wasn't an alien. They have ways to hide their presence in the daylight." Mel was leading this band of merry men. "Unless they're playing games with us."

Mel stopped as though the thought disturbed him.

"I don't think it's aliens." Seth felt a deep need to stop Mel before he started to talk about probes. Mel liked to get real in depth about probing, and he could go into gruesome detail. Apparently Mel had been in the thick of the alien wars for a long time, and being a warrior equaled anal probes. Seth had already decided not to get involved with aliens. Though he did intend to get involved with anal probes. Fuck. He so wanted to fuck Georgia's ass. He wanted to do it in front of a mirror so he could watch the way her eyes widened and her pupils dilated as he entered her. She was so gorgeous. So perfectly sexy. And those damn shoes killed him. She'd been wearing hot pink ridiculously high heels, and all he'd been able to think about was getting those heels around his neck and driving his cock inside.

"Where do you think Momma Marie took her?" Seth asked, trying to catch his breath. Trekking through a mountain at nine thousand plus feet wasn't something he was used to.

But Logan wasn't even breathing hard. He didn't show a single sign that his muscular body even noticed the stress. "I'm sure she took Georgia to her club meeting. They meet on every second Tuesday."

Mel turned, his rifle at his side. "That club keeps growing. I'm the speaker next month. I'm giving the ladies tips on how to take down alien species, but mainly I go for the pie. There's always such good pie there. Not quite as good as my Cassidy's pecan pie, but Lucy's chess comes close. Seth, is it true you're going to pay for alien DNA detection for the upcoming wedding?"

Logan snorted, putting his hand over his mouth to cover his laughter.

Stef Talbot was a son of a bitch. Bastard. Rat-fink motherfucker. He'd sold him out. Seth had talked to him yesterday, inviting Stef and his wife to the cabin sometime, discussing the upcoming wedding situation. Seth was taking about half of the Texas crowd while the rest would be staying at the Talbot estate. Seth didn't know Wolf Meyer, but he'd spent a lot of time talking to Leo Meyer on the phone and he'd sent Julian Lodge some hefty checks for Logan's therapy and club membership. And now he had to pay to keep Mel happy. He was going to kick Stef's ass. "Yep. Can't have aliens disrupting a wedding."

Mel took a seat on a rock. The forest was quiet all around them. "Cass is worried that her boys are marrying an alien. It would be just like an alien queen to come after those boys. They're prime mating material. Sweet boys, of course, but they do have all that alien DNA. And Shelley is averse to beets. Said she wouldn't allow a beet-filled wedding cake."

"We're not having beets at our wedding, dude," Logan said. And then he shook his head. "I mean Georgia is probably going to want something fancy when you marry her."

He'd been right the first time, but Seth was counting the flub as progress. The same way he was counting that damn *G* on Logan's chest. There was no way it stood for Green. That *G*, with its romantic curves, was all about their Georgia, and he wanted a matching one on his chest. Georgia could get a sweet *L* and *S* on that gorgeous curve right over her ass. They would be inked, linked together forever. That was what he wanted. "Georgia can pass the alien test. Aliens can't wear her heels."

Mel nodded. "I've heard that even the females have terrible arches. I wonder if Shelley wears heels. Cass would be much happier if she does. We'll have to see. But we still need monitors. They're making plans, I tell you."

Logan slid him a long look, his lips curling up. "They're always making plans. But I don't think this is an alien invasion we're dealing with. Come on. Let's keep moving. I have a meeting with Nate at one, and I'm on highway duty all afternoon. I get to write tickets to tourists."

He wouldn't have to write tickets to tourists if he would let Seth pay his damn tuition. It was stupid. It was stubborn. Seth had money. He wouldn't miss it even if Logan went to freaking Harvard. But Logan didn't want to hear it. He'd been like a dog with a bone ever since he'd walked out of his room this morning. He'd told Seth to come with him and then they'd spent a whole lot of time at the sheriff's office talking to the park rangers. And then they'd walked like five hundred miles to get to even more trees. The forest was beautiful, but he wasn't sure why they were here. Logan had said something about a light and glinting, and he'd sounded an awful lot like Mel, who was their guide.

Yep. Crazy Mel was their guide, but then he'd kind of, sort of been their guide before. Mel had been a master at taking young men under his wing and teaching them to kill aliens, protect themselves, and to view purely human pornography.

"Logan, come on, man. Why the hell am I up here?"

"Because Nate is in the cabin and Cam has a new baby." Logan kept striding up the steep incline. "And this has something to do with you."

"A glint in the atmosphere has something to do with me?"

Logan stopped and turned, frowning. "Nate is going to call us when he sees the glint off our binoculars. That's going to tell me where this guy was standing. Did you not listen to a thing I told the park rangers?"

He'd kind of been thinking about Georgia at the time. He'd been daydreaming about getting Georgia back in bed and prepping her for what he wanted. Both of them inside her, one in her ass and one in her pussy. Sweet, sweet double penetration. And then Logan had shoved a contract in front of him. He hated contracts. He really hated contracts that put boundaries on sex and love and life.

"Tell me again." He wasn't going to explain that he'd been flustered by that fucking contract.

Logan took a long breath. "I saw something up here earlier today. It was either a scoped rifle or a camera. I suppose it could have been someone's glasses, but the park rangers claim no one is up here right now. At least no one who has clearance. Did you see the footprints on the porch yesterday? They were still there this morning. I didn't make them."

"It rained a couple of days ago. We don't know how long that print has been there." It could have come from anywhere. The contractors had been working on the house right up until the day before they'd come here.

"It wasn't there when I got in the day before yesterday," Logan argued. "The whole place was pristinely clean."

"What was the print like?" Mel asked. He was carrying his ever-present rifle as he walked up the steep incline.

"Round toed. It was totally human unless aliens have started wearing sneakers. It was an asshole human. How much would reporters pay to get a look at your new place?" Logan directed the last question at Seth.

He shrugged. "Not much. Dude, it's not like I'm some celebrity. I'm more likely to be in *The Wall Street Journal* than a paparazzi rag. The *Journal* doesn't want pics of my house. They just want to run my stock into the ground."

But he'd been getting phone calls to his cell that didn't make much sense. He'd paid to have the number secret, and yet someone with an unknown number kept calling him. Maybe it was time to figure out what the hell was going on. He wasn't sure he would find the answers on a mountain on the other side of the river though.

"Someone is watching you," Logan said. "Or maybe me. Or, hell, maybe they're watching Georgia. Do you want to take a chance on that?"

Fuck. The idea that someone might be watching Georgia got his blood pumping. He raced to catch up. "Why would someone be watching Georgia?"

"Aliens are always looking for women to mate with." Mel didn't look back, just kept to his slow and steady climb. "Once they discovered they couldn't get any babies out of men, they started looking at our women."

He needed some of Mel's tonic if he was going to have that conversation. "Logan?"

Logan's shoulders moved up and down. "I don't know. I don't think it's about her, but I have to consider it. If someone's watching the house, they're watching Georgia."

"If it's a reporter, they're likely looking to see who I'm meeting with here. When they realize it's a vacation home, they'll go away," Seth explained.

Of course, he had to consider corporate espionage. There was always some bastard willing to sell him out for a fat paycheck. His processes were protected by about a thousand patents, but that didn't mean someone wouldn't pay to get a look at it. Or at any of the hundreds of projects he had going at any given time. Would they follow him out here?

It would be easy enough to find him. The property was in his name. His flight plan had been logged.

Had he once jogged through the mountains without a single problem? Because he had to stop and take a long breath.

He needed to get back into shape. He was perfectly healthy. He jogged five miles every single day, but it was on a treadmill. The mountains were different. The mountains didn't care that he could run like a mouse on a wheel.

Mel stopped. "I can see the place from here."

Logan picked up the binoculars he wore around his neck. "Yeah. This might be the right spot. I can definitely see the window from here. Nate, can you see me?"

He was talking on the walkie-talkie. The sheriff was watching out of the bedroom Logan had used last night.

Nate's reply came over the radio. "I don't see anything, man. Are you sure you're not being paranoid?"

Mel shook his head, giving Logan a pat on the shoulder. "Don't let them tell you that, son. You're only paranoid if they aren't really all out to get you, and we know they are."

Seth looked down and there was a line of tracks. Athletic shoes like the one on the porch. "I think this is the spot. Look."

Logan glanced down. "Damn. Tell me that's not the same shape as the one on our porch."

"Aliens don't wear sneakers," Mel explained. "Unless they're possessing human bodies. I've heard that's been happening a lot lately. I'm not so sure about Doc. I think they might have taken him over. It makes a person grumpy, having two people in one body."

From what Seth had heard, Doc Burke didn't need an alien possession to be grumpy. He did fine on his own. "Give me the binoculars. I want to try something."

Logan was taking a look around the area. He passed the binoculars before kneeling down. "Fucker smokes. I see two butts here. He hiked in from the road and was here for at least thirty minutes, unless he smokes fast. These are down to the filter."

Seth looked through the binoculars. He had to adjust them, but he could plainly see the cabin in all its glory. It rose from the lush riverfront. It was everything he'd dreamed of when he was a kid, right down to the woman who was living there. Before he'd gone into town with Logan, he'd moved all of Georgia's things into the master bedroom. She was right where she should be, and the idea of someone watching them had his heart racing.

"Do you see any other tracks, Mel?" Logan asked. "It looks like he hiked back out the same way he came in."

Seth could hear them moving around behind him, searching for clues, but he was focused on what this guy had been looking for. From this vantage point, he couldn't see into the master, but he could see the room Logan had taken over. He couldn't see inside. Perhaps at night he would be able to, but Logan said the man had been watching them this morning.

Seth turned the glasses slightly, and Henry walked across the lawn, moving from his small cabin to Seth's.

The walkie-talkie squawked and the sheriff's voice came over the radio. "There it was. I can see it. Wherever you have the binoculars pointed right now is where this guy was looking."

Logan started talking to Nate, but all Seth could see was Henry making his way across the lawn, the way he likely did ten times a day.

Was the person who stood here earlier watching the house or was he watching Henry?

Either way, Seth had to find out.

Chapter Twelve

Logan looked up from his desk. The day seemed to drag on though he'd only been at the office for the last two hours. Somehow time seemed to have slowed to a near stop. He had to admit to himself that he enjoyed certain parts of the job. He really did enjoy helping people, but the rest of it kind of sucked. How had he ever thought he would be able to work here for the next forty years?

But he was starting to think he couldn't work the dungeon at The Club forever either.

There was always college. He would be an older freshman, but lots of people took a gap year. He'd taken like eight.

There was the small problem of money, though.

Gemma stood up, slinging her enormous leather bag over her shoulder. "It's noon. I'm heading to lunch. Can I bring something back from Stella's for you? Cade's already there. He called to let me know that today is soufflé day. Apparently Hal is on a rampage and everyone has to be super quiet. They've made it into a game."

He shook his head. He wasn't hungry. He hadn't been all day. He was stuck and couldn't figure out how to fucking move. Since he'd returned home, it felt like a hundred paths had been laid out for him, and he couldn't take a single step down any of them. "Nah. I got a sandwich in the fridge."

Gemma's perfectly plucked brows formed a *V*. "Really? I didn't take you to be the kind of guy who made his own lunch. You seem like a grab-a-burger guy."

He had been. Except Georgia had made him a sandwich on his way out. Ham and Swiss with hot mustard and one tomato, and absolutely no disgusting lettuce. Exactly like he liked it. He'd seen her talking to his ma as she put the sandwich in a bag along with some chips and the cookies that had been miraculously saved. He said miraculously because he'd actually tried one and, holy shit, they were fantastic. But he wasn't about to tell Gemma Wells that his almost sub had taken the time to make his lunch and send him on his way with a thermos of coffee and a kiss on the cheek he'd pretended didn't mean anything. "I'm trying to cut back on the burgers."

"You know the sandwich would keep," Gemma pointed out. "Come on. Come meet my guys. They're curious about you. You're kind of a legend around these parts, as the locals would say."

Yes, he was a legend for getting his ass kicked and hard. "You go on and have fun. I'm going to keep watch here. Nate is dealing with a problem at the art gallery. Apparently Max and Rachel got into something on Main Street and then took it inside, and now they're locked in a closet. Nate's waiting on a locksmith, but Max keeps screaming something about how nice Rachel's new shoes are. It's a typical Bliss clusterfuck. Literally. I'll stay here. I don't want us to be shorthanded."

She frowned. "Come on. What's going to happen if you step away for lunch?"

Alien invasion? Bigfoot sighting? Assassins. Hell, they had it all in Bliss. He sent Gemma a pointed look.

She shrugged. "Fine. I'll be back in an hour or two."

She swept out of the room, and he was left alone to think about what his momma had said this morning. The idea of Marie Warner having problems with her heart damn near brought him to his knees. She was so strong, so solid. He'd thrown his father out there as a way of getting her off the scent. The truth was he didn't much think about the man who had donated half of his DNA. Momma Marie had been the one to throw baseballs with him. She'd been the one to teach him to fish and how to haul himself up and keep trying when he fell off a horse. He didn't need a man to have a father. He'd had two loving parents, and they'd been enough.

He was the problem. He wasn't trying. She'd been right about that. He'd found a safe place where he didn't ache all the time and he was willing to stay there. Georgia was forcing him to want more.

It wasn't only Georgia. Hell, Seth made him want more. That kid he'd thought had died so long ago was making a return appearance, like a turtle popping its head out of his shell. He'd reached for those dumb comic books not fifteen minutes ago, from curiosity at first, and then he'd started rereading the story and it was only Gemma walking in from the break room that made him shove that shit aside.

Being home after months of therapy with Leo was doing bad things to his defenses.

He hadn't thought about any of this when he was at The Club. He hadn't thought about his friends. He hadn't thought about Jamie and Hope and Noah. They hadn't been quite real when he'd been in Dallas. He hadn't been upset he'd missed their wedding then. Now he thought about the fact that Jamie Glen, the manwhore of Bliss County, had gotten married and he hadn't been around to rib the holy fuck out of him. He'd missed the bachelor party. It had been thrown by Max and Rye, but it should have been Logan. He was closer to them. Once.

He hadn't had to think about that in Dallas.

He hadn't thought about his mommas or how they were getting older, frailer. He hadn't had to consider that they worried about him, that he might cause stress between them. He hadn't worried that he was an irreplaceable cog in the family machine. He'd been single and on his own and thinking of no one but himself. He liked to laugh at the child he'd been, but at least that child had taken responsibility seriously. The adult he'd become seemed to just want to forget.

His eyes stole toward Nate's office. People weren't the only things he hadn't needed to think about. He hadn't thought about that day. Not consciously. Sometimes in Dallas, whole hours would go by before he remembered. Damn, but he remembered that door. He recalled every streak on the wood, every panel. Nate had left the door open.

It hadn't been that day. The door had been closed. He

remembered it vividly. They laid him out on the desk, arms and legs tied down, and he'd looked up and watched the door close. Every inch of the office beyond that disappeared was another mile into hell. When it had shut entirely, his world was changed forever.

Was his momma right? Was he allowing a few hours of pain to take away a lifetime of love and joy? How the hell did he fix it? He couldn't come back here full time. He couldn't be a deputy for the rest of his life, but did he want the half life he had in Dallas? Did he want his only connection to his friend and the woman he cared about to be through a stinking five-page contract that Leo had faxed over? It wasn't even a personalized contract. There were blank lines for the Dominants and submissive to place their name. Shouldn't they at least have a contract that had been written specifically for them?

Stef would be able to write it up, but he knew damn well he wasn't going to Stefan Talbot. Julian wouldn't write a contract for someone he had never met, never put through his rigorous tests and slightly intrusive questionnaires. He could practically see Georgia's face when Julian Lodge asked her about her feelings on having a cock shoved up her ass. He would have to get in between the big Dom and his sweet-faced, smart-mouthed sub or Armageddon would occur quickly.

His eyes strayed back to Nate's office, the door wide open, a gift basket of horrors. Oh, they could clean up the blood, get rid of the implements of his torture, but the room was still there. He could still feel that first breath of horror, hear the slap of flesh striking his. Funny. He'd heard it before he felt it, as though his brain couldn't process what his ears could for the barest of moments. He'd thought, just for a second, that it wouldn't be so bad because it didn't hurt. He could survive. He could make it through this.

And then his nerve endings had screamed to life.

He was taken out of his rotten memories by the sound of his cell pinging. Text.

People here really like their guns. I think I can make them prettier, though. Ordering a BeDazzler ASAP. Having fun with your momma, but what's up with all the tofu? Pick up meat for dinner. Will cook for sex. XOXO, Georgia

And then there was a flurry of emoticons that Georgia seemed to believe every message required. There were three hearts, one red, one blue, one green, and multiple kissy lips and a dolphin. He kind of thought she threw those in to be surreal, but he couldn't help but smile. He quickly sent her one back.

You're not bedazzling my gun, baby, but I will feed you some sausage tonight. You better be ready to open wide.

He stared down at the message. He sounded almost normal, like he was her boyfriend and they were playing. He deleted the message and set down the phone.

Damn it. He liked her. He'd said they couldn't be friends, but they already were. He liked her sassiness and wanted to text her all day. He wanted to take a picture of his dick and see if she was really as sassy as she liked to play at.

But she was with his momma and his momma had no compunction about looking on someone's phone. He could imagine the lecture he would get about sexting and keeping his junk in his pants.

And damn it, she wasn't his girlfriend. She hadn't even signed a contract yet.

The doors to the outer office opened, and he tensed briefly before forcing himself to relax. He wasn't some dumb kid anymore. He had his gun and he wasn't afraid to use it.

And then he was seriously thinking about using it because Alexei Markov walked through the inner doors, the big Russian pulling off his cap as he looked around. "Gemma? Sheriff?"

It would be simple, so easy to shoot the fucker and be done. He could have his pistol out in a second and it would all be over. Alexei had sent him to hell. It was only proper to return the favor.

And what would that solve? You wouldn't be killing the person who truly let you down. That man would still be walking and talking, but he would be in an orange jumpsuit, having brought shame down on everyone he loved.

Sometimes he hated his inner voice. It had started to take on Leo Meyer's deeply reasonable tone. His inner voice was right. Killing Alexei would solve nothing. Logan had his chance that night in Hell on Wheels, but he was always a coward. He'd proven that over and over again.

"Nate's not here and Gemma's gone to lunch. You'll have to come back later." Logan turned to his computer screen, flipping it on. There was always some sort of paperwork to do around the office. They all tried to avoid it like the plague, but sometimes it came in handy. It gave him something to focus on because despite the knowledge that killing Alexei wouldn't solve his problems, he also knew it would make him feel satisfied for a few minutes.

"You are back. This is good."

Logan didn't look up. "I'm filling in for Cam while he's on leave."

"Ah." The fucker didn't seem to be taking Logan's point. Out of the corner of his eye, he registered that Alexei moved toward him, hat in his hands. It was a knit cap, the kind a man wore all year long in the mountains because even spring and summer could be cold at the right time of day. Holly liked to knit. He had a cap from Holly. She'd given it to him for his birthday a couple of years back. It was in a box somewhere along with the rest of his life.

"This is good also. Laura is good mother. I think maybe I convince Holly to give it other shooting one day."

Holly already had a grown kid, but neither Caleb nor Alexei had kids of their own. And none of that fucking meant a thing to Logan. He finally brought his eyes up, his jaw hardening. "Is there something I can help you with, Markov?"

Alexei frowned, that playboy smile of his turning down. He was an intimidating height and bulk, but Logan matched him now. "You are still angry."

"I am nothing to you." It was the truth. Months of therapy had lessened his anger toward Holly. She couldn't help the fact that she had terrible taste in men, but he couldn't fucking stand Alexei.

"This is not true. You are meaningful to me. I think about you many times." Alexei sighed. "I am always saying the sorries in my head."

He could say sorry in that thick Russian accent twenty-four seven and it wouldn't make a difference. "But you would do it again."

The look on Markov's face told the tale. He was resolute. "And I say this, too. And if shoe was tied to your foot, I would expect the same from you. It is contract between men. We take the pain so the women can live. Can you honestly say that you would not place me in same situation were roles turned around? If it had been your mother?"

If it had been Georgia…

Georgia had been taken from him once, and that had been before he'd known what it was like to hold her and love her. He'd been willing to do damn near anything to get her back then. He'd felt powerless those hours he'd spent waiting for her brothers to figure out where she'd been taken. If he could have almost guaranteed her survival, what would he have been willing to give up?

Maybe it was time to have this out with Markov. Leo had wanted him to have this conversation months ago, but Logan had told him he was cool. He'd lied to Leo saying Alexei didn't bother him anymore. He wasn't fucking cool. "You knew what would happen to me. You knew I didn't have the information they wanted."

A deep sympathy came over Markov's face. "I did. I knew how much pain you be forcing to take. I am sorry. Words are harder when they are important. You understand?"

He was struggling with his English. Over the months he'd been here, he'd actually gotten much better, but now Alexei sounded like he'd gotten off the plane today. "You knew they would kill me."

His pitch-black hair shook. "No. I knew they would if I could not find way out of situation. This is something I know. But I also know that Luka like to play. He is sadist. He take his time."

"You asked me to trust you." He could still hear those words right before he'd been kicked in the gut and dragged away. Alexei Markov had sold him to his Russian mob cohorts to buy time to save his own ass.

Except Alexei could easily have saved himself by giving them all up. The mob boss had come for a painting, and Holly had known where it was. Then Jen had shown up and it had all gone to hell, and the only thing that kept those women from being raped and killed was the fact that they'd been too busy brutalizing one Logan Green.

"I know. And I think you will not trust anyone again. I think this break you, but I want to tell you that you do not have to stay broken, Logan. You can to be putting pieces back together. They may not fit as perfectly as once they did, but they can fit. I think I am broken when I lose my brother."

"The one that fucker Pushkin killed?" He knew a bit of Alexei's story. He hadn't been able to avoid it. His brother had been killed by the same mobster who ordered Logan's torture.

"Yes. Pushkin kill Mikhail because he will not pay securities and he tries to talk to others, to band them against the bosses. He was brave man, my brother. I was not so brave. I was angry. You are angry, too. I would hate to be seeing you lose all those years like I did."

"We're nothing alike." He didn't have anything in common with Alexei.

Alexei shook his head. "We both go through pain. We both chose wrong path. We are very much alike."

"I haven't chosen the same path as you, asshole," Logan shot back. "I'm not some criminal."

Alexei's voice went low. "Tell me you don't think about killing. Tell me you don't think about blood and how good it would feel on your hands. You think about killing me because I am one left behind. I am one you can focus on. Tell me how you would to kill me."

How many times had he thought about it? At first it had been Luka's face he'd seen in bloody revenge fantasies, but when Alexei had returned to Bliss and started his happy life, Logan had switched to dreams of him. It had been all right when it was likely that Alexei would go to prison. He could handle it. There was some punishment involved, but then he walked right back into town like a conquering hero. Yeah, Logan had thought about killing him more than once. "I would gut you. I would make you feel everything I felt and then some. I would love the look on your face when you realized what I was going to do to your…"

Fuck. He wasn't talking about that.

Alexei's voice went soft, like he was trying not to spook an easily scared animal away. "I know all of Luka's tricks. I worry he do these things to you. Are you…how to ask? Caleb will not talk about it. He say it is privacy issue. He will not tell me even when I beg to know because guilt eats at me. Are you still whole?"

Logan shot up, his whole body stiff with rage. He never talked about it. Never. Not even to Leo. Not to his moms. Only Caleb had to know because he'd been the one to deal with the aftermath. "You want to see it? You want to see if he cut my fucking cock off? Because he tried. He was going to do it. You fucking knew he would do it, didn't you? Guess what? Caleb is damn good at his job. I can still fuck all I like."

After he'd recovered and the swelling had gone down, that was exactly what he'd done. He'd fucked any woman who would let him climb on top of her. He'd done it to prove he was still a damn man. But the ability to screw a chick, he'd learned, didn't take away the pain.

Alexei held his hands up. "I am sorry. I am so glad to be hearing this. It is thing Luka did before he killed a man. I think he believe it made him strong. I knew it would take a while. And when Luka goes to kill you, this is when I take the chance and follow him in."

"Stef killed the bastard. Not you." Stef Talbot had snuck into the office through the outside window. He'd lain in wait and when the time was right, he'd taken Logan's tormenter out.

But Markov had been there, too. Just as he'd heard the shot from Stef's pistol, he'd seen Markov bring his gun to the back of Luka's head. Stef had simply been faster to pull the trigger.

Would he have sent Seth in? If the situation was the same and someone had to distract them, what would he have done? Would he have asked Seth to take that pain, to risk the loss of all that he was to save Georgia? To save his moms?

Logan slumped down, so weary he could barely breathe because he knew the answer.

Yes. He would send his best friend in knowing what could happen. He would do it because they did have a covenant between them that went far past the damn sterile contract on his desk. There was a promise, never spoken but always alive. A promise to put her first, to protect the people they loved. To kill or die so their family could go on. To build a future.

God, he was so angry with Seth for leaving him behind. He had thought it was all about the incident, but now he realized he was pissed that Seth hadn't been there. He was angry with Alexei for using him even when he knew he would do the same thing. He was angry with the world for changing so suddenly, for being safe one minute and deadly the next.

But most of all he was so damn tired of being angry.

Alexei stood in front of him, his face tight, a sheen of tears there. "Logan, from bottom of heart, I wish you well. You cannot forgive, but I am here to tell that this forgiveness I ask for is better for you. I am not asking for self. I know what it is to walk the world with bitter heart, but I came here and it make me realize that I was the problem. Me. The past is something that cannot to be changed, but self, this you control. And the past was not bad, not all. Just hours. Just days. I betray my brother by seeking revenge. I honor him by living life. I honor him by hoping for son to teach as he teach me."

He could still have kids. He could still make love. He could still have a life. Everything that had been wronged physically had been placed to rights. His body had healed. He'd followed every bit of advice Caleb had given him, trained and made himself stronger. He'd worked his ass off to make sure he wasn't a gangly weak kid anymore.

But Caleb hadn't been the only doctor to treat him.

"I would have done the same. You didn't have a choice. We were outgunned. If you hadn't given me up, all three of us would have died and then they would have started on the rest of the town." The words felt like they were in a foreign language, odd and alien on his tongue. But they were the truth.

But they weren't the whole truth. He wasn't ready to face that. Not yet.

One step at a time. Leo preached it. One step and then another until he would find himself walking and talking and feeling again. He'd worked so hard on his body and neglected his soul.

"This is more than I could hope. Logan Green, I need you to know that my Holly, my heart, she walks the earth because of you, because of your courage."

"Don't say that." Logan couldn't listen to anyone talk about him being brave. He'd been an idiot bumbling his way through life. A joke.

"You may not hear, but I say because it is true. You may never like me, but in my heart, in my soul, you are my brother," Alexei said with deep purpose. "Know that wherever you to go, whatever you to do, I am behind you. I will be there if you need me."

Logan nodded, the only motion he seemed capable of.

"Please to tell Sheriff I come by. I must sign paperwork for the class I teach." Alexei took a step back, his face more open than it had been before. Alexei seemed younger now, happier. "And if you ever want to come to house with your friends, know you are most welcome. Holly would love to see you. Caleb as well, though he will likely only growl your way."

Alexei put his hat back on his head and left, the station quiet again, but nothing could stop the voices pounding through Logan's head.

He could forgive Alexei. He could say the words and know the truth and one day, he might even be able to be friendly. He might be able to sit down to a meal with him and laugh and joke and enjoy time with Holly again. The three of them had survived something together. He could handle that. He might be able to walk into Nate's office and not see himself there.

He could forgive everyone involved but the most important person. For that, he would need to see someone else.

And he would need to be honest for once in his fucking life.

He picked up the phone because his honesty had started in one particular place, with one man. It only seemed fair to continue it. He dialed the number and the phone answered on the first ring.

"Hello?"

Logan took a long breath. It took courage to banish demons. He needed to find some. His hand strayed to the comic book on his desk. His younger self had played at being Superman, had found comfort in the stories. But he was only a man and had to take small steps. He'd held back in the beginning, so damn sure that his real secrets never needed to come out. He'd had people who wanted to help him, but he hadn't let them. "Hey, Leo. I need to tell you a story."

Leo Meyer's infinitely patient voice came over the line. "I'm here to listen."

Logan began again. This time, he began with the truth.

Chapter Thirteen

Georgia stepped inside the sheriff's department hoping she wasn't making a terrible mistake, but after the lovely morning she'd had, she felt powerful. She'd made friends outside her normal circle. Considering the fact that the friends inside her normal circles were well-dressed snakes who already used Botox even before their thirties, she was thinking that Nell, the vegan who needed the tiniest bit of lip gloss, Lucy, who seemed to be pining after some mountain man everyone else was scared of, and Naomi, who sat back and enjoyed the chaos, seemed like the coolest friends ever.

It didn't matter that Naomi was older than she was. She'd gotten along great with the nurse. They'd chatted after the meeting and talked about Chicago, where Naomi was from. Lucy had joined them and asked all sorts of questions about big cities, and Nell had served them vegan muffins, which weren't as good as real muffins, but she'd been able to eat them once Momma Marie had given her a mug of tea with a kicker of vodka. Apparently, Momma Marie knew what it took to get through a vegan meal.

Georgia was starting to adore Momma Marie.

She'd conquered Bliss's social scene, and now she wanted to conquer Logan Green.

Maybe not conquer, but getting through a meal without shouting at each other would be a good start. She owed it to Seth.

No. She wasn't going to lie to herself. Women with the strength to shoot a son of a bitch were honest with themselves and others. It was in the bylaws of the club she'd recently been claimed as an ancillary member of. When she actually shot her own son of a bitch, she would be a full member. Momma Marie had promised shotgun lessons as soon as possible.

She wasn't going to lie. She was doing this for herself. Because she wanted them both.

She walked in and was struck by how quiet the place was.

"Georgia?"

She nearly started, Logan's voice seeming to come out of nowhere. He was sitting at a desk to her left, his face dark, his eyes fixed on her. He looked like a man who hadn't slept much the night before. Maybe this wasn't such a good idea. "Hey."

He flicked his eyes to a place to her right and kept them there. "Go away. I'm not in a good mood."

Immediately her back came up. The instinct to tell him where to shove his mood was right there, begging to be let out. She'd behaved perfectly. She'd spent time with his mom. She'd fit in. She'd done everything right, and he wanted to reject her? Well, she could make that painful.

And she stopped because something was obviously wrong. This wasn't about her, and it would be childish to make it about her. This was about Logan. "Maybe I can help."

His brows came together as though that had been the last thing he'd expected her to say. "I'm not trying to be a bastard. I…just had to admit something to a man I admire very much. I need to be alone for a while."

That was part of his problem. "You're always alone. Even when you're with me and Seth, you're still alone. Have you thought that maybe being alone isn't working for you?"

"Don't push me, Georgia."

Tears sprang to her eyes, but she wasn't going to shed them. She needed to make him understand. "I'm not trying to push you. I'm trying to help you. I'm trying to mean something to you."

His fingers drummed along the desk. "Do you know what I'm going to ask you to do tonight? I'm going to ask you to sign a contract. Before I touch you, you'll have to sign a contract that gives me use of your body. I have to pencil your name in because it's a standard contract I sign with all subs."

Did he think she hadn't grilled her brothers about him? She knew exactly how obnoxious to be for Chase to break down and tell her what she wanted to know. She simply kept asking the question for fifteen minutes in a place where he couldn't escape her and, voila, she knew everything there was to know about Master Logan. "How many?"

Those brows were now a near perfect *V* over his deep green eyes. "What?"

She tapped her foot against the floor, but sneakers didn't have the same effect her heels normally had. "How many contracts have you signed? You say it's standard and you're the big bad Dom, so how many contracts? Kitten's doesn't count because there was no sex involved. Give me this massive number, Logan Green, so I'll know how little I mean to you."

He stared at her for a minute, and she knew they both knew the truth. He hadn't signed a contract before. Oh, he'd slept with submissives. As far as she knew, he'd slept with half the women in Dallas and an even larger percentage of Southern Colorado's female population, but he'd never signed that sacred contract with one of them.

And she wasn't stupid. That *G* on his chest had nothing to do with his last name. He was a foolish male who didn't want to admit he'd gotten caught in her clumsily placed trap, but he was in it and she wasn't about to let him go.

She wasn't letting either of them go.

Logan leaned forward, obviously still looking for a way out. "The amount of contracts I've signed means nothing. You're not at all disturbed that I'm asking you to sign a contract that gives me rights to your body? You're willing to allow our relationship to be limited to what's on a piece of paper? In a standardized contract?"

He needed to get over that contract thing. It was something he hid behind. She grabbed a pen off the big desk beside her and strode to Logan's workspace. Without a second thought, she took the contract, flipped to the back page, and signed her name. "There. Now you can relax."

His jaw dropped open. "You didn't even read it."

She didn't need to. She knew this man. It was funny. Seth had talked about his best friend for weeks before coming to Colorado and how brave and loyal he was, and all she'd been able to think about was that whoever that guy was, he had nothing on Logan Green. God, she'd made him crazy and he'd still come running for her when she'd been in danger. He'd still pulled her out of the fire and made sure she was safe. If Seth was her Prince Charming, then Logan was her Knight in Shining Armor. His armor was a little rusty though. "I trust you. Isn't that what all of this D/s stuff is about? Trust and communication?"

He frowned, looking down at the contract. "I don't know how we can communicate if you don't even read the thing. You need a keeper."

She had to admit, he kind of rocked the khaki uniform. She'd never found the color sexy before, but Logan was hot in everything. He was so big and gorgeous that it was hard to remember how vulnerable he was. "You need the contract. I know what it says. It talks about rights and obligations and sex and weird freaky sex and it makes you feel safe, so I signed it. As to me needing a keeper, I kind of thought the contract gave me one."

His jaw firmed as he looked down at the contract. "I haven't signed anything yet, and I don't know if I should."

His voice was so quiet, her heart nearly skipped a beat. Her first instinct was to panic, but she stilled the impulse. He needed her. She could see that plainly. And she could definitely see that if she wanted a shot with these two amazing men, she needed to grow up. She put her hand over his. "What scares you about it?"

She was surprised when he didn't move away from her. He was still, but he didn't move. "You don't know everything about me."

She knew all the important stuff. She knew he had a big heart and he was stubborn as hell and he was a hero. Even when he'd been a kid, he'd been a hero. Seth had told her a story about how Logan had saved him from a man who'd held a gun to his head years before. Logan hadn't flinched, even as an untested teen. But he seemed to have something he needed to say. "You could tell me."

He shook his head. “I can’t. Not yet.”

Patience wasn’t usually her thing, but since she’d come to Bliss, a lot of things had been changing. When she thought about it, it wasn’t the trip to Bliss that had started her change. That had begun the minute she’d met Logan Green. Without meeting Logan, she never would have been ready for Seth. She would have been a blustery brat throwing up every bit of armor she had to protect herself from rejection. Logan had softened her up, and Seth had delivered the deathblow to her childish persona. “You don’t have to tell me everything, only what you want to.”

Logan stood up. “I don’t want to talk about any of it. I want it to go away. I want to wake up and find out that the last two years were a bad dream.”

She leaned into him. She knew he’d been through something bad. Chase had said Logan had gotten his ass kicked. Ben had called it torture. Georgia had been reading about Dominance and submission, and despite her attempts to look like she couldn’t care less, she knew one of the things in that contract she hadn’t read would be about comfort. She’d read the contract Nat had signed. The Dominant owed the submissive protection and comfort. Maybe that was all one-way in the contract, but there was something implied underneath, the way it was in a marriage. The man could be all stalwart and stuff, but deep down, it went both ways. If she’d become Logan Green’s sub, then she wanted to comfort her Dom. She slowly slid her arms around his lean waist and rested her head against his chest.

It took him a moment, but his arms came up and circled her, holding her more tenderly than she could remember. He’d made love to her before, but this was something even sweeter. This was kindness and caring.

“I think I might be broken inside.” He whispered the words. “I don’t know that I’m good for you. I’ve been in therapy for months and earlier I called my shrink and had to tell him I’d been lying about a whole bunch of stuff. I thought I was fine. I really did, but I’m not, and I don’t know that I should put you through that.”

“Do you care about me?” She tilted her head up, loving the strong line of his jaw and that hint of a beard that never seemed to go away no matter how often he shaved. After the meeting had broken up, his other mom had come in and talked with everyone. Teeny had come armed with some photo albums. She had shown Georgia pictures of Logan as a child, and it had been hard to equate that sweet-faced, gangly kid with the rough man she loved.

"I shouldn't."

"Logan, answer the question."

His lips turned down in a frown, and his eyes got steely.

"Please," she tried and snuggled closer. "Sir."

He sighed, the frown fading. "God, you're a brat. I'm crazy about you, and you know it. You also know I've never signed a contract before and, you're right, Kitten doesn't count. She's the only person I've ever met who's more fucked up than me."

Georgia shook her head. "Oh, no, I think you passed her, Sir. The last time I saw her she was almost normal."

He smacked her ass. "Brat." His cheek came to rest against her hair. "But you're right because at least Kitten will talk about what happened to her. God, she can talk. Like forever. I know more about Kitten's cage and her upkeep than I ever hoped to know."

"So you should talk to me. If you care about me, then I want in. You're not dragging me down. You're giving me the chance to lift you up. I want that chance. I know you think I'm superficial, but I don't want to be. I want to mean something special to you."

"You are special." His hand found her hair, his fingers tangling in it.

"Then talk to me. I'll tell you about my craptastic childhood and you can tell me all the bad things. If you like, we can call Seth and make it a drinking game. We're both kids with crappy parents. Seth and I will get drunk off our butts really fast."

A slow smile slid across his face, and her heart lit up. She'd put that smile there. "Yeah, Seth's dad was pretty terrible, and his mom wasn't any better."

"My mom was a stripper who only married my dad because she got pregnant, and then she took him for everything she could and ran off with a European hustler named Reynaldo. I haven't seen or heard from her in fifteen years."

He hissed a little, a grimace on his face. "Yikes. I can't help you with the 'bad parent Olympics.' I kind of lucked out. I mean, my dad was psychotic crazy, but Momma Marie took care of him."

"I love your momma. I love Teeny, too, but Marie is all shades of awesome."

A laugh shook through him, and she could feel his interest rising. His erection was right there against her belly. Without her heels, she barely made it to the middle of his chest. He was so big and strong, he made her feel downright petite. "I would not have guessed you would get along with my scariest mom, but I shouldn't be surprised. Seth was worried, but I knew you would hold your own."

His hips were moving now. She didn't think he was even aware of it, but he was rubbing his erection against her, and all of her hormones were singing. Her skin flushed, nipples peaking to life, pussy softening right up. And it was okay because Seth was cool with it. Hell, Seth would be thrilled. "I like it here. I wouldn't have told you I would be all nature girl, but here I am. Well, I could do without the moose. And the like nature sounds and stuff, but it's pretty."

He tilted her head up. "Oh, wait until you see the bears, baby. And don't forget all the deer."

Bears? She was pretty sure she didn't want to meet any bears, but a few pretty deer would be nice. "Deer are sweet. Like Bambi."

He snorted. "Yeah, darlin', sweet things. Baby, you don't know much about nature. Those sweet deer will eat a dead body. Actually, they'll eat a live one if it's not moving too much."

"Ewww. That's horrible." And hopefully not true.

"Just about any animal will eat you if you let them." His smile faded and his eyes trailed back to that spot he'd been staring at before.

She turned her head slightly. "What is it, Logan?"

He let her go, taking a step back before sitting down in his chair. He was quiet for a long moment, and she missed their intimacy. "Two years ago, I was working right here. We had one overnight prisoner. He was a Russian mobster, and his boss came for him. Nate was working the Winter Festival so he wasn't in the station house. It was me and Holly and Alexei. You have to understand that Alexei had infiltrated the mob in order to kill the boss. Pushkin had killed his brother, you see. Anyway, when they came for him, we were outnumbered and outgunned, and Alexei needed to buy some time and there was only one way for him to do that. He told Pushkin that I had the information he needed."

She sort of knew the story, but hearing it come out of Logan's mouth in flat, unemotional tones made her stomach turn over. "They beat you up, didn't they?"

"Oh, baby, that is a term you use for a bar brawl. This was so much more. This was an artist at work. A brutal artist, but a master all the same. He kept bringing me right to the edge of death, right where I was certain it would be over and I would be free, and then I would realize there was no freedom. There was only more pain and more loss. He took me into that office right behind you and he showed me how weak I am."

She didn't like the way he was talking. Like he was still in the moment, a piece of him trapped there forever, a sort of purgatory like that never-ending poem she'd been forced to read in college. "Logan, you're not weak."

"You don't know everything. I don't know that I want you to know everything. I only know that I have a lot of trouble being in this place. I used to love it here. I know that sounds stupid, but this job was the first time I felt like I was an adult. It was the first time I was on my own, even though I went home at night. I loved walking in here because I felt like a man. Now I hate it. This is my hometown, and I can't stand being here because of that office."

She looked back. It was a totally innocent-looking office, just a wooden door with an opaque glass inlay that announced Sheriff Nathan Wright worked in there. The door was slightly open, and she could see a bank of bookshelves and the start of a desk. "Is that where it happened?"

He nodded. "They took me in there and worked me over."

And he couldn't get it out of his head. She could see that plainly. Seth had once told her she was his business muse. It was a silly thing to say, but she'd loved the title. Muse. A muse inspired creativity and pushed an artist forward. Logan needed a push. What if he needed a muse, too? She had a stupid plan. It was so dumb, and it might work if she was willing to open herself up to complete and humiliating rejection, but then sometimes the muse had to take a chance.

She kicked off the sneakers she'd been wearing.

"What are you doing?" Logan asked, his eyes widening as though he expected her to do something totally terrible.

"When I was a kid, I ended up getting stuck in my closet while my mom and her boy toy played around all over the house. My dad was gone and my brothers were in school, and the whole thing scared the crap out of me. By the time Dare found me, I was shaking and I wouldn't go back in my own closet for weeks. It was a pain in my nanny's ass because I wouldn't dress myself or even pick up my own shoes."

"Georgia, this is not the same. Are you taking your shirt off?"

She was. She unlaced the top of her blouse and slipped it off. She was lucky she'd selected a halfway pretty bra. It was pink and pushed her boobs up, and Logan suddenly wasn't staring at the sheriff's office door. Yes. This could work.

"Let me finish my story." She started working on her jeans, praying no one needed justice or saving for a while. "So Win finally decided he'd had enough and he came up with a plan. He threw an ice cream party in my closet. I loved chocolate ice cream and I never got any because my mom didn't like fat kids, but she was scared of Win. He was a formidable teenager. He and Ben and Chase and Mark and Dare were eating ice cream in my closet one day, and they wouldn't give me any until I came in. So I got mad and I threw a fit, but they were already good at ignoring me when they needed to. And finally I went in and I sat on Win's lap and I had a chocolate ice cream sundae with pink sprinkles and three cherries. Best ice cream I ever had, and my brothers played with me all afternoon. We had a tea party. You should have seen them, big brawny kids playing with dolls. And I could go in my closet again because I didn't hear my mother screaming. I heard my brothers laughing, and I tasted chocolate ice cream." She pushed her jeans off her hips and tossed them Logan's way. She was down to cotton pink panties and her bra. She knew she was big, but Logan hadn't liked her Spanx, so here she was in her glory. "I'm your chocolate ice cream, Logan. Come and take a bite."

She turned and walked into the sheriff's office and wondered if she could get arrested for being naked in here. Actually, now that she thought about it, she should be damn glad the office was unoccupied. She hadn't been thinking. Oh, god, she was nearly naked in a law officer's inner sanctum. She was going to get thrown in jail. She was going to get laughed out of town.

What was she doing? Chocolate ice cream sex. That was what she was trying to do, but it was dumb. Logan was right. They weren't the same thing at all. She took a deep breath and turned, ready to run, but a big body blocked her way.

He stood in the doorway, his eyes hard and his hand twitching, but he closed the door and locked it behind him. "Take off the rest. I want to see what you're offering me."

She took off the bra and shoved the panties aside because he should know what she was offering him.

Absolutely everything she had.

* * * *

Logan let his back rest against the door as he watched Georgia undress, her hands pushing the pink cotton panties down her curvy legs. He was glad she wasn't wearing that same torture device she'd had on the night before. She didn't need it. She was gorgeous the way she was. She was so fuckable, his dick actually hurt as he looked at her. He could feel his cockhead already weeping because now he didn't have to guess at what it would feel like to slide inside Georgia Dawson. He knew, and it was heavenly.

And he still didn't want to be inside this office.

She started to move toward him. She wasn't as confident as she wanted him to believe. He could see it in the tightness of her mouth and the set of her shoulders. Her smile, usually vibrant and generous, was strained. He was only now starting to understand her, to see past his own shit and get to know what made her tick. She was Hurricane Georgia, an outrageous brat, but she was also a woman who had reached out to Kitten and been a friend. And now she was scared she wouldn't be enough for him so he couldn't walk out of this damn office, no matter how much he wanted to.

Georgia needed him, and she'd signed a contract. She didn't know it yet, but he'd scrawled his name on the line above hers before walking in here. She was his by right of contract, and that meant he owed her. She could be quite fragile at times, and he couldn't break her again.

She wanted to learn D/s? He would concentrate on that and not what had happened to him here. Surely he could do that. Nate's office was the biggest in the building and had its own bathroom, complete with a shower. Bliss County was a small organization with few people on staff. They often worked overnights. Logan himself had slept on the cots in the two cells outside many times before…yeah, he was going there again.

"Knees, Georgia. I don't doubt that you understand what I mean by that." She seemed to have been studying up on the subject.

And apparently, practicing. She fell to her knees before him with the grace of long practice. Her golden head dipped forward, eyes on the floor in front of her. She placed her hands on her thighs, palms up, and spread her knees wide. He didn't have to correct an inch of her form. When Georgia decided to do something, she went all out. He'd learned that she might be lackadaisical in most parts of her life, but when she decided something was important, she was all in.

"Natalie?" He suspected her sister-in-law had been the one to show her the ropes.

"And Kitten, but only for a few days before I left for New York." She kept her head down as she replied.

"Eyes up." He was satisfied that she obeyed immediately and that going into submissive mode didn't take the light out of her eyes. He'd found some subs simply enjoyed giving up control, and submission was like their drug of choice. The minute they found sub space, they zoned out, merely following orders, but staying someplace inside their head where he couldn't touch them. Kitten had been very much like that, but he wanted more. He wanted Georgia's fire. He wanted connection and a flow of emotion from him to her. And he totally wanted a blow job. Seth had gotten a blow job, but none for him. "Very carefully, take my cock out."

There it was. A playful light hit those baby blues of hers, and she immediately went about tackling his belt. Her perfectly manicured fingers worked the belt and then the fly of his pants. She unwrapped him like she was carefully unwrapping a gift and didn't want to mess up the paper. She pushed the front of his slacks aside.

His cock was desperate. Already thick and hard, he could feel himself pulse as she started to peel his boxers off his hips. He looked to the side and caught sight of Nate's stapler.

And his erection dissolved like a pile of sugar in a rainstorm.

"Sir?"

Fuck. He took a step back and thought about running, but she was looking up at him and she deserved the truth. And maybe she was right. Maybe it was long past time to try to reclaim this space. Leo had told him to talk, that keeping it all inside, hiding it, made the whole episode seem like something dirty when he was the innocent one. "Do you really want to know? It's not pretty."

He was back against the door, his fly open and his heart racing. *Let her say no. Please.* If she backed away, then he could, too.

She got to her feet and without a hint of self-consciousness, wrapped that gorgeous body around him, putting her head right against his chest. "I want to know everything, Logan. Sir."

He let his hands wind around her. He'd been able to send her away once, but he wasn't sure he could survive it again. If he wasn't going to let her go, then he had some serious work to do, and it started with talking about what had happened in this room. "The stapler bugs me. I want to throw it out, but I can't tell Nate why."

"Did they hurt you with it?"

"He, Luka, the man who tortured me, thought it was funny to use it on me. He would ask me a question and if I didn't answer it properly, he would shove a couple of staples into me. He started on my chest and worked his way down." The words were difficult to even speak. They felt dumb in his mouth. He'd kept them inside for so long, and now he was telling the story twice in one day. "It sounds like such a little thing, doesn't it? I know some subs who like that spark of pain. It's called needle play."

"This wasn't play. And they work up to it and their Doms are careful. This wasn't supposed to be fun, and don't make light of the pain. I can't imagine it."

"Over and over, he did it. I think when Caleb was done he'd pulled over a hundred staples out of me, and he pulled fifty alone off my cock." There, he'd said it. God, he hated to say it. Leo told him it wasn't something to be ashamed of, but shame was welling up inside him. He'd been laid out and bare, his most private parts on display for rough use and brutality.

"Logan." She breathed out his name, and her hand found his chest. She pushed away, her eyes trailing down. "What did he do to you?"

The question was asked with a tight jaw, her voice shaking, and not with fear. She was angry. Volcanically angry, and Georgia's rage had the opposite effect on him. It calmed him. She was ready to fight, to avenge him when he outweighed her by a hundred pounds of muscle. He pulled her back, a sigh of peace rushing through him. She wasn't disgusted. She wasn't pitying him. She wanted to kill the son of a bitch who had hurt him.

"He's dead, baby. You can't take him out. And I survived." He'd survived. He was alive. He had a chance to make things better. It settled on him. She wasn't pushing him away because of his weakness. Not yet, anyway. "Now let me finish."

She laid her head back on his chest. "All right. But I would kill the bastard if he was still alive."

He had no doubt. She was fierce when she wanted to be. Somehow the words were easier now. "He started out by beating the living shit out of me, but that was only the warm-up. Then came the stapler incident. God, I hated him touching me. He had his hand on me and I thought he was going to rape me. I wanted to die. I really did. I wanted to die, but I couldn't. I got hard. That felt like a betrayal."

"You couldn't help it. It's a biological response."

"That's what Caleb told me, and Leo told me, but at the time, it felt like I was aiding in my own torture." He leaned over and let the smell of her hair wash over him, so different than the smell of sweat and blood. Georgia smelled clean and sweet, like strawberries. And her skin was touching his, a velvety caress to take the place of beefy hands smacking him. He could talk about it because for once he wasn't back there. She was his anchor. "Do you know why I don't have any scars on my cock?"

She nuzzled against his chest. "Why? I wondered because I've seen it up close, and it's perfectly beautiful."

"You're beautiful." And his cock was engaged again. How could he expect it to lie still when she was so close? Even here, in this room where he'd lost so much, he couldn't ignore her. She was right. She was stronger than the memories of this room because all of the sudden, he didn't see himself laid out on the desk. He saw her spread and waiting for his pleasure. When he looked at that desk, he would always see Georgia—her golden body and soft soul—waiting for him.

He picked her up, gripping the globes of her ass in his palms.

"Logan!" Georgia shouted, her eyes widening in surprise.

"I'll tell you the rest, but I'll do it while I touch you. Lie down on the desk." He ran a hand across the top, sending everything to the floor with a crash.

He set her right there, right where he'd been forced to survive. Her hair spread out across the dark wood. He palmed a breast, loving the way her nipples peaked under his hand. She was ridiculously responsive, as though she'd been made for him.

And Seth. But Seth wasn't here. A sliver of guilt pulsed through him. She was supposed to belong to Seth, but he pushed that thought aside. She'd been *his* first. She wanted him and Seth wanted them all to be together.

"Tell me why you don't have scars." Georgia bit her lip as though she was trying not to cry out, and he started to play with her nipples.

He gave one a twist and loved how she wriggled on the desk. It gave him the perfect opportunity to discipline her. He opened the big drawer where he knew Nate kept supplies. He pulled out two binder clips, twisting the silver handles back and forcing them open, bending them slightly. He couldn't use them as they were. They would be too tight. He wanted light pressure, not real pain. Just a bite to let his sub know she should stay in line or there would be some consequences.

"No moving, baby. You're here for my pleasure." He leaned over and let his tongue find her breast. Her skin tasted sweet and clean as he sucked her nipple into his mouth and let his teeth bite down lightly. He played for a minute before allowing the berry to pop out of his mouth. With a quick turn of his hand, he placed the binder clip on her. He moved to the other nipple and gave it the same treatment and then stepped back. He was perfectly satisfied they wouldn't cause damage, but she looked awfully cute in bondage, even off-the-fly, office-supply, perverted bondage.

And he'd spied something else in Nate's desk. His boss liked to complain about people having sex in his office, but he obviously got plenty here himself since he had a tube of lube and a box of condoms stashed right next to his pencils and yellow legal pads. Logan knew damn well which items got used most often. Nate never took notes.

But first, he had to finish the story. "Stay still. You were right. This is calming me down. I'm not even tempted to haul ass out of here anymore. I like it here, but that day was rough on me. I still feel it in my bones."

"But at least you're talking about it now. You have to know that I love your scars. They mean that you're alive."

He shrugged out of his shirt, his fingers finding the circular scars there. "The bastard smoked. He burned me. That was some serious pain. Sit up. I want some therapy." She'd started this, so she could handle what he needed. He helped her sit up, arranging her legs so he was in between them. "Kiss them, baby. You say they don't bother you, but they bother me."

She didn't hesitate. She leaned forward and put her mouth right over the scar, her lips pressing to his skin.

This was what he needed. He didn't need to walk the dungeon, finding comfort in every sub there. He needed one sub. The right sub. The one who could make things bright again. His Georgia.

She kissed the burn scars across his chest, taking her time with each, her fingertips tracing the lines as though memorizing each one before she placed her lips over them—a benediction. With each kiss, each caress, he felt lighter, younger than before.

He touched the small scar on the left side of his jaw. "He smacked me with the landline here when I told him to fuck off."

"Of course you did." She gently pulled his head down and kissed him there. "How about this?"

She touched his left shoulder. He couldn't help but smile. "That one I came by honestly. I fell off my bike when I was ten. But you can kiss me there, too."

She nuzzled against his shoulder.

He pushed at the waist of his pants, shoving them and his boxers aside. "I need you to touch me."

She didn't need an explanation it seemed. She simply reached down, and her palm encased his cock in soft heat. Logan groaned at the feel. "Tell me what happened."

"He hurt me. He got me hard and then stapled notes to my cock. He wrote messages to me. Said I was weak. I was pathetic. I was worth nothing. And then he laughed as he said I wouldn't be able to forget because they were on my dick."

"Logan."

"Don't stop, G. I need you." He moaned as her hand tightened. "I wasn't circumcised at the time. That came later. It saved me, I think, because Luka got bored and took a knife to my cock. He told me he would cut it off, but he only tore up the foreskin before he got called away. He tucked me back into my pants. He didn't want anyone to think he was queer. The asshole. I knew what he was going to do when he came back. But Stef was there."

Georgia hopped off the desk and got to her knees. "I'm so glad he was there. Logan, I don't think any less of you because of what happened. I think more of you because you survived."

She leaned forward and started pressing kisses on his cock. She started at the head, her lips touching him, and then he was the one who wanted to whimper and wail. It was maddening, her slow, methodical work. She pressed chaste kisses all along his straining cock. He clenched his fists at his sides, forcing himself to stay still. She didn't know everything about that day. There were things he couldn't admit even to her, but they didn't matter right now. Right now he was exorcising demons with the only woman he would ever love. He knew it deep down. Georgia was the one. She was the only one for him.

"He didn't actually touch my balls, but they were very scared." Was that him? Was he fucking joking about it?

His eyes nearly crossed as she gently pushed his cock up and laid her mouth on his balls. He sounded like he used to. Everything had been fair game when he was younger. He'd laughed at himself, been open to everything.

He couldn't be that kid again, but maybe he could find a piece of himself he'd thought he'd lost.

"Suck me, Georgia. I want to feel your mouth on me." He tangled his fingers in her hair, pulling her toward him.

She drew him inside, her lips on his cockhead. He hissed when her tongue came out, darting all around his head.

"Did you make Seth crazy this morning? Is this what you did to him, you little witch?"

He caught the hint of a smile on her face. "You listened in, Sir?"

He'd wanted to join them, but they seemed so far away. What a difference one day could make. "I heard you sucking his cock. You think you owe him less than me?"

"No, Sir. I wouldn't dream of it." She leaned back over again and this time she started to properly eat his cock, sucking him inside. She gripped his dick, stroking the stalk while she suckled the head.

So hot. So fucking good. This was what he'd been missing all his life. Sex had been good before. It had been fun and light, totally casual. He'd enjoyed it, but now he craved it, and it wasn't the sex he longed for. It was her. He wanted to be inside Georgia Ophelia Dawson, with her bratty mouth and soft heart. He'd trained to be a Dom, but he only wanted to be her Dom.

He watched as his cock disappeared into her mouth, her lips opening wide to take him deep. Heat scorched him, lighting him up from the inside. Her tongue whirled, caressing every inch of his dick, and he nearly exploded when she started to hum. It wasn't a song, merely a low vibration from the back of her throat that tingled along his cock. Her blonde head moved in perfect harmony with her hand. Over and over again, she sucked him inside, taking a bit more each time. If he let her, he would soon hit the back of her throat, and there would be no going back from that. He would come, giving her every ounce of semen he had, filling her belly.

That wasn't what he wanted to fill. Soon, he would do that. He would wake her up in the middle of the night and settle her on top of him, her mouth to his cock, his mouth to her pussy, and they would lick and suck and eat until they were both full and fell back to sleep perfectly satisfied. He would do it so she knew that he always wanted her. He would take her anytime, anyplace, because she was his.

But this time, he wanted her pussy. He needed to be inside her, connected by their bodies as much as he felt connected to her soul. He tugged on her hair, pulling back, his cock protesting the whole time.

"Am I not doing it right?"

It was so easy to forget how vulnerable she could be. She put on that tough-girl, dumb-blonde act as a way to deflect her fear. It was so simple when he thought about it. Before training with Leo and Wolf and Julian, he would have scratched his head and never wondered why she acted out. He would have assumed she was a little crazy, but now he saw it for what it was. She was scared.

He didn't want her scared. Not ever. He forced her head up, staring down at her. "You are the best I've ever had, Georgia Dawson. You're the only one I want, but I'm not ready for this to end. So obey me now. Get up on the desk."

She hopped up, an eager smile on her face. She seemed so much more open than before. Even last night there had been a tightness on her face, but she seemed sure of him now, sure that he wouldn't reject her, sure that he was going to satisfy her.

He'd done that. He'd made her feel safe. Loved. God, she was so fucking loved.

He got to his knees and pulled on Georgia's ankles, dragging her down the desk so he could do what he wanted to do. "Spread your legs. I want to look at it."

Her pussy. It was really his pussy when he thought about it. She'd signed the contract, so he owned her pussy. It was the prettiest pussy he'd ever seen, with pouty pink lips and that pearl that was the button he liked to push to send her into the stratosphere. Nothing he'd done in his whole life was as satisfying as being the man who made Georgia scream.

"You're making me crazy."

He inhaled her, letting the scent of her arousal coat his senses. "You're the one who started this. Remember. You said you were my ice cream. I want a nice long lick."

He gave in to temptation and let his tongue have its way. He devoured her, settling in and letting all the bad shit fly away.

He licked and sucked and enjoyed her, finally giving way to his impulses. Even the night before, he'd held back because she hadn't truly been his. She'd been Seth's and Seth had generously allowed him to join them, but now…now it was all different. Now he was pretty fucking sure he belonged to her. He was certain he would never love anyone the way he loved her. He had no idea what would happen tomorrow. He was a small-town deputy with very few prospects, and she was a woman who deserved everything money could buy. He wasn't sure how they would work it out, but none of that mattered now. All that mattered was being with her, replacing the bad memories with the good ones.

They would work it out. They had to because he was damn sure he couldn't live without her. "My sub."

He growled the words against her flesh.

And felt her hands in his hair, pulling him up. Her face was flushed, her eyes dark with need, but there was a stubborn set to her jaw, like she knew he wouldn't like what she was about to say, but she was going to say it anyway. "Not just your sub. I love you, Logan. I want to be your woman. I want to be yours."

Oh, she was supposed to be still, but she wanted to make demands? He was so going to spank her for that, but not now. No. Now he was going to give her what she wanted because he fucking wanted it, too. She loved him. Georgia loved him. He wasn't sure what he'd done to deserve it, but he wasn't about to turn that down. He got up, shoving his body off the floor. He could still taste her on his lips, smell her arousal, a spicy, bold scent like Georgia herself. He shoved his pants down and freed his cock. He reached for the condoms and started to roll one on. "Say it again."

She didn't hesitate. "I want to be yours."

"You are mine. You've been mine from the minute I saw you." He'd been too caught up in his own shit to acknowledge it. He'd been a coward then, but he was finding his strength now. Because of her.

"I was yours long before that," she whispered back. She reached out for him. "I've waited for you all my life, Logan. I've waited for you since I knew there might be someone to wait for. I was so nasty in the beginning."

He grinned. "You were a bitch, baby, and I want you to always knock me on my ass when I need it. Don't you ever apologize for trying to get what you want, but all you have to do is ask from now on. You're mine and I'm going to take care of you. Do you understand me? I'm going to be your man, Georgia. I'm your Dom. No one else."

Seth could top her, but Logan needed that place in her life. He needed it all to himself.

Her hand found his chest, covering the tat there with an obviously possessive hand. Yeah, he'd fooled her. "You're already mine. Always mine. I want you to be my man and my Dom."

There was his woman. He didn't want to tame her, just play with her for the rest of his life. He reached down and lightly twisted the clips. Georgia in pervertables was the hottest thing he'd ever seen.

She shrieked a little. "Oh, my god!"

"On your knees. I have more to do." So much more.

She started to turn, and he knew beyond a shadow of a doubt that this particular demon had been permanently exorcised. Georgia had brushed it away like a ghost who was no longer welcome.

His woman. He reached for the lube because he had work to do.

Chapter Fourteen

Seth stepped out onto Main Street and took a long look down the road. Things weren't going the way he'd planned. He was surprised at how much things had changed. There were new people, new businesses. Time hadn't stopped and stood still while he was going to school and building his company. And Logan was further away than ever.

And someone was watching Henry's cabin. Or his. He couldn't be sure. Had he screwed up somewhere along the way? Had he left some thread undone and now it was unraveling? He'd been looking for Henry all day, but apparently he and Nell had left earlier to protest something and wouldn't be back for a few hours, and Henry was currently eschewing cell phones due to radiation or some shit.

The man had been in the CIA for years, but now he acted like a Luddite. Seth's stomach was rolling.

He'd had a long talk with Stefan Talbot about Logan. It was worse than he could have imagined. Somehow he'd thought Logan had merely gotten his ass kicked and he was being overly emotional about the whole thing. Momma Marie hadn't said much when he'd asked her. There hadn't been any press coverage. Logan himself always shut the conversation down when he asked about it.

Stef hadn't pulled any punches or tried to spare Seth the details.

Logan had been tortured. He'd nearly died. Stef had thought he was dead at first, he'd looked so bad. Stef had told him he was pretty sure there wasn't an inch of Logan that hadn't been battered and bruised. Logan's body had healed, but his mind hadn't, and some of the town was worried he never would.

What was he going to do if he couldn't convince Logan to give this a try?

For the first time in a long time, he wasn't sure he would get what he wanted.

He couldn't live here full time. He could be in Bliss for long portions of the year, but he needed to be in New York, too. He'd tried time and time again to get Logan to join him, but he'd always gotten the same spiel.

Logan Green didn't take charity.

He was so frustrating.

"Seth!"

Seth looked up and saw a freaking nightmare coming his way. He blinked because he couldn't possibly be seeing what he was seeing. He'd handled this problem already. It was done and checked off his fucking list.

Win Dawson was walking across the street right in front of the art gallery, moving Seth's way. He was dressed perfectly, as he always seemed to be, as though a designer three-piece suit was his uniform. He would bet Win Dawson would wear Hugo Boss to a backyard barbecue.

Seth turned back and made sure he was still in Bliss because damn Dawson looked out of place here.

"Where's Georgia? I've driven around and around this town, and I can't find her anywhere." Win's face was locked in a grim mask.

"What's wrong? Did something happen to your brothers? Why didn't you call her? Or call me?" God, he hoped they were all right. Georgia worshipped the ground her brothers walked on.

"They're all fine, and I didn't call you because you're the problem, Seth."

He barely managed to not roll his eyes. "What? I thought we cleared this up. I'm marrying her. I'm taking care of her. Go back to California."

"Not without Georgia," Win said between clenched teeth. "And you're not the problem. Your partner is."

Logan? "What are you talking about?"

Win got in his space. "Did you think I wouldn't check him out? Did you think I wouldn't find out everything there is to know about a man who is going to be involved in my sister's life? How the hell did you think that bastard would pass the tests?"

"I'll ask again. What are you talking about? Logan is a great guy."

Win huffed. "Yeah, because great guys get into bar fights and cause thousands of dollars' worth of damage."

Fuck. How the hell had Win found out about that? Seth didn't even know the full story. He'd immediately sent the money when Logan asked for it because Logan never asked for anything. Taking money from Seth was sort of anathema to him. "He ran into some trouble."

"Really? Because according to my sources, he's been involved with drugs."

Alcohol wasn't the problem. Logan had said it himself not two days ago. "He's clean now."

"He never went to rehab," Win said. "Believe me, I checked. You don't kick a heroin habit without help. He's not getting anywhere close to my sister. Now you tell me where she is. I don't give a shit what you do to my company. Take it. I'm not sacrificing Georgia. Do you understand me?"

Seth felt like the wind had been knocked out of him. "Logan wasn't involved in heroin."

He could see a little weed, maybe some valium or pain pills. Maybe he'd gotten addicted after his surgery. According to Stef, the doctor had placed Logan on numerous pain medications for several weeks. Heroin? No. Not Logan.

Win frowned. "You don't know. Damn it." He sighed. "Look, when Ben and Chase talked to me about him, I decided to hire a PI. He's been in town checking Green out. He's been floating some cash for information on the kid. He went into this bar close to here."

Seth knew it well. "Hell on Wheels."

Win nodded. "Yes. The owner threw him out, but there was a guy who followed him and was willing to talk. He said Logan Green bought drugs off him. Ten thousand dollars' worth in the end. Started out on pain meds and worked his way up to one night where he bought heroin. He must have switched dealers then because that was the last the guy heard of him. Green paid off his debt."

Ten thousand dollars. *Fuck.* There hadn't been a bar fight. He was paying off his dealer.

Win continued, every word making Seth's head pound. "This guy told me a crazy-ass story about Logan and some brunette who came and saw him and talked him into turning himself in. He did six months in county on his first offense, but he could have been put away for years. The guy claims that he's been scared straight or some shit. Said going to jail was the best thing that could have happened to him. This idiot actually tried to get my PI to give him Green's number because he wants to talk to him about going to rehab. So even the drug dealer thinks Green needs rehab. And this is the guy you want to share my sister with."

"You believe a drug dealer? It sounds like he's still high." Seth didn't want to believe a drug dealer. He knew Logan, damn it.

"Why would he lie? I haven't been able to locate his dealer in Dallas, but I'll find him, and when I do, I'm going to have a bone to pick with Julian Lodge because my brothers and sister-in-law work in that club of his. Now where is my sister?"

"I don't know." Hopefully she was still with Marie because he needed to have a long talk with Logan. Was any of this shit true? How had this happened? How had Logan slid so far? God, Logan barely drank a couple of years back.

"I'm going to find her and then we're out of here." Win didn't wait for an answer. He simply moved on, taking the steps to the Trading Post two at a time. The bastard had hired a PI.

At least he knew who'd been watching them. He could tell Henry to stand down. He still had the problem of who was looking into Henry Flanders online, but it was very likely Win's PI who'd been on their porch and out on the mountain. Damn, but the fucker had moved fast. How had Win gotten a PI out here before Seth and Georgia had gotten here?

It didn't matter. He needed to talk to Logan because Win was serious. And he wouldn't listen to Georgia's protestations either. Win was a throwback feudal lord and would haul his sister back to his castle and pull up his drawbridge, and then Seth would have to mount an all-out siege.

Damn it. He hated when things started to fall apart.

He looked back, certain Win was safely in the store, likely trying to bluster his way into someone giving up Georgia's location. Maybe Logan knew where she was. Seth jogged up the road, past Stella's, and right to the station house. *Thank god.* Logan's Escalade was sitting in the parking lot, the only vehicle there. Nate must be out. Maybe they could have a private talk before they went after Georgia. It was a long time coming. He needed to know everything. Every dark detail.

Seth walked confidently through the double set of doors. He was going to calmly ask Logan what had happened. He wasn't going to get mad. He wasn't going to judge. They were best friends. They shared everything, well, everything Logan would let Seth share with him. Why hadn't Logan let him help? He would have paid for anything. He would have paid for the best rehab, and it wouldn't have been in a damn BDSM club. He would have sent Logan anywhere in the world if he thought it would have helped. Logan didn't need to hide things from him.

A low moan caught his attention. *Fuck.* He'd found Georgia. Their world was falling apart and what were Georgia and Logan doing? They were fucking. Yep. And they hadn't even thought to call and invite him. Well, he was a part of this threesome, and they could just be surprised when he walked in.

"You were a bitch, baby, and I want you to always knock me on my ass when I need it. Don't you ever apologize for trying to get what you want, but all you have to do is ask from now on." Logan's voice stopped him in his tracks. He stood outside the sheriff's office door. He'd never heard Logan sound so passionate. "You're mine and I'm going to take care of you. Do you understand me? I'm going to be your man, Georgia. I'm your Dom. No one else."

Seth felt his jaw clench. *No one else?* That sounded selfish. He was the one who had brought them together.

Henry's words came back to him. *Logan feels like you*

abandoned him. Why didn't you come back, Seth?

Was this Logan's revenge on him? Georgia would tell Logan off now. Seth was the one who'd taken care of Georgia. Logan fucked her. Seth was the one who treated her like a princess, and she wouldn't let Logan cut him out.

"You're already mine. Always mine. I want you to be my man and my Dom."

Or she could agree with everything Logan said.

Seth practically stumbled back out of the building. His plan had completely backfired. She only wanted Logan. Logan, who had lied. Logan, who had treated her like crap, but the minute he crooked his finger Georgia's way, she ran right back into his arms.

They were going to leave him behind. He'd seen the heat between them. Logan and Georgia could be like an inferno when they started going. Their chemistry was explosive, but he'd thought there was a place for him, too. All of their lives, Logan and Seth had planned for this day, and now Logan had turned his back and wanted to waltz off with the girl.

Seth had to find his feet because he was suddenly completely off-balance. The floor didn't seem to be quite steady.

He started to walk down Main Street. At least he could tell Win he'd found her. Maybe Georgia was better off without either of them.

He turned his face to the sun.

He really couldn't go home again.

* * * *

She had binder clips on her nipples. It was weird and strangely hot. She was so aware of them. Every time she moved, she felt the bite.

Georgia got into position. Logan had ordered her to her hands and knees, and she was in the mood to obey. She had no doubt that she wouldn't want to do the slave thing twenty-four seven like Kitten, but oh, she liked it for play. Logan had brought her more pleasure than she'd ever had in her life, and it finally felt like he was really here with her. He was truly engaged, and for more than a night.

"Damn, girl. You have got the prettiest ass."

When he started talking and his voice went deep and low, she didn't even want to argue with him. She wanted to believe him. When he talked like that, she felt pretty. Right down to her ass. Which he seemed to be playing with.

"Uhm, are you planning on spanking me?"

He sighed as though he'd found his happy place. His big palm was rubbing over the cheeks of her ass. "I'll always spank you, baby, but not right now. Right now, I want to play. This is going to be cold. Don't tense up on me."

"What?" He couldn't tell a girl to not tense up and then not actually expect her to tense up. *Holy crapballs.* Something cool hit her back door and, yep, she tensed.

And Logan proved he was serious about always spanking her. He smacked her ass and chuckled when she yelped.

"I will get you back, Green." But she didn't move because she kind of totally was a freak for the spanking thing. And she loved how he was laughing now. When she'd first walked into the station house, he'd been so grim, and now he was relaxed and happy. If slapping her ass made him happy, then she would misbehave more often.

"I have no doubt you will. Now let me play and then I'll give you some cock."

She snorted. "You make it sound like a gift." Oh, it was, but she couldn't let the arrogance go unnoted.

Another hard smack had her dragging her breath in.

"It's a gift, all right. But I'm getting the best present of all. Have I told you how crazy I am about you, girl? You're a gift. Seth wrapped you up and tied a bow on you. He knew I couldn't handle you all by myself, so he trussed you up and brought you to me."

Seth. If only Seth were here, everything would be perfect. Of course, if Seth were here she would probably have a cock in her mouth. "You like it because when he's around, one of you is stuffing something in my mouth and I can't argue."

His laugh boomed through the room and suddenly there was something right at her asshole. Oh, yeah, he was going to go there. Well, what had she expected? There were two of them. They probably didn't want to take turns.

"Oh, ewww, I just figured out how my brothers have sex with

Nat. Ewwww."

He didn't even stop for a second. His finger started a long, slow sliding circle around her asshole. "I try not to think of your brothers naked. It's best if you put it out of your head, but if you've figured out that sometime in the near future I'm going to be inside this beautiful ass while Seth fucks your pussy, then, ding, ding, ding, you win the prize for smarts, gorgeous. God, baby, you're so pretty. So fucking pretty. Relax and let me in."

He knew how to get to her. There was a plea in his voice that had her forgetting everything she was thinking about. No more Ben and Chase. No worries about whether or not she could handle this. She could because they were her men and she wanted them. She wanted the three of them together.

This could be her life, always between Logan and Seth, always loved and comforted and protected.

And needed. They needed her. She hadn't seen it before, not with Logan. Seth needed someone who would pull him out of that head of his and make him take a look around. He needed someone who loved him enough to pull him out of work and make him spend time doing dumb things.

And Logan needed someone who loved him enough to see through all his shit and not let go. She would never let go. Now that she understood the pain that had molded him, she was determined to ease that and make a life for them all.

"Almost there. This is only a taste, baby, because Seth isn't here." His finger slid inside.

She had to take a long breath because she could feel her asshole clenching around him as he started to massage her from the inside. It was an odd sensation. No pain, just a weird sense of fullness. "You're going to be bigger than that finger."

He started to gently fuck her ass with his finger, circling her and then fucking inside and starting the whole thing over again. Over and over again. "I'm way bigger, but you can handle it. See?"

She gasped as he slid something else inside. Another finger. He groaned as though he loved the sight of watching his own fingers disappear into her asshole.

And then she felt him hold for a second and his cock was

suddenly at the edge of her pussy. His fingers kept up the long, slow fucking of her ass, but his cock was right there, teasing the channel of her pussy. Offering her that taste of what it would be like to have both her men.

He was so big, so dominant. She felt her whole body give over because he really was its Master. Only Logan had ever played her body like an instrument he'd finely tuned. She loved Seth, too, but she had a different kind of sex with Seth. She could see now that she wouldn't be whole without both of them. She wanted the hard-core, rough sex with Logan, and she needed to be made love to by Seth. Maybe, over time, they would switch roles, but for now they each had their place, and she couldn't imagine giving up either one.

"This is a preview of what it's going to feel like when we come together properly." His cock teased at her pussy.

She let her head fall forward as his cock started pressing inside her. With a low grunt, he forced his way inside, filling her up.

"Keep still, baby. I can't hold on the way I should because I only have one free hand." His not so free hand seemed to concentrate on opening up her ass. She felt his fingers scissoring deep inside her as he held his cock still.

What would it be like when Seth was under her and she was riding his cock, staring into those gorgeous eyes of his?

"Georgia, look up."

She brought her eyes up and saw what she had missed before. There was a mirror hanging on the wall in the perfect position to be able to see herself and Logan on the desk. She stared at the erotic picture they made. Logan's beautiful, oh-so-masculine face was hard with arousal as he stared at her. His shoulders were broad and muscular. That tattoo on his chest made her heart soften because it was proof positive that Logan Green was crazy about her.

And she looked like a woman. Not a girl anymore. She couldn't hold on to that youthful vision of herself. She had to be a woman now. Only a real woman would be enough for her men. A real woman would know how to love them and how to accept the love they could offer. It would be so scary, but she was ready to do it. She was ready to leave the selfishness of her youth behind. And she was ready to leave the pain behind, too. She could see now that it was a cage. It was a comfortable cage where she could deflect the rejection, but it was time to grow up now and break free from all of it.

She planted her palms on the desk and curled her lower back up, taking more of him, letting him slide inside until she could feel his balls against her flesh.

"Fuck, Georgia. You're going to kill me."

"Not if you kill me first, babe." She loved the deep laugh that came out of her throat. She sounded like a confident woman, and that woman in the mirror was definitely more than she'd been before.

Logan's mouth widened into a glorious smile. "That's my baby. I don't want Hurricane Georgia every day, but I like a storm from you every now and then. You never bore me. Never."

Life with them wouldn't be dull. They had plenty to work out. Logan worked here or in Dallas, and Seth had to go back to New York. She wasn't sure that she wanted to be his assistant for the rest of her life. But none of that mattered now. All that mattered was Logan was here with her.

"You feel so good. You have the tightest pussy ever." He scissored his fingers again, drawing a moan from her. God, what would it feel like when it was his cock? "You're going to be so much tighter when Seth is in your pussy and I can really be in your ass."

He pulled his cock out and pushed back inside, every centimeter of her pussy sensitive and wanting. How had she lived all this time without this feeling? She pushed back against him, trying to keep his cock inside. It sent his fingers deeper in her ass.

"That's what I want from you. Fight me. Give me everything you have. I want it all," Logan said as he wound his free hand around her waist. "I want you to scream my name when you come."

His free hand found its way down her stomach and started to rub her clit. Tension built, making her lungs work and her heart pump. She let go, fucking back toward him, reaching for the orgasm she knew would come now. She wanted to prolong it, live in the moment forever.

It was too much. Logan pressed down on her clit while his cock stroked inside her pussy and she went off, giving him what he wanted. She gave him everything. She screamed for him, shouting his name and watching in the mirror as he stiffened behind her, his face contorting as he came. He shoved his cock into her one last time before pulling out and lifting her with him.

"That's my girl," he whispered lazily. He kissed her ear, his eyes watching the mirror. "Look at how gorgeous you are."

Her skin was flushed, and the binder clips had come off at some point in time. She hadn't noticed. Her nipples were red and they throbbed, but she loved the bite of pain. It would be a sweet ache for hours that would remind her how well she'd been loved. She stared at that mirror and realized it had already happened. The girl she'd been was gone, and a woman was in her place.

"I love you."

"I want you to always love me. I can't live without it." He paused for a moment. "I love you, too. I hope my love is worth something."

How could he think that it wasn't? It was worth the world to her.

"Logan!"

Georgia nearly screamed at the masculine shout that came from the other side of the door.

And Logan laughed. "Hey, Nate. Uh, you're going to have to give me a few minutes. I probably ought to clean up. The good news is we didn't use your chair at all."

If Logan was worried about his boss catching them fucking in his office, he didn't show it. He winked at her through the mirror as he helped her off the desk.

"Take a shower before you come back out here." There was a moment of silence. "Logan, are you all right with being in there?"

"I am now." Logan towered over her, a gentle smile on his face. "I think I'm going to be okay with this room now. I won't be thinking about what happened then anymore. I'll be thinking about ice cream. Georgia Peach–flavored ice cream." He leaned over and took her mouth in a long, slow kiss.

"You didn't tell me you were eating in there! Damn it. I was serious about that chair. You better not drip ice cream on it."

Logan laughed as he led her toward the shower.

Georgia followed, her heart light.

Chapter Fifteen

Logan reached for her hand as he opened the door and led Georgia out of the bathroom. She was dressed again, and that was a complete shame. He didn't think he would ever forget how she'd tossed her clothes off and boldly told him that she was his chocolate ice cream. She'd been everything he needed her to be in that moment. She'd been his woman.

She'd given him the strength to understand once and for all that he had to figure this out.

She was almost at the door, but he tugged on her hand and drew her back. Now that he'd given in, he couldn't seem to stop kissing her. He'd kissed her during their long shower, crowding her in the small space and running his hands over every inch of her.

"Are you going back home?" Logan asked. Somehow his damn uniform didn't seem so confining anymore.

She tilted her head, golden-blonde hair flowing around her shoulders. "Yes. I have a party to plan and dinner to cook."

Apparently she'd invited most of the women of Bliss out to the cabin for a makeover party that included a metric shit ton of wine and a bunch of appetizers he wouldn't mind trying out for himself. His girl knew how to throw a party.

"And you need to rest because I bet Seth and I will have plans for you." He leaned down and kissed that cute nose. God, she scared the holy crap out of him, but he couldn't turn away. He fucking needed her.

And that meant he needed to sort his shit out. God, he was going to have to talk to them both. Seth and Georgia. He had to get it all out. He had to tell them about what happened that night at Hell on Wheels. And he had to talk to Jen and Stef and Holly. He had to admit what he'd done. Nearly done. Maybe the *nearly* part would save him.

"Hey, what's wrong?" Her hands were suddenly on his face, her eyes searching as though she could see the hurt and wanted to wipe it clean.

He shook it off. He had to find a little faith. Maybe his momma had been right. Maybe a single incident shouldn't erase years of being loved. "Nothing, baby. I still have things to tell you, but you're going to be okay with it, aren't you? Even if it's bad."

She nodded, her eyes teary. "I'm going to be okay with anything you say to me as long as you don't say good-bye."

He wrapped his arms around her, pulling her into a bear hug. He didn't know why the universe had opened up and given him this woman, but he was damn glad it had. She would make him stronger. He would never be weak the way he'd been before. Not as long as he had Georgia.

And Seth.

One more squeeze and he set her on her feet.

She reached over and grabbed the stapler. She'd rearranged Nate's desk to perfect order after she'd gotten dressed. "I'm throwing this out."

She didn't have to. It wouldn't bother him again. It was a freaking stapler. It wasn't evil. Luka had been an evil prick, but he was gone and Georgia was here and Logan was here and it was all good.

But she wanted it gone, so it was gone.

He opened the door and Nate and Gemma were standing at her desk, both of them staring. Gemma had a smirk on her face and held up a sign that gave him a nine point eight.

That was totally wrong because what had happened in that office had been a perfect ten on the fuck scale.

Nate frowned and crossed his arms over his chest. "What the hell is wrong with everyone today? First, I practically have to pry Max off Rachel because she got a pair of fuck-me heels stuck in Max's belt loop in a closet at the art gallery, and they were still managing to go at it when I got the door unlocked. I don't think that position was covered in the Kama Sutra. I might have gone a little blind. And now I can't even go into my own office because you defiled it."

Nate sounded so prim and proper. Logan couldn't help but laugh. "Dude, I found your stash of condoms and lube, and you can't possibly tell me that the mirror is there so you can check your hair."

Nate flushed slightly. "Gemma, we're going to need to run a 1220."

"I'll get the Lysol, Sheriff, but you're going to do the cleaning. I've been very good. I only have sex on my own desk." Gemma turned and disappeared into the kitchen.

"I already cleaned." Georgia was a pretty shade of pink.

"He's being a dick, baby. Don't worry about him."

Nate finally smiled. "Hello, Miss Dawson. It's damn good to see you again. You got him in there?"

"She did," Logan replied. "I'm good. I'm really good, but I have to talk to her and Seth. They need to know some things."

Nate reached a hand out. Logan clasped it in his own. "If they're going to be your family, then they need to know everything. Your family will understand. Your family will forgive you."

Like Nate had forgiven him. Nate should have fired him, but instead he'd talked to Stef about getting Logan help.

"Speaking of family," Nate continued. "There's a shark running up and down Main Street screaming for his baby sister. Six foot six, killer suit, practically shoots laser beams from his eyes."

Georgia's mouth dropped open. "Win. What the hell? I have to find him before he goes after Seth again." She gave Logan a quick kiss. "See you at home."

Home. God, he'd come home, and he might manage to stay here if he was lucky.

She ran out the door, and he was left alone with Nate.

A well of emotion ran through him as he looked at Nate. Damn, what had that girl done to him? He'd felt dead inside for so fucking long. Anger and fear had been all he could feel, but then Georgia walked through the door and he came alive again. He suddenly had the feeling he needed to talk to a whole lot of people, starting with Nate Wright.

"You should have fired me." He'd been a nutbag shithead after the incident. He'd pulled crap that should have gotten his badge taken away about ten times, and nothing had been worse than what happened at Hell on Wheels.

Nate put a hand on his shoulder. "That wouldn't have solved a damn thing. It would have pushed you further into that world. And you got yourself out, Logan. I don't know everything that happened, but I do know that I never once thought you wouldn't make it."

"I did some things I'm not proud of," he admitted.

"And you made them right. You know a few days before you left for Dallas, a guy named Bernie came in and turned himself in. I don't usually have dealers who turn themselves in. He said he needed a fresh start and that he knew he couldn't do it on his own."

That had been more about Hope than him. Sweet Hope had convinced his idiot dealer to turn his own ass in. He'd taken the ten grand Logan owed him and started a new life. Hope told him the worst Bernie did now was have the occasional beer at Hell on Wheels.

God, Nate knew. He'd known and he'd never said a word. "I heard that."

"I wish I could have shut down that bar."

"Sawyer's not bad." Sawyer had taken over Hell on Wheels a year and a half before, after his grandfather died. Nate had it out for him, but Logan owed the man. "Sawyer saved my life. He and Hope did. There wasn't a big bar fight where I broke up the place. Sawyer made that story up because I'd gotten myself in trouble."

Nate held up a hand. "I don't need to know anything else. And my trouble with Sawyer comes from that MC tat he used to wear on his arm."

Sawyer's left bicep was now a mass of pure black ink, but at one time he'd belonged to the Colorado Horde, an outlaw biker club. Nate and Zane had worked for the DEA before coming to Bliss and had their fill of "one percenters," as they called themselves. "I want you to know that I don't bear any ill will toward the man. I'm grateful to him."

He was shocked to find out he was grateful to a lot of people. He felt a little like the Grinch in that story his ma would read to him every Christmas. Somehow, his heart had grown back to its original size—or bigger—and he felt the need to share it.

"You know you're meant for bigger things than this, Logan Green." Nate nodded as he spoke as though this was something he'd been thinking about for a while. "You need to get out into the world, see what you can be."

See the world and not because he didn't want to be at home, but simply because the world was such a thing to see. And he could see it with his best friend and his girl. Their woman. "I've been thinking about that, but I have things I need to do first."

"Yeah, you take care of what you need to," Nate said. "You always have a job here. But I think you're going to find something better."

"There's no place better than here." Gemma was smiling as she walked out of the break room. She had a spray bottle of Lysol and a roll of paper towels. "We have everything here. We have nudists and actors and protesters and vegans and aliens and whatever the hell Henry is. But seriously, everyone should see New York and Paris and London. Go see them and then you come back here and happily live in Bliss."

"Whatever the hell Henry is?" Logan asked.

Nate rolled his eyes. "Gemma's become one of our premier conspiracy theorists. She believes Henry is hiding his background."

"Caleb does, too. I'm not alone in this. We have our own club now. We both saw what he did to my needle-dicked ex." Gemma turned to Logan. "You weren't here for that party. Twelve-Second Patrick. I call him that because of how long he lasted during sex. He was my fiancé, and then he tried to kill me with strawberries and oops, suddenly he spends some time with Henry Flanders in the woods and his head pops off. Oh, sure he was only internally decapitated, but he was decapitated all the same. Henry said he tripped. Yeah, like I'm buying that one."

Nate patted her head. "Sure, vegan Henry Flanders is a super assassin."

But Nate hadn't met Henry before he'd gotten together with Nell. Logan had. He'd been a kid when Henry Flanders had first come to town, but he remembered being afraid of the man. His eyes had been cold, and he'd nearly killed Seth the first time they'd come in contact.

Seth. Seth had been in contact with Henry all these years. It was a weird relationship, but Henry was the man Seth was closest to after Logan. It hadn't made sense then, but years and experience had lent a different light to his eyes.

Henry wasn't what he said he was—or he wasn't what he'd said he'd been. Gemma was right. Caleb was right. They were new eyes looking at something that seemed normal.

Seth knew. *Damn it*. Seth knew the truth. Seth had something to do with this. There was a cover-up, and Seth was right at the heart of it.

"Nate, I need a couple of hours." This couldn't wait. He needed to talk to Seth. He needed to figure out a whole bunch of things.

"Take the rest of the day." Nate had a smile on his face. "We've had our crazy shit happen today. Max was damn near bent in two, I tell you. I have no idea how he kept a hard-on through that. And he kept calling her 'Rachel, Mistress of Pain' through the whole episode. What's wrong with them?"

He didn't think there was a damn thing wrong with them. There was probably a Hurricane Rachel out there and Max loved the winds. It took a special kind of man to take on that much woman, but he was up for the task. And he knew Seth was, too.

Logan hit the door at a run and went straight for his SUV. He had questions to ask and stories to tell.

* * * *

Georgia ran from the station house, up Main and past Stella's, and she caught sight of Win almost immediately. He stood out in any crowd, much less the jeans-loving cowboy crowd. He was still wearing his Armani suit and Louis Vuitton loafers even at nine thousand feet plus above sea level.

"Win!"

He stopped and turned, his whole being laser focused on her.

Win. So much of her life fell into place as he stalked toward her. She'd spent a lifetime depressed because her mommy and daddy didn't love her. They'd been shitastic parents, but that didn't matter. Biology didn't mean anything in the end. It was a starting point, a place on the map, but in the end as long as the destination was reached, it didn't matter which route a person took.

Love was the be-all, end-all of existence, and now that she looked back at her life, she'd had it in spades. It didn't matter where it came from, only that she'd had it.

"Win!" She screamed his name, not to stop him from searching for her, but to let him know she saw him, wanted to be with him. Win. Her rock.

Win had a grim look on his face as he stalked toward her. *Damn.* She had some work to do, but now she was ready to do it and as a woman, not a girl.

She reached for him, her arms open, because no matter what happened, he was her big brother. "It's so good to see you."

He enveloped her in a bear hug. "You, too, sis." He pulled away, and his handsome face became a mask of implacable will. "You will get your things, and we're heading to Colorado Springs and catching a plane."

Oh, how she loved him. And she wasn't about to tell him yes. "What's wrong now?"

His jaw clenched, a sure sign he was upset. "Logan Green. He's not who he says he is."

A deep serenity fell over her. Of course. Win loved her. He'd been her everything for so long. He was just being the superhero he was. "He says he's a fuckup who got into a shitload of trouble."

Win's eyes narrowed. "He's been in a lot of trouble."

Don't engage with the Neanderthal. It was a lot like the granola except with fangs and claws. "He's so sweet. Did you see our cabin? Ten thousand square feet of pure paradise."

She didn't mention the moose. It would only throw Win off. Then he would be worried about her being killed by a moose.

"I don't care about the cabin, Georgie. And that's Seth's doing."

So Seth was good and Logan was bad. It was good to know the score. "It's beautiful, and you should see the closet. It's huge. I need to fill it up."

Win looked down, catching sight of her feet. "What the hell? I haven't seen you out of heels since you were sixteen."

She'd been trying to fit in with the upperclassmen. So much time spent trying to get to a place that she didn't even like. "I let a friend borrow my shoes. It's totally reminding me of what it means to walk without pain. Maybe that's why I've been so grumpy the last couple of years. My feet always hurt."

Win shook his head. "You're not doing this to me. Do you think I don't know all your moves? I'm not going to let you distract me."

"I wish you would." By this point in the conversation, Ben would have handed her a credit card. Chase would have been fixated on something shiny. Mark and Dare would be scratching their heads wondering how to get the conversation back on track, but Win never got the chance to play it dumb. He couldn't.

"Not happening. Now let's go to this amazing cabin and grab your things." He glanced down at his watch. "If we hurry, we can make it to Colorado Springs before dark."

She reached out and took his hand, leading him to the bench that sat right outside of something called Blissful Art. There were lovely pots and ceramic work in the window front along with a bunch of flyers someone had taped on the "public forum" section of the store. From the words "tofu sit-in," "cruelty-free," and "fair wages," she was betting on Nell.

"Georgie, we don't have time for this. I have a meeting in the morning."

Of course Win had a meeting, but he'd made time to ride to her rescue because that was what he did. "I'm not going home with you, brother."

His hands went to his hips—his dad pose. "I don't want to have to tell you this, but Seth's gotten you involved with a rather unsavory character."

Logan was totally savory. He was a big old gorgeous hunk of man meat, but she thought pointing that out to her brother might not be the best way to go. "I was involved with Logan before I ever met Seth."

"Did you know he's been hooked on drugs?" Win asked the

question with the gravity of a man dropping a hammer, about to shatter her life.

She wasn't that fragile. And Win's statement didn't surprise her. After what he'd gone through, she was surprised Logan wasn't still involved with them. "He's perfectly sober now."

If she didn't count the tequila incident.

"I don't care. He was apparently in to a drug dealer for ten thousand dollars."

She felt her eyes widen. "Seriously? Damn. Well, Seth can cover it."

"From what I can tell, he already did. Not that he knew it. Your friend lied."

"My boyfriend lied," she corrected. So much of what Win was telling her didn't make sense. She'd known Logan back in Texas, and he'd been a solid guy then. "And this incident was a while back, wasn't it?"

Win frowned. "It was last year, yes, but people don't change. If he was an addict once, he's always going to be one."

She reached out and put her hand in his. "Oh, Win. We're all addicted to something." She'd been addicted to fitting in rather than making a place for herself. Seth was addicted to plotting and being the king of the mountain, and Logan's real addiction for the past year had been his own misery. "It's how we handle it that makes us who we are. It's easy to get addicted to being the victim, you know."

He frowned. "What are you talking about?"

"I'm talking about Logan. He was brutalized, and I think it was probably the first time he'd had something really bad happen to him so he decided the world was a piece of crap for a while, but he's strong. He's going to come out of it." He'd started today. By the time they were done, he'd been relaxed and happy, as though something had settled deep inside. "I'm also talking about me, though. Logan hasn't been able to let go of what happened to him, but I've been the same way all my life."

Win leaned in. "What happened to you?"

"Mom happened. Dad happened." Vitriolic mother and cold, distant dad hadn't made for the best childhood. "But you happened, too, Winter."

"What are you trying to say?"

She looked at her big brother. He'd been twelve when she'd been born, and from what she could tell, he'd already been looking out for their brothers, keeping them together when all the odds had been against them. "Why didn't you move out when Dad cut you off? Why did you stay and pay him rent?"

Win turned his head, staring off into the distance. "My trust kicked in at eighteen. I had plenty of money, and I was comfortable staying where I was."

"No, you weren't. You could have gone to college anywhere in the world. You could have walked right out of that house and had your own place. You could have partied like a rock star."

"I was never a big partier."

Because he'd had a family to raise. She turned her face up to the sun, letting it warm her as much as the truth did. It was so easy to see now. She'd wasted years playing at being the poor little rich girl when she'd been given everything she'd needed. It hadn't come in a perfect package, but her family had been there all the same. "I've spent years being angry that I didn't have a dad. I need to apologize for that."

Win sighed. "We were all in the same boat. Dad was a bastard. You have nothing to apologize for."

"Oh, yes, I do because never once did I acknowledge how well I was raised. You were the best dad I could have hoped for. I love you so much."

He could have walked away and no one would have blamed him. He'd been a child trying to fill a man's shoes and doing the best he could. He'd been the one to keep his brothers in line. He'd been the one to make sure they had the things they needed. Win had taught her what it meant to love someone. It meant standing with them, fighting beside them—sometimes even fighting with them. Win had done the one thing a true father always did—he'd stayed. He'd done whatever he had to do to stay involved in her life.

Her brother squeezed her hand, his face flushed. She'd never seen him so emotional, but he was Win and it was gone in a flash, replaced with pure Dawson calculation. "I love you, too, Georgie. That's why I'm taking you home with me."

She stood up, a sense of peace invading her bones. If Logan had lied to Seth, then he'd had a reason. He'd been ashamed, but the time for that was over. They were going to be a family, and there was no room for secrets or anything so useless as shame. He'd made a mistake. He'd cleaned up his act. They were moving on.

"I'm sorry, but I'm not a kid anymore. I'm staying here and I'm fighting for what I want. I love Logan. I love Seth. This is my life, and I'm taking charge of it. No more calls to you or Ben. No more screwing up to get attention. No more throwing fits. I'm going to make you proud of me and that starts by telling you that if you try to come between me and my men, we're going to have trouble. This is my relationship and my life and I want you in it more than anything, but Logan Green is my Dom and he's going to be my husband whether he knows it or not. Because I'm a Dawson and we fight for the people we love. We never give up. My big brother taught me that."

Win went still. "Georgia, are you sure?"

She'd never been more sure of anything. She'd loved Logan Green from the moment she saw him, and whatever he was going through, they would get through it together—with Seth. "Promise you'll give me away at my wedding."

Win reached for her hand, squeezing it tight. "He better be worthy of you. If he's not, if either one of them steps out of line, they should know that you have five brothers willing to kill them. And by kill, I mean take the maximum amount of pain before they're no longer breathing."

"He's already been there. He's tougher than he thinks, and he's going to pull through. We're going to be a family, and I think that means spending a lot of time here." It wasn't so bad. She was starting to become rather attached to the community. "I hope you'll visit. Whether it's New York or here or California, I'm always going to want to see my big brother."

Win turned, not watching her, but keeping his eyes on the road. "Ben and Chase are happy. Now you're happy, too. I think Mark and Dare are going to form a ménage with their assault rifles and live happily ever after that way. I'll be honest, Georgie, I'm not sure what to do. This has been my life for so long."

"You're going to find a new one, and our brothers and I will stand right beside you." She couldn't think of anyone who deserved a happy ending more than Win. She felt her face light up because she had the absolute best idea ever.

"Oh, god. What are you going to do?" He practically backed off the bench. "That is the scariest look I've ever seen on your face."

She smiled and shook her head. "I'm going to make it my mission to find you a girlfriend."

"No. No. No. I can find my own sub. No. No. If you ever loved me, don't start setting me up." He stood with a sigh. "I give up. I'll take you to the cabin. I'll pay for your wedding. Anything you want as long as you don't find me dates."

It looked like everyone was afraid of her today, and that was a good thing. She gave him her most harmless smile because she was already thinking about who she could set him up with. Yes, this was a worthy project. "I will totally take a ride, but I make no promises."

Only the best for her big brother. It was time she started to pay him back.

And it was definitely time to let her men know the score.

"My car's in the parking lot." He shook his head as he looked down at her and then ran a hand across her head the way he had when she was a kid. "You turned out okay, Georgie."

He started walking, dragging her along because he was so damn tall. She had to admit that keeping up with him was easier when she wasn't wearing five-inch heels. She just had to jog a little.

And he would look so good with Naomi. Georgia nearly sighed at the thought. Naomi had gorgeous coffee-colored skin and huge brown eyes. She was curvy, and that was the way Win liked his women. He liked his women solid, and she'd heard him talking about his deep love for a truly curvy ass. Naomi's had been perfect.

And they would have the most gorgeous biracial babies ever. She could already see her nieces and nephews. Oh, she would be such a good aunt.

"Seriously, you're scaring me. No setups," Win said as they rounded the corner.

"But I already have you married with two point three kids," she admitted.

"No." He started to say something else, but then a pinging sound hit the air, and Georgia watched in complete horror as her brother's perfectly white shirt bloomed with blood.

"Run," he managed to say.

"Win!" What the hell had happened?

He fell to his knees, his hand over his chest. She dropped to the ground, trying to think of any way to save her brother. She didn't even understand what was going on. One minute he'd been fine and the next he had a hole in his chest.

He couldn't die. Win was too big to die, too strong and powerful.

God, he couldn't die.

"I wouldn't run if I were you, Miss Dawson." A tall man in a dark suit stepped out from behind an SUV. He held a gun with a silencer on it. "I don't think I got his heart. I could try again. I'm not the best shot in the world, but I doubt I would miss at this range." He shrugged. "And if I do, my friends will be happy to fix the situation."

She was suddenly surrounded by men. She counted seven of them and they all had weapons.

"I won't run." She wouldn't leave her brother behind. Her heart pounded in her chest. "What do you want with me?"

His henchmen were rough looking, but this man oozed wealth. Even the gun in his hand looked oddly elegant. He was dressed beautifully, with blond hair and pale skin, but his crew was a motley mismatch of street thugs. "I don't want anything with you, dear, but I've found it's always best to go into these situations with leverage. I believe Mr. Stark will begin to negotiate with me if I have his lover. You will come with me. You will come and then Mr. Stark and I will have a chat about a man who my boss wishes to find."

She stood up, forcing herself to leave Win's side. "I'll come on one condition. You leave my brother here and you don't shoot him again."

"Or I could shoot him anyway. I would still have you."

"You'll find me very difficult to deal with if you touch him again. I don't know why you're here, but I will make your life a living hell, and don't think I can't do it. I'll make damn sure you have to kill me, and then there won't be anything on the earth that will make Seth give you what you want." She'd been in this position before. She had to get through these few minutes and then she would start working on a way out. One step at a time.

"I believe you." He looked to his men and said something in Spanish. They all moved back, one opening the door to a massive SUV and gesturing her inside.

She gave one last look at her brother, praying he would survive.

As they pulled out of the parking lot, she thought to ask one last question. "What do you want from Seth?"

The man with the easy smile turned, his eyes so cold she thought she would freeze. "John Bishop, of course."

Well, of course. She wracked her brain but couldn't come up with the answer to the one question now rolling through her head as the armed escort began to drive toward the cabin.

Who the hell was John Bishop?

Chapter Sixteen

Seth paced the floor and wished he could get the pilot back earlier than tonight. It would be perfect if he could be gone before they returned. Georgia and Logan had made their intentions clear. They wanted each other. Not him.

Was Logan so pissed off with him for going to college that he would steal away the only woman Seth had ever really wanted?

And Georgia. She only wanted a Dom, but Logan couldn't take care of her the way Seth could. Logan would do all the big gesture things, but he wouldn't know how to take care of her on a day-to-day basis because Logan was still a coddled infant when it came to things like that. Sure he could top her in the bedroom, but would he remember how she liked her vodka tonics made? How she loved fresh lilies? And presents. She loved little presents because growing up she'd had all the creature comforts, but her parents never gave her gifts. They'd forgotten her birthday half the time, the same way his parents had.

Was he doing the right thing? The situation seemed to call for a strategic retreat. Or should he start treating Logan like the enemy and come at him hard and fast and utterly annihilate him? It was what he would do to anyone else. He would zero in on a weakness and ruthlessly twist the knife.

He could point out all the ways Logan wasn't good for her. Right down to the fact that he had a drug dealer in the past.

He heard the sound of crunching gravel and knew that he wouldn't. Because Seth Stark had a weakness, and his weakness had two names. Logan and Georgia.

He was going to be a self-sacrificing idiot who walked away. Maybe in a couple of years he might be able to look them up again.

Fuck.

"Seth!" Logan shouted as he walked in the back door. "Dude, what's up with all the luggage? Did Georgia get back yet?"

Just get through the next couple of minutes. Play it cool. They don't need to know how much it hurt. Seth was good at masking his emotions. He was an iceman. "You're a motherfucker, you know that, Logan? Do you know what a son of a bitch you are?"

Yeah. That was real cool.

Logan stopped, his expression going completely blank. "What are you talking about?"

Laugh it off. Tell him that your job is done here and then get the hell out. He doesn't have to know. His inner voice was so rational, and he listened to it ninety-nine percent of the time. But not today. "I was standing right outside the door, asshole. I heard every word you said to her. Tell me something. Were you going to try to kick me out of my own cabin or were the two of you going to use me for cash for a while?"

Yeah, that was a direct hit. He could see plainly the way Logan blanched. "What are you talking about?"

He was totally out of control. He knew he should be cool as a cucumber, but he was eight years old again and lashing out. "I thought you didn't take charity. You wouldn't let me pay for college, but you'll let me pay for your drug habit."

It was so clear now. Logan wouldn't let him pay for college because he hadn't wanted to go with him. He hadn't taken him up on the roommate offer because he hadn't wanted to live in New York. Oh, sure, he'd head off to Dallas with a dude he barely knew, but he didn't want anything to do with his best friend.

"Ah, now I know why Win is here. So big brother dug up some dirt, huh?" Logan pulled off his hat and set it aside. "Well, I was planning on telling you anyway, so I guess this is as good a time as any. Why don't you sit down?"

"Fuck you. I'm not sitting down. I'm not listening. I've finally got the message. I'm the big-city prick who trailed after you every summer. I'm not masculine enough for your world. I'm not the kind of friend you need, and you won't be bought. Because that's what I do. I buy friends because I can't make them. So I get it. You're going to be Georgia's Dom, and I'm going to go back to New York where I belong. Actions. I should have looked at your actions and then I would have known where I stood."

God, he sounded like a whiny chick trying to justify a breakup. He was everything his father had said he was. Not manly. Overly emotional. Useless.

Logan put his hands on the bar and stared for a minute. "What were my actions?"

Logan was so calm, but then Seth was starting to understand that he didn't value the friendship. Seth had managed to turn it into some mythic story. Best friends forever. Such bullshit. Real men didn't act like that. Real men had golf buddies and shared a beer with their "friends" right before fucking the other guy's wife. They didn't get emotional about some other dude.

He took a long breath and then let it out. He needed to walk out of this with as much dignity as he could muster. "I'm sorry. I've been acting like a kid again. This place meant so much to me growing up and I think I'm foolishly trying to get that feeling back again. I'm using you to do it."

"What were my actions, Seth?" Logan repeated the question, but his voice was softer now as though he felt sorry for Seth.

Why the fuck had he started this? "Fine. You got in trouble and you didn't call me. I should have known. You had better friends. I just…you were always my best friend. I was a weird kid."

A hint of a smile curled up Logan's lips. "You still are, buddy."

"It was hard to make friends, but I found that after I met you, I didn't need them anymore. I was content to have one person."

"And I was mad that you didn't come back here to go to college." Logan's face flushed. Maybe he wasn't as unemotional as Seth had first thought.

"What?"

"I was angry that you didn't come back here so we could go to Adams State together," Logan explained. "That was our plan. We came up with it when I was twelve, and then you went to MIT. You left me behind. I was angry for years about that. You didn't even come back for the summers."

Seth had gotten the scholarship to MIT at the same time he'd come up with his software idea. He'd been obsessed with it. He'd known that he could make computers work more efficiently. The software he'd come up with integrated systems with ease, and from there he'd been able to completely transform the way companies did business online. But he'd needed the professors at MIT, the equipment, the connections. He wouldn't have had them here. "I thought you understood I had to go to a bigger school. I needed one that concentrated on technology. I offered to pay for you to come with me."

Logan shook his head. "I couldn't have made it into MIT."

"There were other schools." He'd sent Logan about a thousand enrollment packets.

"And I was scared of them." Logan sat down at the bar. He was calmer, more assured than Seth had ever seen him. God, Logan had grown up and Seth still felt like a kid. "I was scared of leaving Bliss. I was scared that I would get out into the real world and not fit in. I was scared that once I was in your world, you would realize what a completely inappropriate friend I am for you."

"What?"

"Don't play dumb. What would your parents have thought of me? The people around you? I was a hick kid from a small town who was kind of scared of his own shadow. And I was raised by lesbians. And my male role model is a guy who keeps a star chart of all the alien species he's met. Yeah, I would have been totally accepted."

Seth's heart hurt, but Logan was right. "I would have accepted you."

"One of two things would have happened," Logan began. "You would have paid attention to me and not gotten your work done and you would have resented me. Or you would have ignored me and then I would have resented you. I can see that now. Everything happened the way it needed to happen. I wasn't ready then. I am now. I've finally figured out that bad shit can happen to a person anywhere in the world, but that doesn't mean you don't take it on. That doesn't mean a man should hide away. I didn't take the money because I wasn't sure I would make it through school, and I didn't want to let you down. I'm cool with it now. I know what I want to do, and you're the moneybags of this family."

"What?" He was starting to feel like he was way behind in this conversation. He'd kind of thought this would be the place where he stormed out.

Logan leaned forward. "I know we're supposed to be having this massive fight, but I don't want to fight anymore. I'm going to lay it out and I'm going to hope that you can forgive me. I didn't call you after the incident because I didn't want you to see me like that. I was ashamed. I was lost. I was broken, man. I was utterly broken. I let it happen."

"You didn't exactly have a choice."

"I did later. I chose not to call you. I chose to beg my moms to understate my injuries to you. I chose to keep taking those pills even after I didn't need them because I didn't want to have to feel anything. Caleb cut me off, and I went out and found some more. The asshole didn't even charge me at first, and then he told me I had everything on credit. Yeah, I bought that. He was paying me off to not turn his ass in. I chose to do that. And I chose to buy heroin one night because I was going to go out in a blaze of glory."

Nausea hit suddenly, like he'd been kicked in the gut. "Oh, god. You were going to kill yourself."

"Yes," Logan admitted. "I didn't actually try, but I went so far as to buy it. I sat in Hell on Wheels. I had a couple of beers. I walked into the bathroom because I didn't want my moms to be the ones who had to find me. It seemed fitting to die in a toilet because that's where my life was."

His best friend had nearly died—twice—and he hadn't realized it. "What stopped you?"

"You sent me a text. I was sitting there staring at it and wondering if I would feel good for a few minutes before I died and my phone buzzed and you were asking if I'd seen the new Marvel movie and, just for a second, I wanted to. I wanted to see the movie. I wanted to grab some popcorn and sit in a theater and do something normal. I had one fleeting second where I wasn't thinking about what a piece of shit I was."

He forced down the need to cry. All of his anger was gone in a rush of empathy. "Logan, how can you think that way?"

"I'll tell you, but not without Georgia. I only want to say it once, and there are a few people I need to say it to, but I felt that way then. There's a piece of me that still feels that way. But that night, I knew I wanted to do one thing and that was see a movie. Silly thing, really, but it had been months and months since I wanted anything beyond feeling numb. So I dumped the drugs and I called my friend Hope, and she marched into that bar and she sat up all night with me and in the morning I knew I was going to try to find my way out. That started with paying off my dealer. I am sorry about that, man. Sawyer helped me out by making up the whole barroom brawl story so you and Nate didn't have to know how far I'd fallen. Hope convinced me I should talk to Bernie when I paid him off. At first I was going to drop a tip and have the bastard arrested, but Hope is convincing. She seems to think we all deserve the chance to change. Do you know what happened? After an hour with Hope, the dumb fuck used every dime I paid him—your money—and he got himself clean and right with the law. Who does that? I remember watching him and I couldn't quite believe it. At the end of the day, he was a scared fuck like the rest of us. But he took the out when it was given to him. When he walked into the station house, I knew I had to go to Dallas. If a low-life drug dealer could change, I had to. I called Wolf and he talked to his brother, and I tried to get out. There's the truth. I shamed this badge. I shamed my family."

"You made a mistake, and you're correcting it. Logan, you could have told me then and all I would have done was gotten my ass here as fast as I could." He would have done anything to help his best friend.

"I know that now. And Georgia will forgive me, too. That's not the problem. I haven't forgiven myself, and I'm not sure how I'm going to do it, but I know what Leo was trying to tell me now. I have to figure it out because I'm not willing to lose anything more. I've chosen to be afraid to move, to see the darkness. I think you would have handled it better."

"I don't know. I'm not into pain, man. I don't know how you survived."

"A part of me didn't," Logan admitted. "Georgia handled it better than me. She's a tough one, our girl. She figured out early on that the world isn't perfect, and she didn't wilt under the pressure. I damn near did, but I won't anymore. I've figured something out about families. If we let them, the people in our lives can get lost. How long have you planned this trip to Bliss?"

Seth knew what he meant. How long had he been plotting to get Logan into a position where he had to come home? "Over eight months. If we're coming clean, then you should know that I did pay for your membership to The Club and I paid all of Leo's fees, too. I paid for your moms' anniversary party because I needed an excuse and I helped grease the wheels for Laura's adoption. I didn't have to do much. Caleb and Stef have a lot of pull, but I've done a bunch of business in China, so I made it work."

So many plots, so many balls up in the air.

A smile tugged Logan's lips up. "You wouldn't let me stay lost. If I hadn't come home, I probably would have hung around in Dallas for a couple of years and we would have gotten involved in our own lives, and we would have drifted apart. Eventually you would have married Georgia, and we would have missed out on something amazing because we let it break down. A friendship is like a marriage. We have to work at it. We have to put energy and love and kindness and, yeah, sometimes we have to pray that there's a ruthless prick in the relationship with a complete control disorder. I love you, Seth. I know your father told you that makes us queer, but I'm okay with that. I kind of like the hell out of my moms, so if I turned out like them, I would be damn lucky. I love you, Seth. I don't want to get physical, but you've got a big part of my soul and I want to thank you for not letting me get lost again. I want you to understand that I know you'll get lost in another project, but I'll let you and when you're done, me and Georgia will be waiting right there."

A massive wave of relief rolled across him. This was what he needed. He could handle anything as long as he knew they were going to be okay at the end of the day. But he needed one thing cleared up. "I thought you said she was yours."

Logan rolled his eyes. "Dude, I was balls deep. She is mine when I'm balls deep and you're not around. I'm not going to stop in the middle of fucking our woman to say you're mine except you belong to Seth, too, and we share you in all ways. Sex is not the time for clarifications." He made a totally juvenile vomiting sound.

"God, you're obnoxious." But he couldn't help laughing.

"Yeah, well, you've known that for about twenty years, so if I'm obnoxious, then you're dumb as dirt because you're still here."

And he always would be. "So you're taking me up on school?"

"Fuck, yeah," Logan said with a grin. "And she doesn't know it yet, but Georgia is, too. She's got a business degree, but she hates it. She's going to find her passion if it kills me. I think I already know what mine is."

Seth stared at him. "I thought you would join me."

"Not even. Nah. That's your business and I'll always help out, but I'm going to do something else. I'm going to follow in some big footsteps because Mel isn't my only role model."

There was only one man Logan truly looked up to. "You're going to be a shrink like Leo."

"I'm going to be a therapist," Logan corrected. "I'm going to help dumb assholes like me. I'm going to do something good because if I learned that the world could be a bad place, then I also learned that we can make it good again. With hard work and the right people. Maybe I can make something good come out of this. Leo. He's like Superman. I want to be, too. And I kind of torched my comic book collection. I want it back."

Seth laughed, all of his tension leaving. "I can handle that. We'll have fun putting it back together." He took a long breath. He hadn't lost. He'd fought and he'd won.

Logan's phone went off. He looked down. "Damn. Nate. Sorry, man. It's only for another couple of weeks." Logan touched his finger to the phone. "Nate? What? Are you fucking kidding me? Is he alive? Where's Georgia? She was looking for him."

Seth felt his whole body go on alert. Where was Georgia? She'd been with Logan.

Logan shoved his phone back into his pants. "Win's been shot. Nate said a tourist found him behind the art gallery, and Caleb and Naomi are working on him right now. They couldn't wait to get him to Del Norte. A bus is on the way."

Seth's head whirled. What the hell? "Bus?"

"Ambulance. They're going to stabilize him and then Caleb will ride with him and make sure he makes it, but there was no sign of Georgia. I have to go find her."

Seth heard another low crunch of gravel. He rushed to the window.

"Get back, Seth," Logan shouted. "You don't know who that is."

"It could be Georgia." He ran to the front door and threw it open in time to see an SUV he didn't recognize pulling up to the house. The door opened and a man in dark clothes hopped out. "Fuck. Logan, it's a bunch of guys with guns."

He turned around, but Logan was at the back door. "How many?"

"Six, maybe seven."

Logan's face was tight with anxiety. "I can't handle seven on my own. Where's the gun locker?"

Oh, fuck. They had Georgia. She was small and pale as they hauled her out. This wasn't about Win's private detective. No fucking way. These were serious players, and that meant one thing. He kept his mouth tight as he spoke so maybe they wouldn't see him talking. They had one shot at this. "I don't have a gun locker yet. You need to get Henry."

Logan's mouth closed, his jaw forming a hard line. "Fuck all. They're here for Henry, aren't they? They're here about Henry's past."

Seth nodded slightly. He didn't speak because he didn't want the Colombian cartel enforcers to know he wasn't alone in the house. He'd done his homework. Henry had been trying to shut down a cartel before he'd faked his death. It was a cartel that worked with jihadist sects, money that fueled terrorism around the world. They'd found him. Somehow they'd figured out that John Bishop wasn't dead, and they'd tied him to Seth Stark.

He couldn't see Logan now. Not even out of the corner of his eye.

"Survive," Logan said. "Do you understand me? Don't give them anything because they will kill you and they will kill Georgia if they have her. Fuck. I understand it all now. I want you alive no matter what they do to you. They can break you both and I swear to god, I'll put you back together. Do you understand? I won't let you down. I won't leave you alone for long."

Seth didn't turn back, merely let Logan's words sink in. He felt his eyes widen as Georgia was hauled toward the cabin. They'd shot Win. Her brother might die. They would shoot her, too, if he didn't find a way to keep them talking.

A man in a suit stepped out of the SUV, his elegant form moving with ease. The gun in his hand was an extension of his arm.

"Hello. You must be Mr. Stark." The blond man in front of him was cold. So fucking cold, and he had an arm around Georgia. Her blue eyes looked out at him, but he didn't see weakness there. Hell, no. She was pissed and her will was plain on her face. "We can make this easy or we can make it very difficult. Where is John Bishop?"

Fuck. This was going to hurt. He finally turned, and out of the corner of his eye, he could plainly see that Logan was leaving, his big body moving out the back door. He was alone and responsible for his and Georgia's survival. "What's going on here? Who's John Bishop?"

A mean-looking dude with a gun in his hand stepped up, bunching his fist. "*Jefe*?"

The man with a gun against Georgia's head smirked. "*Sí*."

He heard Georgia's scream before he felt the pain hit his belly. The breath left his body and all of his senses flared in horror.

His agony had just begun.

* * * *

Logan slipped out the back door and made sure he didn't make a damn sound as he moved around the house. He had one gun on his body. One gun versus seven.

Fuck. This was what Alexei had felt. The brutally painful knowledge that he was outgunned and needed a distraction. Logan had been the distraction. He'd paid in pain and suffering, and now he was asking Seth to do the same. And potentially Georgia, because there was no way they didn't have her. Her brother had been shot. She'd been with him. She was in danger, and he was buying time because he finally understood.

Life was worth everything. There was no pain that was worth more than life and love and a future. There was no suffering that a person couldn't come back from if he had enough love. No situation that good couldn't bloom from.

He'd suffered and he could choose to find good in it. He'd suffered so he could make the right choices, help people. Even his own. Would he put Seth through hell if it meant they all survived?

Yes. And yes. And yes again.

He would ask them to suffer and survive because life was worth more than pain. More than pride. Life and love were everything.

He heard a low grunt. Seth. God, they'd already started. His county vehicle was to the right. He hadn't parked up front. They didn't know he was here. He pulled his cell, dialing Nate's number. It was only a second before Nate answered.

"He's still alive, Logan, but I haven't found your woman, yet. I've called in Zane and Max and Rye. Max is moving slow because apparently he slipped a disc, but we're all looking."

Logan kept his voice low. "She's here at our cabin by Nell and Henry's place, but you got to come in real quiet or we're all dead. I don't know who the hell it is who has her, but they're damn serious. Seven guys, every one of them carrying semiautomatics. Do not come in here sirens blaring or they'll kill Seth and Georgia. I'm getting Henry and we're going to handle it, but you get your ass out here pronto."

"Henry?" Nate asked. "What the hell is Henry going to do? Protest them? Logan, just hold tight."

He cut Nate off because he wasn't going to listen anyway. He'd said what he needed to say. Logan shrank against the cabin, looking out over the yard between their place and Henry's. If he was smart, the big boss would leave at least one guard, probably two. One at the front and one at the back.

Sure as anything, a thickly muscled man barged out the back door. Logan whipped his body around though his every instinct told him to kill now. He pushed them all down deep. Killing now would alert the herd that there was a predator around.

The guard took up his post at the door and stared at the river, like something would come up from the water or the forest behind it. He yawned as though taking over someone's house for a torture session was an everyday occurrence. His neck was covered in tattoos. Cartel. Logan would bet the man was either cartel or mob, and there wasn't much difference in the two these days.

What did they want with Henry? What had Henry been involved in before he'd come to Bliss?

The guard leaned against the back door and closed his eyes for a moment as though he needed a nap. Logan would give him a nice long one once he had some backup.

This was his shot. He took off, moving as quietly as he possibly could. He hit the ground with as little of his weight as possible, keeping everything in the front of his feet, stepping lightly. He sprinted across the yard, expecting to get hit at any moment.

He heard a low shout. Georgia. She was screaming for Seth. God. He was leaving them when they needed him the most.

He had to. If he charged in without backup, they would all die.

Nell and Henry's cabin was situated slightly up the river bend, so their front door faced the side of Seth's cabin. Logan made his way around the back. It was the most protected place. No one would see him there. His breath was sawing in and out of his chest as he made it to the cabin. The backyard had a small vegetable garden with a view of the river. Two Adirondack chairs faced the river, but they were both empty.

He turned and found the door. The screen was closed, but the door was open and Logan could hear humming. Nell was in her kitchen, humming as she shoved her hands in a big bowl and started working some dough.

"I'm better," Nell said. "You worry too much, Henry. It's perfectly normal. I'm actually quite hungry now."

"I don't know. I think you should see Caleb." Henry was suddenly at the back door, the screen shadowing his face. If Logan thought he was sneaking up on Henry, he'd been very wrong. Logan suddenly got the feeling Henry had known he was coming. Henry put a finger to his lips.

Silence.

Nell's voice floated through the house. "I need some rest. That's all. Caleb would try to prescribe things, and you know how I feel about big pharmaceutical companies."

"They're not all bad," Henry replied.

Nell was off, her voice rising though she didn't leave her place. She started talking about all the different ways drug companies hurt patients and consumers, and Henry silently slipped outside.

"What's going on? I caught you running across the yard with a gun in hand about thirty seconds ago and then that big guy stepped out onto your porch. Have you called Nathan?"

"Yeah, though I think this is your problem. You tell me something and you tell me now because my partner and my wife are being held by some sort of drug lord. Did you work for them before you came to Bliss?"

Henry went the slightest bit pale. "They're from a cartel?"

Logan ran a hand across his hair, frustration welling up. He didn't have time for this. "I could be wrong. They could be mob. They could be a traveling circus. I don't give a shit because they're going to kill my people and I think they're here for you. So I'm going to ask the question and you're going to answer. Were you on the payroll?"

There was a short shake of Henry's head. "No. The cartel was the target. If it's who I think it is, they were mixed up with a terrorist cell. I was CIA, but then I wasn't. Damn it. They're supposed to think I'm dead."

"They seem to have caught on. Nate's on his way, but I don't have time to wait so I need you to get your freak on. You owe Seth." It had to have been Seth who had helped him, protected his identity. Seth was smart enough to do it, even all those years ago. Logan remembered all the times Seth would close his laptop when Logan walked in the room. He'd hidden Henry's secrets, even from his best friend. Logan wasn't mad. That was just who Seth was. He was trustworthy. "You owe him, Henry. And you damn well know it."

Henry nodded and disappeared back into the cabin. "Hey, baby, Logan's here. He says there's a problem with the plumbing. I'm going to go check it out. You knead your bread, okay? I wouldn't want to ruin it. And I'll turn up the music. I know you love this aria."

The sound of an opera filled the house and spilled over into the yard.

"I could come help." Nell had to yell over the music. Clever Henry, trying to hide the inevitable sounds of death and destruction with wailing opera singers. Actually, Logan thought he might like the sound of gunfire more.

"No, baby. You stay here. It's just a little wet work. I'll be back in ten minutes. I love you, Nell."

Henry slipped back outside and suddenly there was a nasty-looking knife in his hand. It looked like he'd raided the kitchen for his arsenal. While the knife was long and sharp, it wasn't what Logan had in mind.

"Can't you get a gun?"

Henry shrugged, the knife held easily in his hand. He stared down at it, a stricken look on his face. "I don't keep one in the house. I don't keep one at all anymore. I am exactly who I say I am. I'm Henry Flanders. I gave all of this shit up a long time ago."

The truth was right inside Logan's cabin. "It didn't give you up, Henry."

Henry's eyes went cold. Yeah, that was the dude who had first shown up here. Somber. Dangerous. An elegant viper waiting to strike. "How many?"

"At least seven. And they've had Georgia and Seth with them for a good five minutes now."

"They'll play with them for a while," Henry explained. "They don't understand this place. They'll think they're isolated. As long as they don't think the police are going to blaze in, they'll take their time because you soften up a target before you go in for the kill. They want information."

"I suspect they want you."

"I can walk in there and give myself up," Henry started.

He wasn't about to let him do that. No matter who he'd been before, he was Henry Flanders now. Henry was the guy who'd fixed his ma's sink and helped work on their roof when it needed fixing. He was the man who winked as he protested. He was Henry. "They would kill them quickly and then take you. I was never planning on trading you in. I need someone to watch my back. I have to save them."

Henry's hand tightened around the knife, and he edged up to the side of the cabin, his face turning slightly away. "The guard they put on the back door is half asleep. I'm going around the back, like I'm walking up the river. You got a knife? Because that gun is going to be too loud. The minute they hear gunfire, they'll scatter. We need them securely in the house."

He reached down into his boot. Of course he had a knife. It was utilitarian, but it would get the job done. Quiet. He had to keep quiet.

Henry took off, his bare feet moving silently across the grass. He went the opposite direction from the house, around a set of trees, but in mere seconds, Logan saw him walking down the river.

And so did the guard who hopped off the porch and started walking toward the intruder.

Logan took off the minute the guard's back was turned. Henry was right. This guy was pure muscle, not trained to keep quiet and move in for the kill. He would simply shoot whatever came his way. Logan silently thanked Mel for all the training. He might not be trying to take down an alien horde, but the idea was the same. He could hear Mel talking in his head. *Move quick. Move silently. Take down the prey without alerting the rest of the herd.*

Save your town, son.

Save his family.

He'd never done this up close and personal before, but there was a time for everything. He didn't hesitate, didn't feel any fear beyond what would happen if he didn't get this done. The guard raised his gun to take Henry down, and Logan quietly shoved his knife between the man's ribs, his free hand knocking the gun away and then covering his victim's mouth so he couldn't shout out.

It was hard, but he was strong. A knife didn't merely slip in, it required force and movement. It required upper body strength. The man in his arms was a bull, all sinewy muscle. Logan had to force the knife past his ribs and up, into his heart. Two years ago he'd never lifted a weight, didn't think to train.

It was his own torture that brought about the change, but now he knew if it hadn't happened, he would have been helpless to stop this.

His past pain might be Georgia and Seth's salvation, and suddenly he was grateful. Grateful for the time he'd spent on that desk. Grateful for the lesson it had taught him. Grateful that he was alive in this moment to save them.

He held the guy close, adrenaline pumping through his veins. He didn't feel remorse. This man would have killed Georgia. He would have taken everything that was beautiful and lovely and precious about her and ground it into dust. Logan had already decided to give up law enforcement, but he would never give this up. This was his job in life. To protect them. To love them. To do anything he had to do to ensure their survival.

Henry was suddenly in front of him. "He's dead. You can let him go now."

He let the man slide away as Henry picked up his gun and checked the clip. For a man who hadn't used firearms in years, he still knew his way around one.

"Are you ready? This is your op, Logan. I'll do what you need me to," Henry said.

"I'm going to slip into the master bedroom window. Georgia left it open earlier. You go in the back door. Kill anyone you see. Use the knife if you can until we're in the living room. Once we know we have them trapped, all bets are off." He wouldn't care how much noise he made once he knew they couldn't get away with Georgia and Seth. He looked down, expecting his hands to be shaking, but they were stone-cold steady. It was only his heart that was shaking. He gave Henry what he hoped was a confident grin. "Hey, Henry, I won't tell your wife if you won't tell my moms."

Henry put a hand on his shoulder. "Deal."

Logan jogged around the back of the cabin, his whole being set on doing his job. On getting them back.

Chapter Seventeen

Georgia winced as the man in the suit slapped Seth full across the face. A stream of blood began to flow, racing down Seth's blue and white button-down, but when his eyes came up, there wasn't pain in them. He swayed on his feet, but it was obvious that Seth was angry.

"Is that the best you can do?"

The man who had taken her prisoner gave him a reptilian smile. "Oh, Mr. Stark, I assure you, I can do so much better. My men are simply playing around right now. *Amarralo, por favor*. I think it's time we had a chat."

Seth's eyes found hers as he was pulled into one of the dining room chairs and bound by the chest to it. Two of the boss's henchmen had already zip tied his hands, and now they wound a thin rope around his torso. She could see where it cut into his skin.

Her own hands had been left undone. She'd been careful to be pleasant since she'd gotten in the SUV. All the long trip from town to here she'd wondered if her brother was dead. She couldn't stand to think of Win's big body cooling in a parking lot while life went on around him. Tears seeped from her eyes.

"Hey, gorgeous. Don't cry." The man with the gun reached up and casually wiped a tear off her face. "You're very beautiful when you cry, but I haven't given you anything to cry about. Not yet."

She shivered, her every nerve in pain at the thought of his hands on her. She didn't want anyone except Seth and Logan. Not for the rest of her life. The love she felt for them was sacred.

"Don't you fucking touch her." Despite the fact that he was tied up and bleeding, Seth growled the words. He struggled against his bonds, the chair moving back and forth.

"My name is…well, you can call me Jones. I work for a very particular business." Jones straightened his tie as though he couldn't stand the thought of being unkempt. "I guess you could say I'm the North American manager for my firm. It's a family-run business, and they'd prefer to stay in their country. I handle issues that tend to come up for my boss back in Bolivia. I suppose you could say I'm the public relations and the security guy all rolled into one. You understand business, don't you, Stark?"

Seth's eyes were clear as he spoke, though she could still see the blood on his chin. She wanted nothing more than to walk over there and wipe his face off and kiss every place where he surely ached. He took such good care of her. Standing idly by seemed wrong, but it was her only play now. "I understand that a man like you will do anything for money. I happen to have my checkbook handy. Unfortunately, I can't write one out because you seem to have tied down my hands."

Jones walked a circle around him, making a *tsk tsk* sound, like a disappointed mother. "Oh, you underestimate me. I'm a company man, if you know what I mean. Once in, you're in for life. That life can be an amazing one, or it can be short and tragic. I personally enjoy the perks of being employed by one of the largest drug cartels in the world, and I also enjoy my head being on my body. So I do my job."

"What exactly is your job today?" Seth was cool as a cucumber. He sounded like he was in a Friday afternoon meeting with his management staff.

Jones laughed, a sound that contained no humor. "I'm going to tell it to you straight, Stark, as one businessman to another. I'm looking for a man, and I think you can help me find him. I brought along my Spanish-speaking compatriots because the last thing I want to do is fail at this. Right now, they think this is a simple shakedown. I've been trying very hard to solve a problem for my bosses. I want to move up. They can be generous when they're pleased."

"And when they're not?" Seth asked.

"Oh, well, that doesn't tend to go well for anyone. Like I said, I'm doing this on the down low because I would rather like to beat the man they actually hired for the job. He doesn't have my brains. He's still trying to figure out where Bishop is. Bishop is gone. We won't find him on our own. But I have a suspicion that you can. So you're going to be a good boy and tell me that my hunch is correct, and I can prove to everyone that I'm the right man for the job."

"I'm not feeling particularly chatty today." Seth struggled against his bonds.

Jones shrugged as though he'd expected that. "There's only one way this goes down. You're going to die. I can't leave behind a bunch of witnesses. This is a bit of a covert mission, and I don't want it getting back to the big boss if I fail, so your death is absolutely going to happen. Now, it can happen quick and painless, or my friends there will enjoy dragging it out along with your intestines. They're good at it."

At least he was honest. Georgia's eyes struck on the bar and something that shouldn't be there. Logan's hat. Her heart rate tripled, and it had been pounding hard before. Logan's Stetson was right there along with the keys to his county-issued vehicle. Logan was here somewhere. Was he hiding? Had he gone for help?

She knew one thing. He wouldn't leave them behind. If he was hiding, then he was waiting for the right time to pounce. He would come for her. He'd promised her that a long time ago when she'd been taken by another douchebag. *I'll always come for you, Georgia.* She'd sobbed in his arms and felt safer than she'd ever felt before.

So she had to stay alive because Logan would be here. She had to make sure Seth was alive, too. She had to do whatever it took and that meant getting the attention back on her. If she didn't, all the focus would be on Seth and it would be all violence. At least when it was on her, it was a slight bit softer. Gross, yes, but not all knifey and stuff.

"You don't have to kill me." She said it in that oh-so-breathy way that let a guy know she was soft and pliable and very dumb. Guys, idiot, nasty assholes like the one in front of her, tended to like their women dumb.

Jones turned and sure enough she had his attention. "Really? You weren't so keen on me killing the other one."

"He was my brother. I love my family." He'd called the cartel a family business. It was a gamble. "A brother is different from a guy I've been banging and you know it. You let him live." Hopefully.

Jones's eyes flared, and she knew she had him. "Now that is a surprise, sweetheart. I thought you were going to be trouble. I'll be honest, the whole way over here I was thinking what a shame it would be to have to kill someone so sexy. Isn't this your boyfriend?"

She shrugged. He was so much more than a boyfriend. He was half her soul. She'd figured out this afternoon that her soul wasn't her own. It belonged to Seth and Logan. She belonged to them. "I was with him because he's rich. You're rich, aren't you? I can see plainly that you're powerful. Power can be very attractive to a girl." She'd seen him staring at her, his eyes going right to her breasts. When he'd helped her up into the car, his hands had lingered on her hips for a few seconds too long.

Jones assessed her, his gaze moving up and down her body. "You're living with him. Do you think I haven't done my homework? I checked you both out." He turned to Seth. "She's been living in your condo for months."

"Wouldn't you have invited her in? Look at her, man," Seth said. "She's not exactly the best assistant. She's good for one thing. And I've had that for months and months."

Yes, Seth was damn good, too. It occurred to her a little drama could buy them some time. She huffed and rolled her eyes. "I was his secretary. He's handsome and rich. A girl's got to eat, you know."

Jones frowned her way. "You didn't seem so happy with me before."

She hated him and, at the time, she hadn't known she would need to flirt with her horrific kidnapper and potential rapist. "But you were kind. You didn't kill my brother when you so obviously could have."

"I didn't have to. I believe in a measure of mercy." He stared down at her.

She giggled like a schoolgirl. She wanted to throw up, but that wouldn't further her cause. "I do, too."

Jones put a hand on Seth's shoulder. "You got a good one there, buddy. You chose well. Don't blame yourself. You're young. You think with your dick, so it's no wonder you picked a whore. That's what happens when you trust a chick, especially one with great tits and a heart-shaped ass. She'll throw you over for the first guy who comes along and chooses not to put a bullet through her brother's heart."

"Georgia, what are you doing?" Seth sold it. And she knew he was acting because she'd seen him do it before. Seth was a master. A deep peace settled in her despite the fact that they could still die. It was the peace that came from having a great partner.

She shrugged, hoping her eyes were properly blank. "Sorry. I'm going to go with the best bet."

A long laugh boomed through the room as Jones winked her way. "I thought I'd put a gun to her head and threaten to shoot the bitch if you didn't give up Bishop, but I think that might be doing you a favor now. Maybe she can blow me while I have you tortured. A blow job makes everything so much more pleasant, don't you think?"

Georgia smiled because she would bite his dick off the first chance she got and then they would see who had the upper hand.

"I was in love with her," Seth said, his voice bitter.

A bit of worry ran through her. God, he was either really good or not lying at all. What was his game? Had he caught on to hers? She would rather suffer through seriously icky sexual stuff than have Seth's inner parts get used as playthings. She could survive the ick. She couldn't survive watching him die. Her stomach rolled at the thought of any of these men touching her, but she would do it with a big smile on her face if it bought Logan the time he needed.

Jones got closer to her. "I'm not kidding. I would enjoy watching his torture while you service me. I don't actually like to get my hands dirty. I've moved past that. It's like asking an executive to pass out the mail. But I don't mind getting my dick a little filthy. Not for a woman who looks like she'd be worthwhile."

And then she would require some serious bath time in which both of her men took special care of her. They wouldn't leave because she'd played a part and pretended to want the gross criminal guy. Oh, she was going to get her ass smacked hard. She might become deeply acquainted with floggers and whips and that spanking bench thing, but then they would kiss her and love her and make her forget because she'd figured out that she could make it through anything now.

She walked up as boldly as she could and cocked a hip at Jones, whose eyes went right to her chest. "I'm game. You said you would be honest, well, I will, too. I'm a practical girl. I'll go with the guy who offers me the best deal."

No lying there. The best deal was the one Seth and Logan offered her. Pure, no-holds-barred, stick-together-even-when-the-going-went-to-complete-shit love. They offered her nothing less than a life where things could go wrong and they could fight and make each other crazy and still know that they would get in bed at the end of the day and turn to each other because they were in it together.

So she didn't even have to lie to him. She was telling him flat out who she would choose.

"I can offer a lot," Jones said.

He had nothing on her men. "I imagine you can. So who's this Bishop guy? I want to help if it gets me out of this dingbat town." She loved Bliss. She could stay here. She would even get used to the moose and stuff, but she would bet that Mr. Big Suit didn't love small-town living. "I don't know why he dragged me here."

Jones smirked her way. "You're a big-city girl. That's obvious. So you've never heard of John Bishop? Think hard, sweetheart. Any information you can give me would help."

She scrunched up her face, pretending to tax her brain. "I've worked for Seth for months. I don't think there's a Bishop on the payroll, but I could find out, maybe get you an address. I need a computer. Or I could call in to the office. We don't have to make this bloody. This flooring is like expensive and stuff. I think the blood would make it less pretty."

Yeah, she was good at this.

Jones smiled at her, watching her lips as she wet them with her tongue. If she only had her heels, she would bring one very slowly down on the bridge of his foot, letting it sink into the skin, and then she might actually get to shoot a son of a bitch. "Bishop isn't working for Stark, sweetheart. I rather think it's the other way around. You see, John Bishop was a ghost, a spook."

"You're a ghost hunter." A little blondeness never hurt. It always got the guys to think she was cute and stupid and harmless. Why was Seth involved with the CIA? She knew exactly what a spook was. Her brothers were Delta Force. "Do you have one of those EMFBS thingees? Like on TV? They like hear ghosts and stuff. I don't think Seth believes in ghosts."

Jones laughed. His right hand relaxed. That was his gun hand. Yes, he was relaxing around her because he believed she wasn't a threat. She was sweet and pretty and only good for a fuck. Oh, she was going to show him. "I wish these guys understood a lick of English because they would be amused by you. So pretty and so vacant. Exactly how I like my women." He turned to his henchmen, giving them a shorthand gesture.

The man closest to Seth planted a fist in his gut. She heard the air whoosh out of his lungs and then his harsh moan of pain wracked her. She rolled her eyes as though the sound annoyed her when it hurt her down to her soul. She wanted to take the pain for him, but he would never allow it.

Where was Logan? She needed Logan. They needed him so badly. Had it only been a few hours before that she'd held him tight and promised him everything she had? Logan was the hero. He was the one who came out of nowhere and saved the day. Seth was the one who held them together. She needed them both.

"No, sweetheart. Bishop is supposed to be a real ghost, but after my counterpart in South America got through…interviewing…an old barkeep who thought he could get away from us, well, we found out that Bishop isn't exactly as dead as he should be. If only his counterparts in the CIA had as good intelligence as we did."

She had no idea what any of this had to do with Seth. There was no way Seth was John Bishop. Was he related to him? She knew how close family could be, even when they were miles apart. *Please let Win be alive.* "It sounds like a tough situation. I don't like it when people come back from the dead. It's confusing."

He actually purred as his free hand came out to pull her close. She was dragged hard against his body, his hand going low to cup her ass. "You are a bundle of joy, aren't you, blondie? You're going to be a lot of fun to keep around."

She forced herself not to stare at Seth. How much could he take?

They were using him like a punching bag.

And Jones, the giant asshole, had an erection he was rubbing against her. “We knew we didn’t kill John Bishop, so we did some investigating. My boss found the last man to see him alive. Bishop faked his death. After we paid a hacker a ton of money, all we were able to find was a cell phone we suspect belonged to Bishop. It was used shortly after his car exploded and he went up in a ball of fire and smoke. Do you know who he called?”

She shook her head.

He turned his eyes to Seth. “You, Mr. Stark. He called you. Why would a CIA operative contact a college kid? Is Bishop your father? Or just a guy who liked to bugger college boys?”

He held a hand up. Apparently his henchmen were well trained. They stopped immediately, and Seth’s head rolled forward, his exhaustion and pain apparent. “Don’t know what you’re talking about, man. I don’t know anyone named John Bishop.”

Georgia looked around. She’d lost track of two of the men. One seemed to have stayed out front and another had walked to the back door. There was a man hovering in the hallway to her left, leaning against the wall, watching the action. The last man she could account for had walked back toward the bedroom looking for anyone else in the house. He’d been gone for a while. She couldn’t stand the thought of that man walking into their bedroom, the room where she was safe and loved.

There was a banging noise that came from that direction and a crash as something broke.

Jones’s head whipped around. “What was that?”

Seth spit blood before talking. “That was very likely a priceless antique. Your men don’t seem to appreciate the value of fine vases. If they destroyed the one I think it was, it was from China. Ming dynasty. Or they might have smashed a couple of Fabergé eggs. Idiots.”

There was nothing like that back in the bedroom. It was tastefully decorated, but not with antiques. What was Seth doing?

A light hit his eyes even though he was in rough shape. He gave her a wink.

Logan was coming for them, and Seth knew it. She had to be

ready.

She put a hand on Jones's chest. "He's not lying. He's got some seriously amazing stuff back there. We don't want to leave without it. There's a fortune sitting there and collecting dust. And I have the code to his safe."

She looked over at the hall that led to the secondary bedrooms. The man who was leaning there so negligently didn't see Nell Flanders's husband walking up behind him. What was he doing here? God, she hoped he didn't get hurt. Nell was such a sweetheart.

And then he very casually and with utter silence slit the man's throat and got him to the ground and was out of sight before anyone could look his way. It had been like one of those nature videos she'd watched. The lion had taken down the rather unattractive and mean gazelle without breaking a sweat.

Wow. That explained a whole lot.

So Henry was John Bishop. Yeah. She hadn't guessed that.

Jones spoke in rapid-fire Spanish and another of his goons stalked down the hallway, rushing off to the master bedroom. "Sometimes these guys from down south get distracted by shiny things. I think it's about time we finish up here and take this party somewhere else. No matter how quiet we are, we're not isolated enough to fire up the chainsaw and start hacking off Stark's body parts here."

Henry was suddenly back in the hallway. Kent had been right. He moved like a ghost. He caught her eyes and nodded to a place behind her.

"Where are we going to go?" Georgia asked the question like she couldn't care less. She yawned and turned her head.

And her heart nearly stopped. Logan was walking down the hall. His shirt was ripped and completely covered in blood. His hair was wild as though he'd been in a fight. His eyes, oh, his eyes were focused on one thing and one thing only.

Her.

He was a magnificent beast, and he wasn't going to allow anyone to take his mate. He'd killed both men who had walked back there. They were dead on the floor because they'd threatened her. She had no doubt about that.

He was so getting sex tonight.

But between Logan and Henry, they still only had two against three as the guard outside walked back in. She needed to even up those odds. She wasn't going to sit back idly. Logan and Seth needed her. Her magnificent beast and her Prince Charming were getting help from her.

"Someone is coming," he said in slow, deliberate English. "Two cars. I think it is the police. No sirens, though."

They needed a distraction because someone was about to get shot and it wasn't going to be her men. Luckily, she was damn good at distractions, but she was done playing a role.

As quickly as she could, she brought her knee back and up, catching that fucker right in the erection. It was a move she'd perfected on LA casting directors who got too handsy. It was also probably why she'd never been cast. She was okay with that now.

"Son of a bitch!" Jones yelled as he doubled over. His gun dropped to the ground with a clatter. "Kill them."

But Logan and Henry were already on the move. Shots began raining around her, and she ducked, her hand going straight for that gun. She sent a silent prayer of gratitude to her brothers, who were gun nuts and wouldn't allow their baby sis to walk around in blissful ignorance. Oh, no, they'd taken her to gun ranges. She'd looked ridiculous shooting at targets in designer heels and the full Chanel treatment, but she knew what to do with the one in her hand.

She lifted it and fired the minute she got a good aim. Jones was reaching for her when the bullet hit. His chest pounded with metal as she got three shots off in rapid fire.

His eyes went glassy as he looked down at the mess she'd made of his chest. He slumped to the side like a marionette with his strings cut.

Her hands shook as she clutched the gun and thought about emptying the clip.

"Georgia, baby. He's dead. They're all dead. It's all right." Logan eased the gun out of her hand and then helped her up. She shook, trying to get her arms up so she could touch him. God, she needed to be between them. "Baby, I'm covered in blood."

She didn't care. She threw her arms around him, reveling in how tightly he held her. Now that the danger had passed, she was shaking, unable to control her hands, her tears, the way her heart pounded. "Seth."

Oh, god, Seth. She let go of Logan, but the scary dude she'd formerly thought of as a mild granola was slicing through Seth's bonds. She got to her knees and caught Seth as he fell forward. She would have dropped to the floor, but Logan was there, a strong body, holding her up. Seth's arms went around her, his head slumping forward onto her shoulder.

"You did so good, Georgia. Logan, she was so good," Seth managed to say.

She let her hands find his hair, pulling him close, trying to lend him whatever strength she had left. She breathed in. She breathed out. Her men were alive, and that was all that mattered.

Chapter Eighteen

Seth didn't want to move. Moving hurt. Everything fucking hurt, but Georgia surrounded him. Georgia had moved onto the couch with him and snuggled close. She'd been so strong. She'd taken the burden off him. If he'd had to watch that man put a gun to her head, he wasn't sure what he would have done. He likely would have spilled everything the minute they'd started to hurt her and then they would both be dead. She'd been smart and fast on her feet.

"Marry me." She was everything he wanted in a woman. He'd known it before, but he couldn't wait any longer to claim her. Screw his timelines. Screw his plans. The only plan that mattered was sitting right here with him. He felt Logan's hand gingerly touch down on his shoulder, a simple sign that he was there with them. They were together.

"He's a little loopy in the head, baby," Logan said. "What he meant to say was marry us."

"Marry us." It was all he'd wanted since he was a kid, a family with his best friend in his hometown.

A brilliant smile crossed Georgia's face. "Yes. I'll marry you. I love you both so much."

Seth stifled a groan when Georgia hugged him tight. It wasn't the most romantic proposal, and he would fix that by giving her the wedding of her dreams. After he regrew all the organs that had been pounded to dust inside his body cavity.

The front door swung open and Nate Wright moved into the room, his gun drawn. He looked around and then sighed. "You can come on in, Ty. It's all corpses. Henry, that look is so not vegan. Fuck all. I'm going to owe Caleb and Gemma some serious cash, aren't I?"

Fuck. Henry was here. Henry had been forced to take out a bunch of dudes. Henry, who just wanted to live his life in peace, had a whole cartel coming after him.

Seth forced himself to bring his head up, finding Henry standing in the middle of a bunch of dead bodies, covered in blood. It dripped off his hands. Seth knew he'd finished the job with a gun, but it looked like he'd done some knife play somewhere in there because a big-ass butcher knife was in his hands, the one he'd used to cut through Seth's bindings. It wasn't clean. It was coated in blood, and obviously not his. Henry stared down at his hand as though he couldn't believe there was a knife there.

Seth wasn't the only one who'd gotten the shit kicked out of him. Henry's whole world had ground to a halt. The cartel knew he was alive. They would come after him. Even if that Jones asshole hadn't told anyone what he was planning, they wouldn't give up.

"Holy shit." A man in blue pants and a white shirt walked in carrying a huge medical bag. "That is a lot of corpses. Caleb is going to be pissed. Is there anyone left alive for me to treat?"

Seth held his hand up weakly, gesturing the guy over. "I will take any drugs you will give me. Logan, dude, all is forgiven. This shit hurts and I only had to survive it for like ten minutes. Motherfucker, I think I felt my spleen go." Georgia's blue eyes went wide with terror. Seth shook his head. "I'm joking. I'm fine, baby."

He let the EMT help him lie down. He so wasn't fine. He was pretty sure he was about to spend some time in the hospital, but he didn't want to scare Georgia.

"Are you going to get as fucked up as this one did?" Nate asked, proving he could joke even in the worst of circumstances. He pointed to Logan, who was helping Georgia up.

Seth managed a grin and shook his head, which also hurt. "Nope. I already knew the world kind of sucked. This is no surprise to me."

Logan flashed him his middle finger but smiled as he did it.

"Hi, my name is Ty. I'm going to be your paramedic today, but honestly, I think I'm going to be the dude who sits here with you until the ambulance comes. Tell me how this feels." Ty barely touched his stomach and Seth nearly screamed. Yeah, he wasn't going to win tough guy of the year.

He left that up to his best friend.

"You're probably going to need surgery. I think it's likely you have some internal bleeding." Ty stood up. "Don't move. There's a bus on the way, but I'm going to make sure Caleb knows to stick close to the hospital. He got out of surgery a couple of minutes ago. Gunshot wound. It must be the day for them."

"Did the patient make it? My brother. Is he alive?" Georgia managed to get the question out even through her tears. Logan wrapped his arms around her as though bracing her for some ugly truth.

Ty smiled. "Yeah, he's alive. Caleb said he's going to be fine."

"Your brother is a tough son of a bitch. He was barking orders at me even as they loaded him into the ambulance. He's the reason we were already looking for you," Nate said. "Logan, why don't we take Georgia outside to wait for the ambulance?"

"I can't leave Seth," Georgia argued.

"I'm fine, baby," Seth replied. There was someone he needed to talk to, and he couldn't with an audience. "Logan, please?"

Logan nodded, and over her virulent protests, picked her up bodily and hauled her outside. She was cursing him as he carried her out the door.

"Hurricane Georgia," Seth whispered with a smile. She was awfully pretty when she was pissed.

Nate knelt down. "Are you sure you're all right?"

Seth nodded. "I'll live. Henry?"

Henry moved quietly, standing over him before kneeling down. "I'm sorry, Seth. I can't tell you how much."

He managed to reach out a hand. He could see Henry's reluctance to take it. "I'm not mad. I think we've got time. The asshole in charge said he'd been keeping it all on the down low because his bosses hate leads that don't pan out. They're not going to charge in here tomorrow."

"Henry, I respect a man's privacy." Nate's voice was grim. "You know I do, but if something's heading into my town, I need to know."

Henry's face was a blank, as though he didn't have an ounce of emotion in him. His words were dead, too, just combinations of letters that came out of his mouth. He could be talking about the weather for all the fire he put into them. "Hell, Sheriff. Hell is coming to Bliss, and I invited it in."

Nate closed his eyes as though he'd been dreading that very response.

Henry stood up. "I can't tell my wife. I can't. She's pregnant." Now the emotion seeped through, his face flushing and a hand running across his hair. "Nell is pregnant, and I don't want her to know the father of her baby has been lying to her for years. I need time."

"Who are you?" Nate asked.

Henry turned, and there was no blankness to his face now. There was pure will there. "I am Henry Flanders. I am Nell's husband. I am fucking Henry Flanders because that is who I choose to be."

"I don't think they're going to stop looking." Seth could hear the distant wail of the ambulance Ty had called. Soon he would be happy with an IV filled with mind-numbing drugs, but he had a few things to say first. "Henry, I can start again and build a whole new scenario. I can place Bishop somewhere else, leave a trail even an idiot could follow. I can do it."

He'd screwed up once. He was going to make it right this time. He would save Henry and Nell would never have to know.

"You would help me after all this?" Henry asked.

How could he think for a second that Seth wouldn't? "What's a ruptured spleen between family? I won't let you down."

He could have sworn he saw a sheen of tears hit Henry's eyes. "I thank you, son. But I know I have to tell her. Just please, not today. After the wedding. She's so looking forward to Wolf's wedding. I'll tell her then. Maybe she'll be comfortable with the pregnancy at that point."

Nate shook his head as though he couldn't quite comprehend everything he was hearing. "I thought you two weren't planning on having any."

"She changed her mind because she loves everyone else's kids so much," Henry explained. "She decided we could have one. Nate, we've been trying for a while. She's had two miscarriages. God, I can't tell her. I can't be the reason we lose another baby. I fucking can't."

Nate put a hand on Henry's shoulder. "Then you won't. We'll fix this. I don't give a shit who you were before. You're Henry now and you belong to Bliss. So go get cleaned up. I'll tell Nell you got caught in the crossfire. I'll make it look good. This was a robbery. Seth is a wealthy man. Everyone will buy it. Go take a shower. She can't see you like this. And the ambulance is here. Be quick. She'll be over here in a minute."

Henry nodded and walked back toward the master bath.

Nate smiled down at him. "So now that you've been back for a while, is everything the way you remember it?"

Just the same. "Yep. Gorgeous mountains. Beautiful women. High body count. Some things never change."

* * * *

Logan looked out over the assembled crowd and wondered how he was going to get through the next few minutes. He hadn't intended to make his confession today, but Holly and Caleb and Alexei were here. And Jen and Stef were here. When would he get them all in the same place again? And he couldn't wait any longer. He had to get it out. Something fundamental had changed inside him, and the need to tell the truth had become a fire in his blood.

His moms were here. He wished they didn't have to know this truth about him. But it was good. Confession was good for the soul. He hoped.

His ma was covering Seth with a quilt she'd made. Hospital blankets weren't nice enough for Teeny Green. And Momma was watching him with suspicious eyes, as though she knew he had something to say.

"Whoa. Is this what it looks like when you buy a damn hospital, Seth?" Jamie walked in the room followed by Hope and Noah, who carried a tote bag in his right hand, proving he was totally trustworthy. He'd found what Logan had been looking for. Jamie caught sight of Momma and grimaced. "Sorry about the 'damn,' Momma Marie."

"You speak nice around ladies, James Glen," his momma shot back. Everyone else was giggling at the sight of a grown man with his own ranch flushing like a schoolboy who'd been caught doing something naughty, but Logan understood.

"He didn't buy the hospital. He merely made a nice-sized donation, since apparently so many of you end up in here," Georgia explained.

She was sitting on the hospital bed, her hand wrapped in Seth's. Since he'd come out of his surgery, neither one of them had left the hospital. Two days later and Georgia had managed to grease the wheels enough to get a double room converted into a nice big suite for all future Bliss patients, courtesy of the new Seth Stark wing of the hospital. Actually, she'd convinced them to make two since gunfights had become a regular occurrence in town. Her brother was quietly recovering in the suite next door. He was grumpy and caustic to the nurses. All of them except Naomi. When Naomi walked in, Logan had noticed that Win was suddenly on his best behavior.

"He seems like he's trying to buy the whole town," Stef grumbled.

"Hush, babe." Jen Talbot had a smile on her face. She pretty much always did, as though the world amused her to no end. She settled her hand on her belly. She looked ready to pop, but someone had told Logan that she still had some time left.

Would she find what he had to say next amusing?

"I think Stef here just likes to be the richest man in town." Caleb snorted Stef's way. "Not that he is. My bank account is way bigger."

Stef rolled his gray eyes. "Yeah, well, you're also the stingiest man in town."

Caleb shrugged. "Hey, it's how I keep being the richest man in town. I don't go around buying a bunch of crap."

"Except for the massive cabin, all the new medical equipment, and the brand-spanking-new ambulance," Holly murmured.

"Do not to be forgetting the new bed. Yes, that was good purchase. That bed is not a California kingdom. It is much bigger. I swear this new bed is from Russia," Alexei said with a smile and his patented bad English. "It is bed for Russian acrobats."

Momma looked at the big Russian. "Are you going to start talking nasty around the young'uns, Markov?"

The ex-Russian mobster shook his head. "Oh, no. It is plain to see Miss Georgia here is very innocent."

Georgia didn't even blush. "Thank you. I am a delicate flower."

Holly laughed. "Sorry about that. Neither one of them has a sense of decorum." She stood up. "Seth, I'm glad to hear they're letting you go tomorrow. I'm going to take my gorgeous monsters home. I look forward to the makeover party."

"Oh, yes, we're still having that. And Nell said she would bring a soothsayer along to bless the cabin after all the death and destruction," Georgia said. "Hey, I bet someone who makes a living off of soothsaying probably needs a makeover, too."

Georgia would make over the world if it would let her. She would make it beautiful and cover it in rhinestones so it always shined. God, he hoped she still looked at him the same way. He closed his eyes and said the words he'd been holding inside for two years.

"I was going to tell them."

He opened his eyes. The whole room turned to him. His ma was holding hands with Momma, both of them watching and waiting. Standing by as they always had.

"What are you talking about?" Seth asked.

Holly seemed to understand. "Logan, you don't have to do this."

Alexei shook his head. "He does, Holly. He needs this. He needs to be a man. That was taken from him. He take back by talking and doing the right things and letting himself love."

Logan felt a well of emotion. It had been blocked for so long. He'd shoved it down and ignored its existence, but he couldn't now. "You're wrong about one thing. I wasn't a man before. I was a kid, and maybe that would have changed on its own. Or maybe not. I lived this charmed life, and I didn't have to see the sacrifices that were made for me. I didn't have to see them as sacrifices at all. I saw it as my due. My moms sacrificed. They could have gone somewhere where they would have been easily accepted, had friends like them, but they stayed here because of me. Because they thought this was the best thing for me. God, I can't imagine what it was like all those years ago. It's great now, but it had to have been hard in the beginning."

"Logan," Ma began, but Momma shook her head.

"You let him talk, Teeny. He's finally doing what we asked him to do. He's dealing with it," Momma said. "And it wasn't so bad, son."

"She's being Marie, Logan. They had tough times here. Stella talks about it. Sure, it's good now. It's great because of people like Marie and Teeny," Stef said. "Because they helped change the generation that came before. They were strong, and now the world is a little better."

"I didn't see the pain they endured. I was a child and the world revolved around me until one day it didn't. The world revolved around my pain and my sacrifice and it was all bullshit because I broke. God, I broke." He didn't want to say the words. He hesitated and then felt a hand in his. Georgia. She threaded their fingers together, and he noticed that she reached for Seth, too. Their strength was his, an offering of love. This was what he'd had growing up. A family that held on, that gave each other strength to do the things that needed to be done.

He brought his head up and looked Alexei in the eye. "I apologize. I would have done the same thing. And I would get on that desk again myself if it meant saving my people."

Alexei nodded. "This I know. You say you were child, but even then you had heart of a great man."

"I didn't. Did you not hear what I said? I broke. I wanted you and Holly and Stef and Jen here because I have to tell you that I was going to tell them everything I knew. It wasn't much, but Luka had beaten me so badly. I just wanted it to stop. I was going to give you all up. I am so sorry."

There it was. The heart of all his pain. His shame.

Seth sat up, moving slowly. "How many times, brother?"

Jamie came to stand beside him. "Yeah. I was thinking the same thing."

"What?" What were they talking about?

Noah shook his head. His three childhood friends stood together.

"Damn, man. Don't you remember? When we were kids, we would see how long we could stand things. Like how long we could run in place. Or how far we could swim. You had a ritual when we would do it."

Jamie took over. "You would talk to yourself. You would say just one more minute and I'll get to stop. And then the minute would be up and you would say it again. You were such a stubborn shit. He actually passed out once when we were trying to see who could go the longest without taking a breath. The sucker turned blue."

Seth nodded. "So we'll ask again. How many times did you say it?"

It came back to him in a great rush. God, how could he have forgotten? He hadn't really. It had been an incidental thing, something meaningless in the great nightmare that had been the day. Even as they'd pulled him into the office, he'd already been at it.

Ten minutes. I can take ten minutes and that's all Alexei has.

Ten minutes had become an hour, until he counted the time in blows and lashes and bites of pain.

Two more and I can be done. Just two more.

"I don't know. I lost count."

Jen Talbot stepped in front of him, her gentle hands reaching for his face. "Logan Green, you never would have said a thing. You had every opportunity to stop it. You took that pain for me and Holly and, Logan, you didn't know it then, but you took that pain for my baby and any babies we have later. This baby is going to live and breathe and grow because of what you did."

"You never would have said it," Stef agreed. "I saw some of it. That was not a boy on that desk. That was a man I was damn proud to know. That was a man I'm going to name my son after because I hope he has half your courage."

Holly was surrounded by her men, their arms around her, somber looks on their faces as she cried freely. "I…we are so grateful to you. We love you."

"I love you." Georgia wrapped her arms around him. "I love you so much. I'm so proud to be your girl."

Seth reached for his hand. "Hey, of course you are, baby. Logan Green is a big fucking deal. He's my hero. Always has been."

"You're my boy. You're our boy and we're proud," his momma vowed.

Logan let go. He'd held it for so long, but there was no need now. He cried. He let it out in a great yell that had the nurses rushing in, but he barely saw them because he was surrounded, protected. Arms came around him, hugging him, and familiar voices soothed him and somewhere in that great show of love he did the one thing he hadn't managed to do.

He forgave himself.

Chapter Nineteen

Georgia walked into the dungeon prepared for almost anything. After all, this was her wedding night.

"What do you think?" Seth looked entirely perfect in his Armani tux. Prince Charming in the flesh. "I tried to get it right. I wanted it to be a perfect mix of romance and, well, whatever it is that Logan does to you."

"Dude, I do dirty things to her. This place is sweet. What's up with the flowers?" Logan walked into the dungeon, his hands already going to the buttons on his dress shirt. He'd dumped the tux coat the first chance he'd had. He turned and winked at her as he questioned the flowers.

"The flowers are romantic," she countered.

"Baby, so are these handcuffs," Logan said, holding up a shiny pair and giving her a wolfish leer.

Somehow everything was romantic with these two. "I love the handcuffs. And I love the flowers, too." They were calla lilies, her favorite, of course. Seth would never get anything less.

They were so beautiful, her men. Logan was all alpha male hotness while Seth was the perfect modern male and somehow, someway, they fit perfectly together. She thanked the heavens for that day so long ago when two boys from different worlds had become friends because she hadn't known it at the time, but her life had started in that moment.

"Hey, this is supposed to be a happy day." Seth crowded her, reaching up to brush away tears she didn't realize she was shedding.

Logan crowded her other side. "She is happy. She's just Georgia. She's feels everything strongly, and I love her for it." He bent down and kissed her cheek. "And she should be happy I didn't kill her brothers."

She smiled brightly. It had been a hell of a wedding. She'd only had two weeks to plan it, but she'd discovered that Seth's checkbook opened many doors. And the ones that had remained closed came open once they had been met with the one-two-three punch of Georgia, Nell, and Rachel. Nell and Rachel had done their good cop-bad cop routine and then Georgia had cried. Those poor florists hadn't stood a chance. Georgia had argued that they needed at least a year, and Seth had negotiated her down to six months. Then super Dom laid down the law. He wanted to be married like right now. She'd thought Seth was the ruthless one, but Logan had it in spades when it came to making things legal. She was now legally married to Seth Stark, but she had signed a contract with Logan and the ceremony they'd had hours ago might not have been perfectly legal, but it was binding to them.

She'd pulled off a gorgeous, intimate wedding, but Logan was right. Her brothers had been obnoxious. "Sorry. I think Mark and Dare wanted to make sure you were all right, you know."

"They jumped me at my bachelor party," Logan shot back.

She winced, but then remembered what Logan had done. "You managed to take them both out."

"Only because I had Jamie and Noah and Seth with me. Seth was the one who figured out it was an ambush, and Jamie is damn nasty in a fight. They turned my bachelor party into *Fight Club*." Logan had a grin on his face. Despite his grumpy complaining, she knew he'd enjoyed the exercise. He totally fit into her crazy-ass family and so did Seth.

"Hey, Win is on board now." Only because he and Logan had a man-to-man where she happened to know that Logan had promised to lay down his life for her and, more than that, he'd promised to help her find what she wanted to do with her life.

She'd been thinking a bit, and she liked the kids of Bliss. They didn't have a school to call their own. It might be fun. She knew damn well she could raise the funds. A private academy that the town would control, would decide on, would prepare their kids for the future in.

Her kids. One day, but not like now or anything. It was her time to have fun, to explore, to see the world, and she got to do it with the loves of her life.

"I like your brothers. I intend to get along with your brothers. But you need to understand one thing." Logan's eyes had narrowed in that sexy look he gave her right before he tossed her over his knee and started in on her ass. "You belong to us now. This is our family, and I'm the head."

Yeah, that look totally made her girl parts start to sing. *We're getting some tonight!*

"You're in charge of part," Seth said, squaring off with Logan.

"I'm in charge of part." Logan put a hand on Seth's shoulder. "And you're in charge of part. And she's totally in charge of our dicks, so she's the really big fucking deal."

She was in charge of more than their dicks. They were guys. It was the way they talked, but she was totally in charge of their hearts, and that did make her a big deal. "Are you two going to congratulate yourselves on being the tough guy and the rich guy? Because the last time I checked, the hot chick was still in her wedding dress."

It was a gorgeous confection of silk and lace, a Monique Lhuillier she'd selected with Nat's help. It was hard to believe that her whole family was under one roof and she was about to have crazy, whacked-out sex with her husbands. Luckily, Seth had promised her the dungeon was completely soundproofed. Earlier when she'd given her brothers a tour, she'd offered to show them the dungeon because they were all in the lifestyle, but Mark had pretended to vomit and Dare and Ben had shaken their heads. Only Chase had been willing to explain that no matter how high tech the dungeon was, he didn't want to see where his sister got her ass whipped.

They whipped so much more than her ass and she loved them for it, but it had been days and she was dying.

Seth sat back, looking at her, his eyes roaming. Logan stood beside him. Neither one said a thing, just stared, emotion plain on their faces.

"Guys, you're going to give me a complex, and I already have like ten of those." Why weren't they attacking her?

"Give us a minute, baby," Logan said. "Tell her what we're doing. You're better with words."

"We're memorizing you," Seth explained. "We've been doing it all day. We stare and make sure to take in every detail of the way you look and smell and feel in this moment because you're the most beautiful thing either of us has ever seen, and when you're ninety years old and we have great grandkids running all over the cabin, you should know that what we'll be seeing is you, the way you look today."

Seth really was good with words. "I love you."

And they would always be these men, young and strong and so beautiful it hurt to look at them. No matter what would happen in life, they would always be the way she'd seen them on their wedding day.

"Seth, would you please present our sub to me?" Logan asked as he shrugged out of his shirt and sank onto one of two leather chairs she liked to think of as their thrones. There wasn't one for her because, they'd explained, she was always to sit in their laps. She didn't need a chair when she had her men.

Seth got up, striding across the gleaming dungeon like a panther who'd scented prey. He walked straight up to her, but she knew the drill. She didn't flinch when he got into her space. Presentation. Logan loved this part, seemed endlessly fascinated with Seth slowly peeling back the layers of her clothes and unveiling her to the Dom. Sex with her men could be hard and quick and satisfying at times, but she loved it most when they took their time, playing with her for hours, bonding the three of them together.

Seth gently pulled the pins out of her hair, letting the waves cascade over her shoulders, arranging them to his liking. He pushed the straps of the gown down, his hands caressing her shoulders. Ah, the warm-up, as she liked to call it. It could last for hours. Hours where they simply worshipped her skin, running their hands all over her, staring at her body like she was a work of art they were studying.

It was guaranteed to have her begging before they took her.

He leaned over, softly rubbing his lips over hers, nibbling on her bottom lip and drawing it inside before planting soft kisses all over her face. "What part should I present first, boss?"

Logan was the boss in the bedroom. Seth made the financial decisions. And they had a mutual agreement that as they both learned the other's roles, they would make the decisions together because they were a family.

"I want to see my sub's breasts."

Seth's hand briefly toyed with the small platinum and diamond collar around her neck. Along with two wedding rings, she had taken their collar as well. Every time she touched it, she was reminded of how loved and protected she was.

She had her collar and they had their tats. Seth had a matching one to Logan's, a gorgeous *G* on his chest proclaiming to all the world that he was taken. And Logan couldn't ever claim again that it was for his last name because his last name wasn't Green anymore.

Tears threatened when she remembered the moment. "I can't believe Momma Marie actually cried."

The sweetest smile came over Logan's face. "It was a long time coming. I'm just glad Ma was able to keep the secret and Seth was able to push it through so fast. Marie Warner is the head of our family. It was long past time we took her name."

At the anniversary party the night before, Logan and Teeny had given Marie a gift. Their change of name certificates. Logan and Teeny Warner. As it should always have been. Momma Marie, the toughest woman in Bliss, had broken down and cried because after all this time, her family shared her name.

And she'd told Georgia how pleased she was that she would be known as Georgia Stark-Warner. It was kind of the best name ever.

"It was a perfect idea," Logan said. "It was the best gift I could give them."

She felt Seth's hands start to undo the tiny buttons at her back. Nat and Kitten had taken their time buttoning each one carefully, and Seth seemed determined to take it off just as slowly. Each button would come undone and she would feel a kiss on her spine.

All the while, she watched as Logan eased the zipper of his

slacks down. He ran a hand over that cut chest of his all the way to his pelvis, and with slow deliberation, eased his cock out. He was a delicious sight, his eyes on her as he stroked himself. His cock was so gorgeous, big and full and already wet at the tip because she knew he'd been thinking about her.

Seth eased her bodice down and pulled at the cups of her corset. Her breasts, the same ones she'd always hated, spilled out, but she kind of loved them now because Seth's hands were cupping her, Logan's eyes heating at the sight. And her nipples were practically singing a hallelujah chorus.

The pads of Seth's thumbs brushed her nipples, his voice low against her ear. "Someone's excited about her wedding night."

Damn straight she was. They'd held out for the last five days. Nothing but cuddling. The boys had spent the night before at Logan's childhood home and she'd been left here with Nat and Kitten. It had been fun, but she needed her men. They had gotten her used to regular freaky, awesome sex. And they'd gotten her used to more than that. "Well, I'm ready to see what all the fuss is about. Logan's made me wear a plug for three hours every day."

The bastard. He'd explained that he wanted their wedding night to be special, but she thought he was trying to make her insane. Every day he would spend time on "training." He would get her naked and introduce her to a flogger or the spanking bench. One time he'd spent three hours on touch play, as he called it. He'd used a bear claw on her, sensitizing her skin, and then ran a long feather all over. He alternated between warm wax and ice cubes, making her squirm and writhe. And then he and Seth would go to other bedrooms and she would want to scream. The one time he'd caught her trying to relieve herself, she'd been treated to a long time over his lap.

But he was right because now all that waiting made the night feel special.

Logan's cock seemed to pulse in his hand. "Oh, you're going to find out."

Seth moved behind her, rubbing his erection against her backside. "Do you know how long we've wanted to do this to you? To get you between us?"

"Forever." It seemed how long she'd been waiting for them.

"Absolutely, baby. Forever." He rolled her nipples between his thumbs and forefingers.

She couldn't help but respond, her whole body feeling languid and soft, ready for anything. Logan could be deeply inventive, and not all of his topping her was purely sexual. Some of it was merely sensual. He'd spent an hour working her over with a deerskin flogger that was buttery soft on her skin. She'd been wary at first but after a couple of minutes, she'd found herself drifting, relaxing. And he found the act relaxing, too. They hadn't had sex, but they'd cuddled afterward, perfectly content. He was teaching Seth to use it, too. Soon she would have two Doms, like she had two husbands.

"Georgia, get out of those clothes and present yourself to me." Logan's hand gripped his cock, and she could tell he wasn't going to torture her tonight. No. He wasn't going to wait at all.

Seth helped her out of the rest of her clothes, skimming his hands across her skin, making her shiver with excitement. He held her hand as she stepped out of the dress wearing only a pair of lacy white panties and pearly white Christian Louboutins.

"Off with the panties, but leave those shoes on," Logan ordered.

Seth winked as he got to his knees in front of her. "You know how attached we've become to your footwear."

Her men had a footwear fetish. If she bought a new pair of shoes, she had to give them a fashion show, and they claimed they couldn't appreciate the shoes unless she wasn't wearing anything with them.

She groaned as he put his mouth on the mound of her pussy, wetting the thin fabric with his tongue.

"God, you smell so good, baby." He dragged the panties down her hips, but his mouth stayed where it was, his tongue licking up her labia and worrying her clitoris. "You taste even better."

He left the panties where they were and parted her labia with his thumbs, opening her for better access. His tongue played all around, licking and sucking and laving.

"Only one, Seth." Logan was watching through narrow eyes, his hand working up and down his cock.

"Just a little starter, baby," Seth said.

Oh, yes. Her every pink part was playing the cheerleader now. *Go, Seth! Go!*

"Don't you move, Georgia. You let him play with you." Logan couldn't give up control even halfway across the room, but she'd come to adore him for it.

She held herself still, giving over to the husband kneeling in front of her. He slipped a finger inside, unerringly knowing exactly where to go. One finger and then two foraged inside her pussy as his tongue traced circles around and around her clit, sliding over her with feathery pressure. So close and so far away, and Logan had forbidden her to move. Clever bastard. He knew damn well she wanted to sink her hands in Seth's hair and hold him where she needed him the most. Now she was trapped and at Seth's will or she knew exactly what the Dom would do. He'd put a halt to everything and she'd find herself bound to a spanking chair with no hope in sight of a starter orgasm.

"Oh, Seth. Please."

"Yes, baby. I want to please you." The pressure on her clit tripled and he rubbed her G-spot in exactly the right place.

The orgasm swallowed her, racing along her skin, wakening her every cell.

She wobbled on her heels, but Seth was there, catching her before she fell. He hauled her to him, kissing her with abandon. She could taste herself on his tongue.

Some starter course.

Now she was ready for the main event. Her men. Together.

* * * *

Seth took his wife's mouth, letting his tongue slide in and sharing the taste of her pussy with her. She should know how amazing she tasted, that he craved her like a drug. She was everything he'd wanted, and she'd been the one to bring them all together. She'd been the one to save Logan, to show him he could come out of the darkness. She was their light.

And their wife. It was hard to believe it, but she belonged to them now. She wore their rings and Logan's collar, and they were tied together in so many ways, he could never be free. And that was just how he liked it.

"You're a pussy, man," Logan said, but he was smiling.

Seth kissed her again. He didn't mind being a pussy for her. And her pussy was totally worth being a pussy over. She was curvy and so feminine in his arms that he felt like he was ten feet tall. He carried her toward Logan the way they'd planned. While Georgia had orchestrated the wedding, he and Logan had planned the wedding night. For them, it was sacred, even more meaningful than the vows. They had pledged to love her and take care of her, and now they would worship her with their bodies and souls.

"Steady, baby. I'll help you down. Find your position." He had to admit, he rather loved watching her in slave position. She held his hand as she dropped to her knees, spreading them wide, displaying herself to her Masters. Her golden hair spilled around her shoulders, and while her head went submissively down, her blue eyes were sparkling with mischief. Hurricane Georgia was always simmering below the surface, and he wouldn't have it any other way. He wanted a woman who would put him on his ass when he screwed up. He found it incredibly sexy, but he also liked spanking hers.

It was the best of both worlds.

"Perfect, Georgia. You have that down. You know you look for all the world like the sweetest submissive ever." Logan placed a hand on her head. When he had a hand on Georgia this way, he always looked so peaceful to Seth, as though they were deeply connected.

And Seth didn't feel anything but a fierce joy. He had his own connections to Georgia that Logan likely never would understand, but that was okay. Seth finally got that they both had their roles. It was why the relationship worked. Even he and Logan had a relationship slightly apart from Georgia. When she went shopping or to her meetings or out with her friends, he and Logan became teenage boys again, reading comic books and playing video games. He had his best friend and the most beautiful girl in the world.

Lately, he and Logan had been talking to Henry, trying to figure his situation out. The cartel would find him again. It might take them a good long time, but they would find Bliss. Hell, they would find him anywhere he went. There had been long discussions between Henry, Seth, Logan, and Nate. Henry had thought about running. He wanted to protect the town. He'd decided he would wait until Nell was out of danger with the pregnancy, and then he would disappear.

Nate was completely against that plan of action, and so were Seth and Logan. When the time came, they would make a stand.

"Are we boring you, Seth?" Logan asked in that deep voice he used in the dungeon. Logan's eyes narrowed as though he could read his mind. "Henry's going to be okay."

Georgia reached out a hand, grasping his own. "He'll be okay. And if the time comes, if we have to defend the town, I'll be right there because I'm an official member of the club."

Logan paled and Seth was damn sure he did, too. The "I Shot a Son of a Bitch Club" had welcomed Georgia with a T-shirt and lemon crème cake.

"Let's talk about that later," he said because he could see Logan was about to do something stupid like interrupt their honeymoon by forbidding something.

Logan met his eyes, and he gave him a nod. When the time came, Seth would make sure Georgia was otherwise occupied while Logan stood on the front line. That was his job.

"Baby, I do not remember giving you permission to move. Hands and knees. That's a count of twenty." Logan's palm twitched as though he couldn't wait to spank that ass.

Georgia smiled Seth's way as she leaned forward and assumed the position. Seth couldn't help but groan at the way her ass swayed as she moved. Heart-shaped and round, her ass was as perfect as the rest of her. And it looked so damn good with a flush of pink.

"Count for me, baby," Seth said. He loved how breathy and sultry her voice became.

A hard smack tore through the quiet of the dungeon followed by a gulp from Georgia. "One."

"Seth?" Logan was kneeling beside her, but he gestured Seth down. To share in the punishment, the pleasure, the joy.

Seth dropped to his knees and let his hand find her cheek with a hard smack. He wasn't afraid of hurting her anymore. Georgia loved this.

"Two."

They took turns, each slapping a cheek until both were rosy and pink. Her skin was always silky smooth, but now there was a lovely heat to it, and he'd put that there. And he could smell how much she loved it.

He was already hard, but his dick stiffened further as he looked at her. She was exquisite, from her golden-blonde hair to those breasts he couldn't get enough of. He loved her breasts and the way they bounced when she rode him.

"Very good." Logan's hands ran across her ass before he stood up. "You took that well. Now let's see if we can move on. Georgia, baby, we need to get you ready for this, but since Seth warmed you up, I think you should return the favor." Logan grabbed the bottle of lube he'd set out this morning.

And Seth got up and out of his pants faster than a speeding bullet. Yeah, he could use warming up. Not really because he was about as fucking hard as a man could be, but he definitely wanted what Logan had in mind.

When he was naked, he got back to his knees in front of her. She was still in her position, waiting for Logan to start preparing her, but she leaned forward slightly, her tongue swiping across the head of his cock. He loved that. She always acted like she couldn't get enough of them. It made a man feel like a superhero.

"She likes a cock in her mouth," Logan said with a smile. "I think we should accept that our wife is a complete, gorgeous pervert."

"Only for you two," she said before pulling his cockhead into that sultry mouth of hers.

"Thank god for that." Seth was enveloped in heat. It was so fucking good.

Logan smirked as he settled behind her, but only after he'd gently pulled her hair to the side. "I know you like a show."

He did. Now he could fully watch as his dick sank into her mouth. Those gorgeous lips of hers were opening around him. She pulled back and her tongue darted out like lightning strikes all over his flesh.

And then she groaned around his cock, the vibrations damn near causing him to lose it. He took a deep breath and looked across her body. Logan was busy. "She likes having her ass played with, too, brother. Definitely a sweet little pervert."

Logan's face was flushed as his arms moved in a rhythm. "I've plugged this gorgeous asshole every day for the last couple of weeks.

I've moved her from a starter plug all the way up to very near my size, and she still is tight as a goddamn drum. She's going to kill me."

She *was* killing him. She sucked and then dragged her tongue up, finding the spot at the back of his head and giving it a long rub with the flat of her tongue. He had to steel himself. He couldn't come yet. Not until he was inside her.

God, it was the first time he got to be inside her with absolutely nothing in between them. She was on birth control, and he and Logan had a clean bill of health from the most invasive, gruffest doctor he'd ever been examined by, and it was all worth it because he got to feel that silky smooth pussy on his cock tonight.

"Just a bit more, Georgia."

His blonde minx set in, sucking and dragging hard, as though she was a woman on a mission. She worked her mouth around his dick, eating it down inch by inch. Seth felt his eyes close, his balls start to draw up.

And he pulled out.

"Not until I'm ready, Georgia."

"You seemed ready to me."

Little brat. He moved around and smacked her ass five times in quick succession. His cock pulsed as she squirmed and squealed sweetly because Logan still had two fingers securely in her asshole.

"See," Logan began with a grin. "You're learning. And *she's* ready. Get inside her. I'll be right back."

Seth felt savage. So this was why cavemen dragged women around. He wasn't about to fist her hair or anything, but he lifted her easily into his arms. Conquering. That was how this sex felt. He'd conquered the business world, had more success than most people twice his age, but he hadn't felt like he'd truly won until he looked down at the woman in his arms and realized she'd utterly submitted to him. Not for his money or for power, but because this woman loved him with her heart and soul.

"You're the prize, Georgia. You're the prize." Logan had accused him of getting lost in his work, and he did, but he'd always known that whatever software he was developing or company he was building wasn't the endgame. *This* was the endgame. This woman and his best friend and the life they could have together. That was the ultimate win.

Her hand came up, running through his hair. “I love you. I love you both so much. I want to be with you.”

She was always with him. He set her down on her feet. “Get on top, baby. I want to get inside you.”

He stretched out on the big bed he’d had custom made for them. It was one of the romantic parts of his third-floor dungeon. The bed was huge and covered in soft Egyptian cotton sheets that tastefully hid the restraints that ran under it. They could tie their wife up all they liked and keep her screaming. But that was for later.

Seth groaned as she straddled him. This was right where he wanted to be. She enveloped him with her heat, her beauty. She grasped his cock as she began to lower herself on him.

He closed his eyes because this was heaven.

* * * *

Logan washed his hands and then glanced in the mirror.

Who the hell was looking back at him? He’d been a boy for so long, even after he’d started wearing a badge, and then he’d been so fucking angry, he hadn’t recognized himself. So who the hell was this man? He was peaceful. He was happy. He read comic books again and loved bad science fiction, but he also worked out and was serious about going to college and seeing the world.

He was a friend and a husband. One day he would be a father.

And he was not going to fucking cry again. God, he was like a baby sometimes when he truly felt the love around him. He was blessed beyond measure. They should have run. His moms, his boss, his friends, Georgia. He’d practically been an animal. He’d shamed himself and shamed his badge, but when he was at his lowest, his family sent him to a place where he’d found more friends. Leo and Julian. Ben and Chase. Fuck, even Kitten had helped him. Maybe she had most of all because nothing would have been possible without Georgia, and Kitten had made sure Georgia met Seth.

The man staring back at him was the man who had taken his real family name. Logan Warner. He was a man who had stepped up. His momma might not have liked it, but she was on a diet now. She’d laid down the law with him. Well, he'd done the same with her. He was out of the woods, and he wanted his momma to live a good life, and if that meant giving up bacon, that was the way it was. He could still remember the horrified look on her face when he'd explained that Nell was now in charge of the food for the anniversary party. And the way his ma had cried because she'd been so worried after they had told her about Momma Marie's heart. If Logan had his way, Marie and Teeny Warner would be together for another twenty-five years. They had to because they would make the best grandparents in the world.

They'd certainly been the best moms.

No, he wasn't sure about this man yet, but he knew one thing. This man would work it out. This man had hope. After all, the world could be cold, but there was always warmth waiting for him.

And if he waited too long, Georgia would talk Seth into another orgasm. Logan knew what his place was. He was the hardass. He was the Dom. Seth was getting there, but he still melted the minute she turned those eyes on him. That was perfectly fine outside the bedroom, but a man needed to be in charge of at least one segment of his life.

Logan ditched his overly expensive trousers. His cock had been ready for hours. He'd made them all wait, but anticipation could be sweet, and now all that sweetness was about to come to fruition.

He threw open the door and groaned at the sight in front of him. Warm? The world was hot right now.

Georgia was riding Seth, her head thrown back, her hips rolling. Seth gripped her waist, forcing her on his dick over and over again. Logan knew that most men would be horrified, but he wanted to join in. He didn't give a flying fuck what most men would do. Most men didn't have his family.

"Don't you come, Georgia. Not until I'm inside." Most men didn't get to be a warlord in the bedroom and then cuddle up afterward secure in the knowledge that they always had someone to watch their backs.

"But I'm so close." She was using that breathy sex kitten voice that let him know she wasn't joking. She really was about to come.

"I will pull you off and get the violet wand out. I'll tie you down and shock your nipples until you scream for me to let you come and then I'll keep doing it." His sub had loved the violet wand. On a low, playful setting. She'd loved the way the blue sparks hit her nipples. She'd giggled and talked about how they were singing a rock song.

Exploring her unique sexuality was the light of his life. He had so much to show her, so much to discover with her. They could play forever.

He grabbed the lube but not the condoms. They didn't need them. He didn't want anything between him and his woman. And when the time was right, she would toss out the pills and he and Seth would take turns filling her up, getting her pregnant, creating their family.

But not for a while. He had more exploring to do, more time to spend with them before they settled back here in Bliss to raise their family.

Seth went still. "Listen to him. He will do everything he says he will. He will torture you all night and then none of us will get any until we hit Hawaii tomorrow. Do you want to wait that long? I have a private plane taking us. He made sure it was stocked with floggers and nipple clamps and a whole bunch of rope."

"The mile-high dungeon." Logan was going to have so much fun on that flight.

Georgia gasped and went still and then slowly lowered her body to Seth's, chest to chest. She was graceful and playful because she never lost that cock seated deep inside her. She even managed to shake a bit. "Yes, Master. Please, Master. Don't punish your poor sub."

Who said she couldn't act? She knew exactly what to do to get his cock tight and weeping for her. A pulse of arousal wept from his slit. He stroked himself once and then again before he climbed on the bed.

"I'll punish my sub any way I like, darlin'. You belong to me. That's my collar you're wearing. You're mine to punish." He loved how soft her eyes got when he started in with his Dom growl. She loved this play and he needed it. She was his perfect match. A sub in the bedroom and a fiery, loyal partner outside of it. "Lucky for you, your Master is in a giving mood. I'm going to take this ass, baby. I'm going to split it with my cock and make you feel the burn."

He'd taken his time. He'd prepared her day after day, making sure to open her up so all she would feel was some pressure and a whole lot of pleasure.

Georgia groaned as he planted his hands on the cheeks of her ass and pulled them wide.

He'd lubed her up before, so the rosette of her ass was pink and shiny and looked so tight he nearly came right then and there. She was going to test him. He had to pull through. He lubed up his cock, praying for patience.

Seth had his hands in her hair, whispering in her ear. He told her how gorgeous she was, how good it was going to feel, how tight she would be. His lips played along hers, distracting her so she wouldn't tense up.

Logan took a deep breath and lined his cock up. Heat immediately invaded his veins and he'd barely touched her.

Her spine shook. She felt it, too. She had to feel it. He pressed in, gaining the tiniest bit of ground. His jaw clenched as he forced his dick inside, fucking into her in small nudges. Patience. Just a little bit more. Three seconds more and he would shove in hard.

And three seconds passed and he gave himself another three and another, all the while finding the patience to go slowly, to make it good for her.

First the head disappeared inside and then a few inches more. Heat and pressure were building inside him. She was strangling his cock and it felt so damn good.

"Oh my god," Georgia breathed.

He knew she was serious when she didn't abbreviate. OMG was the brat, but "Oh my god," was the woman. Yeah. And it meant he was doing it right. "What's wrong, baby?"

"You're too big. You're bigger than the plug. Seriously," she complained.

He felt Seth laugh. Felt it. When Seth laughed, the sensation rumbled along Logan's cock because they were separated by nothing but a tiny piece of Georgia's flesh. It was a hell of a sensation. "Is your Master torturing you with his cock, Georgia?"

"She's the one torturing me," Logan shot back with a laugh of his own.

"Fuck," Seth said.

"You can feel each other, can't you?" Georgia asked, looking back over her shoulder. "That is so incredibly sexy."

Of course she would think that way. "Relax. We're almost there. Let me in. Kiss Seth. Kiss him and let my cock in."

Seth took her lips and Logan watched as they kissed, their tongues tangling in obvious passion. Her hand came around her back and stroked the hand that held her hips. She wouldn't leave him out. Not ever. That was his woman.

Her hips lifted slightly and he was pulled in, his dick foraging fully past the super tight ring of her ass. His eyes nearly crossed at the pleasure. She was tight and hot, and it was so different from her pussy. He pulled back a little and then thrust in.

Georgia moaned. "Oh, the plug doesn't feel like that."

"No, I'm sure it doesn't." It was going to be all right. She could handle anything he could give her. He dragged his cock out, feeling her asshole clenching around him while Seth's cock slid next to his. So much pleasure. So much intimacy.

"I can't hold out forever, man. She's too tight. Her pussy is always tight, but that giant cock in her ass is making her so snug I can barely breathe." Seth's face was contorted. Logan could tell he was on the edge.

Logan pulled his cock out almost to the tip. He loved how he'd stretched her, how her asshole gave way to welcome him inside. "Then let's not wait a second longer. Hold on, baby."

Seth sighed with pleasure as he twisted his hips up and took the first thrust. Then it was Logan's turn. As Seth pulled out, Logan fucked in, their cocks sliding against each other and rubbing every inch of Georgia's pussy and ass.

She moved between them as they set a punishing pace, her body flowing, connecting the three of them together. She was the missing piece, the one who completed them. Since the day he'd met Seth Stark all those years ago, he'd felt incomplete, like a piece of himself was missing when his friend was gone, but Georgia bound them together.

They rode her, worshiping her. Logan let his free hand circle around her waist to nestle between her body and Seth's, finding her clit and making circles as he fucked her ass.

She clenched down as she came, her head falling back against his chest as she screamed her pleasure.

Seth shouted out, thrusting his cock deep, riding up against Logan's, and suddenly there were no more seconds to wait, no more patience to be had. His balls grew tight. Pure pleasure shot up his spine causing him to thrust as far as he could, giving Georgia everything he had. Wave after wave took him, and he fucked her mindlessly, letting himself go.

He finally fell over, his cock slipping out as he rolled to the side, bringing Georgia with him. She lay back, that gorgeous face looking utterly exhausted as she snuggled down between them.

Peace. Comfort. They settled over him like a blanket.

"Oh, we have to do that again," Seth said.

Georgia weakly slapped at his chest. "Not until I've soaked in a tub for about a day."

Such a princess. Logan palmed a breast. "I can arrange that."

He would take care of her. Always.

* * * *

The next morning came and Logan Warner jogged up the steps to the private plane. Georgia and Seth were already inside, but Logan turned and looked out. He took in the mountains and the river. He couldn't see the cabins in the valley, but he didn't need to. He had this whole town memorized. All he truly had to do was close his eyes and he could be back in Bliss. No matter how far he roamed, his town would be in his heart. This was where he'd grown up, found his friends, his family. This was where he'd truly found his heart and soul.

He was going out to see the world, to become the man he needed to be. He was going to explore with the other parts of his soul. But he would always return here.

Home. To Bliss.

* * * *

Enjoy the chaos as your favorite characters from Texas Sirens and Bliss, Colorado, come together for one eventful weekend in *Sirens in Bliss*, now available.

Author's Note

I'm often asked by generous readers how they can help get the word out about a book they enjoyed. There are so many ways to help an author you like. Leave a review. If your e-reader allows you to lend a book to a friend, please share it. Go to Goodreads and connect with others. Recommend the books you love because stories are meant to be shared. Thank you so much for reading this book and for supporting all the authors you love!

Sirens in Bliss

Nights in Bliss, Colorado, Book 10
By Lexi Blake writing as Sophie Oak

What happens after happily ever after?

It's the event of the year. The wedding of Leo and Wolf Meyer to their beautiful sub, Shelley McNamara, has all of Bliss up in arms—and makes everyone think about love and marriage and family.

Wolf and Leo have to deal with the sudden reappearance of their father. Rafe Kincaid is handed an opportunity that might take him and his family away from Bliss. Aidan, Lexi, and Lucas O'Malley find themselves at a crossroads in their marriage. And Stefan Talbot must face his biggest fear—possibly losing his wife in childbirth.

So come to the Feed Store Church, pick a seat, and enjoy the chaos as all your favorite characters from Texas Sirens and Nights in Bliss, Colorado, come together for one eventful weekend.

And some of them may never be the same again.

Note: This is a reunion book, which shares an overall story arc and many crossover characters with the Texas Sirens and Nights in Bliss series. This is not a stand-alone.

About Lexi Blake

Lexi Blake is the author of contemporary and urban fantasy romance. She started publishing in 2011 and has gone on to sell over two million copies of her books. Her books have appeared thirty-three times on the *USA Today*, *New York Times*, and *Wall Street Journal* bestseller lists. She lives in North Texas with her husband, kids, and two rescue dogs.

Connect with Lexi online:

Facebook: Lexi Blake
Twitter: authorlexiblake
Website: www.LexiBlake.net
Instagram: www.instagram.com/lexi4714